# A DARK LEGACY

*Love can be a dangerous game!*

From the moment Bethany Lyall first saw Greg Randall he haunted her dreams ... and her every waking moment too. But two other men were showing an interest in her. Duncan was as blond as Greg was dark, while Paul seemed to offer Bethany loads of uncomplicated fun. Before Bethany could follow her heart, she had to conquer the demons from her past and face the dangers in the present. Of the three men in her life, only she could decide who was her friend, who was her enemy and who would be her lover!

# A DARK LEGACY

# A DARK LEGACY

*by*

Benita Brown
writing as Clare Benedict

**Magna Large Print Books**
Long Preston, North Yorkshire,
BD23 4ND, England.

British Library Cataloguing in Publication Data.

Brown, Benita writing as Benedict, Clare
    A dark legacy.

    A catalogue record of this book is
    available from the British Library

    ISBN   978-0-7505-3435-2

First published in Great Britain in 1996 by Scarlet

Magna Large Print is an imprint of Library Magna Books Ltd.

Printed and bound in Great Britain by
T.J. (International) Ltd., Cornwall, PL28 8RW

# CHAPTER 1

Whenever I see coloured lights reflected in a rain-wet pavement, I think of the first time I saw him. Everyone else on the promenade was hurrying to escape the sudden downpour, but he just stood there, looking at something in a shop window.

He was very tall; his hands were pushed into his pockets and his broad shoulders were hunched slightly against the rain as he stared intently at the display. He was wearing jeans and a creamy Aran sweater and, as I got closer, I could see the raindrops glistening on the oiled wool and on his dark hair.

A crowd of youngsters pushed past, laughing as they ran into the brightly lit amusement arcade. I gripped my case and travel bag more firmly and started to hurry. The illuminated sign of the taxi office beckoned from the end of the block, but to reach it I would have to walk past him.

I couldn't resist turning my head to look. I am five foot nine, so I guessed he was well over six foot. But now, rather than his appearance, I was interested to see what it was that had commanded his attention. It was a large map of this part of the Northumbrian coastline. The top was the local Tourist Information Office.

Then, just as I was behind him, the man stepped back and we collided. His reactions were quick. He reached out to save me from falling. As his arms went around me, instinct made me raise my own to grab hold of him. Of course, in doing so, I let go of my luggage. My case landed on his foot and he gasped in pained surprise.

I cried out, too, but not in sympathy – my travel bag had landed in a puddle and books and papers spilled out across the wet pavement.

'Oh, no, look what you've done!' I pulled away from him and crouched to gather up my work.

There was a moment's silence and then he said, 'Well, that's all the thanks I get.' He hunkered down beside me and began to help. 'It could have been you sitting in this puddle and not your drawings, if I hadn't caught you.'

I raised my head and was disconcerted to find how close his face was. Brown eyes stared into mine, humorously, and I was sure his lips were twitching. But then, as he looked at me, his eyes widened. He frowned.

I was, instantly, aware of the picture I must present; my blue linen dress and jacket were rain-blotched and my long fair hair was plastered in wet strands across my face.

I pushed it back from my eyes and, because I was so embarrassed, I snatched the last smudged paper from his hand. Putting it in the bag, I muttered, 'You expect me to be grateful – but if you had been looking where you were going, this wouldn't have happened!'

He didn't respond. He was fiddling with the zip of my travel bag. 'I'm afraid this is broken,' he said at last.

'I know – it already was.' I couldn't have him

thinking that was his fault, too. I took the bag from him.

We stood up and I felt a familiar stab of pain in my right ankle. I must have ricked it by pulling away from him too quickly. Now, for a while, I would have to concentrate on walking properly if my foot was not to drag as it sometimes did when I was tired.

He had picked up my case. I reached for it, but he swung his arm away and, with his other hand, took hold of my elbow and propelled me towards the nearest café.

He grinned when I started to protest. 'I think we could both do with a drink – let's say I owe you one!'

By drink, of course, he meant a soft drink or a cup of tea or coffee, for this was Seatoncliffe, a small resort on the north-east coast, and the cafés lining the promenade were not the kind to have a liquor licence.

He opened the door and we paused and adjusted to the fuggy atmosphere. Damp holiday-makers crowded round the tables and lined up at the counter near the hissing coffee machine.

We stepped inside and sand gritted underfoot. He steered me to a table near the window and then went to join the queue.

The café was a cheerful enough place. The table tops were covered with formica patterned like red and white checked gingham; in the centre of each there was a tall, old-fashioned sundae dish made from heavy, greenish, fluted glass. Each one contained paper napkins folded into long triangles. I helped myself to a couple and patted my face dry.

9

Then, using the window next to me as a mirror, I surreptitiously tidied my hair. It had grown quite dark outside and the entire room behind me was reflected in the glass. I saw him threading his way back through the tables, carrying a tray.

He wasn't looking at me and I studied him properly for the first time. For a moment I thought his face was familiar, but how could it be? I was sure I'd never met him in London – how could I forget him? – and the last time I had been in Seatoncliffe he wouldn't have looked as he did now.

I glanced away as he came nearer.

'Frothy coffee!' He pushed the gold-rimmed bistro cup across the table. Curled shreds of chocolate bobbed amongst the cinnamon-coloured bubbles. I couldn't speak.

'You don't like cappuccino! I should have asked you, but it's such a magnificent old coffee machine they have here that I couldn't resist it!'

He sounded disappointed and I forced myself to look up. 'No – I mean, I love cappuccino, it's just...'

'Just what?' He looked puzzled.

I stared back into those dark brown eyes, but I couldn't answer him. Nothing I could say would make sense.

How could I tell him that at the same moment he had said, 'Frothy coffee', I had heard another voice ... a masculine voice, deep-timbred just like his, but not his ... an echo from some other time, a happier time, that I had forgotten...

I stared down into my cup and it took all my self-control not to seize the teaspoon and scoop

10

up the tiny flakes of chocolate as a child would have done...

He was still looking at me curiously, so I forced myself to let go of the disturbing images that hovered just out of focus. I brought my mind back to the present. 'I'm still getting my breath back, I suppose.'

I reached for one of the little packets of sugar and concentrated on tearing it open and sprinkling the brown crystals into my coffee. I was relieved to see that he was doing the same.

For a while we sipped our coffee in a silence that neither of us seemed willing to break, then he turned to stare out of the window towards the North Sea.

He had a strong profile, well-defined and well-proportioned, and I itched to reach into my bag for the pencil and sketch-pad that were never far away. But, of course, a pencil drawing would never have captured the smooth texture and the subtle olive shading of his skin. He was very handsome.

Then he turned and smiled; it would hardly be fanciful to say that my heart stopped – that was the effect the slow and easy lifting of the corners of his mouth had on me.

Then he asked me, 'Do you live here or have you come on holiday?

I frowned. 'Well, not quite – I mean, I'm just ... visiting ... I think...' I managed.

I was hesitant because I was undecided about the final outcome of my visit, and I was inarticulate because I was still a little shaken by what had happened when I stared into that innocent cup of cappuccino. But he was not to know that – I must have sounded strange and even hostile.

'I didn't mean to pry.'

I felt myself flush. He was no longer smiling and I thought I had offended him.

'Oh, that's all right,' I said. 'And you? Are you on holiday?'

'No, I'm not on holiday.'

His answer was no more forthcoming than my own had been and I took this as a rebuff. I imagined that he thought I had been stand-offish and so he had given up any attempt to make conversation.

The moment for exchanging names had passed and we were silent again.

But I wondered at his answer to my question. If he was not on holiday, why had he been staring at the map in the Information Office just like a tourist?

Outside, the dark clouds passed over and the sky lightened as the rain eased off, a little. The café began to empty. Some of the customers ran out as the bus pulled up at the seafront terminus where I had alighted just a short while before.

Soon it drew away to return to Newcastle; as it went it sent huge sprays of rainwater across the deserted pavements. The shops lining the promenade began to put up their security shutters. It was after five o'clock and, once the day-trippers had gone, it wasn't worth staying open.

A girl in a red-checked pinny began to clear the tables and wipe them down and I looked around to find that we were the only customers left.

'I suppose we'd better go,' I said. 'Mrs Bertorelli will want to close now.'

'Mrs Bertorelli?' He looked surprised.

I smiled and pointed to the menu which was propped up against the sundae glass. 'Yes, look, "Bertorelli's Ice-Cream Parlour"...'

He picked it up and studied it for a moment. Then he turned it round so that I could see the words printed at the top and, as I stared, he read them out loud.

'"The Gondola"', he said. 'What made you think this café was called anything else?'

I looked at him, helplessly. 'I don't know...'

And, of course, I didn't. Not exactly. But there were two possible explanations. Either this café had belonged to Mrs Bertorelli when I was a child and it had changed hands since then, or the café that I must have visited with my father had been very similar to this one.

But how could I possibly tell which of these suppositions was correct when I couldn't remember *anything* about the first seven years of my life?

'The rain's stopped,' he said. 'I think it's safe to leave now.' He was looking out of the window and up into the sky, which was almost blue again. No doubt he was relieved that he had the excuse to escape from my awkward conversation and long silences.

As he got up, his foot caught my case, which we had stowed under the table, and it began to topple so he stooped to straighten it. His whole body became tense. I knew I was not imagining it; I leaned over to see what he was doing.

He was holding the name tag. It was one of those imitation-leather label holders that you get

13

with some package holidays. Josie had given it to me when she had come back from Tenerife, but it was not the cheerful logo he was looking at. He was looking at the label.

Josie had told me not to put our address on because she had a theory: thieves study luggage labels on long-distance trains and then go and rob your home address. My flatmate works long hours and she said she didn't want to come back from the hospital and find our flat 'done over'. So there was only my name on the label, *Bethany Lyall;* that's what he was staring at.

He straightened up and looked at me. His eyes widened and I was reminded of the look he had given me outside on the promenade. Then he breathed, 'Of course...'

Surely I didn't imagine that the air between us became as wintry as the North Sea? But the next moment his face was totally expressionless and he said, 'Goodbye, then – Bethany?'

There was a question in his voice. Did he want me to say, 'Oh, Bethany Lyall, that's not me, I've only borrowed the case from a friend?'

But I didn't say that, of course, I just murmured, 'Goodbye.'

He turned to go and I almost called out to him. Perhaps he had lingered for a moment because he wanted me to ask him what his name was? No ... he could have offered that before...

The door closed behind him and he walked away along the deserted promenade. My head was aching and I leaned forward to rest it against the cool glass of the window. He was heading south towards the curve of the bay where most of

14

the hotels and boarding houses were situated.

But, in spite of that, I thought I knew the answer to my own question. He was not on holiday, but must live in Seatoncliffe, otherwise why had he reacted like that when he had seen my name?

I knew, then, that my father, David Lyall, was still hated here.

'Here, this is on me!'

The girl who had been clearing the tables had brought me a fresh cup of coffee. She looked about seventeen or eighteen and was pretty, with a clean pink and white complexion, blue-green eyes and dark hair. A name badge attached to her pinny read 'Mandy'. She was smiling sympathetically.

'Thank you, but why...?'

She didn't answer directly but patted my shoulder and said, 'You just sit there and drink it and, whatever you do, don't go running after him!'

'Running after him?'

'Yes. I can see you've had a tiff – and not to say he's not worth catching – but that would be the worst thing you could do, take my word for it.'

'What on earth do you mean?'

She flicked her long ponytail back over her shoulder and grinned knowingly. 'I see it all, working here, believe me, and it does no good at all to let them think they own you!'

She returned to her work behind the counter and I tried to come to grips with the startling idea that, to the casual observer, the man and I had appeared to be intimate – to be lovers, perhaps. Lovers... I didn't even know his name.

The door opened and the youngsters who had

15

hurried into the amusement arcade when the rain started now came crowding into the café. They brought with them the smells of the outside world; the smell of wet tarmac drying as the sun grew warm again, the pervasive smell of cheap food from the fish and chip shops and the hamburger bars, but above all the smell of the sea.

I looked at Mr Simpson's map. Dune House stood on a promontory of land that jutted into the ocean some miles to the north of Seatoncliffe; it was time I resumed the journey that had begun in London that morning.

Or perhaps it had begun when the letter from my grandmother's solicitors had arrived some weeks before...

*'You've inherited a house? I don't believe it!'* Josie was excited. 'Just think, all this time I've been sharing a flat with an heiress – you might have told me!' She put her mug of coffee down and put both hands on the table, leaning towards me accusingly, but grinning, just the same.

'But I didn't know. Believe me...' I stared at the thick, creamy paper and its heading: Tompkins, Simpson, Brown & Hathaway, with an address in Dean Street, Newcastle. 'They want me to go up and see them...'

'Shall I come with you?' She got up as if I were going to set off that minute.

'No!'

The answer was too emphatic and Josie looked hurt. 'It's not that I wouldn't want you to come, it's just that I may not go at all.'

'But, Beth, you'll have to! I mean – your grand-

16

mother has left *you* the family home. Surely you don't mean to let the others have it?'

I had read the solicitor's letter to her over the breakfast table in our tiny kitchen. The gist of it was that the house was mine if I wanted it; if not, it would revert to my grandmother's other heirs, as it also would if I died childless and unmarried.

'I may just sell it...'

'No ... let me see.' Josie came to stand behind me and she read the letter over my shoulder. I had been quite open with her about its contents so she wasn't being pushy. 'I don't think you can do that.'

She pointed to one of the paragraphs. 'I think this means that you've got to live there – or at least be responsible for the house until you die – and, although this letter isn't very precise, it doesn't look as though you'll be short of funds!'

I stared up at her helplessly, and she squeezed my shoulder before she said, 'Why don't you go up to Newcastle and talk to Mr Simpson as he suggests? Go and look over the house while you're up there. That will help you decide.'

Josie began to put her coat on prior to leaving for the hospital where she was a staff nurse. She was small and wholesome-looking with naturally curly brown hair; her pin-neat appearance was completely at odds with the total chaos she left behind her in our flat each morning.

At the door she turned and smiled. 'Do you want me to phone and tell them you're not coming in to work today?'

'Why should you do that?'

'Because you look as though you're in a state of

shock, that's why.'

'No, I've got a slight headache, that's all.'

'I'm not surprised. Look, if I were you I'd take the day off.'

'No, really, I've got an important client coming in today – Patrick trusted me with a real live duchess – and I must be there.'

'OK. But try and get home early and we'll have a pizza and a bottle of wine to celebrate!'

She opened the door, but then hesitated and turned to look back at me, wonderingly. 'Do you know, you've never really talked about your grandmother, yet you and your parents lived with her until you were seven years old, didn't you?'

'Yes.'

'She must have thought a lot about you to make you her heir. Do you remember much about her?'

'No, not much.'

The truth was that I could not remember her at all.

When Josie had gone I finished my coffee and washed the breakfast dishes. I still had plenty of time to get to work so I wrote to my grandmother's solicitors, acknowledging their letter and telling them that I'd be in touch.

Since leaving art college, I had been working with a firm of interior designers in Kensington. I had been very lucky to get the job, as Patrick Collings usually preferred to employ people who were older than I. He believed that you needed a little more experience of living before you could adequately design and oversee the decoration of other people's homes.

However, my portfolio had impressed him and he had taken me on to cover for one of the designers who was on maternity leave. My contract had only a few more weeks to run, but Patrick had promised me good references and useful introductions.

When the time came to leave, I told Patrick that my grandmother had died and, very briefly, what my situation was. He was pleased for me and told me that if I decided to stay in the north country – he made it sound more like another planet – he would send some freelance work my way. He wished me well.

Up until the last moment Josie offered to come with me. I did not know how to refuse her – after all, our friendship had started in the most emotional of circumstances.

My father had become ill during my last year at college and Josie had been a staff nurse on the ward where he was cared for during his final stay in hospital. At work she was efficient and compassionate. She had been more than kind to me, then and ever since. So, I felt guilty but relieved when she couldn't get time off work because I sensed that, whatever it was I had to face in Seatoncliffe, I needed to face it alone.

It was one Monday morning at the end of August when I finally left London. Josie insisted on coming with me to King's Cross before going to the hospital. She lingered on the platform until the train began to pull away, then she cupped her hands and shouted, 'Remember – phone me tonight!'

She ran along the platform, following the train, and I leaned towards the window and mouthed, 'I will – don't worry.'

And then the platform receded rapidly and Josie was lost amongst a rush of travellers hurrying for another train.

The sun was beating on the windows and the train was warm. My head was aching, so I bought myself a large waxed carton of tea from the buffet counter and tried to relax for a while.

When my headache receded I read the magazine that Josie had bought me and then glanced at some of my preliminary notes and sketches for the renovation and decoration of a small terrace house in Putney.

The clients were friends of Josie's – a girl she had trained with was just about to marry a doctor she had met at the hospital. Josie had asked me do this as a favour to her and I wanted to do my best for them.

Just over three hours later I glanced out of the window and recognized the famous outline of the Tyne Bridge. We were crossing the river on another one of the six bridges and the train was already slowing down to enter Central Station.

I took a taxi to Tompkins, Simpson, Brown & Hathaway, only to discover that I could have walked if I'd known the city. The Victorian building near Dog Leap Stairs had once been very grand, but now each chamber had been partitioned off into a series of tall, narrow rooms equipped with modern office furniture and new technology.

Mr Simpson faced me across his desk, which

was the one good traditional piece of furniture that I had seen since entering the building; from its size alone I guessed he must be very senior. If I were right and he were the senior partner, then 'Tompkins' was probably dead, for Mr Simpson seemed to be incredibly old.

'I was at school with your grandfather, Ralph Templeton, you know, but of course he died long before you were born...'

He opened a large brown envelope and, with great precision, laid out several keys on the desk top. They were all carefully labelled in a copperplate hand. 'I am assuming you will want to go and look at the house. In fact, although the will is not yet through probate, there is no reason why you should not take possession.'

'Take possession? You mean ... stay there?'

'Yes.' He glanced through some papers. 'The electricity and water are still on and we asked the cleaner, Mrs Doran, to continue going in twice a week. She would be willing to come in every day and do a bit of cooking for you as well, if you want her too.'

'Oh, I don't know about that.'

The idea of having someone working for me was strange. I must have betrayed my surprise for he looked at me keenly before he asked, 'Do you mind telling me what your intentions were when you set off from London this morning?'

I realized that I had puzzled him. Surely heiresses did not usually appear so diffident?

'Well ...' I hesitated. 'I had planned to come and see you ... talk things over ... perhaps stay in a hotel in Newcastle overnight...'

'Just overnight?'

I blushed when he glanced at my case and travel bag. His old eyes were shrewd. There was more there than was necessary for one night's stay.

'Well, a day or two, perhaps. I mean, I didn't know if you would want to see me again, to-morrow...?'

'No, not tomorrow, not as soon as that but... Tell me, aren't you at all curious? Don't you even want to look at your house?'

'I suppose I do...'

At that moment I knew that that had been my intention all along. Josie had told me that I should at least visit Dune House before deciding whether to renounce it and I had half agreed that she was right. But, now, I acknowledged that it was more than that.

Suddenly, I knew why I had come north. I wanted a family history – roots, if you like. In all the years that my father and I had lived happily enough in a series of rented flats in London, I had never questioned my lack of any other relatives except him.

I knew that he was an orphan and that my own mother had died when I was seven. I knew that I had a maternal grandmother because she sent me a card and a small gift every birthday. My father always made me write a 'thank-you' letter, but he never ever added a greeting of his own.

When I was twelve I had asked my father why we never went to visit my grandmother as other children seemed to do and he had given me a searching look. Young as I was, I got the impression that he wanted to know if my question was entirely innocent or whether I was testing him in some way.

But it must have become obvious to him that I genuinely wanted an answer so he said simply, 'Because she hates me. They all do. I wouldn't be welcome there.'

I had stared at him, uncomprehendingly. How could anyone hate my father? I wanted to ask him to explain but his grey eyes were full of pain so, instead, I flung my skinny arms around his neck and hugged him.

'Well, then, I hate her!'

He didn't say anything. He held me, tightly, and I realized he was crying.

The thought that anyone could even dislike my father would have been unbelievable. He was the kindest of men and our life together was haphazard but happy. He had a series of poorly paid clerical jobs, but we always had enough to eat and I was always respectably clothed.

Now, here he was telling me that, somewhere, there were people who hated him. I decided that I never wanted to meet anyone who could hate my father and, after that, my thank-you letters to my grandmother became so short as to be rude.

After a while, my brief curiosity about her died. Strange that it never occurred to me at the time that I should have been curious about my mother, too. My father never offered any information. Was he waiting for me to ask?

Much later I understood that the pair of us had, on some very deep level, entered into a conspiracy of silence. It was the only way to block out the hurt.

After he died, I had the job of sorting through his belongings. I had the strangest sensation that someone had been there before me – recently.

Had my father, knowing he was dying, been getting his affairs in order? All our photographs had been neatly arranged in albums, but there was only one surviving from my first seven years. I have it still.

My grandmother had never sent Christmas cards. Christmas is a time when families exchange greetings and I had realized very soon that she and I and my father were in no way a family.

No greeting or gift had arrived on my twenty-second birthday. That had occurred just before I received the letter telling me about my inheritance so my grandmother must have been already dead and buried.

Mr Simpson was looking at me, consideringly. 'Do you have any questions, Miss Lyall? Is there anything you want me to tell you?'

'Yes ... there's something in the will ... Mr Simpson, who exactly are my grandmother's other heirs?'

The old man drew his brows together and sighed. Then he answered, 'Mrs Deirdre Templeton and her daughter Sarah, of course.'

'Templeton? But that means-'

'Yes, they are connections of your grandfather's. After your mother ... er ... died, your grandmother, Frances Templeton, had no surviving relatives of her own except you – she may have thought that Dune House should return to the Templeton family if you did not want it.'

*I suppose Helen and David will inherit Dune House – there's no justice – there's always been a Templeton here...*

The voice came from nowhere and I looked keenly at Mr Simpson but he went on talking as if nothing had happened. I realized that I must have imagined it, but had no time to wonder why – the old gentleman was questioning me.

'But surely you met the Templetons when you were a child? They stayed at Dune House for a while, don't you remember?'

'I...' My head had started to ache again. The atmosphere in the room was close and I felt breathless.

'Are you all right, Miss Lyall?'

'Yes ... just ... tired ... I set out early this morning...'

'My dear young lady, forgive me for being so inconsiderate. I should have offered you some refreshment.'

'No, that's all right.'

'But I insist. A cup of tea, at least.'

He called for his secretary to bring a tray of tea and biscuits. This arrived very quickly but, by the time he had poured the milk and tea into the bone china flower-patterned cups, he had forgotten that I had not answered his question.

'You could move in to Dune House immediately if you wanted to.' He smiled over his cup. 'You would be in possession. Lawyers like possession.'

'Because it's nine-tenths of the law?'

He shot me an appraising look. 'Something like that.'

25

I had made my decision – or at least part of it. 'Mr Simpson, I think I'll go to the house today. It's not too late, is it?'

'No, of course not. You can get a bus – two buses, to be precise. The journey will only take little more than an hour – I'll write the directions and draw you a map – but before you go, I must explain some points to you. Also, I want to make absolutely sure that you understand the terms of the will.'

I was rich. After Mr Simpson had finished explaining my grandmother's bequest to me, I realized that my life would never be the same again.

Part of the land could be sold if I wished – in fact, there had already been some interest expressed by Paul Mitchell, a local businessman. But in order to come into my full inheritance, I must agree to keep Dune House.

# CHAPTER 2

The sun was shining when I left the café but the warmth was evaporating and I realized how cold even a late summer's day could be here on the north-east coast. The waves were choppy and white-crested, the wind was driving in from the east, all the way from the Scandinavian Arctic.

A few grey clouds lingered and, high above the water, seabirds wheeled and shrieked as they rode turbulent currents of air. I shivered. For as long as I could remember, I had never liked the call of gulls.

The taxi office was at the end of the block, next to a small general store that was still open. A dripping green-and-white striped canopy protected trays of fruit and vegetables that had been set up on a wooden stall on the pavement. There were apples, oranges, scrubbed carrots and dark green cabbages alongside purple aubergines and scarlet capsicums. The lucent colours caught my eye and I hesitated.

The open door gave a glimpse of an Aladdin's cave, with well-stocked shelves of groceries all around and, in one corner, the light glancing off wine bottles stacked from floor to ceiling. There was a gentle aroma of exotic spices. I suddenly realized that, if I were intending to stay in Dune House, I ought to have some provisions.

I stepped inside and found a young prince

behind the counter, who was wearing jeans and a pale blue T-shirt. There was no other word for the Asian youth except beautiful, although his delicate features were in no way feminine. A struggling moustache proclaimed his burgeoning manhood and the voice which greeted me was confident and courteous – and disconcertingly Northumbrian.

I chose tea, coffee, milk, bread and all the basic essentials of modern living as well as some in-essentials such as chocolate biscuits and a bottle of wine.

The youth packed them in a cardboard box and, as I paid for them, his eyes narrowed and he stared at me almost as if he were trying to place me. Then he saw that I had noticed and he smiled. He asked, 'Do you have far to go?'

'Dune House – do you know it? It's a few miles north of here.'

There was definitely a reaction to my words but, whatever it was, he struggled to cover it. I was puzzled but he hurried on, 'Yes, it's on the lighthouse road.' As he spoke, his head tilted to one side and back, in what I was to learn was a characteristic gesture. 'The local bus goes past there every twenty minutes but I think, with all this, you should take a taxi.'

'That was my intention.'

'I'll get one for you.'

'No, really, that's not necessary, the taxi office is only next door.'

'I know, it belongs to my brother.' He grinned and disappeared into the back shop. I heard him open a door and call out something in another language.

28

A moment later he returned. 'Imran will bring a car to the door for you. My name is Ahmed – Ahmed Hussain. I'll put one of our business cards in with your groceries. If you need a taxi, or if you want anything delivered-' he indicated the shelves all around him – 'please don't hesitate to phone.'

His older brother, more Asian in his speech patterns and handsome in a worldly-wise way, was equally courteous. He helped me carry my shopping and my luggage to the car; his fashionable cream chinos and biscuit-coloured polo shirt made me aware once more of my crumpled state, that the classically simple outfit, which had seemed so right for a journey combined with a visit to a solicitor, was decidedly tired.

Dune House was approached by a narrow coast road which ran parallel to the cliffs so that the sea was in sight all the time.

'This is the Viking coast, you know ... Norway, Denmark, they lie out across there...'

Imran had been observing me through the driving mirror whenever he thought I wouldn't notice. I smiled and he continued, 'It is also called the "Heritage Coast". It is an area of great natural beauty and, as such, it is very fitting that you should come here!'

I laughed. 'You say that to all the girls, don't you?'

'Only to the pretty ones!'

I knew that his flirting was not serious.

He half turned and his eyes narrowed as he looked at me. As with his brother, I got the impression that he was trying to place me. Did he imagine that he knew me or was it just the kind of curiosity that you find in small towns?

Whatever the case, he gave a small shrug and his concentration returned to the road ahead. In the ensuing silence I gazed out across the sea. I found myself remembering the man who had been standing looking at the map in the information centre, so intent on it that he had seemed to be oblivious to the rain...

Then Imran spoke again. 'Look – there is Dune House.'

I craned forward. The house stood alone on the promontory. Mr Simpson had given me a few brief details. The family home had been built in the middle of the nineteenth century by a Templeton ancestor who had made a fortune from a munitions factory on Tyneside. He had bought up the site of a ruined priory, abandoned after the dissolution, and he had built his Victorian Gothic pile.

It was not as big as I had feared, but it dominated the headland. It was turreted and battlemented and, although it was obviously not a real ancient building, it was impressive.

The clear, cool light of the northern sky was a perfect backdrop for the grey stone, and the house could deceive you into thinking it had stood there for centuries just like the clutch of Norman castles a little further north.

There was no parkland or ornate garden at the front of the house, no stately avenue of trees. Low walls surrounded a turfed area and, once through the tall gates, a wide sweep of gravel led straight to the house. A fork in the driveway led round to the back but I told Imran to drive to the front door.

Imran stood with me on the top step and watched while I pulled the neatly labelled bunch of keys from my handbag.

'You have a key?'

'Mmm.' I concentrated on fitting the key and turning it.

'You will be living here? In Mrs Templeton's house? You knew her?' His curiosity had got the better of him at last and the questions came tumbling out.

I turned to smile at him. 'Mrs Templeton was my grandmother.'

He looked puzzled.

'Is something wrong?'

'No, of course not, but forgive me, I should not be questioning you like this, but I did not know she had another granddaughter.'

'You knew Mrs Templeton?'

'Oh, yes.' The cheerful sideways nodding of his head was more pronounced than his brother's. 'Mrs Templeton used my taxi service and sometimes she would phone the shop for groceries to be delivered.

'She would joke with my brother and say she did not mind paying our outrageous prices because she knew we always stocked the very best!'

He had liked her. I could not reconcile his fond smile with my idea of her. Not only had my grandmother hated my father, but he had also given me the impression that she had turned others against him. The woman that Imran was remembering did not match my picture of her.

And then his smile faded. 'It was so sad, the way she died, was it not?'

'I ... I suppose so.'

For the first time it occurred to me that I had no idea how my grandmother had died. Mr Simpson hadn't broached the subject and I hadn't asked. I felt uncomfortable, realizing that he must have thought I was unfeeling.

So, obviously did Imran for, now, the look on his face was one of gentle reproach. 'You have never been to visit her, here?'

'No. Well, I mean, not for a long time...'

I turned away from him and pushed the door open but held back for a moment before stepping inside. Was it fanciful to wonder whether the act of opening the door of Dune House would invoke the shade of the woman who used to live there?

But the hall was empty.

A moment later, we stepped into a scaled-down version of a Great Hall in a medieval house, galleried and oak-panelled. A tall, stained-glass window on the half-landing spilled jewelled light down the stairs to mingle with the patterns on the traditional Turkey carpet.

No one had lived here since my grandmother had died and yet the house smelled well aired, dried and clean. But it was cold and that was probably why I shivered violently.

Imran looked concerned. 'Are you all right, Miss Lyall?' He must have read my luggage label, too.

'I'm fine. But it's cold in here, isn't it?'

He was too polite to contradict me. 'Yes, it is cold. If you will permit me, I will find out how to turn on the heating for you.'

'The heating?'

He grinned and pointed to a bronze-coloured grille built out from one of the walls. 'Yes, look, that tasteful contraption conceals a radiator. Now we must find the boiler.'

The boiler was in a utility room behind the kitchen. Imran turned it on and set the timer for me, then carried my box of groceries through and placed them on the kitchen table.

I paid him the taxi fare and, as he was leaving, he paused on the doorstep. 'If you need anything, just–'

'I know, your brother gave me your card.'

He got into his car and drove away. I closed the door and leant back against it as I gathered my strength. I knew what I had to do.

From the moment I had craned forward in the taxi I had been hoping that the sight of the house would bring back some memory of my years here. So far there had been nothing. Then I argued with myself that it was likely that I had never approached the house in a car when I was a child.

I could not remember if my father had ever owned one. If not, I might never have seen the house from precisely the same angle.

Had I hoped for some dramatic revelation the moment I opened the front door? Well, it hadn't happened. I decided I would have to walk through the house, visit every corner of it in the hope that something would jog my reluctant memory.

It was only at that moment that I finally admitted the possibility that something very disturbing must have happened here to make me block out my childhood so completely.

Nothing.

Wielding the keys that Mr Simpson had labelled so carefully, I had opened doors and walked along corridors, climbed the stairs and looked into more rooms. I had switched on all the lights, looked into cupboards and out of windows.

Nothing had come back to me.

It was easy to see which room had been my grandmother's – her belongings were still there. It would be my task to sort them out but, for the moment, I simply shut the door.

None of the other bedrooms looked as if they had been permanently occupied for a long time. There was nothing to suggest which room my parents had shared or which room had been mine.

At one stage I stood at the top of the stairs with my eyes closed, hoping that some kind of knee-jerk response would set me going in the right direction. I suppose I hoped that my feet might take me automatically the same way they must have done so often when I lived here.

But I merely became aware that an empty house is never really silent. A grandfather clock was ticking in the hall, the sound echoing up the stairs towards me. The central-heating boiler fired now and then and the pipes made disconcerting cracking noises as they heated and expanded.

Outside the wind had risen and was whining around the corners of the house and buffeting the windows. I decided to give up my search for my past for the moment.

But even if I had not discovered anything about myself, I had learned something about my ancestors. Later, I learned that William Templeton, the Victorian industrialist who had built Dune House, had been a labouring man made good. He had been a self-taught, resourceful engineer who had ended up owning a munitions factory and making his initial fortune out of the Crimean War.

But on that first day, before I knew these facts, I realized that here was the creation of one of the *nouveau riche*. I knew enough about the history of dwellings and their interiors to grasp at once that the man who had caused this house to be built had also been trying to invent an ancient lineage for himself.

The house was a pastiche of Gothic and Elizabethan and something older. It seemed that William Templeton had instructed his architect to give his new home the appearance of having grown and developed over the centuries from a medieval manor. The landing suggested a minstrel's gallery, a design in the stained-glass window gave the effect of a coat of arms.

But, thankfully, the founder of the family fortune had been a practical man. He may have had a sentimental yearning for nobility, but he also had a working man's craving for creature comforts. Whatever the fanciful embellishments, Dune House was entirely well proportioned and designed to be run without huge numbers of servants. It had the air of a comfortable family home.

It was obvious that my grandmother had refurbished and redecorated whenever it became necessary. Everything was solid, comfortable and practical – and the overall result was haphazard.

An entire mismatch of colour and style.

Even as I looked around the house that evening, I longed to put my training to good use. My imagination ran away with me and I stopped only when I realized that I had spent several thousand pounds. This thought was immediately followed by the realization that I could well afford it now – if I chose to stay.

Then I realized something else. I was hungry. The box of groceries was still on the kitchen table, so I made myself unpack it and put everything away. I was too tired to actually cook anything, but I assembled a snack and decided to find somewhere comfortable to eat it.

Balancing the tray on my hip, I switched on the lights in the large sitting-room at the back of the house and looked around. When I had looked into this room earlier, I had noticed that there were large French windows on one wall.

I put the tray down on a small table near the fireplace and went over, thinking I would draw the curtains. They were draped elaborately and looped back with heavy cord ties. After struggling for a moment to unhook them, I decided that they were more for show than for use and gave up. After all, there wasn't another house for miles. No one would look in on me.

I looked out of the window just to confirm that this was the back of the house. Outside, a paved terrace and stone steps gave way to a large sunken garden which stretched a long way back. Bearing in mind the stark simplicity of the grounds at the front, the lush beauty that was revealed now was totally unexpected.

As there was no hot food to spoil, I went to get the keys. The air was fresh and sweet after the recent rain and the smells of roses and damp earth mingled strangely with the smell of the sea.

I knew nothing about gardening – my father had never kept so much as a house plant – but I could see that Mr Simpson had slipped up at last. In the weeks since my grandmother's death, the lawns had not been cut and the flowers looked overgrown and uncared for. Unexpectedly, I was moved at this sign of neglect.

The light was fading now and the shadows of the old trees were lengthening but I could just make out what looked like a summer-house at the far end of the garden. It looked as if it were built into the high boundary wall.

The door of the summer-house was swinging on its hinges, creaking and slamming against its frame in the strengthening wind. I started to descend the steps with some idea of securing the door.

Strange that I should have thought it my duty to do so. Until a short while ago I had not been accountable for anything that happened here. Had I already begun to accept responsibility for my inheritance?

Halfway down I stopped. As the daylight fades your sight can play tricks with you and I imagined that a darker shadow crossed in front of the others at the bottom of the garden. The door of the summer-house slammed once more but this time it stayed shut.

Seabirds wheeled over the house, their cries sounding eldritch in the half-light. I looked up at

37

them, fearfully, and then I saw the lights of Dune House – my house – spilling out across the terrace to meet me. I hurried back inside and closed the door. My heart was racing.

'Beth, I've been so worried, why haven't you called before now? Is everything OK? Your voice sounds funny ... shivery...'

'Everything's fine, I'm just cold.'

I stood in the hall, clutching the telephone. My experience in the garden had unnerved me but I could not pinpoint why. The shadows shifting in the dusk, the summer-house door banging in the wind, the gulls calling – it was all eerie enough, I suppose, and I was alone and a long way from home.

At that moment I still thought of the familiar little flat in Fulham as home; I had rushed to phone Josie the minute I had shut the French windows behind me. The relief when she heard my voice made me feel guilty.

'Honestly, I'm all right, just cold and tired. I'm sorry that I haven't phoned before but there hasn't been a minute, really.'

'Well, what's it like – the house?' Josie sounded excited and eager and my heart sank. She would be hurt if I didn't give her a full description, but I really was tired.

'There's too much to tell you all at once. Look, I'll write you a long letter, with sketches, I promise, but ... Josie, I'm exhausted, do you mind?'

'Well, all right...'

She was hurt – her subdued tone was a giveaway – but she simply told me to take care and, after giving her the number and saying good-night, I put the phone down and hurried back to my supper tray.

The central heating had hardly had time to warm such a large room so I lit the fire. It was gas, one of those simulations with mock coals. I turned the control knob to full power and soon the coals were glowing and the flames flickering cosily.

I dragged a large, comfortable chair nearer to the hearth and pulled the coffee table up beside me. I had set out buttered crackers and cheese, fresh apricots, chocolate biscuits and slices of iced fruit cake. It was an indulgent meal, almost like a child's midnight feast, I thought.

I had found a corkscrew in the kitchen but no wine glasses. Rather than go and search for one, I had settled for a tumbler.

Josie usually bought any wine we drank from an off-licence near where she worked. Faced with the large array of bottles in the Hussain's store, I hadn't known what to buy. Then an attractive label with a drawing of a French château had caught my eye. Ahmed had assured me that I would enjoy it.

It felt pleasantly wicked to pour myself a glass of wine and to drink alone. I began to unwind a little.

Without warning my thoughts returned to the man I had met earlier that day. Perhaps it was the second glass of wine but I began to fantasize that he was sitting at the other side of the hearth, sharing my meal...

He was sitting on the floor, his long limbs

stretched carelessly across the rug towards me as he relaxed in the warmth... His dark hair had dried into unruly curls... He held his glass up and the wine shone like rubies in the firelight... Then he put the glass down and reached forward to cover my hand with his own... I looked up into his eyes...

And then, of course, the romantic fantasy ended. When I looked into his face I could only see the withdrawn and guarded look he had given me when he had learned my name.

I sighed and allowed the pictures to fade.

Outside the wind was still clamouring to be noticed and it had started raining again. I could hear it spattering against the windows. But now I was warm and well fed and the most important decision to make, as far as I could see, would be which bedroom I should have.

I realized I should have done that before my meal because now I was comfortable and sleepy and reluctant to move. I thought it would do no harm to close my eyes for a while.

But just before I drifted off, something came back to worry me. Something Imran had said... What was it...?

I was still trying to puzzle it out when the wine and the warmth and my own tiredness overcame me. I fell asleep in front of the fire.

*She was looking at me...*

I was pretending to be asleep with my eyes tight shut but I had sensed the moment when she had crept into the room and now I could hear her breathing as she stood over me.

40

I had come in here to get away from her but she had waited until I'd curled up with my dolls beside the fire and now she'd chosen this moment to tyrannize me.

'Beth – Bethany, open your eyes. I know you're not asleep!'

Reluctantly, I did as I was told. She was standing, arms akimbo, her blue eyes blazing with scorn. Although she was small and underdeveloped, she was four years older than I was and, ever since she had arrived at the beginning of the school holidays, she had assumed leadership.

'Go away. I'm tired.'

'How can you be tired? It's only two o'clock in the afternoon!'

'I'm tired because you wouldn't let me get to sleep last night!'

She had kept me awake for half the night, as she had done every night since she had arrived, coming to my room to chatter and tell stories. At first it had been exciting, especially when we crept downstairs in the middle of the night to raid the pantry.

'They have midnight feasts at boarding school, you know. We'll eat this in your room, it's much more comfortable than the attic they've given me!'

I had been impressed by her and her knowledge of other more exciting worlds than my grandmother's house at Seatoncliffe, but now, on this rainy summer's afternoon, I was bone weary and beginning to wonder how long it would be before she and her mother went away again.

'Come along, you can't lie there all day, we're

meeting Gyp in the summer-house.'

That made me sit up. 'Don't call him that, he doesn't like it.'

She tilted her chin in a superior way. 'I'll call him what I like and do hurry up, you're keeping him waiting.'

Usually, I would have done just as she told me, especially as I liked our new friend, the slim, dark boy with his ready smile and his patient tolerance of Sarah and I. He was fourteen years old, almost grown-up as far as I was concerned, but he seemed content to go where Sarah led. And I usually tagged along behind.

But today I was tired and out of sorts. 'We're not supposed to play in the summer-house, it's dangerous.'

'Oh, for goodness sake! They only say that because they don't want us getting out into the Priory garden. Now are you coming with me to meet Gyp or not?'

'No, I'm not and you shouldn't have told him to meet you there. If you get caught, you'll get him into trouble too!'

'Stay here, then, baby! Baby Bethany's too scared to come and play with the gypsy boy!' She turned and marched across to the French windows.

A draught of rain-sodden air invaded the room and then she pulled the door shut after her with a thud.

I woke up with the sound of the door closing still ringing in my ears. My heart was beating, painfully, and I gripped the arms of the chair with both hands. I knew at once that I had been dreaming and yet the sound had seemed to be part of the real world and not just an echo from my unconscious.

I looked around me. Everything looked normal. The fire was burning in the hearth, the tray with the remains of my supper was on the coffee table and the door into the garden... I forced myself to look over at the French windows.

It was dark outside now and I could see nothing beyond the rain-speckled panes of glass. I got up and a sharp jab of pain in my right ankle almost made me sit down again.

I stood still for a moment until the pain subsided and then went over to the door. The neatly labelled key was still in the door. I remembered that I had not locked it.

I reached for the key and then paused. My attention had been caught by a pattern of water on the wooden-tiled floor – as if the wind had blown the rain in when the door was open.

Had the rain started before I came in from the garden? I supposed it must have. I should have forced myself to remember that more clearly but there was something else fighting for my attention.

I turned to face the room. I saw the beautiful faded colours of the Persian rugs on the parquet floor. I saw the matching chintz covers on the armchairs, the oak panelling halfway up the walls, the gilt-framed mirror above the fireplace, the Jacobean pattern in the plasterwork of the ceiling and the ormolu chandelier. The room had not changed so very much over the years.

For now, I knew that even if I closed my eyes I would still be able to describe this room – to sense its proportions. At last I could see it through the eyes of the child who had once lived here – the child that I had been. The room had been restored to me.

But of course I had remembered much more than a room. In my dream I had summoned up the image of one of the people who had lived in this house with me.

Why did it have to be her? Why did the first person I remembered have to be the girl whom everyone assumed to be Frances Templeton's other granddaughter but was, in fact, her great-niece – my cousin Sarah?

# CHAPTER 3

The next morning I woke to the screaming of gulls and to the sound of the waves dragging back across the shingle on the shore below. My room faced the sea and I had come to it unerringly. Remembering the sitting-room seemed to have unlocked my memories of the rest of house at last.

It was as if, like some rogue computer program which had been filed away in my unconscious mind, the missing data had made itself accessible once more now that I had keyed in the required code.

But what was the code? Was it a pattern of physical actions – the things I had done since entering the house – or was it just simply being there?

If that were the case, I wondered how long it would be before the other people and the things that they had done came back to me...

After locking the French windows, I had not stayed downstairs long. I had turned off the fire and put my tray in the kitchen and then, picking up my luggage, I had gone upstairs. My old bedroom had its own bathroom and there was clean, warm bed-linen in an airing cupboard.

The room had been redecorated since the last time I had slept there, but there was no sense of being in a strange room or in a strange bed and I went to sleep very quickly. As far as I knew, I did not dream again.

Of course, the wraith of Sarah that had appeared to me the night before had not just been acting out or a dream or a fantasy. The incident had really happened, so it was more like a replay of an old movie and, the next morning, something Sarah had said came back to nag at me.

*Your room's much more comfortable than the attic they've given me!*

I could almost hear that her shrill little voice, which I remembered now, was only a sound mirror of another voice, an older, more sophisticated voice, and it expressed the same sentiments.

It was still very early but I got out of bed, pulled on my robe and headed for the stairs that led to the north tower.

I had looked up here the night before, of course, but now, as I opened the door and stepped inside, I heard the dismal echo of my aunt's nasal tones, on the day that she and Sarah had arrived...

*For goodness sake, Helen, why have you put the poor child in the attic?*

My mother answered her. 'But, Deirdre, we thought Sarah would love to have the top tower room. We thought it would be a treat for her. And with you just in the room below, it will be like having your own private suite. You've even got a bathroom. You'll be able to shut the door at the bottom of the stairs and keep yourselves to yourselves if you want to.'

'And out of your way, I suppose. I know how tiresome it must be for you to have the poor relations staying, especially now that David is beginning to be a success, but you needn't make it quite so obvious!'

My aunt was dark and elegant, but now her thin face was blotched with anger and my mother stared at her in exasperation.

My mother: small, blue-eyed, long fair hair caught back in a ponytail, looking very much like she looked in the one photograph that my father evidently could not bring himself to destroy. The same, that is, except for one detail. She may have been pregnant when the photograph was taken, but the picture does not show it.

But that day, as she faced aunt Deirdre across the tower room, her pregnancy could not be disguised. Her figure was rounded under the loose summer dress and she stood with one elbow crooked and the palm of her hand supporting the small of her back. She was exasperated.

'Deirdre, it's not like that. You're welcome here–'

'And so we should be!' my aunt hissed.

Sarah had not spoken since we entered the room, but she had never taken her eyes off her mother. Her attention was absolute. She was listening to every word.

Another voice.

'Is something the matter?'

My grandmother's voice. We all turned as she entered the room. She was much taller than my mother. I suppose she must have been well into middle age, but her hair was still a glossy chestnut and she was beautiful, imperious, exciting to be with, but frightening at the same time. When she and my mother crossed swords, my father and I took to the hills!

But that day mother and daughter were allies.

'Deirdre is unhappy about the rooms, Mother. She thinks we're hiding her away in the tower because we're embarrassed about her crooked husband.'

When I saw the effect her words had on my aunt and my cousin, I knew my mother should not have allowed herself to be provoked. When she lost her temper she spoke without judgement, and now she had gone too far.

Deirdre and her daughter were cowed and silent – they had already conceded defeat – so there was no need for my grandmother to add, 'Nonsense. Whatever Raymond has done, it is his guilt alone and he is paying the price for it. No one here will treat you like pariahs, Deirdre.'

The irony was that it was true. Neither my grandmother nor my mother were the kind of people to censure someone whose only crime was to have married a criminal. But they had never cared much for her in the first place and Deirdre knew it. It must have galled her that she had nowhere else to turn except to the more fortunate members of her black-sheep husband's family. She would never be able to forgive them for the fact that they were too decent to turn her away.

My mother left the room at that point and I followed her. Halfway down the stairs she met my father coming up. 'David, where on earth have you been? I could have done with some of that bohemian charm of yours to deal with dreary Deirdre!'

Her voice was clear and angry and I knew it

would carry up the stairs and through the open door. For a moment my father looked irritated, but he must have glimpsed my worried face peeping out from behind my mother because his features cleared and he winked at me before he answered her.

'Hush, Helen, it's time you rested – no, I insist. Bethany, why don't you go and rescue Sarah? As soon as I've settled your mother, I'll take you both for a walk along the beach to Seatoncliffe. We'll go to Bertorelli's for an ice-cream.'

He had put his arm around my mother's shoulder and, all the time he was talking, he was coaxing her the rest of the way down the curved staircase of the tower.

'But, honestly, David,' I heard her saying as they walked away from me, 'the woman is impossible! I've put her in my favourite place in the whole house and she's not a bit grateful.

'You do know that she believes they have more right to Dune House than we have, don't you? Raymond has told her some ridiculous story about my grandfather cheating his brother out of the inheritance. She believes there's another will somewhere...'

The voices faded and the images wavered and lost substance; my throat ached with grief and the desire to recall them all. There were tears in my eyes as I stood in the centre of the room.

It was empty now, literally. Not even a carpet to cover the floorboards, no pictures on the walls. I remembered there had been pictures, but not like the heavy oil paintings in the rest of the house, the worthy biblical allegories and the gloomy Scottish glens. The pictures in the tower rooms had been delicate water colours of the sand and the sea and the sky, and of the seabirds that always seemed to be circling over the cliffs and over the dunes.

I looked around at the bare walls and at the four windows, one set in each wall. This room at the very top of the tower was the only room to have a view of all the points of the compass. North to the dunes and south to Seatoncliffe, east towards the sea and west across Templeton land towards the countryside and the rise of the green hills.

In the morning it was full of the light of air and sea. My mother had been right – Sarah should have been delighted with this room.

Now I stared out across the dunes. From my enclosed vantage point, the marram-covered ridges, stretching for miles to the north, seemed remote and silent.

Then my eye was caught by something. The sun was flashing on glass, or was it rooftops? Inland from the dunes, towards the hills and just beyond the drystone walls that must have been the boundary to my own land, there were rows and rows of caravans.

It was the caravan park that Mr Simpson had told me about. Its owner, Paul Mitchell, wanted to buy some land from me to extend his site. He had offered a great deal of money, but I could not think about that yet.

I had begun to people this house with my forgotten family and I was puzzled by some of the things that they had said. What had aunt Deirdre meant when she said my father was beginning to be successful? As far as I knew, my father had never made a success of anything in the material sense.

What had my mother meant by his 'bohemian charm'? And the man that I had just remembered – exasperated, but laughing and confident as he coaxed my mother out of one of her arrogant moods – that was not the sad, diffident man I had lived with for all those years in London.

I looked around the room. They were all gone but something lingered ... the sweet, cloying smell of aunt Deirdre's perfume...

I pushed my fingers through my hair in sheer vexation. Why should I have remembered that? I had not liked her perfume when I was a child and I did not like it now. I hurried down the tower stairs and back to my room. I had decided to get dressed and walk in the dunes.

What had made me think that this was a silent landscape? The dunes depend on the wind for their very existence and here, even as the sun grew warmer, the breeze was constantly shifting through the marram grass and the air was full of bird calls.

Not just the sea birds; the rich vegetation and insect life in the dunes attracts linnets, meadow pipits and skylarks. A kestrel hovered, waiting to swoop on some unfortunate mouse or vole.

I watched, fascinated, yet not wanting to see the moment when the hawk began its deadly dive. I could visualize only too well what the outcome would be, so I turned quickly and headed towards one of the gaps in the sand ridges that I knew must lead to the beach.

I remembered the island as soon as I saw it – or perhaps even a few moments before that. The path I followed cut down, steeply, through two high banks of yellow sand crowned with vegetation; but before I had even stepped out from the shelter of the overhanging grasses onto the sloping beach, I knew what I would see if I turned towards the north.

It wasn't very big – more an outcrop of rock than a proper island – and you could walk to it when the tide was out, as it was that morning. The ancient, manmade causeway was plain to see, rising about a foot above the glistening tide-ridged sand. I remembered being fascinated by the island when I was a child. I was always asking to go there, but it was forbidden.

A cloud covered the sun and at the same time the wind died and the air grew silent. Even the gulls stopped crying as they hung over the water. The sea was as smooth as glass, the breaking waves merely frothing gently on the pebbles at the shoreline.

I walked down towards the start of the causeway; when I reached it, I stopped and tried to judge the distance. I guessed the island must be about a quarter of a mile away – not too far, then. I started to walk across.

'Stop!'

I was almost there when the shout rang out and I spun round in shock.

'I wouldn't do that if I were you!'

It was a man's voice, authoritative and urgent,

but where was he? Behind me the causeway and the beach were empty. I looked upwards towards the ridge of the dunes.

He was standing at the top of the path that I had just descended, a tall, very masculine figure in jeans and a grey cotton sweatshirt. I caught my breath and my heartbeat quickened. But the sun emerged from behind the clouds and I saw the bright blond hair. He was a stranger.

'Did you hear me? Come back!' He started hurrying with awkward, long-legged lurches down the bank. Small avalanches of displaced sand plunged down ahead of him.

'Why should I?' I yelled, indignantly.

'For goodness sake, woman, don't argue with me and don't just stand there – do as I say!'

The lilt of his voice became more attractively Scottish in his anger and, for some reason, that made my spirits lift. I was still standing where I had stopped, smiling foolishly, when he reached the beginning of the causeway.

'Why shouldn't I go to the island?' I shouted.

'No reason – that is, if you don't mind waiting there until the tide goes out again!' He wasn't shouting now but his voice carried clearly in the morning air.

*The tide*, I thought, but it was low tide, wasn't it?

He had read my mind. 'It's on the turn.'

And then I remembered with a stab of fore-boding why the place had been forbidden to me. Once the water had reached the far shore of the island it divided and came racing round to meet up again and cover the causeway in a matter of minutes. If you were caught there, at best you would get a soaking; at worst there was a strong northerly current that could sweep you away.

'Will you look behind you, woman?'

I turned round. In the few minutes since he had shouted for me to stop, the rocky outcrop had become an island again and the waves were surging in from each side and forming angry cross-currents as they met each other.

'I think you'd better hurry.' He was quite calm but, even as he spoke, the advancing water began to lap around my feet.

I ran. It probably took me no more than two or three minutes to reach the end of the causeway and yet, by then, the water was ankle deep and I could feel my bare skin stinging from the assault of the grit and small pebbles carried in the swirling foam.

Since telling me to hurry, my rescuer had walked towards me and stood with one arm outstretched ready to grab at me and pull me the last few steps onto the beach.

At one point I caught my foot on a large pebble and almost fell. Out of the corner of my eye I saw him start forwards, as if to come and help me, but I righted myself quickly and he stopped. I was panting slightly when I reached him and took his outstretched hand.

We looked at each other and something in his face made my eyes widen. What was he staring at? Merely a slim girl in blue shorts and a long red T-shirt? Or something unexpected that had surprised him?

I was wearing old training shoes without socks

and I had combed my hair and let it hang loose to my shoulders. I did not think it was because he thought me beautiful, yet he was staring so intently. Had I imagined it, or had his first expression been one of shock?

I lifted my chin and stared back, coolly. He had a strong-boned face with regular features and he was very attractive in a rugged, outdoors way. His skin crinkled slightly at the corners of his clear blue eyes. His hair was straight and surprisingly soft looking. At that moment it was flopping down across his brow, almost covering one eye. He raised one hand and pushed it back. I think he sighed.

We walked up the beach together. He went ahead up the steep dune track, pulling me up behind him; at the top, we stopped. He let go of my hand and looked down at my face. He was smiling, quizzically. 'Have you hurt yourself?'

'No, why do you ask?'

'You're dragging one foot a little – your right one. Perhaps you twisted your ankle when you stumbled?'

'Yes, perhaps...' I frowned. I remembered the moment when I had almost fallen. I had not been conscious of any pain at the time. I realized I had not thanked him and I did so, shyly.

He laughed. 'Don't mention it. I'm always rescuing damsels in distress – it's part of the job.'

'Job?'

'I'm the warden of the Nature Reserve, here.' While he was speaking, he turned to look across the dunes.

'I didn't know there was a Reserve – have I

been trespassing?'

'No, of course not.' He looked at me and smiled. 'Anyone can walk here – that's the trouble, of course. It's natural for people to want to enjoy such a beautiful coastline, but trampling can destroy huge areas of vegetation. I try to work out ways to help strike the balance-' he broke off. 'I won't bore you with the details.'

'I'm not bored!'

'Thanks, but I know I get carried away whenever I've got a captive audience! My name's Duncan, by the way, Duncan Alexander.' He held his hand out towards me.

A skylark soared overhead, its sweet clear singing filling the air around us. I took his hand.

'Bethany Lyall.'

We shook hands, formally. He was standing with his back to the sun so that I could not see his expression clearly, but when I said my name something changed between us. It was as if I was only telling him something that he had already guessed but did not want to believe. This time I did not imagine the sigh.

'I'd better get home...' I looked down at my feet. 'My shoes are wet and full of sand.' They would dry in the sun, of course, but I was suddenly on edge and it was as good an excuse as any.

'OK. I'll take you back to the road – that will make for more comfortable walking.'

I followed him through the dunes. The path twisted and turned around the uneven parallel ridges and, in places, the sand banks towered over us. It was like walking into enclosed pockets of heat. I had no idea which way I was going and

I realized how easy it would be to get lost or at least temporarily disorientated.

When we emerged and walked out onto the road it was as if we had returned to civilization after having been trapped in a strange alien world – a landscape from a science-fiction movie.

We had hardly spoken until then; now Duncan put one hand on my shoulder and with the other he pointed along the road to our left. 'That's the way back to Seatoncliffe. I presume that's where you're staying.'

He knew it wasn't.

'No, I'm at Dune House. It – it belonged to my grandmother.' I was not ready to admit to owning it.

'I see.'

His voice was subdued, but I didn't take too much notice at the time. I was perplexed. The dunes were behind us, across the road farmland stretched away towards the hills. I could not see the sea at all.

When I had left the house earlier I had turned to the north and followed the road until it struck inland. At that point the coastline bulged out into the North Sea and the road obviously took the more direct route across to where the land curved in once more. In doing so, it cut off a large area of the sand-dunes. This was where I had been walking.

I realized that Duncan had brought me back onto the road at a point much further to the north than I had left it. I was still some way from home.

He said, 'I'll have to leave you, now, Bethany.

I've left some film washing in the tank.'

'Film?'

'Yes, it's a bonus having a job like this if you're a keen photographer!' He had already moved away from me, back towards the dunes. He must have seen my puzzled expression.

'I live in an old fisherman's cottage near the lighthouse,' he explained. 'The road gets there eventually, but it's quicker this way. If you're staying here long enough, you're welcome to come and visit. I can tell you all about conservation and your responsibilities as a landowner.'

'Landowner?'

'Yes, well, I mean, if you've inherited Dune House, you've also inherited a tract of land and that means all the wild life that goes with it...'

He sounded awkward and, for the first time since I had met him, seemed lost for words. He had realized that he'd revealed that he knew too much about me, but I was not perturbed. Seatoncliffe is a small place and no doubt everyone would know that my grandmother had died recently, so if I suddenly turned up it did not take too much intelligence to guess that I might be the heir.

I smiled and tried to put him out of his misery. 'All right, then, I may take you up on that.'

'Goodbye, then.' He turned and walked away.

The sun grew warmer as I walked back but again there was a strong wind blowing in from the sea. It skimmed the tops of the dunes and whistled through the grasses; soon my hair was full of windborne sand. I was looking forward longingly to reaching the house and having a shower.

I hadn't gone far when, on my right, I noticed a dusty cart-track heading inland across the fields. It led to the caravan park. I imagined that there must be a better road from the Leisure Park directly into Seatoncliffe, but this track would be handy for anyone from the site who wanted to go to the dunes or the quieter beaches.

I stopped and looked towards the caravans. Even at this distance I could hear a radio blaring out pop music and I could smell the breakfasts cooking. I began to hurry; I was hungry.

Soon the area of sand-dunes on my left shrank to a few feet as the road approached the coastline again and the dunes themselves gave way to low sandstone cliffs that seemed steeper as the land rose towards the vantage point where Dune House stood.

By the time the house was within striking distance, the cliffs plunged, dramatically, to the beach below; there was only a foot or so of grassy land dividing the edge of the road from a sheer drop.

I remember the next few moments vividly. I can still smell the warm, sea-scented air, feel the sting of the sand on my face and, if I close my eyes, I can see the sun sparkling on the water and the wind slicing in across the waves to hurl the spindrift against the foot of the cliffs below me.

Because of the wind, I didn't hear the car until the last moment. By the time I had registered the crunch of fast wheels on gravel, the loose stones scattering across the road, it was almost too late.

I sensed rather than saw the dark shape looming up behind me and I flung myself sideways. As I fell, I felt a glancing blow on my right foot and I cried out in pain. The next moment I gasped and reached out both arms to hang on to the grass around me for dear life. I had landed on the very edge of the cliff.

# CHAPTER 4

I was face down on the ground and there was a gritty taste in my mouth... What was it? Sand...

I had lost all sense of time and place – only the wind from the sea was constant.

I frowned and tried to concentrate on the frantic movement in front of my eyes... Insects, no bigger than the tumbling grains of sand, scurried away from the disturbance I had caused.

Then I remembered that I had fallen and had flung my arms out in front of me to grasp at clumps of grass.

I raised my head a little but my vision blurred – instead of my own forearms stretching out in front of me, I saw the skinny, sun-tanned arms of a young child.

*I was seven years old and I had hurt myself badly. My right ankle was caught somewhere behind me and the pain was intense...*

The sense of the past was strong, but instead of welcoming the knowledge it might bring, I closed my eyes and fought my way back. For, with the vision had come a thrill of fear and something else – a gut-wrenching anguish.

I had to fight down the sense of terror and desolation that was beginning to overwhelm me – I was not prepared to face whatever it was that had marked me so deeply.

The moment passed.

The sound the waves made as they crashed onto the sharp-toothed rocks at the base of the cliff below was only too real. At high tide those rocks would be ten or twelve feet under water – and the tide was on the way in.

If I fell now, my body would almost certainly be broken in the rock-filled surf. If I hung on until the tide came in, I could be washed out to sea.

*Just as she had been...*

I had to save myself. My right leg was half on the road – splinters of gravel dug into my flesh – but my left leg was dangling over the edge of the cliff. It should have been easy enough to push off with my left hand and roll over onto my back, bringing me safely onto terra firma, but I just couldn't bring myself to let go of the clumps of grass.

Then I heard footsteps.

I was too disorientated to tell which direction they were coming from. They crunched towards me and then stopped.

There was a silence which went on for too long. I gripped the clumps of grass so hard that my muscles began to lock. An icy surge of panic engulfed me. I certainly couldn't bring myself to move my head and look round.

Then, at last, a man's voice said, 'Here, let me help you.'

A moment later I stood on the cliff road staring into the face of my rescuer. He was not much taller than I, but he was heavily built and muscular. He had blue eyes and dark hair that was curly and slightly too long. And, to complete his Romany appearance, his skin was tanned.

His black sports shirt and stone-coloured slacks were obviously expensive, but the gold chain glinting at his neck and the flashy wrist-watch gave him a showy air.

'We–ell, hello...' He raised his eyebrows and I thought he was being fresh – and found time to wonder why he found me worth the effort in the state I was in.

He stared, curiously, at my scowling reaction and then, I realized to my embarrassment, that, since he had hauled me to my feet, I hadn't uttered a word.

'Thank you,' I gulped and it was only then that I began to shake.

His blue eyes filled with genuine concern. 'Were you jogging? Did you stumble?'

'No, I didn't stumble – someone tried to kill me.' I'd had no idea that I was going to say that. In fact, I surprised myself, but his reaction was unsettling.

I was sure he looked frightened but when he spoke his voice was firm enough. '*Kill* you? How?'

'A car ... it came up behind me ... knocked me over ... deliberately.'

His eyes narrowed. He turned and looked each way, up and down the deserted road, and then he faced me once more and I felt myself flushing.

'I'm not making it up.'

'I wasn't going to suggest that you were – about the car, I mean. But surely it's more likely to have been an accident?'

'Then why didn't he stop?'

'*He?*'

'The driver – he or she – it all happened so

quickly, I didn't even see what kind of car it was...'

I stopped and chewed on my lip as I recalled the impression of the dark shape hurtling up behind me... Surely if I concentrated I would be able to describe it, tell him something about it-

But he went on quickly, 'I can guess.'

'Guess what?'

'Why the driver didn't stop. Even now some young tearaway's probably panicking – thinking that he's in real trouble. But there's no harm done, thank God.

'All the same, I think I'd better call the police.'

If he was acting it was very good. His expression conveyed indignation being overcome by reason. 'Look, I know whoever did this deserves to have the law on him, but I really don't think there's much point.'

'Why not?'

'Can you describe the car?'

'No.'

'Can you describe the driver?'

'No.'

'Can you even prove it happened?'

'What do you mean, can I prove it happened? You found me on the cliff's edge, hanging on for dear life!' I was so angry that I began to shake again.

'Look, calm down, please, no offence, but when I found you, I thought you'd stumbled and fallen. There was no sign of a car.'

'Don't you believe me?'

'Well, yes, but I wouldn't be able to back you up if the police asked me to.'

'Thanks. Great.'

'Look, I'm sorry, but that's the truth.'

And, of course, it was. He was being utterly reasonable, so why did I have the impression that there was more to it than that? That he wanted me to forget the incident and not cause trouble?

When I smiled he must have thought he had convinced me, but I didn't leave him long with that comforting illusion.

'Well,' I said, 'there would be no need for you to say anything. The police could see for themselves that I wasn't just a hysterical woman.'

He became very still. 'How?'

'Look.'

I pointed and he stared down at the disturbed surface of the road. The scattered chips of gravel didn't prove very much, but the deep imprints left by the tyres in the soft, sandy soil at the road's edge were unmistakable – as were the flattened swathes of grass, some of it pulled up by the roots.

'Yes, well, that's evidence, I suppose, but I still don't think there's much chance of catching the culprit – and if they did, what would they charge him with? Dangerous driving? They're not going to believe that anyone would want to murder you.'

I didn't answer him. I couldn't because I had no answers to the questions he had raised. I don't know whether he thought that, at last, he'd convinced me not to call the police but, eventually, he seemed to relax.

'Now don't you think I'd better get you home?'

'Home?'

'Yes, home. Can you walk? I'd go and get my

car, but you're shocked and I don't like leaving you. Here, lean on me, luckily it isn't far.'

He reached out to take my arm but I backed away in confusion. 'What's the matter?' he asked.

'How do you know it isn't far?'

'Excuse me?'

For a moment he looked as confused as I was, then he began to grin. When he smiled he looked years younger and very attractive – I couldn't help being drawn to him. Nevertheless, I was suspicious.

'I mean, you seem to know where I'm going.'

'Of course I do, Dune House. You may have grown up, but you haven't changed much, Bethany.'

As my eyes widened his smile became rueful. 'I knew you hadn't recognized me. I'm Paul – Paul Mitchell.'

'The caravans...'

'You do remember, then?'

'No, I'm sorry, I don't really ... in fact, not at all.'

'Then how...?'

'Mr Simpson – my grandmother's solicitor – he told me you were negotiating to buy some land...'

'Yes, that's right, but I'm disappointed that you don't remember me. Vanity, I suppose. I know I'm not the skinny kid I used to be, but otherwise I don't think I've changed that much.'

He grinned but he couldn't quite disguise his sense of pique. He obviously wasn't used to any female forgetting him.

We began to walk towards the house. It would have been easier if he had allowed me to link arms as I hobbled along, but he insisted on putting his arm around my waist. As well as giving me some support this brought me very close to him and I could feel the warmth of his body through my cotton top and smell his aftershave.

'I recognized *you* straight away, you know–' he still sounded a bit peeved '–even though you've grown so tall. It's not just that you haven't changed much, but the family likeness has grown stronger, if anything.'

'Family likeness?'

'Yes, in spite of the difference in heights, you could almost be Sarah's sister.'

'Sarah.'

I barely whispered the word. Suddenly it was all moving too fast. Paul Mitchell could have no idea that until last night I had had no conscious recollection of my cousin – nor any of the people or events of my first seven years.

I decided not to tell him. I persuaded myself that it was because it was all too complicated and I didn't want to appear foolish but, in reality, a deeper instinct was guiding me. Something had happened here in the past, something that had terrified me and, until I remembered what it was, I was convinced that I had to be cautious.

On another level, I had the hunch that he might talk more easily and I would learn more if he just assumed my poor memory was due to the natural passage of the years.

But for a while he didn't say anything at all so, eventually, I asked, 'Do you still see Sarah?'

'Well, I can hardly avoid that, can I?'

He was laughing and I was vexed. His answer

had told me that my cousin was probably still here in Seatoncliffe, but it had also thrown the ball back into my court.

Luckily, he didn't notice my predicament and he went on, 'I don't know why I let her get away with it, but I allowed her to take up residence in one of my best caravans after your grandmother threw her out.'

'*Threw her out?*'

'You didn't know?'

My surprise had been so evident that I could hardly deny it. 'No. Why did she do that?'

'I'm not really sure. At first the old girl seemed pleased when Sarah came back from Spain – I mean, she must have been lonely rattling around in that great house all on her own. But, clever as she is, Sarah obviously didn't play her cards right...'

'Play her cards right?'

He hesitated; when I glanced up at him, he couldn't meet my eye. 'Well, you know what I mean. Sarah was skint and Deirdre wouldn't have her back. She had nowhere to go. You can't deny Dune House is a cosy billet – and your grand-mother–'

'Was loaded.'

'Yeah, well... You know what a charmer your cousin can be; it was silly of her to have fouled it up. She could have been living the life of Riley instead of waiting for her next social security cheque and slumming it along at the caravan park.'

He saw my surprise and he jumped to the wrong conclusion. 'Oh, I'm not saying Prior's Park is a slum. Far from it. My caravans are the latest word in luxury, but it's not quite the same, is it?'

I decided to reveal some of the truth. 'Paul, if I looked surprised, it's because I knew nothing of the quarrel.'

He looked at me and, for a moment, his expression of easy-going charm sharpened into something much more shrewd.

'Sarah told me you haven't been in touch with her or her mother since you and your father left. I'm not surprised, really, not after the scandal Deirdre and – Deirdre caused, but I thought your grandmother might have told you about her quarrel with Sarah in her letters?'

'No.'

He was cleverer than I was. My answer had been short enough but, when I saw the way he looked at me, I was sure that he had guessed, there and then, that my grandmother and I had never corresponded. And I had the uneasy feeling that it mattered.

Was he playing games with me? Did he know that I knew nothing of what had been happening in Seatoncliffe for fourteen years or more and did he want me to admit that, or was he unsure and trying to fish for information without revealing anything, just as I was?

What had I learned? That Sarah had been in Spain ... that her mother wouldn't let her live with her. That surprised me – they had always been so close.

He had mentioned some kind of scandal that Aunt Deirdre had caused ... puzzling. Hadn't I just remembered that it was Uncle Raymond who had been sent to prison...?

I was so concerned with covering up my own ignorance of everything that it didn't fully register, at the time, that Paul's reaction had been as guarded as my own. It wasn't until I thought about it later that I wondered why he had acted as if he had something to fear...

'Here we are, Dune House.' We had stopped by the entrance to the drive. 'Do you want me to come inside with you?'

'Mmm?'

'I said do you want – for God's sake, why are you looking at me like that?'

'Paul ... why were you walking on the cliff road?'

'What do you mean? What are you getting at?'

'I mean, how did you just happen to be there when–?'

'Lucky I was!'

'Yes, but where were you going?'

'Can't I just go for a walk? Lots of people do – every morning, in fact.'

He was grinning, but I was determined not to be deflected. 'Do you? Go for a walk – every morning?'

'Usually. Even when the weather isn't as nice as this – dogs don't care about the weather.'

'Dogs?'

I stepped back from him and stared up into his face, then glanced all around in bewilderment.

Paul was laughing. 'One dog to be precise. Benjy.'

Before I could question him further, he crossed the road to the cliff's edge and scanned the beach. Then he gave a piercing whistle and waited, looking south towards the town, where the cliffs dipped down again.

Seconds later, and some way off, the long grasses that overhung the cliff's edge rustled violently and then parted to reveal a sleek, yellow Labrador.

'Here, then, Benjy. There's a good lad.'

The dog bounded up the road towards him and Paul crouched down to fondle its head. Man and dog were obviously fond of each other.

He stood up again to find that I was staring at them. 'Benjy's young, he has twice as much energy as I have – and I'm pretty fit,' he couldn't help adding.

'Sometimes, I let him go down to the beach without me – back there' – he turned towards the north – 'there's a path and some steps cut into the cliff. I walk along the top. I call him back when I think he's had enough.'

We stared at each other. I could hardly disbelieve him – the dog was there, living evidence that he was telling some version of the truth.

And yet, just a few seconds before, I had remembered, without warning, that moment on the cliff top when I hadn't known whether the person who stood over me was friend or foe.

All the terror I had experienced then had come flooding back. And, whether or not Paul Mitchell wanted to harm me, I knew that someone did and I couldn't rid myself of the suspicion that he knew about it. I turned from him and started hurrying towards the house.

'Bethany – I'll see you again?'

'Yes, I suppose so,' I called over my shoulder.

'I mean, I'd like to see you, show you around a little. And it's not just for old times' sake – I think we could really enjoy getting to know each other all over again.'

'Well, we'll see.'

Even the open admiration in his eyes couldn't make me smile; considering the man had just hauled me up from the cliff's edge and probably saved my life, my behaviour must have appeared offhand, to say the least, but I just had to get away.

The past was beginning to resurrect itself, whether I wanted it to or not, and was trailing with it some horror that had never been laid to rest.

I didn't know whether I had the strength to face it.

# CHAPTER 5

'Miss Lyall, is it? I'm Mrs Doran. Mr Simpson will have told you about me.'

The woman who met me in the entrance hall was middle-aged and comfortably plump with a round, friendly face, so it was disconcerting to sense that she hadn't warmed to me.

Before she had even spoken, she had glanced down at the trail of sandy footsteps I had left across the expensive carpet. This made me feel uncomfortable and out of place. I was just re-minding myself that this was *my* house, not hers, when she spoke.

'That's all right, Miss Lyall, it's easy enough to sweep up.'

I hadn't apologized – hadn't said a word. One to her!

She waited for a moment, then realized that I wasn't going to beg her pardon. She accepted defeat, philosophically, and was quite unruffled as she informed me, 'You've had a visitor while you've been out.'

'Visitor?'

I was puzzled. Who did I know in Seatoncliffe? Who knew me? Who knew I was back here? Unless it was Sarah...

'Said his name was Greg Randall.'

*Greg Randall* ... the name was familiar... I'd heard it before ... no, I knew the name... I knew

73

the man ... and yet I couldn't place him.

'Mrs Doran, what did he look like?'

'Gorgeous.'

'I beg your pardon?'

I looked at her in astonishment. The woman had forgotten her animosity long enough to smile – if somewhat cynically.

'Gorgeous. You know, tall, dark and handsome – not the kind of man you forget in a hurry. He said, not to worry, he'd catch up with you later.'

It had to be him. It had to be the man I bumped into in the rain, the man whose chilling look in the café had so disturbed me, the man I had shared a fantasy meal with in front of the fire last night. But why would he be calling on me this morning?

And, more important, why had his name, Greg Randall, meant something to me? He hadn't told it to me.

'Did he say what he wanted?'

'No. I told him he could wait for you if he was a friend of yours, but he said that you hadn't really met properly – whatever that means – and that he had to get on with some work.'

What kind of work? I wondered. I'd had the impression that he might be here on holiday.

'Miss Lyall, would you like some breakfast? Or would you like to freshen up first?'

I would have loved to have gone straight upstairs and had a shower and changed into some clean clothes. That's what I had intended to do the moment I got into the house, but the very suggestion that this woman was trying to tell me that I *should* do so before I contaminated the house any further made me decide against the idea.

'I think I'd like some breakfast, but it's all right, I can make it myself.'

She stared at me, assessing me, and I have no idea what she decided, but the result was a slight sniff and something that almost resembled a smile of welcome.

'Don't be daft, that's what I came in early for.'

For such an amply proportioned woman, she moved very quickly. By the time I reached the kitchen she was already laying rashers of bacon on the grill pan.

'You can sit here in the kitchen if you like.' Over her shoulder she nodded towards the end of the table. Had she thawed sufficiently to desire my company or did she just want to keep me and the mess I was out of the other rooms?

Whatever. I decided to take her up on her offer – the kitchen was warm and appetizing smells were beginning to fill the air.

'There's knives and forks in that drawer and the crocks are on the dresser.'

I set my place and sat and watched as she sliced tomatoes and cracked two eggs into a bowl before tipping them into the frying pan.

'Tea or coffee?'

'I'd like some tea, please, Mrs Doran.'

'Betty.'

'OK.'

She poured boiling water into a large teapot. 'I'll have a cup of tea with you, and mebbe a slice of toast.'

'Of course. Did you bring these provisions, by the way? I mean, I didn't find bacon and eggs in the fridge when I put some things away last night.'

'Yes, I noticed that you'd done some shopping, but I couldn't be sure that you would, so I told Mr Simpson that I would make sure the pantry was filled for you.'

'Thank you. Tell me what I owe you.'

'No, Mr Simpson will see to everything like that until it's all sorted out.'

She paused and faced me. 'You mean to stay, then?'

'Well, yes, for a while...'

'Not for good?'

'I haven't decided yet.' Even as I said it, I knew that I wanted to – in spite of everything that had happened.

'Here you are, then.' Betty Doran set an enormous plate of breakfast in front of me. I stared at the bacon, eggs, tomatoes and fried bread in dismay.

'Go on, you look as if you need feeding up. I'll start making some toast for us both.'

I was hungry. It was probably the sea air, or maybe the luxury of having someone cooking for me, but I enjoyed my breakfast and we didn't say much until I had cleared my plate.

Although I did make her promise that, if ever she cooked breakfast for me again, she would aim for more ladylike proportions.

'Yes, well, muesli and orange juice, I know the kind of thing. As a matter of fact I used to squeeze fresh juice every morning for your grandma.'

'Did you?'

We stared at each other over our teacups and our plates of toast and marmalade. This had been the first mention of my grandmother, Frances Templeton, and I knew that we could no longer avoid discussing her.

The cosy atmosphere that had lasted as long as we shared the kitchen table for our meal had gone. The assessing look was back on Mrs Doran's face.

'I came in every day, cleaned, washed and ironed and did a bit of cooking – although she didn't eat enough. Actresses and models – all the same, aren't they?'

'Actresses? Models?' I looked at her wildly; I thought we had been discussing my grandmother. 'What are you talking about?'

'Well ... it was a long time since she'd made a film – I think she only made one after she and your grandfather got married–' so we were talking about my grandmother '–but she never gave up her glamorous ways, did she?'

'I don't know ... it's been a long time since...'

I was reeling under the influence of this new information. I was already grappling with the problem of gradually remembering the years I had spent here as a child, but now I realized that I needed to know so much more. Like all the stories and the family history that other people accept as facts about the people they grow up with.

That had all been taken away from me by whatever had sent my father and me scuttling to London fourteen years ago. My grandmother a movie star? I was mad about the old black and white movies... Josie and I watched them whenever we could on television. I might even have seen her in one of them and never known it was her.

'She was lonely, living here on her own, you know.' Mrs Doran's look was accusing.

'I didn't know ... I mean, how could I?'

'That Sarah ... she livened her up for a while, but the arrangement didn't work out. I didn't think it would.'

Did I dare ask her what had happened? Before I had made up my mind, she hurried on, 'Of course Mrs Templeton had friends in Seatoncliffe. The ladies she played bridge with, especially Mrs Bradfield, a retired theatrical herself. It was Mrs Bradfield who organized the funeral, as a matter of fact.'

'The funeral...'

Betty Doran got up and reached for my empty plates. 'But friends aren't the same as family, are they?'

I couldn't meet her eyes. 'No.'

'I'm not blaming you, it's not my place to. I know your father and your grandma fell out many years ago. I don't know much about it, I didn't live in Seatoncliffe then. I just wanted you to know that I think it's a shame, that's all.'

She turned away to dump the plates on the kitchen bench, then filled a plastic bowl with hot water. She squeezed some washing-up liquid through the rising steam, but turned to face me before she started washing the dishes.

'Do you want me to come in every day, then?'

'No, no, I can manage quite well, thank you.'

'That's as may be, but this is a big house and Mr Simpson said I should go on keeping it in order until the question of the inheritance was settled.'

I could hear him saying just that, with his precise old-fashioned delivery, but it also occurred to me that Mr Doran might need the job and didn't like to admit it.

'We–ell, I don't think I need you every day...'

'Twice a week then, like it's been up to now?'

'Why don't we make it three days, say, Monday, Wednesday and Friday? But I don't need you to make my meals–'

'I could easily make your breakfast; if there's any washing, just leave it–'

'OK, that's great. Now I think I'll go up for a shower.'

After my shower, I dumped my shorts and T-shirt in the laundry basket and pulled on some jeans and a pale blue, long-sleeved sweatshirt. Through my bedroom window I had noticed that the skies were clouding over again and I had already learned how cold it could be here.

The only place to plug in my hairdryer was the single socket which had been installed for the bedside lamp. As this would mean crawling under the bed, I used the socket on the landing near the top of the stairs. Luckily my hairdryer had a long flex; by standing in my bedroom doorway, I got a half-decent view of the dressing-table mirror.

I smiled when I thought how this would amuse Josie. Here I was, an 'heiress', and having the same kind of trouble as we both had in our inconvenient little flat.

When I was ready, I went downstairs and made a phone call.

Paul Mitchell had almost convinced me that it would be pointless to tell the police about my 'accident', but I found that I couldn't let it go. Somehow, I felt I would be safer if I at least registered with someone what had occurred.

So what happened next was all the more frustrating – and worrying.

It wasn't too long before the patrol car arrived. Two young constables listened courteously and one of them took notes while I told them what had happened.

Mrs Doran had shown them into a small, cosy room she called the 'morning-room'. She hovered for a moment but I didn't tell her what it was all about.

The taller of the two policemen, who had introduced himself as PC McKenzie, asked me, 'Are you injured at all? I noticed that you're limping slightly.'

'Well, that was the leg that was knocked...'

'But?' He was shrewder than he looked.

'I've an old childhood injury. It was so long ago that I can't remember exactly what happened – but I do limp now and then. Usually when I'm tired.' Or stressed, I could have added.

Then his colleague, PC Robson, who wasn't that much smaller – Northumbria police seem to recruit fine young giants – said that we should visit 'the scene of the crime'.

They took me in the patrol car to the place on the cliff top where I was sure it had happened – but could no longer prove it. The tyre tracks had been obliterated. Someone had smoothed over the sandy soil at the road's edge for some distance in each direction until the marks could have been anything – and certainly were no use at all as evidence.

Mac and Rob, as they called each other, looked at me doubtfully.

'It would be very hard to prove anything, Miss Lyall,' McKenzie said.

Wordlessly, I pointed to the clumps of disturbed and uprooted grass and he sighed. 'That could have been dogs, kids, anything.'

I knew it was hopeless. 'You don't believe me, then?'

'No, I'm not saying that.'

Rob was already back inside the car, radioing back to control. He confirmed their attendance at the scene and I heard him say, 'No, no description. Nothing to go on...'

McKenzie spoke quite kindly and his freckled, rawboned face looked almost handsome when his blue eyes smiled. 'I'm just saying that without a clear description and with the physical evidence gone, we stand very little chance of catching the culprit.'

'You do believe there was a culprit?'

'Aye, I do. We've had complaints before about some of the people who stay at the caravan park using this road like a race track. But we're not going to nobble any of them this time.'

'You think whoever did it came back and wiped out the tyre tracks, then?'

'Aye, well, I hadn't put them down as being as smart as that, but, yes, that's what must have happened.'

I watched their car heading back towards

Seatoncliffe. They had offered to take me back to the house but I preferred to walk and think things over.

I was glad that I hadn't told them that whoever had run me down had done it deliberately.

They had classed the incident as a 'hit and run' and it would be logged in the computer as such. I wanted, very much, to believe that version of events. It was much better than having to accept that someone in Seatoncliffe wanted me dead.

A brisk wind had sprung up. In spite of the sunshine, I grew quite cold on the walk back along the cliff road, so it was a pleasure to enter the walled garden at the back of Dune House. The sunken garden faced southwest and, being sheltered from the north-easterlies by the bulk of the house, it was as if it existed in a different climatic zone.

As I crossed the lawn towards the summerhouse, it was easy to imagine that it also existed in a different time zone. The lawn, the winding paths amongst the shrubberies, the rose garden with the old statuary were all laid down in more gracious days. Days when the owners of a house like this would be able to afford a full-time gardener or two.

But everything was sadly neglected. I gazed round at the unpruned roses, the overgrown shrubs and the straggling lawn, helplessly.

Dad and I had never had a garden and I had no idea how to tackle what was obviously becoming an urgent problem. I would probably do more harm than good if I tried to do anything.

I would phone Mr Simpson, I decided. Whatever I did in the long run, whether I stayed and accepted my inheritance, or relinquished it in favour of the other heirs, my grandmother's solicitor would understand that the garden of the house must not be neglected so.

Surely he would be able to release some funds, especially as the grounds at the front of the house were obviously being taken care of. But I hadn't come to make an inspection of the garden. I had come to have a look at the summer-house.

Even now, with the sun high and the shadows almost non-existent, I shivered as I remembered that moment the night before when the gulls had screeched and the door had creaked and banged in the greyness at the bottom of the garden.

The building looked ordinary enough now. Quite large, but, nevertheless, it was only a wooden lean-to attached to the boundary wall. The windows, at each side of the door, were dirty and cobwebby.

The roof of the summer-house sloped down to shade a veranda that ran along the front of the building and was enclosed by a wooden balustrade, once ornate but now in a state of disrepair. It must have been years since my grandmother, or anyone, had sat here to enjoy the sun.

To one side of the summer-house, set into the high garden wall, was a heavy, old wooden gate. I had only just noticed it, so I turned and looked back the way I had come. I realized that the gate would be difficult to see from the house.

*We're not supposed to play in the summer-house, it's dangerous.*

I remembered my words and my cousin Sarah's answer.

*They only say that because they don't want us getting out into the Priory garden...*

But who had said the summer-house was dangerous?

Not my grandmother or my parents for I remembered that I had been allowed to play in there before Sarah and Aunt Deirdre came to stay with us.

Aunt Deirdre then? Yes.

*The floorboards on the veranda are rotting, Sarah.*

Her thin, complaining voice came back to me over the years.

'You are not to go anywhere near the summer-house, you could fall and hurt yourself, badly.'

After her mother had gone, Sarah had scowled. 'That's because she can't be bothered to look after us.' She was annoyed enough to criticize her mother for once. 'She doesn't see why your mother should be allowed to rest and she should have to be responsible. If she confines us to the house, she thinks we won't come to any harm and she won't have to bother herself.'

Sarah loved her mother fiercely but she was not unaware of her faults and there was no denying that Deirdre was lazy.

But there was something nagging at the fringes of my memory... Sarah had been only half-right... There had been another reason why Deirdre had wanted to be sure we didn't stray...

Two shallow steps led up onto the veranda. The floorboards were not rotting, even now, all these years later, and the building itself looked safe enough. The door was fastened with a latch, the kind that gives trouble if the bar doesn't fall exactly into the catch.

That could have explained why the door had been swinging to and fro in the wind the night before – and then one rush of air more violent than the others could have slammed it shut with such force that the bar fell into place and the door stayed closed.

I lifted the latch and stepped inside. What had I been expecting? The stench of damp and decay? I found that the interior was pleasantly warm and, although there was a faint smell, a kind of spicy, musky odour, it was not unpleasant.

After a moment or two, my eyes adjusted to the dimness and I looked around. The place was clean enough, considering how long it must have been since anyone had used it.

An old but decent carpet covered most of the floor, deck-chairs were stacked in one corner next to a folded parasol, and a table and two chairs were placed against the back wall.

In one corner there was an armchair piled up with scatter cushions and a couple of rugs.

*We've made our own den in the summer-house, you can come if you want to, Bethany, Gyp's going to bring food and something to drink...*

Sarah's voice rang out stronger than ever as the events of that last summer in Seatoncliffe came tumbling back at me again.

I had to grip the edge of the table with both hands for support.

There was a bottle on the table, a wine bottle covered in melted candle wax. Surely it couldn't be the same bottle that Gyp had brought all those years ago? The tall green bottle had been in the cardboard box along with the cans of coke, the packets of crisps, the bars of chocolate and the individual sandwiches wrapped in cellophane...

*This is great, Gyp, but wasn't it risky?* Sarah had been admiring, her eyes wide.

'Don't worry, nobody saw me take anything and the café's so busy at this time of year that this lot won't be missed.'

'But the wine? Where did you get the wine?'

He grinned. 'Let's just say I know where there's a private supply.'

Gyp had brought a corkscrew and Sarah was impressed with the way he opened the bottle, as if he'd done it before.

She poured a little of the dark red liquid into each of the three yellow and white melamine cups that, along with some paper napkins, was our contribution to the occasion.

I was seven years old, remember, and I didn't much enjoy my first taste of wine. After the face I pulled, I wasn't offered any more. Sarah and the boy she called Gyp finished the bottle between them.

Afterwards Gyp tidied away the remains of our secret feast. For a fourteen-year-old boy, he was incredibly neat and methodical. When Sarah mocked him about it, he explained that he couldn't help it, it was the way he lived.

I didn't always go with Sarah to meet Gyp; she didn't always want me. Sometimes the two of us had gone there and he wouldn't show up, then

Sarah always pretended that she knew what he would be doing.

As my mother's pregnancy advanced, we were left more and more to the care of Aunt Deirdre. She didn't seem to care what we did so long as we caused no trouble and turned up, clean and tidy, on time for meals.

My father wasn't much in evidence, either, but I had long accepted that he needed to be alone when he was working...

The memories faded. But as I stood there, looking down at the wax-encrusted wine bottle, which surely couldn't have been there for fourteen years, I wished I could remember just exactly what it was that kept my father so occupied.

The musky warmth inside the summer-house had made my head ache. I straightened up and turned to leave. And then, without warning, Sarah's voice came to me again across the gulf of years.

*Are you coming with me or not, Bethany? I can't wait all day for you to make your mind up!*

'Sarah, I can't – and you mustn't!'

'Don't be such a spoilsport! They'll never know where we've been.'

'But it isn't safe.' I wanted to go with her but it would be breaking all the rules.

'It's all right, Gyp has checked the tides and we've got ages before they turn. Oh, come on! He's waiting for us on the beach!'

'All right, I'll come.'

If only I hadn't agreed to go with her that day!

Then, suddenly, some powerful force, some form of self-preservation, made me abandon my journey into the past – there was something too awful waiting for me there, something that I never wanted to remember.

I had the sensation of fighting my way back against the tide and, as the brief burst of memory receded, it left me shaking and with tears streaming down my cheeks.

I stumbled out of the summer-house and across the veranda to grip the wooden balustrade for a moment before going down the steps into the garden.

I had to get away. Not just away from my memories but away from the place that had conjured them up for me.

I didn't want to go back to the house, either, so I turned towards the gate that led out into the Priory garden.

The gate was old and studded and the wood had a greeny-grey patina that was peeling off in places. There was a large, metal-rimmed keyhole but no sign of a key, and a bolt that had been shot home, but the staple was hanging loose. So, as long as the door had not been locked, it would be easy enough to open – from either side.

The gate pulled inwards, quite easily, and soon I was staring out across the area which had once been cultivated by the monks of Seaton Priory. The Priory itself, or what was left of it – mainly a series of beautiful arches – was only about two hundred yards from the garden wall.

Mr Simpson had explained that the historic buildings had been given by my grandmother to English Heritage, although the surrounding land was still part of the Templeton estate. The public were allowed access to the ruins – so long as they kept to the designated path.

I began to walk towards it along the path, which led to the Priory and then on towards the high road into Seatoncliffe. There was someone approaching from the other direction.

It was past noon and the sun was high, but the clouds were racing across the sky and throwing an ever-changing pattern of shadows on the rough turf ahead of me.

I knew it was him. But, although I continued to walk towards him, he hadn't noticed me yet. He was striding towards a collection of gravestones at the further side of a small chapel that looked almost perfect – except that it didn't have a roof.

He had a camera bag slung over one shoulder and, that day, he was wearing a black shirt and a dark leather jacket. This made him stand out against the pale greens and greys of the background. Although I still couldn't see his face clearly, I didn't need to.

Then he saw me. He stopped walking and became very still and so did I. The sun was high, the wind from the sea had swept the clouds inland towards the distant hills and the sky was clear.

*Greg Randall.* Of course.

Now I knew why the name had meant something to me and why, when I had studied his face for that surreptitious moment in The Gondola, I had thought it was familiar.

I knew who Greg Randall was, all right. But I could not imagine why he should want to see me.

# CHAPTER 6

'*Greg Randall?* You're joking!'

'I'm not, honestly, I've just spent the day – well, most of it – with him.'

'Bethany! Tell me all about it!'

When I phoned Josie that night she could hardly contain her excitement. Greg Randall had long been an unlikely hero of hers. She had every one of his television programmes on tape – even the ones he'd made for the Open University!

That was why his face had seemed familiar to me. I had seen it when I had been watching television with my flatmate.

On the screen he had been earnest, excited, passionate, his dark, mobile features lit by an inner fire of enthusiasm. That day, as we stood looking at each other in the ruins of the Priory, he was merely smiling.

There was no hint of the coolness he had shown the day before when he had learned my name and I began to hope that I had imagined it.

Besides, how could Greg Randall know anything about my father or my family history? He wasn't from Seatoncliffe.

And I guessed that he probably wasn't here on holiday, either. Greg Randall was an historian, or an archaeologist – I wasn't sure which – but he had left the academic world for a career in television, which was growing ever more successful.

I remembered the evening Josie had arrived home with stuffed vine leaves, feta cheese, olives, crusty bread and a doubtful-looking bottle of Greek wine – doubtful because neither of us could decipher the writing on the label.

'What's all this? I was expecting a Chinese take-away!' I protested.

'Greg Randall's on the box tonight. It's the first in a series about the ancient Greek theatres – you know, Epidaurus and the like – so I thought we'd get in the mood.'

It was the first time I'd heard of Greg Randall and, until then, Josie hadn't revealed her passion for him. 'I didn't know you were interested in ancient Greek drama, Josie.'

'I'm not, really, but that man could make even an inner-city shopping precinct sound interesting!

'Do you know that woman I told you about, the television researcher who came in to my ward to visit her brother? Well, she worked on this series with Greg – imagine spending all those months in Greece and on the islands with that gorgeous hunk of a man!'

Remembering Josie's words and her almost-teenage hero worship made me smile. He must have caught the faraway look in my eyes.

'What is it?' he asked.

'Oh, nothing... It's just that I know who you are.'

That must have sounded imbecilic and he frowned.

'I mean, I didn't recognize you yesterday when we ... when we bumped into each other on the sea front, but you left your name at the house earlier, and when I saw you I knew ... and I thought of my friend who ... oh, dear...'

It wasn't getting any better and I just hated the amused look that was beginning to make the corner of his eyes crinkle.

Two thoughts collided in my mind. One was that I must sound like one of his fans, overcome to be actually meeting him in person; the other was that he was used to it and he was about to be patronizing. That was the thought that damned him.

But all he said was, 'I'm sorry, I should have introduced myself yesterday.'

'No doubt you thought there wasn't any need.'

'I beg your pardon?' He looked surprised.

'I mean, you probably thought that I should know who you were.'

'Not at all.' No smile now and, in spite of my pique, I was sorry.

But then he went on, 'Even though my academic colleagues class my television programmes as popular entertainment, I know they have a selective audience.'

*Wow!* And I'd thought he was about to be merely patronizing. He'd gone straight for the jugular. He'd implied that he didn't think I was intelligent enough to watch cultural documentaries.

What could I say? On the contrary, I *do* know who you are, because I've watched every one of your programmes with my deranged friend, Josie. Deranged because she actually imagines that you're a nice person!

What I did say, after a long pause, was, 'Is that why you're here? Are you making a television programme now?'

I think he was relieved that I had decided to act like a grown-up. 'Yes,' he said and the smile came back. And suddenly the sun seemed to shine more brightly – yes, really.

When he spoke to me it wasn't a bit patronizing. 'At least, the programme is still at the planning stage, but I've sold them the idea and we've agreed a budget.'

'Them?'

'The independent film company who's backing me.'

'But why Seaton? I mean, I didn't think these ruins were very important...'

'Would you like to sit down?'

'Where?'

'Here, on this stone, or perhaps you'd rather go into the chapel?'

I looked at the upturned gravestone lying on its side amongst the long grass. The ravages of wind and rain and time had been so intense that it was impossible to make out any of the symbols that were carved there – except something that looked like a skull. 'I think I prefer the chapel.'

'Good.' He led the way to the ancient building. 'Actually, I came here today to get some shots of the ruins. I'm no photographer, but I like to give the cameraman an idea of what I'm after. After he stops laughing, he usually goes along with it.'

I couldn't help responding to him and I smiled. 'Hadn't you better take your shots then? I might even be able to help you.' At college I had discovered that I was good with a camera.

'There's plenty time for that, although I might take you up on the offer, when I get round to it. Right now, I think the time will be better spent explaining things.'

He pulled open the heavy wooden door. Strange that the door should be so solid and yet the chapel was open to the sky.

There was nothing remaining of its religious life, no altar, no pews – in fact, it was almost completely empty. The walls were bare of plaster and the stone slabs of the floor were uneven and covered with a faint dusting of sand. Brought by the wind, no doubt.

I said almost empty. At one end there were two stone coffins with broken lids. I wandered across to look at them. The pieces of broken stone were propped up against the sides of the coffins. The lid of one of them was almost intact; it had only one corner missing. The coffins themselves were completely empty.

What had I expected? Each to be filled with an arrangement of old bones?

'They look as if they're very old,' I said.

Greg had come up to stand beside me. 'They are,' he confirmed. 'There's a legend about these coffins; one of them is supposed to have belonged to one of the monks, the other one ... I'm not so sure. I'm trying to track the story down.'

'A monk? I thought they were children's coffins – especially that one.'

'No, they were both for adults. People were smaller then.'

That corner of the chapel was in shadow and I

shivered. It wasn't just the cold ... there was a pervasive sense of melancholy which seemed to be seeping out from the stone coffins and across the floor towards us. I moved back quickly.

All the windows were empty of glass, mere arched frames letting in the wind and weather. That day, sunlight streamed in to warm the centre of the floor space and the wall at one side.

'We'll sit here.' Greg put his camera bag down, carefully on the flagstones and took off his jacket. He spread it out in a pool of sunlight. He sat down, patted the place next to him and turned to open his bag. My hesitation made him look up and grin.

'Come on, I won't bite.'

I avoided his eyes as I lowered myself to sit beside him and, for a while, stared straight ahead as he busied himself finding a notebook and some loose papers from a pocket at the back of his camera bag.

It seemed so strange, so intimate, to be sitting here in the ruined chapel as close as I could be to a man I had only just met and yet, on another level, had known and admired for some time.

For, of course, I did admire him and, although I had never admitted it to Josie, I had been half-way along the road to hero worship, too.

'This foundation was never as important as Lindisfarne, of course, or even Tynemouth to the south of here.'

He was turning over the pages of a reporter's notebook. I glanced at his writing, large but completely indecipherable. I wondered if he'd developed that style on purpose so that no one could steal his research.

He glanced up and saw my expression and he grinned. 'I know, it's terrible. My excuse is that my formative years were spent travelling about the country so I never got a proper schooling.'

'But it couldn't have done you any harm?'

'What?'

'The travelling about – I mean, you got to university, didn't you?'

'Yes, well, we settled down eventually. I caught up.'

There was a certain bleakness in his expression that made me sorry I had opened up the subject. Now, I decided to change it, or rather bring it back to our reason for being there.

'So? Your programme?'

'Well, at first I thought I might do something about early Christianity – you know, the Venerable Bede, the Lindisfarne Gospels. They were exciting times...'

I could just see him on television, dressed in something rugged, Northumbria's dramatic scenery the perfect backdrop as he set about convincing his audience that the early days of Christianity in these islands were indeed very exciting.

'But suddenly I came across this other manuscript. It must have been gathering dust on the shelves in the cathedral library for years ... for centuries. Bethany, it's marvellous!'

When he said my name and looked straight into my eyes the way he did, something inside me, my heart probably, thumped against my ribcage so violently that I thought he must have heard it – or even felt it, that's how close we were.

'Marvellous,' I squeaked. 'Marvellous? Why?'

'Because all the time Bishop Eadfrith was writing his version of the gospels up on Holy Island, there was an unknown monk, here in Seaton, writing this marvellous stuff! Look, I've copied some out...'

He thrust his notebook in front of me and I gazed at the page, helplessly.

'Oh, I'm sorry, my writing, but if you concentrate, you'll get used to it.'

I concentrated in vain. After a while I said, 'Look, it's not just your writing, it's a language problem. Is this Latin?'

'Yes, Latin of a kind. I'm sorry, my fault.' He wasn't being a bit patronizing. When he got carried away by his enthusiasms, he seemed genuinely to forget that not everyone was as erudite as he was.

He took the book back and began to turn the pages, frowning. 'I thought I'd made one or two translations ... no, not here...'

He closed the book and stared down at it, thoughtfully.

'Why couldn't you just translate it for me?'

'Mmm?' He was avoiding looking at me.

'I mean, read it to me, now – in English?'

He seemed to consider my suggestion for a moment and he even opened his notebook at the page and studied the writing for a while. 'Ridiculous,' I heard him murmur.

'What's ridiculous?'

He turned to me and grinned, at the same time snapping the book shut, decisively. 'I can't, Bethany. Don't ask me to explain why, because I don't know. I've never had this problem of embarrassment before.'

If I felt a sudden heat as I held his gaze, it was because he had flushed, not me. The motes of ancient dust danced in the sunlight all round his head and the way we looked at each other for that long, long moment was as ancient as time itself.

'Embarrassment?' I whispered.

'You see, these are not sacred writings, they're ... I suppose you would call them profane.'

'Profane?'

'Yes, but you mustn't call them blasphemous!'

I wasn't going to – I hardly knew what profane meant – so I just shook my head earnestly as if I agreed with him.

'They're not religious writings at all,' he said, 'they're secular, but they're wonderful, full of life, full of joy, perhaps representing another way of life that was being experimented with here.'

He'd retreated into the television screen again, trying out his script with me a willing audience. Oh, Josie, I thought, how you would love to be here!

'You see, that example I showed you is a love poem.'

'Lo-ove?' I was annoyed with myself for the way my voice had cracked.

He was back in the chapel with me and he was grinning, 'And the language is very forthright.'

'You mean...?' Now it was my face that was pink.

'Yes, it's poetic, beautiful, but decidedly, dreadfully, bawdy. I may send a translation for you to peruse but I definitely can't read it to you here, face to face.'

'So, you're going to make a programme about monks who wrote rude rhymes?'

It wasn't that funny, but the tension that had built up between us snapped at my words and we both began to laugh, helplessly.

I leant back against the warm stone and so did he. It seemed perfectly natural when we both toppled sideways until our arms were touching and my head came to rest on his shoulder.

Our laughter subsided and, for a while, I just sat there, my eyes closed, and gave myself up to a growing awareness of his physical presence. I could feel the heat of his body through his fine linen shirt and indescribable sensations began to charge through me.

It was Greg who moved first, drawing away, almost imperceptibly, but enough to break our contact – and the mood.

'That's one way of putting it, but it's much more than that, of course. There was something going on here, something wonderful, not at all debauched or evil, some way of life that embraced every aspect of living, the joy of existence–' He broke off when he saw my expression. 'I'm going on a bit, aren't I?'

'Yes, but I don't mind. Just wait until I tell Josie.'

'Josie?'

'A fan of yours.' I didn't mind giving him that.

He turned to put his notebook away and I pointed to a sketch on a loose piece of paper that drifted to the floor. 'Is that a drawing of the Priory?'

He picked it up and gave it to me. 'Yes, but, as you can see, I've attempted a reconstruction – tried to make it look as it must have done in its glory days when it was one of the centres of early learning. I'm no artist, though.'

'No, it's quite good.'

I was given no warning.

'Nowhere near as good as this.'

He brought out a cardboard folder and opened it to reveal another sketch.

'This is a photocopy, my – someone I know has the original.'

He leaned towards me and my heart thumped again, but not because his arm accidentally brushed my breast, nor because his face was so close to mine that I could see the long, dark curve of his eyelashes.

It was the picture of the Priory that he had placed in front of me that had suddenly become the focus of my existence. I stared at it. I had never seen it before, never, and yet it was totally familiar to me. The swift, bold lines, the confident style, the beauty of the composition.

'He signed it, of course.'

Greg sounded subdued, but I was in no state to wonder why.

'Who?' The sound I made was more of a whimper for, before Greg answered me, my eyes had already found the flamboyant signature in the corner of the picture.

I was staring at it when he spoke. 'The artist, David Lyall.'

'My father.'

You know the expression, 'the earth stood still'?

Well, it did. Or it seemed at least to halt on its axis. There was a sickening lurch and the daylight dimmed until I was surrounded by a crimson darkness.

Only the picture resting on my knees in front of me continued to reflect a glaring light. I couldn't take my eyes away from it.

There was no sound either. I suppose that, until that moment, I had been aware of the wind soughing through the grass outside and the distant call of the sea birds, but now everything ceased – even the sound of my own breath.

Did I stop breathing?

'Bethany? Are you all right?'

His voice. Greg's voice. Why was he here? What had he to do with this picture and everything I now remembered about my father?

'Bethany – for God's sake!'

The picture vanished and the red dark whooshed in to enfold me. Just before I sagged forward, he swung round and took hold of my arms, gripping them fiercely.

'Bethany! Breathe!'

I did. I pushed away from him and took in a great gulping breath and then another and another until the next one caught in my throat and I began to sob.

'That's better.'

I didn't, couldn't, protest as he pulled me into his arms and held me there crying like a child. He held me close and soothed me, his hands gentling across my back ... his fingers pushing wisps of tear-dampened hair back from my face.

My sobbing subsided. One of my hands was

trapped between our bodies, my palm directly over his heart, and I became aware of its strong, steady rhythm. And, also, that there was a growing patch of damp on his shirt front.

I pushed myself away from him. 'I'm sorry.'

'Why?'

'Your shirt...'

He shook his head. 'That doesn't matter. But...'

'But what?'

'Bethany ... if it wouldn't upset you too much, I wonder if you could tell me why you had such a violent reaction to seeing one of your father's pictures?'

*One of my father's pictures!*

Greg could have no idea at that time how strange those words sounded. I had only just remembered what it was that my father did with his days and, besides that, there were still so many questions. Such as how had Greg come by this particular picture and who had the original.

It was obvious that he had no idea that, at some stage, I had blanked out my past. Life was complicated enough – I didn't feel like burdening him with my present troubles.

I decided to offer him only part of the truth. 'My father died, not so long ago. Perhaps you didn't know?'

'Of course not, how could I?'

I was sure he was speaking the truth, not because I was foolishly trusting, but because of the genuine shock I saw in his expressive face. And yet, as I sniffled into a tissue that he produced from his camera bag, I couldn't forget the momentary spark of bitterness that flared in his eyes, following the shock.

'Bethany–' he was packing up his notes and his papers '–I'm sorry to have upset you like this but, of course, I had no idea...'

'It's all right, really. Don't feel guilty, I'm glad you showed me the picture, I've never seen – that one before.'

He stood up and offered a hand to haul me to my feet. 'Come on, you need a drink, or perhaps more than that. Have you eaten today?'

'Yes, breakfast, but... Greg, must we go? There's so much more I want to know – about your pro-gramme–'

'And I'll tell you. But not here and not now.'

'But–'

'I insist. I'm hungry whether you are or not and I fancy a good meal somewhere rather more relaxing than my hotel dining-room. Oh, there's nothing wrong with it. It's just these modem hotels are a bit deficient in atmosphere.'

It didn't occur to me at the time that he hadn't actually told me which hotel he was staying in.

Greg put on his jacket and slung his bag over his shoulder. He pushed the door shut behind us and we started to walk away from the chapel and the rest of the ruins towards the road.

'Look, my car's over there, there's a small car park, although the Priory doesn't get many visitors now.'

'That will all change after your programme.'

'I know, that's one of the things I've got to talk to you about. Well ... although English Heritage have given me the go-ahead, the surrounding land belongs to you. It's only courtesy to let you know what I'm up to.'

'Oh, I see.' So that was why he had called at the house earlier. Not because our meeting yesterday had made him want to see me again...

Greg had a midnight-blue Volvo estate car. He explained that he needed the space for the camera equipment he usually carried, plus the fact that he sometimes camped out when he was doing his research in remote places.

Oh, Josie, I thought, how you'd love to camp out in a remote place with Greg!

He didn't take the road into Seatoncliffe, but began to head north.

'Where are we going?'

'Don't really know. I just fancy getting right away for a while. We'll find a quiet village and a quiet village pub. That suit you?'

'Perfectly.'

'Bethany, he didn't? All that way!'

'Yes, he did. It's not that far, actually.'

When I told Josie on the phone that night that we had almost ended up in Scotland, I think the first thought that leapt into her head was Gretna Green. But I assured her that Greg's intentions were strictly business – not the abduction and forced marriage of an heiress.

I was lying, of course, because we didn't talk business at all. We simply enjoyed ourselves.

The lounge bar of the Bluebell Inn was a long, low room, with exposed ceiling beams and a copper jug of dried leaves and grasses filling the grate.

Greg looked at the fireplace, approvingly.

104

'Mmm, that looks like a real hearth, not one of those simulated gas effects. We'll come here again when the weather turns colder and there's a blazing fire going.'

I didn't say anything. The fact that he had just assumed my consent and, also, that he had suggested that we would be going anywhere together in the future, made me happier than I had been since ... no, not since any time. It made me happier than I had ever been.

We had arrived just before they stopped serving bar lunches, but nobody complained. We chose a window seat which gave a view of the narrow road winding up into the green hills. Drystone walls divided the landscape and hardy Cheviot sheep grazed as they had done for centuries.

This was so different from the flat, coastal plain we had left behind us and yet it was so near. Josie would love this, I thought, and then realized that, already, I was beginning to conjure up a future in which I stayed here.

Over our meal, Greg and I discussed the usual topics, the music we liked, the books we read and the films we had seen.

That night, when I told Josie all about it, she was very disappointed. She thought that someone like Greg Randall should be far above admitting that he liked Simply Red, was a devotee of *The X-Files* and would queue round the block to see any movie with Meg Ryan in it.

'Are you going to let him make the television programme, then?' she asked.

'I told him I'd think about it.'

'Bethany!'

'Josie, remember that I haven't decided to stay here yet. If I give up the house, it will be up to my aunt Deirdre and Sarah to decide.'

There was a silence at the other end of the phone and I could almost see my friend biting her lip as she tried to control herself. Josie had never swerved from her opinion that I should keep Dune House. At last she said, 'Well, you will let me know first, won't you?'

'Of course, I promise.'

'Oh, by the way, Beth, have you had a chance to work on the designs for Tom and Alison's house?'

I'd forgotten all about them.

'I'm working on them tonight, as a matter of fact.'

'Great. It'll be a marvellous wedding present – just remember that their budget will be limited.'

'I will. Take care, Josie.'

'And you.'

I missed her, but saying goodbye and putting the receiver down wasn't as hard as it had been the night before.

It was still quite early and I really did get some work done as I'd promised. I decided I would sort out a room that would do as a studio another day but, that night, I settled for the kitchen table.

There was a note lying there, from Mrs Doran. The note informed me that she would start the new arrangement the next week and that she would try to fit in one more day this week – she couldn't say when that would be. She made it sound as if she was doing me a great favour. One to Betty.

It was wonderful to lose myself in my work for a

106

while. I had always intended to try and achieve an effect of light and space in a house which was only one room wide and two rooms deep and, somehow, it was easier now. Perhaps the wide, Northumbrian skies, the sea and the open countryside were beginning to take hold of me.

*Aren't you glad we moved back, here, David?* My mother's voice. *These pictures are wonderful! You could never have produced work like this in London!*

No. Go away. My mother and father were beginning to materialize in my memory again and I didn't want them there. I closed my mind to them. I still could, then, although a time would come when there would be no denial.

I knew that I would have to confront my past, eventually, but, that night, I wanted to be left in peace.

# CHAPTER 7

Someone had placed flowers on my grand-mother's grave.

She had been dead for some months now and I had been half expecting decaying wreaths with brown-veined petals and yellowing sympathy cards, but the plot was tidy and a narrow vase held a spray of carnations and gypsophila that didn't look remotely withered.

Who cared enough to do this? Sarah?

The church was in the centre of Seatoncliffe; it had been many years since anybody except my grandmother had been buried in the churchyard.

Burials and cremations now took place at the municipal cemetery to the north of the town, but when I had phoned Mr Simpson that morning to tell him what I wanted to do, he had told me that Frances Templeton's case was an exception because there was a family plot with a vacant space. I would find it easily as there were other Templetons buried all around.

The day was bright but there was a slight breeze and I had pulled on a long-line cardigan over a cotton dress. I pushed my hands into the pockets and looked down at the memorial stone. It reaffirmed the fact that Frances Templeton, the beloved wife of Major Arthur Templeton, had finally joined him. He had waited a long time.

Mr Simpson had told me that my grandfather,

a professional soldier, had only been in his thirties when he was wounded in action in Korea. That was long before I was born, of course. My mother had only been a child when her father had been sent home to die.

From the other headstones I had discovered that each family plot contained at least three coffins – more in the older ones.

So where was my mother?

The churchyard was enclosed by a low wall, but that formed a sufficient barrier from the bustle of the Wednesday market in the pedestrianized high street behind me.

Here, under the sheltering branches of a few old trees, only the cooing pigeons disturbed the peace of those who were past caring.

'Hey, there!'

At first I took no notice when I heard somebody shouting but, when I heard the footsteps, I turned towards the sound. A girl was hurrying up the path towards me.

'He–ey! Miss Ly–all! Hello–oo!'

She stopped beside me and I suppose I frowned, for she raised her hands, palms up, fingers spread, to gesture. 'It's me, Mandy, from the café.'

'Oh ... I didn't recognize you.'

'I could see that. I look different when I'm wearing my own clothes, don't I?'

She certainly did. When I had first seen her in The Gondola, she had been wearing her waitress's uniform, no make-up and her dark hair had been tied back in a neat ponytail. Now it hung loose and shining and make-up had transformed a pretty girl into someone who could have passed for a model.

She was wearing flower-patterned leggings and a long, white cotton top. She looked terrific.

'What's the matter? Aren't you pleased to see me?'

'Sorry, of course I am, Mandy, it's just that ... how do you know my name?'

I was sure I hadn't introduced myself, why should I?

'Oh, that. Word gets round. Small town, isn't it? You know, I should have realized who you were, if I'd looked at you properly. But then you were giving a good impression of a drowned rat, weren't you? And miserable, with it, when *he* marched off!'

'Thanks.'

'No offence.'

'None taken, but...'

'That's better, you look much nicer when you smile!'

'Mandy! Let me get a word in! Why should you have realized who I was – am?'

'Because you look just like your cousin Sarah.'

My, this really is a small town, I thought, and fleetingly yearned for the anonymity of London. 'Do you know Sarah?'

'She's been in The Gondola now and then.'

For once, Mandy didn't seem to have much more to say.

'Damn pigeons!'

We both turned at the expletive and Mandy began to giggle. The fierce language had come from an angel-faced old lady with a halo of fine white hair. She was standing beside a grave. She held a glass jar full of marigolds in one hand and a walking stick in the other. Water slopped from the jar as she shook the stick to shoo away the pigeons.

She saw us watching her and glared, balefully. 'I hope you two daft lasses haven't been feeding them. Stupid folk putting crumbs down and then the benighted birds shit all over the gravestones!'

Mandy looked as if she was going to explode. I reached for her hand and pulled her away. We ran down the path, through the lych-gate and out into the bustle of the market.

There was the usual assortment of fruit and veg, cheap clothes, jewellery, household goods, secondhand books and tapes and CDs recorded by groups that no one had ever heard of.

Mandy had linked her arm through mine, taking care to secure the strap of my shoulder bag as she did so. 'Villains everywhere,' she muttered.

We wandered aimlessly in amongst the stalls for a while. She seemed to have taken it for granted that we were passing the time of day together and I didn't really mind.

There was much that I had to do ... people I had to see ... but it could all wait. I had decided that for the sake of my health and sanity, I wasn't going to rush anything.

'Aren't you working today, then?' I asked her.

'Day off. All day doing just as I please, then into the town tonight.'

'Town?'

'Newcastle. Pictures probably.'

'With your boyfriend?'

'Cheeky!'

She laughed but she didn't tell me whether she had a boyfriend or not, or whether she was going out with him that night.

At the end of one of the walkways between the stalls, we found our way blocked by the open door of a red transit van. A man dressed in smart black slacks and a camel-coloured polo-necked sweater was unloading armfuls of polyester blouses and handing them to the stall-keeper.

'Morning, Mr Hussain.'

He stopped and looked at Mandy. 'Good morning, Miss O'Connor.' Not a smile passed between them.

Mr Hussain just had to be related to Ahmed and Imran. He was handsomer than both his sons put together, in a more mature way, of course. Imagine Omar Sharif at his best, well, Mr Hussain had that same heartbreaking attraction – but not the charm that should have gone with it.

The way he was scowling at Mandy was decidedly uncharming, not to say totally off-putting. I tried to pull her away but she stood her ground.

'Mr Hussain, I'd like you to meet my friend, Bethany. That's Bethany Lyall, you know, from Dune House.'

My eyes widened as I glanced at Mandy but I was more taken by the change in Mr Hussain. The ice melted as he metamorphosed into an urbane, even courtly, man of the world.

'Delighted to meet you, Miss Lyall. I'm sure Imran has already told you, but if my family can be of any service, any service at all...' He inclined his head graciously.

'Oh, thanks ... that's very kind...'

Exactly how many people had remarked my return to Seatoncliffe, I wondered, and how long was my every move going to prove a topic for conversation?

Mandy suddenly tugged at my arm. 'Well, we've got to go, now, Mr Hussain. Byeee.'

She whirled me away, dodging past Mr Hussain and his van and around the corner into the next walkway between the stalls.

'Snob,' she muttered. 'I've tried my best to be polite to that man.'

'Was that what it was, Mandy? Snobbery?'

She glanced at me, appraisingly. 'Sharp, aren't you? But, yeah, basically, that's what it is. The Hussains started off with one shop on the seafront, living in the flat above. Now, they have a string of corner shops, a taxi business, a clothing factory on the trading estate and a new five-bedroomed house with a Victorian conservatory.'

'So?'

'They've changed as they've moved up in the world. The lads are all right, I was at the High School with Ahmed, but their father thinks they're too good for the likes of the O'Connors. Mind you, a lot of people think the same!'

Her wide smile took all the bitterness away from her words. I realized that not many people would ever get the better of Mandy O'Connor; she had a sharp brain, a keen wit and was completely unpretentious. A lethal combination.

We had emerged from the ranks of market stalls and were crossing a paved area towards a line of ice-cream vans, mobile snack bars and chip vans.

The delicious smell of hot chips drenched in

113

salt and vinegar wafted towards us and Mandy grinned. 'Fancy some? My treat!'

'Yes, I do, but I'll pay, it's my turn.'

'Your turn?'

'The coffee, remember?'

'Oh, that. Cost me nothing and you looked as if you needed it. Have you made it up, by the way? You and Mr Scrumptious?'

My answer was the same as Mandy's had been. 'Cheeky!'

The attractive, middle-aged woman in the Tourist Information Office wore a navy skirt and a crisp blue and white striped blouse. Her back-combed hair was gold-streaked and she favoured chunky costume jewellery with a ring on every finger, including a wedding band. She also wore a name badge which told me that she was called 'Kate Sorensen'.

She seemed far too glamorous to be actually working here, but the promenade was deserted, probably because any tourists that might be in town were at the market, and Mrs Sorensen was only too pleased to help me. All she had was a few leaflets giving very basic information about Seaton Priory.

However, that was interesting enough. I glanced at it as she searched in her filing cabinet. I was surprised to read that the existing ruins were relatively modern, merely twelfth century! The original religious house had been a seventh-century monastery, or rather a double foundation. That is, there had been a house for nuns as well as a house for monks, served by the same chapel.

I learned that these men and women, some of them from noble and even royal families, had decided to renounce the world's pleasures and devote their lives to God.

The Priory was to become a centre for learning, although there was a curious hint of something more – something about the religious community at Seaton 'striving to create a broader, more humane type of monastic life'.

I began to have an inkling of the way Greg's programme was going to go. He had said he would get in touch 'soon' and I wanted to find out as much as I could before we discussed his plans again.

'I'm sorry, dear, that's all I've got. We did have some copies of that beautiful map in the window – that one that shows all the important religious buildings in the whole area – but I sold the last one to a very nice young man just a short while ago.'

It had to be Greg she was talking about. The way her eyes sparkled at the memory proved that he had the same effect on respectable, middle-aged women – Betty Doran, too – as impressionable young nurses.

I remembered the day I had arrived and the way he had been staring into this very window, oblivious of the rain. The idea that I might have just missed him was disconcerting. Disconcerting because disappointment hit me like a blow to my stomach.

'Do you know, I think I recognized him...' Kate Sorensen had a faraway look and, although I could have enlightened her, I didn't. Greg would have introduced himself if he'd wanted to.

'This is the office copy, I'm afraid.' She laid a map out on the counter top. 'It's not an accurate map, but I think he was more interested in the lady who drew it.'

I suffered a stab of jealousy, even although I realized that Greg might want to get in touch with the artist because of his projected programme.

For the map really was striking. It was imaginatively bold and simple, almost like a computer graphic, showing the grey-hued religious buildings, springing up from the green land to stand out against the blue sky, bounded on the east by the rolling sea. I could easily imagine this map being incorporated into the titles of a television programme.

I leant over the counter and examined it more closely. The drawing didn't tell me much. Even that one devastating glance at my father's sketch the day before had been enough to tell me that this was only an artist's impression without real knowledge. But what was interesting was the tiny cell-like building on the island.

'What's that?' I asked Mrs Sorensen.

'Oh, there used to be a hermit's cell there, part of the monastery, but there's nothing left of it now – well, perhaps a few stones. Although there is a rumour that there's a tunnel starting in the cave below which goes under the sea to the Priory itself.'

'Really?'

'I don't think it's true, though. The cave is pretty boring – but that doesn't stop kids exploring it and trying to find the tunnel. They're always having to be rescued. Ah, the man himself!'

I didn't know what on earth she meant by her last exclamation and I couldn't concentrate on making sense of it. Something was happening to me...

*Where's Gyp? He said he'd wait by the causeway. Sarah, let's go back.*

*No, I want to see the cave. He must have gone on ahead. You said you'd come with me...*

Stop it! I wanted to scream. My own voice and that of my cousin Sarah were invading my mind again. My memory was thrumming and clicking like an old film projector about to whirr into action and I didn't want to see the movie!

I gripped the counter top in front of me. What had Mrs Sorensen just said before the past had started to force its way through again? 'Ah, the man himself...'?

The effort of staying in the present was actually making me feel physically sick. I must have looked it, too.

'Are you all right, dear? You've gone ever so pale.'

Kate Sorensen leaned across the counter towards me and at the same time someone grasped my arms from behind.

'Steady ... steady, lassie... It seems I'm just in time again. Here, lean on me.'

'No, no, I'm better now.' And I was. The moment had passed and I shrugged my arms out of his grip. I turned to smile at the man who had stopped me from slumping to the floor. It was Duncan Alexander.

'Did you *really* say that?'

'Say what?'

'"Steady, *lassie*"?'

'*Och, aye!*' He laughed as I shook my head. He said, 'Too much of a cliché, am I?

'No, I love it.' And I did. The lovely lilt of his voice was reassuring as well as very attractive.

He was wearing jeans, a blue and white checked shirt, and one of those photographer's padded, sleeveless jackets with pockets all over the place. It was dark blue and really set off his Nordic looks and blond hair.

He looked so steady, so reliable. How nice it would be to be in love with someone like Duncan Alexander, I thought – and tried to suppress the disturbing image of the man I was comparing him with.

Mrs Sorensen was smiling. 'You're a real charmer when you want to be, Duncan, but have you got those new posters for me?'

'I have, and the leaflets, too. They're in my car outside. I'm parked on double yellows so I'll bring everything in right away, if you don't mind.'

'Of course.' She nodded and Duncan propped the door open with a wedge before going outside.

'Mr Alexander is the warden of the Nature Reserve,' Kate Sorensen informed me, but, of course I already knew that. 'He's the one who has to rescue the kids when they go exploring the cave on the island.'

And damsels in distress who might get caught by the turning tide, I remembered.

After Duncan had finished bringing in the posters and leaflets giving information about the reserve, he offered me a lift home.

We walked out to where his car was parked. It was a dark green, four-wheel drive, off-roader; more of a Jeep, really, and, I suppose, the most sensible kind of transport for a man with a job like Duncan's.

I wavered for a moment. There had been someone else I had intended to visit that day. 'It's OK, I can get the bus, you know.'

'Well, actually, I was wondering if you'd like to come along to my place? If you remember, I said I'd like to talk to you about the Reserve, and now seems as good a time as any.'

I agreed. Why not? Duncan was an interesting and cheerful companion and I welcomed the chance to get right away from my own problems for a while.

'Sit in the car in case the traffic warden comes along,' he said. 'If he does, say I'll be back any minute.'

'OK, but why?'

'I just want to dash into Hussain's and get some provisions – we'll make a meal of it – a late lunch.'

'No, that's all right, really...' But he had gone, leaving me regretting the double portion of chips that Mandy had talked me into.

A few moments later he was back carrying a cardboard box full of groceries. He dumped them in the back and we set off.

We left town by the same route Imran had taken the day I had arrived and, once we had passed Dune House, it seemed to be as far again on the road skirting the sand dunes until we pulled up before a terrace of three one-storey cottages.

'Those two have been knocked into one to form the Visitors Centre and my darkroom,' Duncan said, as he unloaded the box of groceries. 'That one is where I live.'

I followed him towards the end cottage, which was nearest to the sea.

'This row of cottages are all that's left of what used to be a thriving fishing community. The other dwellings fell into disrepair and local people carried off the stones for building.'

'What happened?'

'To the fishermen? As inshore fishermen, their first problems came with competition from the steam trawlers in the last century – and, then, when the Scots came down from Eyemouth after the herring, that finished them off.'

'It's a wonder you sleep easy.'

He smiled over his shoulder as he unlocked the door. 'Yes, I know, it's ironic that it's a Scotsman living here now. If I believed in ghosts, I wouldn't want to be alone here in the long winter nights.'

As I followed him in, I couldn't help wondering if he always did sleep alone here. He didn't act like a married man, but he was so attractive that I would have been surprised if he didn't have someone in his life.

He had no sooner put the box down in the tiny kitchen, than he picked up the wooden table from the centre of the living-room and carried it outside.

'I like to eat outside whenever possible. It's a more relaxed way of living, don't you think?' He placed the table alongside a wooden bench that was already there, along the front of the cottage.

'Sit down, Bethany,' he said. 'Make the most of the sunshine.'

'But can't I help you with the meal?'

'No, it won't take long.' He vanished inside the cottage. He had to duck under the lintel, I had noticed, but was very soon back with the cutlery and a glass of red wine, which he gave to me. 'Here you are. Just relax, for a while.'

I leaned back against the cottage wall and sipped my wine. At this point the coast curved round and reached out into to the sea so that the cottage faced due south. From here I could see the island, Dune House on the promontory and, beyond it, Seatoncliffe and the stretch of beach that attracted most of the holidaymakers.

But in between the cottage and Dune House, beyond the area of sand-dunes, much of the cliff road was visible. I imagined that I could almost make out the very spot where I had been knocked down and left on the cliff's edge.

'Here, have a look at these.' Duncan had re-appeared with a selection of the same leaflets that he had left with Mrs Sorensen. 'And you might like to use these.' He placed a pair of binoculars on the table and retreated into the cottage.

The leaflets were like any that are supplied at country parks and other places of interest, except that the photographs were stunning. I had guessed that they were his even before I read the small print saying that the copyright belonged to Duncan Alexander.

Wildflowers, butterflies, seashells, birds – the photographs didn't just show Duncan's skill, they revealed how very patient he must be – and how much his job must mean to him.

I picked up the binoculars and tried to identify the birds who were running so comically up and down the beach, following the waves, like clockwork toys. They were sanderlings, the leaflet told me.

And then my eye was caught by something diving through the air. I re-focused in time to see a huge white bird with black wing-tips plunge into the sea. It seemed to stay submerged for about twenty seconds before it appeared again.

'That was a gannet. It swallows the fish whole as it surfaces. Are you ready for another glass of wine?'

Duncan was standing in the doorway behind me, but I didn't answer him straightaway. As I followed the gannet up into the air to hover over the cliffs, my attention had been caught by something else.

I thought I had seen a movement in an upper window of Dune House. I held the binoculars steady but, whatever I had seen, it did not occur again.

A flash of sunlight on the window glass, I thought. Or perhaps Mrs Doran had decided to come in today and had arrived after I left to find my grandmother's grave...?

Duncan moved forward and began to fill my wineglass anyway. I put the binoculars down and turned to smile up at him. 'Thank you, but I shouldn't drink so much without eating something.'

'It won't be long now.' He left the wine bottle on the table and took the binoculars back in to the cottage. 'I'll put these away.'

And it wasn't long before Duncan reappeared with two plates, and a large blue and yellow bowl full of pasta smothered in a rich, red, winy-smelling sauce.

'Duncan, that looks marvellous, and you've been so quick!'

'I cheated. The onions, green peppers and mushrooms were all prepared by my own fair hands, but the other ingredients came out of a wine bottle and a jar of ready-made sauce!'

For a while we just sat and enjoyed the food and the wine but, soon, without any prompting from me, Duncan began to talk about his work.

He told me how windblown sand is trapped by sandline plants to form the dunes, the whole process sometimes taking thousands of years. He told me about the plants that grow there, the insects they give shelter to and the birds who feed off them in turn.

And, most of all, how fragile the habitat was. He had pushed his plate aside and leaned both elbows on the table but he turned his head to look at me as he said, 'Trampling can destroy large areas of vegetation, you know, and that could cause serious erosion.'

'Then why do you encourage people to visit at all?' I asked him. 'Surely it would be better to keep this area a secret, yet you actually provide leaflets to the Tourist Information Office.'

'My job is to balance protecting the wildlife against legitimate demands of public access. It's better to educate people rather than to ban them. I depend on the good will of local people and the visitors alike.'

For some reason I had the feeling that his arguments had become personal, that they were directed at me, and I couldn't imagine why.

Had I done something dreadful the day I had attempted to set off for the island? Had Duncan observed me from somewhere, with his binoculars, perhaps, and come running after me, not just to save me from the tide but also to read me the riot act about destroying the natural habitat?'

He was still talking. 'But not all the local people or the visitors are sympathetic to my aims–'

Here it comes, I thought. This is the end of our promising friendship.

'Some of the people who stay at the caravan site, for instance. They light fires – have barbecues in the dunes, destroying the plant life, scaring away the birds who nest there. They race up and down the cliff road in souped-up cars, killing any wild creature who is unfortunate enough to cross their path–'

Is that what really happened? I wondered. Had I been a hit-and-run victim of one of the loutish youths who stayed at Paul Mitchell's caravan park? The thought had distracted me momentarily and I looked back to find that Duncan was staring at me.

'I hope I'm not boring you.' His tone was cool.

'No, no, I was thinking about what you said, really. But I'm not quite sure why–?'

'Why I'm telling you all this.' He smiled. 'Remember, the other day, I made a joke about telling you of your responsibilities as a landowner?'

Had it been a joke? I didn't think so. It was

obvious that Duncan took responsibilities of any kind very seriously indeed. However, I just smiled and nodded in reply.

'Bethany, I wouldn't mention this if it wasn't for the fact that it's common knowledge' - I had no idea what he was going to say – 'but everyone knows that Paul Mitchell wants to extend his site and that he made an offer to your grandmother to buy some land. I don't know what her decision was and neither does – neither does anyone else, but if it's up to you, I beg you to consider my arguments against it very seriously before you decide.'

'I see.'

I stared down at the table. I had come along here, thinking I was going to get away from my problems, for a while, but another problem had just been presented to me.

I really hadn't given any thought to whether I was going to accept Paul's offer for the land because I hadn't finally decided that I was going to stay here. I sighed and Duncan reached out and took my hand.

'I'm sorry, Bethany.'

'Sorry? Why?'

'Perhaps I've spoken out of turn?'

'No, it's all right. I'm glad you've told me and I promise that if – I promise that I'll talk to you again about this. That's all I can say at the moment.'

'That's fine. Now I think we'd better go inside before this rain gets any worse.'

'Rain?'

'Yes, look.'

He picked up the empty wine bottle, it was beaded with moisture and then, suddenly, larger drops of rain spattered on to the wooden table top and the dregs of the sauce in the pasta bowl, curdled in the growing pool of water.

We grabbed the dishes and ran inside and then Duncan dashed out once more for the table.

'Is the weather always as uncertain as this?' I asked him when he came in again.

'Yes, but you'll learn to appreciate the good spells, believe me. That is, if you're going to stay...'

# CHAPTER 8

Duncan and I faced each other across the table. Had that been a question? Was he asking if I had decided to stay here and accept my inheritance? Did he even know that there was a choice? No, he couldn't.

And yet the way he was looking at me suggested that my answer was important to him. I didn't say anything and, after a moment, he walked over to the fireplace.

'I'll get this fire going,' he said. 'We'll have some coffee.'

I settled in an armchair and watched as he knelt by the hearth. The grate was already set with paper and kindling and, after applying a match to it, he carefully added a few logs from a basket at one side of the fireplace. Some of them looked like pieces of driftwood.

The skies had darkened with the onset of the rain and not much light came in through the two small windows. But there was soon a warm glow from the fire.

Duncan tidied the hearth using a brass hearth-set. Every move he made was spare and efficient. When he went into the kitchen to put the kettle on, I looked around curiously.

The floor was covered in plain dark-grey carpet and the walls were white. Behind me was the wooden dining-table and chairs. Near the fire there were two armchairs with a low, rectangular coffee table between them. The chairs had loose-covers that had a faded blue and grey pattern. The curtains were made of the same material. The place was comfortable but sparse.

There was an alcove at each side of the fireplace and, here, bookshelves had been built in. None of the books they contained looked like works of fiction.

So, no cosy nights sitting by the fire, while the wind howled around the cottage, with a good murder mystery, then!

But, apart from his work and his photography, what did Duncan do? These books, which a cursory glance had told me were mostly scientific, seemed to be his only possessions, apart from a radio and a small lamp on the top of one bookshelf; surprisingly, on the other, there were two of those glass carafes with long drinking spouts.

Surprising, because they were the kind of thing people bring home from holidays and nothing in this room suggested that Duncan Alexander went in for frivolous souvenirs – or even holidays!

But perhaps he had chosen them for the lovely, pale golden colour of the glass. They certainly looked well against the white wall, especially when they were beginning to reflect the light of the fire.

The only other things in the room that were not functional were the beautiful framed photographs on the walls. Even from a distance, I guessed they must be Duncan's work.

I got up to look more closely at the largest one which was hanging above the fireplace. It showed a flock of birds; they looked like gulls of some kind, coming in to land over some marshes. The different patterns their wings made against the sky, the glint of the water amongst the reeds, the white, star-like flowers – it was magnificent.

The other photographs, none of them as big as this one, looked as if they had been taken in the same location. And, even before I saw the fantastic shot of four flamingos in flight, I had decided it wasn't England. There was something about the colours and the quality of the light...

'Are you coming to sit down?'

'Oh, I've been admiring your work – I mean, it is yours, isn't it?'

I was startled. I wondered how long he'd been standing in the doorway which led to the kitchen. This room was in semi-darkness and the light behind him was bright, so I couldn't make out his expression.

'Yes, it's mine. Now, why don't we have this coffee?'

He crossed the room and put the tray on the low table. It contained not only the coffee he had promised but a bottle of brandy and two glasses, as well. While he was busying himself with the cafetière, I visited the bathroom.

When I had asked where it was, Duncan pointed to the only other door which led from the main living-room of the cottage. This doorway opened onto a small lobby with two doors.

'The door on the left,' Duncan called out just as I hesitated. The other door must lead to his bedroom, I thought, and resisted the temptation to open it and look in. I thought I knew what it would look like – a monk's cell.

When I returned to the fireside, he had switched on the lamp in the alcove and the area near the fire looked like a small haven of peace and warmth.

Perhaps this was the way to live, I thought. A time-consuming, rewarding job and the simple pleasures of good food and a fire to sit by.

Duncan told me a little about the Visitors Centre next door, and the schoolchildren and students who were his regular clientele. But then we fell silent and, for a while, the only sound was the crackle of the flames.

After we had finished our coffee, I sipped my brandy and glanced at Duncan nursing his glass in one, large capable hand. I couldn't help wondering if he was as self-sufficient as he seemed to be, or whether he ever yearned for someone to share his passions with.

By passions, I meant his fervour for his work, of course. And yet, something moved me. Blame the brandy, but sitting there, in the firelight, I was suddenly shaken to the core.

There was a feeling of such potency emanating from the man sitting barely a couple of feet away, that my hand shook and the glass jarred against my teeth.

I finished my drink, quickly, and put the glass down on the table. 'I suppose I'd better go.'

He didn't hurry. He looked down at the glass cradled in his hand and swirled the liquid round before draining it. 'Yes, the rain's stopped now.'

'The rain?'

I had forgotten why we had dashed indoors so suddenly; now I glanced at the windows and saw that the sky had lightened. My watch told me it was five o'clock. I had not intended to stay here so long.

Duncan was on his feet. 'I'll walk you home. What with the wine and the brandy, I don't think I should drive. Do you mind?'

'Of course not. In fact I'll find my own way, there's no need–'

'Look, I've got to do my rounds, you're not taking me out of my way.'

We took a short cut through the dunes – I would never have been able to negotiate the way myself. But, after a while, I thought I was on familiar ground. I saw the gap in the ridges and the start of the path I had taken to the beach on the first morning I had been here.

Something started to nag at me, reach out towards me. I turned aside. 'Do you mind?'

'No.' Duncan followed me and we stood together at the top of the steep path that led down onto the beach. I looked at the island.

'Do you really have to rescue kids from the caves?'

'Cave. There's only one, although at some time in the past there was a rock fall and there's probably another behind it. But, yes, I do. Every now and then. They get excited by tales of secret passages and smuggler's caches full of hidden treasure. They dare each other to spend the night there. You know, the usual kid's stuff.'

I was pleased to see that he was smiling. I had almost forgotten that he had a sense of humour.

'Why aren't there notices giving clear warning?'

'The local council keeps putting them up, but

131

the yobbos, both the local sort and the visiting kind, keep tearing them down and chucking them into the sea.'

'Is the cave so dangerous, then?'

'Not in itself. The trouble comes when the tide comes in.'

*You can't leave her there – she'll drown!*

The voice came screaming across the years, ripping through the fabric of time. There were no pictures, this time, just the voice, but whose voice? Whoever it was, was hysterical, sounding high-pitched and unnatural...

*Don't leave her!*

*Shut up! We have no choice...*

Another voice, low, whispering, frightened, hardly to be heard above the screeching of the gulls.

*And in the background the sound of the sea, great masses of cold, grey water, rolling, shifting, getting nearer...*

'Aaah!' My voice, here and now.

There was a sharp pain in my right ankle and I cried out again. Then I felt myself, slipping, the sand beneath my feet giving way and beginning to slide down the steep path.

Everything gathered momentum with alarming speed and I felt myself sliding down with the sand, in the sand and under the sand, as the whole bank seemed to give way and come crashing down on top of me. I flung my arms upwards as if I were drowning in the sea.

'Hey! What's happening there?' A new voice, definitely right here in the present, and one I thought I recognized.

'It's all right, I've got her.' And, at the same moment that I heard Duncan say that, he grabbed hold of both my hands and yanked me up and backwards so that we both fell onto the crown of the dune.

I lay there gasping and spluttering and spitting sand; I remember feeling childishly, tearfully, grateful that my shoulder bag had somehow actually managed to stay hooked over my shoulder!

When I had rubbed the sand from my face, I concentrated on the large pair of feet planted in the sand directly in front of me. Large feet in shiny, black shoes and long legs encased in smart black uniform pants.

I looked up – a long way up it seemed – into the quizzical face of PC McKenzie.

Duncan was scrambling to his feet and, at the same time, PC McKenzie reached out to help me up. 'Grab a hand, miss.'

'Are you all right, Bethany?' Duncan asked a moment later.

'Yes, but what happened?'

'That's just what I was going to ask.' The policeman was looking at Duncan, who was shaking his head.

'I'm not sure. We were standing there looking at the island when Miss Lyall suddenly seemed to sag. It was as if one of her legs gave way and, in trying to right herself, she started a landslide.'

'Is that how you remember it, Miss Lyall?'

'Yes, I think that's what happened...'

'But?' Mac was getting good at this. I smiled as I remembered the first time he'd said that.

'No, that's it, really, my ankle–'

'An old childhood injury, I know.'

Duncan looked puzzled. 'Do you two know each other?'

'We met yesterday.'

Had it really only been yesterday? But that's all PC McKenzie said and I was grateful for his discretion. I hadn't told Duncan what had happened to me on the way home and I didn't really want to – my life was complicated enough – but I could see that he was slightly irked.

'It's a good job that Mr Alexander caught you so quickly, Miss Lyall. These sandslides can be dangerous. It's been known for people to be killed in a matter of minutes.'

'Killed?' I was horrified.

'Yes, crushed or smothered, if you like. By the time we dig them out, even after a short time, they could have stopped breathing.'

'Shall I take you home, now, Bethany?' Duncan sounded concerned and that hint of kindness got to me. I blinked back tears.

'Yes, please.'

The three of us began to walk through the dunes together, PC McKenzie leading the way. I was glad that neither of them had persisted in finding out the reason why I had suddenly sagged and fallen. My friend the policeman had accepted that my weak ankle had suddenly given way but, of course it wasn't just that.

What had I just remembered about the island? Something that had really happened there, or some long-ago childhood nightmare about abandonment? The gulls had been screaming ... and I had never liked the sound of gulls...

I realized that we would soon come out on the cliff road. 'By the way,' PC McKenzie threw over his shoulder, 'I don't suppose you saw a young lad running through the dunes?'

'No,' Duncan said. 'No one at all.'

'Nah, too much to hope for. He'll be long gone by now.' He didn't explain himself.

When we reached the road, PC Robson was just returning to the patrol car from the direction of the track that led to the caravan site.

'Any luck?' he asked his colleague.

'Why, no, man.' PC McKenzie had never sounded so Northumbrian. He saw our puzzled expressions and grinned. 'We were called out to the caravan site – Prior's Park, spot of bother there.'

'So what's new?' Duncan looked bitter. 'Come, on, Bethany. I'll see you home.'

'No, that's all right, sir. If you don't mind, I'm going to insist that we take Miss Lyall home in the patrol car.'

'But–' I began to protest but he simply opened the door and indicated that I should get in.

'Now don't object, you've had a nasty shock and I can see you're limping again. Do you want Mr Alexander to come with you?'

'No, that's all right. I mean, I don't want to take him out of his way, he has his job to do.'

Duncan didn't insist. Did I expect him to? As we drove off, I saw him standing and watching us for a moment; then he turned and began to walk back into the dunes.

My new friend insisted on seeing me right to the door and even took the keys and opened it for me.

'Now, get yourself in and make a nice cup of tea.'

I was cheered by his homely manner. 'I will. Thanks for bringing me home.'

'I'll be off, now, but, Miss Lyall?'

'Yes?'

'Try not to make a habit of this!'

He was smiling but there was a hint of something else in his intelligent eyes. Unease? Watchfulness? Circumspection?

He probably has me down as a complete basket case, I thought, as I shut the door. He imagines that I fling myself onto the edge of cliffs and down sandbanks just to get attention – probably all to compensate for some long-ago childhood trauma.

I made my way across the hall, leaving a trail of sandy footprints. Betty Doran's pained expression the first time it had happened came to mind and I began to laugh, weakly.

Then, as my policeman friend had just ordered, I made myself a cup of tea.

I had stayed out much longer than I had intended to. When I had left the house that morning, I had planned to visit my grandmother's grave, then call on Mrs Bradfield, the friend who had arranged the funeral.

I had asked Mr Simpson for her address. When he offered to arrange a meeting, I told him that I wanted to keep it casual. I'd had no idea that I was going to meet Mandy, or Duncan Alexander and spend so much time with both of them in turn.

And there was another thing. I'd given Greg my telephone number when he said that he would be in touch. I wondered if he'd called. I didn't want him to think I was avoiding him.

As if that would bother him, I told myself.

The tea had revived me and the next thing I did was to sweep up the sandy footprints from the hall. I'd always intended to – really.

I tried to decide whether Mrs Doran had been in the house that day. Everything looked tidy, but, then, I had left the place tidy. Just because I shared a flat with Josie didn't mean that I was a slattern.

Betty Doran could have come and gone, I supposed – after all, she had her own key. But, on the whole, I didn't think she had. She was a sensible woman and would have left a note for me. So how to explain the movement I had seen at an upper window?

I wandered round the house, uneasily. Had someone else been here? But who?

I looked out from my bedroom window and from every other window at the front of the house. Of course, that told me nothing.

Now that I knew where they were, it was easy enough to make out Duncan's row of cottages to the north. His binoculars were powerful. If he were outside his cottage now, and he trained them on this window, he would be sure to see me standing here – if I stood still long enough, I thought.

That was when I decided that what I had seen was probably only a momentary flash of sunlight on the glass or even the reflection of one of those large seabirds.

I lingered for a moment, looking for the island, but I discovered that, because of the shape of the headland and the rise and fall of the cliffs and dunes, it was only possible to make out that there

137

was an island at all if you knew exactly what you were looking for.

I went to one of the windows at the back of the house which gave a view of the ruins. I suppose I half hoped that Greg might be there. It was still light enough to take photographs.

But he wasn't. Nobody was there. I was just about to turn away when something much nearer caught my eye, something in the garden of Dune House. The door of the summer-house was very gently swinging to and fro.

I knew the catch was difficult, but I was so sure that I had secured it properly that I ran straight downstairs and across the hall towards the sitting-room and the French windows.

Then I remembered that I'd allowed Mrs Doran to hang all the keys on a special key-rack in the pantry and time was wasted as I went to get the key.

What was I expecting to find? As I hurried across the garden I had no fear. Ghosts couldn't hurt you, nor could memories – at least they could inflict no physical hurt.

My imagination was running riot, but my reason was telling me that neither ghosts nor the images I had summoned from my past could actually open a door.

The door was still swinging as I mounted the steps on to the veranda. I hesitated only for moment before grasping the handle and pulling it open all the way. Then I took one step forward and halted on the threshold.

I stood in the dimness, my heart racing while my eyes accustomed themselves to the shadowed interior. The summer-house was empty. No one was there, nor were there any obvious signs that anyone had been there recently. And yet...

I sniffed the air. That spicy smell still lingered. No, it was stronger, if anything. But the place looked cleaner, surely it was cleaner than before... And the wine bottle had gone from the table.

Could Mrs Doran have been in here to tidy up? The smell could be polish of some kind – perhaps she came in here regularly. I would have to ask her.

I made sure that the door was secure and walked back across the garden. The high walls retained the heat and the scents of the shrubs and the roses.

I had just locked the French windows when the phone started shrilling and I forced myself to walk calmly into the hall.

It's Greg, I told myself. Who else would call me here at this time? It was seven o'clock. The fact that it might be Josie never crossed my mind.

But it was neither.

'Miss Lyall?'

'Oh, hullo, Mrs Doran.'

'You could sound more pleased to hear from me!'

'I am, really. Betty, did you come in today?'

'No, that's why I phoned. Is it all right if I come on Friday? We arranged that I would do one more day this week.'

'Yes, that's fine.'

'Righto.'

She almost put the phone down there and then. There are still some women who will only use the telephone if it's absolutely necessary and, even then, they are as brief as possible.

'Betty! Are you still there?'

'Yes.'

'Does anybody else have a key to this house?' It sounded bald but there was no other way of putting it.

'No, why do you ask?'

'Oh, I just wondered.'

There was a kind of 'Harrumph' from the phone and then she said, 'If you were wondering if any of your fine relatives have keys, the answer's no.

'Your grandmother wouldn't let your cousin Sarah have a key of her own, even when she was staying here. That was part of the trouble.'

'Trouble?'

'They used to quarrel about it. It interfered with Sarah's life too much having to come and go at hours to suit your grandmother.'

'Yes, I can see it would. Why would my grandmother not give her a key? Do you know?'

'Well ... yes.'

'Please go on.'

'I heard her telling her friend, Mrs Bradfield, that she may have made a mistake having the child in the house and she wanted to make absolutely sure that the mother couldn't get in, too.'

'The mother? I suppose you mean my aunt Deirdre?'

'I imagine so.'

'But I thought ... I mean, someone told me my aunt was in Spain.'

'I don't know anything about that.'

And it was obvious that she didn't otherwise, having told me so much, I'm sure she would have told me more.

She gave me her phone number in case I changed my mind about the day. I assured her I wouldn't and we said goodbye. I still had the key to the French windows so, after I put the phone down, I went to return it to its place in the old-fashioned pantry.

I had kept the key for the front door, but all the other keys that Mr Simpson had given me were hanging on the key-rack.

Mrs Doran had said that, so long as I seemed to be staying for a while, they might as well be in their proper place. It was safer than someone trying to carry round a great bunch of keys and perhaps losing it. I looked at them more closely now.

There was a labelled hook for each one, back door, French windows, cellar – where was the door that led to the cellar? I'd opened every door in the house that first night! Garage – I had never looked in the garage...

Like Scarlett O'Hara, I decided to sort that out another day. I was weary, now, and my conscience was telling me that I ought to try to do some more work on the designs for Josie's friends.

But was this a safe place to leave the keys? I wondered. It would be easy enough for anyone living here to have one copied. Betty Doran couldn't be ever vigilant.

I remembered the first night I had spent here, falling asleep in front of the fire... The sudden noise that had woken me and not being sure whether it was part of my dream...

Then finding the pattern of raindrops on the parquet floor ... not being able to remember whether I had locked the door after I had been in the garden...

I should have asked Mrs Doran about the summerhouse! It would be foolish to phone her just to ask if she had cleaned it recently, but I was sorely tempted. She would be here in two days' time, I reasoned, but Friday suddenly seemed so far away.

I still hadn't sorted out a studio for myself so I settled at the kitchen table, again, and tried to do some work. I'd had so much to eat that day that I decided not to stop for supper but, even so, I got very little done.

There was too much on my mind. Eventually, I found an unused notebook and began to make a list.

My father had never spoken about our lives before we had fled to London – I was sure we had fled but whatever it was that had driven us, I had still to discover. On the contrary, he had encouraged me to bury my memories.

*It's all right, sweetheart, it wasn't your fault ... just try to forget...*

I must have buried them very deep, for, even when birthday cards arrived, regularly, from my grandmother, she had remained an elusive, insubstantial figure.

But, since I had returned, since the very first night I had spent in Dune House, I had begun to remember my family.

Sarah.

I wrote that name at the top of the list because

she was the first person who had come back to me. But who had been next?

The very next morning I had remembered aunt Deirdre, my mother, my grandmother and my father.

My list grew and I stared at the names.

My mother had not lived long enough to have the baby she was expecting. My grandmother had lived on here alone, having lost all those she had loved. And my father? In later years my father had become a pale shadow of the handsome and carefree man he had once been.

There was another name.

Paul?

I added the question mark because it was Paul who had remembered me and, as yet, I hadn't placed him in the past.

But who was Gyp?

The boy that Sarah had befriended had been fourteen years old that summer. Grown-up as far as a child of seven was concerned. What would he look like now?

As I stared at the names I tried to make sense of the snatches of past reality that I had glimpsed. I was convinced that they were reality and not just pan of some ongoing nightmare.

And it suddenly became glaringly obvious that, in amongst all the missing fragments of my past life, there was one piece of the puzzle that was avoiding me right here in the present.

There was something I had to do if I was ever going to find out what it was that had changed my life so dramatically.

It was time to confront Sarah.

# CHAPTER 9

WELCOME TO PRIOR'S PARK!

The entrance to the caravan park was dominated by a huge billboard and at each side of the gateway there was a giant flagpole. One flew the Union Jack and the other a brightly coloured pennant with a logo involving a caravan and a jolly monk.

The flags were doing their best to flutter in the breeze, but they were wet and heavy because it had rained all night.

I had gone to sleep to the drumming of the rain on my windows and woken to the same sound but I was still determined to go and seek out Sarah.

So, this Thursday morning, after tea and toast, I rummaged around in the cupboard under the stairs and found a waterproof coat and some wellingtons. The coat was old but respectable enough, with a hood, raglan sleeves and patch pockets.

I guessed it must have been my grandmother's, especially when I pulled it on and found that it fitted me perfectly. I had remembered my grandmother as being taller than my mother. The wellingtons were just a little tight so I wore them without the socks which had been stuffed inside them.

In spite of the driving rain, I went the long way round. Somehow, I didn't fancy the cliff road which led to the track across the fields, so I walked almost into Seatoncliffe before turning back on myself and taking one of the main roads out of town.

Once past the built-up area, there wasn't much of a pavement and I had to side-step into the dripping hedgerow each time a car or a bus sloshed by, spraying me with dirty water from the roadside puddles.

There were very few people about. Of course, it was still early. In fact, the red Post Office van was just leaving Prior's Park, but already the smell of frying food hung upon the air.

It may be possible to be a cordon-bleu chef in a caravan, but life and holidays are just too short to make it worth the bother.

On my left there were rows and rows of cara-vans, shining and clean-looking in the struggling sunlight. Some of them had small fenced-off 'gar-dens' with pots of flowers. I guessed that these home-from-home caravans would be owner-occupied rather than rented from Paul.

At the beginning of each long row there was a signpost, but the arrangement of letters and numbers seemed to follow no logical pattern. If the postman had to deliver mail here, I hoped he had been provided with a code-breaker.

Or perhaps he left it all at the Reception building. I could see it at the other side of a large area of open ground to my right. Someone in a bright red top was moving about in the brightly lit office behind a large plate-glass window.

Next to Reception there was a shop and then a café. The windows were steamed up, but I could see that it was already busy. Some people preferred others to do their frying for them.

These buildings were all single storey but the last in the row was a large square two-storeyed building with no windows, at least on the front wall. There was a large double door, now closed, and a neon sign proclaiming this to be the 'Clubhouse, Disco & Bar'.

In front of the café there was an area with coloured flagstones set in geometrical patterns; here there were some tables and chairs looking on to both a children's playground and a swimming pool.

At one end of the pool, a youth in a yellow plastic raincoat with a hood was scooping litter out of the water with a net on a long pole, placing it in a plastic bag.

At the other end, there were actually two children in the water, enjoying themselves as rain slanted across and chopped up the surface. Their mother watched, patiently, from under an umbrella and called out to them now and then.

I had been expecting ... what, exactly? A sleazy dump with battered old vans and dirt and litter scattered around? Duncan's strong feelings about the place had been leading me in this direction but, in fact, it looked – well ... attractive.

Prior's Park was clean and well laid-out and seemed to be the perfect place for a family holiday. And the only noise, at the moment, was the inoffensive sounds of a couple of children playing.

Beyond the swimming pool, set well back in a small landscaped area, was a caravan that was much bigger than the rest, probably about twice the size. It looked positively luxurious. But I hadn't time to wonder about it because a movement on the periphery of my vision caught my eye.

I turned back towards the row of buildings. The girl in Reception was staring at me. She had crossed to the window and, even from this distance, I could see that she was leaning forwards. She was shielding her eyes against the fierce strip lighting inside to peer into the relative darkness of the morning, outside. There was no doubt that she was staring in my direction.

I must have looked a strange figure. My coat was belted at the waist but it was long, falling below the tops of my wellingtons, and I had pulled the hood well forward to shield my hair and my face. The coat was green but age had added a brownish tinge and, with my hands pushed into my pockets, I fancied I might look like a cartoon drawing of a comic, ghostly monk.

She stood back from the window as I hurried towards her and, by the time I had pushed open the door, she was standing behind the counter, ready to deal with whatever fate and the morning were going to throw at her.

She was probably about my own age with long, dark blonde hair, blue eyes and a dusting of freckles and, although she was decidedly overweight, she looked cheerful and businesslike in a red sweatshirt and jeans. The sweatshirt was decorated with the words 'Prior's Park' in fancy white lettering and the collar of a red and white checked blouse showed at the neck.

I pushed the hood of my coat back from my face and down onto my shoulders and I saw her expression change from bemused perplexity to one of surprise and then puzzlement.

But she recovered quickly and said, 'Good morning, I'm Liz Davison, can I help you?'

'Yes, I'm looking for Miss Templeton, Sarah Templeton. I wonder if you would give me the number of her caravan.'

'Is she expecting you? She doesn't seem to have left word here...' She had turned to look in a pigeon-hole in a row of shelves on the wall beside her. I noticed that what looked like this morning's mail was on a table below.

'No, look, she won't have left word that I'm coming. She doesn't know.'

'Then I'm sorry, I can't help you. We're not allowed to give out our tenant's site number without notice from them. But you can leave a message, if you like. She'll be coming in to see if there's any mail, later.'

She pushed a notepad and a pen helpfully towards me.

'No, that's all right.'

I didn't want to leave a message for Sarah, I wanted to see her right now. I hadn't trudged through the rain to leave it to my cousin's whim whether or not we had a meeting. I had remembered how capricious she could be.

But, I knew, immediately, that I would get nowhere with Liz Davison. She would abide by the rules of the establishment, which were like those of a good hotel, and she wasn't going to bend them for a strange, wet-looking apparition. Even if she had worked out that, from the look of it, the apparition might be related to the tenant in question.

She was still smiling, helpfully – and probably wishing that I would go away and stop dripping all over her carpet.

But I tried another tack. 'Well, is it possible to speak to Paul, then?'

'Do you mean Mr Mitchell?' Now I *had* surprised her.

'Yes,' and I couldn't resist adding, 'He'll definitely want to see me.' I smiled confidently. 'Tell him it's Bethany.'

She raised her eyebrows only slightly before retreating to her desk and picking up the phone. She kept her voice low and I really think it was because she didn't want to offend me.

The thought dropped into my head that she was probably used to protecting her boss from importunate female callers. Almost at the same time, I wondered if he lived here on the site, in that luxurious caravan which was set apart from the rest.

A moment later she was smiling. 'Paul's in the Viking Bar. Just go along.'

'The Viking Bar?'

'It's in the clubhouse at the end, there – don't worry, he's going to meet you at the door.'

She was obviously relieved that, in spite of my appearance, I had proved to be a friend rather than a problem and she managed to keep smiling until the moment I left her domain and closed the door behind me.

The rain had stopped and a few more children were in the swimming pool. One or two people were hurrying towards the camp shop. The young

149

mothers, and even the not so young, all seemed to be wearing the same uniform of bright, stylish jogging suits and expensive training shoes. Two of them glanced at me, disdainfully.

Well, perhaps disdain is too strong a word, but the sight of me had certainly amused them and they giggled as they hurried by with their bread and their milk and their eggs and their bacon.

It took less than a minute to reach the ugly square building at the end of the block and, as I waited outside, I had time to take in the fact that it looked more like a fortress than a clubhouse.

Soon, the door opened a little way and Paul appeared. He was smiling.

'Bethany, come in. I'm glad you've called.' He did glance down at my wellingtons but, to his credit, he didn't say anything.

I stepped inside and he pushed the door closed behind us. We were in a square lobby and the low lighting showed me that every conceivable bit of wall space was taken up with gaming machines. There were doors leading to the cloakrooms and a wide staircase rising up into impenetrable blackness.

'The disco's up there,' Paul gestured as he led the way past the stairs towards the back of the building. 'There's a separate bar without dancing down here.' He pushed his way through a set of double swing-doors, 'Welcome to the Viking Bar.'

We stepped into a fug of stale tobacco smoke that had lingering overtones of spilt beer. There were some very dim blue-tinged wall lights and the only other light came from a mirrored bar area with lights focused on the glass shelves.

150

A woman in an overall was polishing the tables and emptying the ash trays into a large bin bag and another was moving the chairs and stools around as she vacuumed the floor.

The pile of the carpet had worn thin and, around the tables, there were black, shiny patches that had lost the pattern altogether.

Paul stopped at one of the tables and pulled out a chair. 'Wait here, I won't be long, then we can talk business.'

He was gone before I could tell him that I hadn't come to discuss the sale of Templeton land. He lifted up part of the bar counter and retreated behind it.

Soon he was poring over a book – it looked like a ledger – and was deep in muted conversation with an extremely thin older man whom I hadn't noticed until that moment.

I guessed he was the barman. He was in shirt-sleeves, but the shirt was clean and he had a smart red bow tie. Each time he looked up at Paul I could see that his bony face was taut with worry.

Eventually, Paul snapped the book shut. 'OK, Geoff, but I still can't see how you could have been so stupid yesterday.' He was angry so he had raised his voice a little.

'It was so quick, Mr Mitchell. He asked for the cigarettes after he'd given me the money for his drink and as I went to get them he just leaned over and–'

'Grabbed everything he could reach! You should have closed the till. That's an old trick.'

'I know. But he didn't look the type–'

151

'They're all the type!'

'Such a nice-looking lad, I'll know him the next time.'

'It won't be him the next time, it'll be one of his pals. They know you're stupid, now.'

'It won't happen again.'

'If it does, you're out of here.'

I remembered my friends PC McKenzie and PC Robson. They had been called to Prior's Park yesterday and now I thought I knew why.

'Why the frown?' Paul was standing over me.

'Nothing, really. It's just that I heard what you were talking about and–'

'Look, Bethany. That kind of thing can happen anywhere, these days. I don't want you to think that Prior's Park attracts trouble in a big way.'

'Especially as you need my co-operation if you want to extend it.'

He smiled. 'I don't know how much you've seen, this morning, but this is a well-regulated site–'

'Paul, wait a minute. I didn't come here to talk business. I want to see Sarah.'

'Yes, I know. Liz told me that was who you asked for when you arrived. But Sarah won't be out of bed yet, believe me.

'Usually I don't see her out and about until nearly mid-day. So why don't we have a drink while I tell you about my plans?'

He returned to the bar before I could stop him. The cleaning lady with the vacuum had reached the table behind me and Paul had to almost shout, 'What would you like? G and T? Whisky?'

'Nothing! It's too early!'

'What about coffee?'

I nodded and he smiled. 'Wait a minute! Irene – switch that damned thing off!'

The lady with the vacuum cleaner switched it off and looked towards him and he continued, 'Pack it in for a while, will you? You and Val go and have your coffee break and, while you're about it, please bring a cup for Miss Lyall.'

Irene pushed her vacuum cleaner safely out of the way and smiled at me. 'Milk and sugar?'

'No, thank you. Just black.' I felt as though I was getting a hangover just sitting here.

'Geoff, I'll fix my own drink. Here's my key, go over and let Benjy out, will you? Take him down to the beach for a while, then make sure his water dish is full before you leave him.'

'Righto, Mr Mitchell.' Geoff looked pleased to be escaping for a while.

Paul came and sat down at the table. He had poured himself a whisky. To my inexperienced eyes it looked like a double, and I just didn't know how he could drink it at that time of the morning.

'I'd take you over to my caravan, but the girls would talk!' He grinned and I didn't imagine it was his own reputation he was worried about.

'Do you live here, then? On site?'

'Always have. I was born here. My mother didn't survive the experience.'

'I'm sorry. I didn't know.'

'How could you? I don't think I ever told you and Sarah much about myself when we were kids. And, of course, you were never allowed to come and visit me here. Your aunt Deirdre saw to that.'

I knew he had just said something important but I didn't know what, exactly. 'Paul, did aunt Deirdre know about you ... I mean...' To be honest I only had a vague idea of what I did mean.

Paul reached over and took my hand. 'Bethany, you still can't remember me, can you?'

'Well, I think I can.' Had the slim, attractive and serious boy that I remembered as Gyp, grown into this good-looking but very worldly man? 'But I'm not sure...'

'Look, perhaps it's better if you don't try.'

'What do you mean?'

'Well, there might be a reason – I mean, poor kid, it was a dreadful time for you.'

'Dreadful time?'

I looked into his eyes as he leaned towards me across the table. Here he was, beginning to tell me something about my past and I felt completely detached.

No voices, no snatches of remembered action – the screen in my mind remained blank. At that moment, I was the same person I had been for all those years in London, someone who had had part of her past erased.

I realized that Paul was looking at me just as intently as I had been looking at him. Whatever he saw, or didn't see, in my eyes, he suddenly seemed to relax.

'I mean, your mother dying, the way she– I mean, you were as upset as any kid would be, losing a parent. Your father did the right thing taking you away.'

Irene appeared with my coffee. 'Oh, thanks, Irene, just put it there,' Paul said.

I sipped my coffee. I could have asked Paul to explain more but, even though my ability to conjure up the past seemed to have deserted me, there was that same feeling of danger – yes, it was as strong as that – that there had been the day I had met him on the cliff top.

I was sure that it would be chancy for me if Paul was to discover how much, or how little, more like, I knew of past events. And I didn't know why. Although I could no longer avoid the conclusion that he must have been involved in whatever had happened that had frightened me so badly.

Otherwise, why did I get the feeling that the conversation we had just had was as significant for him as it had been for me?

'There's no question of my ruining the area, you know.'

'I'm sorry?' I was puzzled for a moment, but I quickly realized that Paul was talking about his plans to extend Prior's Park.

'I mean – look, I don't know how much your solicitor has told you?'

'Not much. Only that you've made a generous offer for the land.'

'Well, you can check with him, if you like, but planning permission wouldn't be any problem. What I have in mind would enhance the area–'

'More caravans next to a wildlife park? That would enhance the area?'

'Don't talk like that. You sound just like that mad Scotsman.' Even in the dim light, I could see his eyes suddenly widen. 'Don't say he's got to you already!'

'If you mean Duncan Alexander, yes, I've met him. Why do you call him mad? Because he disapproves of your plan?'

'Look, I don't intend to put in any more caravans,' he hadn't answered my question, 'I want to build some log cabins – they'd be tastefully designed, upmarket – attract a better class of tourist–'

'Stop, Paul.'

'Why? Won't you even consider it?'

'No ... yes, but not now. I'll talk to you about it again, I promise you, but right now you're wasting time. You see, I haven't–'

'You haven't decided whether you'll be staying here, have you, Bethany?'

We both spun round to face the woman who had just walked into the room. It was Sarah.

# CHAPTER 10

She was beautiful. Smaller than I, but slim and elegant, even in jeans and a pale blue, cropped cotton top. Her long fair hair had been cut and styled so that it looked like a lion's mane. A silver lion's mane – or so it appeared in the blue-tinged lighting of the Viking Bar.

I could see why people thought we looked alike – we had the same colouring, the same shaped face with recognizable family features – but she was like a hard, bright crystal, sharp and clearly defined, whereas, beside her, I suppose I looked pale and diffident.

Perhaps I had wasted my genetic bounty by growing too tall, spreading everything too thinly, whereas Sarah was the exquisite ideal.

As far as looks and confidence go, it had always been so. When she and her mother had come to stay, I had been a lanky, skinny child and she had been approaching adolescence without a single spot or blemish.

No wonder Gyp – Paul? – had followed her so slavishly when we were children.

She drew nearer and I smelled the same cloying perfume that I had imagined I could smell in the tower room on my second morning in Dune House. Even after all those years I had remembered it as aunt Deirdre's – now it seemed Sarah wore it, too.

I wasn't surprised. Sarah had always admired her mother and championed her fiercely, even although she recognized her faults.

*My mother had had faults, too...*

My memory clicked and brought me another scene from the past...

*Helen, you must rest, your blood pressure is too high and you are endangering the baby as well as yourself when you get excited like this.*

'Are you surprised? Mother, have you seen David? He's gone missing again!'

I was standing on the landing outside my parents' bedroom. The voices belonged to my mother and my grandmother.

'For goodness sake, Helen, the man is an artist. You must leave him alone to get on with his work.'

'But where does he go? What does he do? He says he's sketching ... gathering material ... but he stays away for hours on end ...'

'Can you blame him, when all he has to come home to is a nagging wife?'

'I don't nag... I just want a little attention ... this pregnancy ... it's much worse than the last... I feel so ill ... and where is Deirdre? She is supposed to be looking after Bethany and Sarah and half the time they just run wild...'

'Helen, I love you and, God help me, I've spoiled you – but this man you've married – you'll have to go carefully ... you might lose him...'

'You shouldn't eavesdrop, Bethany. It's not nice to sneak about and spy on people.'

A different voice. Sarah had come up behind me and I turned to find her watching me. She was amused by my confusion and her smile was sly.

I had been pleased when she first came to stay at Dune House but I had soon come to resent her assumption of leadership. At that moment I hated her.

'I'm not a sneak. You're the one who's always creeping about in places you shouldn't! I wish you'd never come here. I wish you'd go away!'

The way she had looked at me then was the same way she was looking at me now, cool, superior, assessing. I had risen from the table in the Viking Bar and, even though she had to look up to meet my eyes, she managed to maintain a superior air.

'Well, well, Bethany, what *do* you look like?' She emphasized the word 'do' and raised her eyebrows. She was behaving as though she had become an adult since we'd last met and I had not.

I was furious with her. She still felt that she could criticize me.

'Why should you care?' I retorted. And, then, I was equally furious with myself for falling back so quickly into the bickering way we had developed of talking to each other when we were children.

'Oh, I don't. I don't care at all if you prefer to dress in an eccentric fashion. I was just surprised that *you* don't seem to care.' She sounded just like her mother. Aunt Deirdre's most effective weapon had always been sarcasm.

I didn't answer her. I suddenly realized that her power in years gone by had come from the way she could manipulate me – and nearly everyone else. But I was not an inexperienced child, anymore. She would have to be more subtle.

Paul had risen to his feet. His usual self-confident expression was overlaid with unease. 'Sarah, that's no way to greet your cousin, especially when Bethany doesn't remember anything about–'

'Be quiet, Paul.' She didn't even try to be polite. 'And Bethany is not my cousin, you know. The relationship is quite distant.'

I knew that. When I had spoken to Mr Simpson on the phone the morning before, I had been concerned enough to ask him and he had explained that it was in fact, my mother and Sarah's father, Raymond Templeton, who were first cousins, making Sarah and I second cousins once removed, or something like that.

'But we were all closely enough related for your mother to exploit the connection when your father went to prison, weren't we, Sarah?'

In that instant I knew I sounded just like my own mother and I had the satisfaction of seeing Sarah's eyes widen.

Her voice was husky. 'You remember that? But I thought...'

I didn't answer her. Irene had started vacuuming again and Val was polishing the tables. Geoff was arranging bowls of nuts and savoury biscuits on the bar top. I guessed it wouldn't be long before the bar would be opening for business.

Sarah was silent. It was Paul who spoke. 'Bethany, perhaps I should have told you, your uncle Raymond–'

Sarah drew her breath in sharply and her eyes flashed and Paul paused as he glanced at her, but

160

then, he went on, 'Your uncle Raymond died in prison.'

Did he expect me to say something? To say, sorry? I'm sorry I said something to hurt you, Sarah? I didn't respond to his unspoken plea. The expression in her eyes wasn't grief, it was anger.

Eventually, Sarah shrugged. She had regained her poise. 'Liz Davison told me that you came to see me. Was it just to trade insults or was it something important?'

She had managed to wrong-foot me again and it took all my new-found control not to retaliate.

'No, Sarah, nothing important.'

I had come here this morning, hoping that more pieces of my past would surface when I saw Sarah. Well, they had.

I had believed, until then, that Sarah and I had not been enemies when she had first come to live with us. I believed that the dislike had grown gradually – at least on my part.

But as we stared at each other in the stale atmosphere of the Viking Bar, I knew that Sarah had always disliked me. I supposed it was connected with her mother's belief that Dune House should belong to their branch of the family. Yet there was something else, something stronger than cupidity.

Sarah was frightened. Of me? Or of something I might remember? I didn't know. I only knew that for one split second her mask had slipped and I had seen something approaching terror in her eyes.

Whatever had happened in the past was reaching out to taint the present and I feared that my life – all our lives – would change irrevocably once it was revealed to me.

'So, why did you come?'

I had no answer for her. I couldn't tell her that I had been hoping that she would help me somehow to regain my memories of the day my mother had died. For I was sure, by now, that that was the crux of it. But I had seen by her reaction that she would not help me willingly.

'Perhaps Bethany just wanted to be friendly?'

'Don't be stupid, Paul.' There was a long pause before she said, 'Well, Bethany?'

I turned and walked away.

'I'm sorry Sarah spoke to you like that.'

'It's OK, Paul, it's hardly your fault.'

We were standing near the entrance of the caravan site. When I had walked out of the bar, Paul had hurried after me.

He looked genuinely upset that my meeting with my cousin had gone the way it had but. suddenly, he grinned and said, 'And I think you look terrific, even if your outfit is eccentric!'

He achieved his aim. I smiled and he looked relieved. 'I'll give you a lift home, if you like?'

'No, thank you.'

'It wouldn't take long to get the car, it's parked just behind my caravan.'

'No, really, I need some fresh air. But, Paul...'

'Yes?'

'I didn't know that Sarah's father had died.'

'But you did know he was in prison and that's why they had to come and live with you?'

'Yes.'

'How? Had your father told you? Had you remembered?'

'Why is it so important, how much I remember about the time I lived here?'

Suddenly he had trouble meeting my eyes. 'I don't know what you mean ... it's not important... You were only seven years old when your father took you away from here. I'm assuming your memories of that time may not be very clear.'

He could have assumed much more but, again, I knew that I should not be completely honest with him. Something told me it would be better – safer? – to keep him guessing.

'Well, that's true.' I smiled with what I hoped was innocent candour and he relaxed visibly. So I had not guessed wrong. 'But this is a small town and I've been here long enough to hear some gossip...'

He was smiling now. 'Yeah, well, there's always gossip, don't I know it! And you'll find people willing to tell you more, so you'd better hear it from me.

'Raymond Templeton was an accountant but he was crooked. When it was discovered that he'd been fiddling some of his accounts in a big way, he went to gaol. Judges don't like people who abuse a position of trust. Your grandmother took pity on Deirdre and Sarah and took them in.'

'And uncle Raymond died in prison.'

'He couldn't stand it, he committed suicide.'

'I'm sorry, I really am.'

I was shocked and I suppose I showed it. No wonder Deirdre and Sarah had behaved so wretchedly that summer. These days they would have been offered counselling and support from some prisoner's aid society. Deirdre and Sarah got my mother and my grandmother who gave them refuge out of a sense of duty and expected them to get on with life.

'Don't waste your sympathy on your aunt.' Paul guessed the way my thoughts had gone. 'Raymond might not have topped himself if she hadn't – if she'd been more supportive.'

Paul's smile was cynical – no, it was more than that, it was bitter, as if he really cared, and I wondered why.

'Well, poor Sarah, then.'

'Yeah, it really messed her up for a while.' For a moment he looked as troubled as I had ever seen him. But then his expression cleared and he smiled. 'Bethany ... we will talk again, won't we? About my plans?'

'I've told you, you'll have to give me time. But, Paul, there is one thing I'd like to know...'

'Sure, what is it?' I imagine he was expecting a question about the size of the proposed new site, or the number of log cabins.

'Do you know the conditions of my grandmother's will?'

'No, why should I?' But he couldn't hold my gaze again.

'Oh, no reason. Now, I really must be going.'

I didn't look back so I had no idea how long he stood there, watching me walk away.

Paul wasn't a good liar. The closed look that came over his face when he'd answered me had told me that he probably did know that if I did not want to accept my inheritance, it would revert to the remaining Templetons.

Paul knew because Sarah knew. They were thick, those two, even if the admiration was one-sided. Mr Simpson had told me that he'd informed all interested parties.

He really should have told me about uncle Raymond, I thought. But, as I had never queried the fact that only aunt Deirdre and Sarah were the alternative heirs, perhaps he assumed that I knew. Perhaps he thought that my father had informed me of any necessary family history.

My father had told me nothing. His reasons for conspiring to blank out my past were surely good. I was beginning to suspect that it was to protect me from grief. But, by denying me the knowledge of my mother's death, he had never allowed me to mourn her.

Why had he given up his work?

My childhood in London had been happy enough but, looking back on it, I knew that both of us had only been half-alive. My father had taken one humdrum clerical job after another and his whole life had revolved around me.

But there was something he had denied me. Until I had grieved properly for my mother I would never be whole.

That was the moment I decided to stay and take up my inheritance.

On my way back I found myself having to stop and lean into the hedgerow even more than I'd had to on the way. I should have been walking on the other side of the road, facing the oncoming traffic, but at that side there was no footpath at all, only the high stone wall that surrounds the municipal cemetery.

So, I kept to the narrow path – which the traffic coming up behind me did not respect at all. The cars sped by without even slowing, spraying me with muddy water from the roadside puddles. My grandmother's wellingtons were beginning to chafe my heels and my ankle was hurting again.

Have you ever limped in wellingtons? My feet, getting hotter by the minute, flopped down so awkwardly out of step that I must have looked like Rumpelstiltskin.

I was hot and bothered and I could feel that my face was flushed with the effort. When I turned to face the car that I could hear pulling up behind me, I was ready to swallow my pride and thank Paul for coming after me.

It was Greg.

'Are you all right, Bethany?'

He got out of his car and came hurrying round and put a hand under one of my elbows to support me.

'All right? Yes.'

'You were limping quite badly. You haven't had a fall, have you?'

'No, it's these wellingtons, they're not mine and – please don't laugh!'

'Look, Bethany, I'm not going to even ask you why you're hobbling about the countryside in someone else's wellies and a coat that may or may not belong to you either, although I hope it doesn't. Just get in the car and I'll take you home.'

He was smiling the way he'd smiled at me the first time we'd met, when we'd bumped into each other on the seafront, but this time I hadn't the strength to be cross or embarrassed about the state I was in. I got in the car.

We drove in silence for a while and he didn't take his eyes off the road ahead when he asked, 'Been to the caravan site?'

'I thought you said no questions.'

'Sorry, just idle curiosity. I just assumed you'd been there as, after Prior's Park, there's only open country.'

'So where have *you* been?'

He ignored my note of belligerence and answered me quite agreeably. 'The Lake District.'

'The Lake District?' Surely he'd been in Seatoncliffe only yesterday? I was sure that he had been the 'very nice young man' who had so impressed Kate Sorensen in the Tourist Information Office.

'The Lake District isn't that far away, you know.' He was almost correct in interpreting my perplexed expression. 'I had to chase up an artist I'd like to do some work for my programme...'

So I'd guessed correctly.

'I discovered that she lives in Keswick so, instead of phoning, I went to see her, it only takes about an hour and half. Then I was able to travel just a little further and spend a night at home.'

'Home? You live in the Lake District?'

'Well, I'm not there very much, probably not as much as I should be.'

Suddenly I wanted very much to know about his home and who it was who thought he ought to be there more often, but he was changing the subject, rapidly.

'Prior's Park looks much better than it used to, of course.'

167

'Used to? When?'

'Years ago it was just a collection of battered, old caravans in a muddy field – oh, there was a shower block and a draughty wooden pavilion that served as a café.'

'It sounds as though you stayed there?'

'I did, one summer, with my mother. Here we are, Dune House.'

The car had stopped but my world was still moving, spinning, shifting on its axis. Until that moment I had believed that Greg Randall's only connection with Seatoncliffe was his interest in early Christianity and the ruined Priory.

Now he had told me that he and his mother had stayed here one long ago summer... He must have been just a boy at the time ... a tall, dark boy...

Greg had got out of the car and come round to open my door. He was carrying a document case. 'I've got something for you – some translations, remember? I had quite a few at home.'

I swung my feet out and put them down on the gravel, gingerly, but even the short rest had helped. I was only limping slightly as we mounted the steps.

'Are you coming in? Would you like a cup of coffee?'

'Yes, please. I was on my way to see you, you know.'

I eased the wellingtons off and dumped them on the top step before shutting the door. Inside I began to unbutton my coat. Greg put his document case down and reached out for it.

'Give that to me. Are you sure you don't want

to dump this outside, too?'

'It's not as bad as that and, no, I like it. I'll hang it up somewhere to dry.'

Greg followed me through to the kitchen and, while I was hanging the coat over a rack in the laundry room, he took off his leather jacket and put it over the back of one of the chairs.

Then he filled the kettle and took a couple of mugs from the dresser. 'Look, just show me where everything is and I'll make the coffee. You might want to go up and dry off.'

'Dry off?'

I looked down at myself in dismay. I discovered that my grandmother's old raincoat had not been totally waterproof and there were damp lines on my dress following the lines of the raglan seams. Also the front of the coat must have been flapping open as I walked and there was a huge wet and muddy stain obliterating the flowery pattern.

At least the hood had been adequate and my hair isn't wet and plastered over my face this time, I thought. Then I looked up to find him staring at me.

'What is it?'

'Your hair...'

'What about it?'

'It's beautiful. What have you done?'

'Nothing, it's the damp air, it makes it curl a little ... the effect won't last...'

I saw him raise his arm and I couldn't move. His hand brushed my cheek as he lifted my hair and let the strands ripple through his fingers. Then, his hand went round to the back of my head, his long fingers moving down to caress the

169

skin at the nape of my neck. I knew I was trembling.

His eyes held mine as his face came nearer. I think I moved first. I brought my arms up between our bodies, but not to push him away. My fingers moved up his arms and then tightened round his shoulders. I pulled him towards me, but he came willingly.

One arm went around me, his hand holding me close to his body in an intimate contact that left me breathless. His other hand cradled my head, drawing it towards him until his mouth found mine.

There was no force, no urgent passion in his kiss and yet, that gentle voyage of discovery as his lips moved against mine, probing, slowly, sweetly, left us both shaken and me clinging helplessly to him when it ended.

I left him spooning instant coffee into the mugs, and it was gratifying to see that he was as dumbfounded as I was. Neither of us had said anything when we eventually moved apart.

I fled up to my room. The landing was always dark and I switched on the light at the top of the stairs, but nothing happened. The bulb must have gone, I thought, as I hurried on towards my door, which wasn't far away.

My hairdryer was lying on the floor, still plugged in to the wall socket near the top of the stairs. I managed to kick it as I hurried by, but I didn't think I had done it much damage. I pushed it further to the side and hurried to my room to change my clothes.

By the time I had thrown my dress in the laundry basket and pulled on a pair of jeans and a cotton top, Greg had made the coffee and carried a tray through to the sitting-room. I found him staring out of the French windows at the garden.

'It's lovely, but it looks neglected,' he said without turning round.

'I know, I'll have to do something about it but I know nothing about gardening. I'm useless – in fact, my friend Josie calls me "Death to house plants"! I must take after my father.'

'Your father? But, surely…'

I had come to stand next to him and he turned, looking puzzled.

'Surely, what?'

'Well, I thought your father loved his garden – this garden. I'm sure he laid it out the way it is today.'

'How … how do you know that?'

He looked at me and then, instead of answering, he said, 'Bethany, how much do you know about your father?'

'Not very much, it seems.' I felt bitter and I turned away and went to sit in one of the armchairs near the fireplace. The tray with the coffee was on the table there. I picked up one of the mugs and held on to it with both hands.

After a moment, Greg came and sat opposite. I remembered my wishful dreaming on the first night I had sat here, he and I sharing an intimate meal in front of the fire. My fantasy had ended when I had looked into his face and seen his withdrawn and guarded look. Well, that was the way he was looking at me now.

'I'd be glad if you'd answer my question,' I said.

171

He didn't, not directly. 'I knew your father was an artist–'

'Well, that's more than I knew.'

'Because I've seen some of his work.'

'And that's more than I have.'

'I think I realized that the other day, in the Priory. Your reaction when you saw the picture was so ... so violent. But, to answer your question, I've seen sketches, work plans, really, with explanatory notes, of this very garden.'

'Where?'

'In a gallery.'

'My father's work in a gallery? Why have I never seen any?'

'Probably because it seems he stopped working when he took you away from here. Any work of his in circulation, and I don't think there can be much, is from long ago.'

'Greg, when you decided to make a television programme about the Priory, did you know I would be here?'

'Of course not. I had no idea who would be living in Dune House now.'

'Now?'

He smiled at my suspicious tone. 'Now as opposed to then, you mean? I've already told you, I spent one summer in Seatoncliffe when I was much younger.

'Your father was an up and coming artist and this is a small town, there was always plenty of gossip about the inhabitants of the big house!'

'Did you know that I'd only just come back here?'

'Well, I guessed that, too, when I remembered

172

your reaction to my question about being on holiday.

'You know, I'd only arrived in Seatoncliffe a couple of days before you,' he continued, 'and I doubt if I would ever have come here again if I hadn't discovered that old manuscript.'

'And you're not staying in Prior's Park this time?'

He smiled at me. Was there a hint of a challenge? 'You know I'm not.'

Well, I wasn't going to ask him outright where he was staying. Let him play his silly games if he wanted to. I went back to what we'd been talking about before.

'I came back because my grandmother left me this house – that is, it's mine if I want it.'

'And do you?'

'Yes, I think I do.'

'Good, I won't have to explain all my plans to someone else! Now, those translations I promised you...' He drank up his coffee and went into the hall to get his document case.

'Here they are, I'll leave them with you, I'm too bashful to stay while you read them.' He put a folder on the coffee table.

'I've put some of my preliminary programme notes in there too. I'd like you to know what will be involved.'

I stood in the doorway and watched him drive away. There was so much more I had wanted to ask him, but, although he had seemed willing to answer my questions, he had set the limits, and I wasn't even sure if he had been completely truthful.

I think I believed he was telling the truth about his reason for returning to Seatoncliffe. But I couldn't help feeling that he knew far too much about my family for someone who had simply spent one summer here in a caravan with his mother.

And how did he know that my father had 'taken me away from here'?

The most likely explanation was that the summer he had spent here had been the summer that my mother died.

# CHAPTER 11

Neither the moon nor the stars showed that night and a patchy mist lay over the sea. Here, thick and impenetrable, and there, thinning to a mere haze to allow the darker grey of the water to show through.

I couldn't sleep. I had lain in bed growing more agitated by the minute and burning up as though I had a fever until, eventually, I got up and went to look out of the window. I opened it a little to allow the cool night air to enter.

The translations of the poems Greg had left had unsettled me. They were simple and full of vigour, they celebrated the life that men and women know on earth and they speculated about the uncertain nature of the eternal life to come.

But, if the monks had been pious, they had definitely not been prim. Some of the verses described the love that man has for woman and the things they do together.

The poems were in no way obscene, not even suggestive. They were exuberant, full of life and even innocent. But when I remembered who had translated them, disturbing, too.

The notes he had left gave a brief outline of the kind of television programme he wanted to do. The background of the foundation of the religious communities was fairly straightforward.

Greg wanted to show how the monks and nuns

175

had lived and worked, in their separate monasteries, only joining together in prayer in the little church which served them both.

But there was a hint of a mystery, an old tale he wanted to follow up, concerning a young woman who had not wanted to become a nun in the first place and a monk who had started writing poetry, inspired by her youth and beauty.

Then they had started meeting on an island where he was supposed to be building a hermit's cell...

I looked in the direction of the island and, even though I couldn't see it, I could imagine the rugged outline against the sky; the rocky causeway that was quite safe until the tide came in; then the narrow beach of silvery sand that encircled the island and led the way round to the seaward side where the entrance to the cave lay, the cave that could not be seen from the mainland. A perfect trysting place for secret lovers...

I shivered, suddenly, and something made me fold my arms across my body, protectively, and grasp my bare arms. My flesh felt cooler, now, and I was growing tired.

I stood there for a while longer, listening to the sound of the water dragging heavily back across the shingle, but, eventually, sheer weariness forced me to return to bed. I slept, only to be further troubled by my dreams.

But when I woke up, after only a few hours' sleep, the only image I could recall was a woman's face, a drowned face, a swollen, sodden face with seaweed tangled in her streaming yellow hair...

I wasn't sure what had drawn me back to the stone coffins. I stood in the ruined chapel and looked down at them and I wondered if I was beginning to see where Greg's research and his imagination were taking him.

It would make a dramatic hook for his programme, a story of forbidden love and the tragedy it led to...

It was very early, just after six-thirty, but last night's haze had cleared and there was the promise of a fine, late summer's day. The birds were already singing and sunlight flooded into the roofless chapel but, once I drew near the two coffins, there was that same aura of timeless melancholy that I had sensed the other day.

On my way back I met Paul's dog. I had just pushed the door of the chapel closed behind me when I saw him racing and twisting through the toppled stones of the old monks' burial ground. He stopped when he saw me and moved forward more cautiously. He seemed as surprised as I was.

'Hello, Benjy. Where's your master? Where's Paul?' The dog put his head on one side and looked at me, intelligently, but, of course, he couldn't answer.

I looked the way he had come. There was no sign of Paul, but Liz Davison was hurrying towards me. She was not quite so agile as the young Labrador and, by the time she had negotiated the old graves, she was red in the face and out of breath. Her hair looked as if she hadn't had time to comb it.

'Oh, hello, Miss Lyall.' She took a gulp of air. 'Thank you for stopping Benjy.'

'I didn't, he stopped of his own accord.'

'Well, thanks for keeping him here!' Her smile was friendly.

Liz had obviously decided that I was OK because Paul had said so. And, of course, even although I was pale and tired, I suppose I looked more normal in jeans and a sweater with my hair tied back, neatly, than I had when I first appeared to drip all over her office at the caravan park.

She knelt to attach a lead to Benjy's collar. The dog didn't object, in fact he started to lick her face. She spluttered and laughed, 'Gerroff, you big daft dog!'

When she stood up she grimaced and wiped her cheek with the back of her hand. 'Come on, mutt, I suppose I'd better get you back to your master.'

Then, her smile faded to be replaced by an anxious expression and I asked, 'Is there a problem?'

'No. Well, yes ... oh, I shouldn't say anything–'

'Is something the matter with Paul?'

'No more than usual.'

She looked so worried that I said, 'I'll walk back part of the way with you, if you like. You can tell me what's worrying you or you needn't.'

We headed across open land towards the cliff road, leaving Dune House behind us to the south. At first she didn't speak at all but, when I asked how it was that Benjy was running free and why she'd had to run after him, she explained, hesitantly, that he had woken her up by scratching at the door of her caravan.

'It's not the first time it's happened, so I'd already pulled on my jeans by the time I opened the door.

'Well, by then, I just saw the tail end of the young devil racing towards the track and I had to run after him.'

She sighed heavily and I thought that was all she was going to tell me. So I asked, 'You live at Prior's Park, then?'

'Only in the summer months. Usually from the beginning of June until about now, the beginning of September. In fact, next week, when the school summer holidays are over and the bookings drop off, I'll be back to part-time work.'

'Then you won't have to stay there?'

'That's right, I'll go home to Mum and Dad and travel in every day.'

'Does your mother live far away?'

'Newcastle.'

'Anyway, Benjy woke you up, this morning?' Gently I returned to the subject that was worrying her; she seemed more confident with me now.

'Yes.' There was a pause. 'You see, sometimes Paul doesn't make sure that the door of his caravan is locked properly at night... I mean, he's just not careful enough because—'

'Because he's had too much to drink?'

She gave me a sharp look but she nodded her head. 'Yes, I'm afraid so.'

I had guessed what she was going to say. Anyone who could start the day with a double whisky might possibly go on to finish the day with a good deal more. But I don't know what prompted me to ask the next question.

'Has he always had this problem?'

'Oh, I don't think you should call it a problem, I mean if you say that it's a problem, it suggests that he's an al– I mean...' She had flushed and her willingness to talk to me was evaporating, fast.

'Look, I can see you like Paul and you want to be loyal to your boss, and I'm not suggesting that he's a drunk.'

I glanced sideways at Liz and saw her flinch at the word, but she didn't say anything so I hurried on, 'I just wondered if there was anything on his mind, anything that had happened, lately, that would make him drink more than he used to?'

She was quiet for so long that I began to think that she wasn't going to answer me. But when we reached the cliff road, she stopped and faced me.

'Paul has always liked a drink – just like his father used to. You should hear the tales that the older members of the staff can tell about the old days. But Paul seemed to be able to handle it until – until a few months ago.'

'What do you think happened to change things?'

'Well, at first I thought it was because his father was so ill – I mean, he hasn't lived here for years, but he came back to go to hospital and, even though they're not close, Paul must be concerned.'

'So that's why you think he's drinking too mu – I mean, more than he used to?'

She grinned. 'Oh, you can say it, if you like, and I might as well admit it. He's drinking too much. And it might be his dad being ill or it might be something else.'

'What else could it be?'

'I don't know.'

But she did. I knew she had her own theory to explain why Paul had started to drink more than usual. She just didn't want to tell me.

'Well, I'd better be getting back. Bye, Miss Lyall.'

She hurried away with Benjy bounding joyously beside her.

'Bethany ... call me Bethany,' I called after her, but she didn't turn to acknowledge that she had heard me.

I had caught her at a vulnerable moment when she was overworked, tired and extremely worried about the boss she was more than likely half in love with. By now, she was probably wishing that she hadn't said anything at all.

I decided to walk back along the cliff road, seeing I had come this way. I knew I must be very near the place where I had been run down, but there was nothing to show that I had almost been killed there.

The tyre marks in the soft sand at the side of the road had gone, probably smoothed over deliberately, and the tufts of grass that I had pulled out as I tried to save myself had been blown away by the wind.

The road stretched ahead of me, totally empty, and down on the beach there were only a few dog-walkers. It was still too early for any holidaymakers to be about.

I had almost reached Dune House when I heard someone calling my name and I turned back to see Duncan Alexander running towards me. I stopped and waited.

Unlike Liz Davison, Duncan was hard and supremely fit and was hardly out of breath at all when he reached me. 'Good morning, Bethany, you're out early.'

He was wearing a checked shirt with the sleeves rolled up; it was open at the neck and I could see the fine, golden hairs in the V and also on his tanned forearms.

'So are you.'

'Och, well, that's pan of my job. But you could surely be taking it easy if you wanted to.'

I smiled. 'Duncan, I've decided that you do that deliberately.'

'Do what, might I ask?'

'That ... what you're doing now! The accent!'

'Good heavens, woman, I'm a Scot. Can I help the way I speak?'

'Yes, I think you can, because you don't do it all the time ... speak like that ... well, not so noticeably, I mean. I think you lay it on only when you want to be charming.'

'And who would I want to be charming to?'

He grinned and, to my chagrin, I felt myself flushing. 'Well ... me, I suppose, although I don't know why – and Kate, Kate Sorensen in the Tourist Information Office. I could see the effect you had on her. Although she has you sussed, of course.'

'What on earth are you talking about?'

'She said you could be a real charmer when you *wanted* to be.'

'I had no idea that I was so transparent.'

'No, you're not transparent, Duncan. You're not transparent at all.'

And, of course, he wasn't. The day I had gone to his cottage to have a meal with him I had discovered that he was a very complex man. He lived like a monk, I had seen nothing in his house that had anything to do with a life other than work, and yet he enjoyed good food, drink and sitting in the sun.

He was both an ascetic and a hedonist, a self-denier who could be self-indulgent, a hermit who could leave his cell and still have the ability to attract women.

For there was no denying that he was sexually attractive and, if I had not met Greg Randall, I wondered if I would have been more susceptible to his magnetism.

I found myself wondering, again, whether there was a woman in his life and, if there was, how she coped with his single-minded passion for his work. Or whether his passion for her, if she existed, would take first place.

'Well, whatever I am, I'm glad I've met up with you this morning.'

'Why's that?'

We began to walk towards the house. Far ahead of us, I could see the houses, shops and hotels of Seatoncliffe hugging the curve of the bay. A bus had just left the town behind and was heading north on the cliff road, but it was still quite far away.

'Well, obviously, I've been worried about you … since you had that fall in the dunes.'

'Yes, that was frightening. But I'm OK, really.'

'I've noticed that you're not limping today. Is the ankle better?'

'For the moment.'

'You'd better explain.'

'My right ankle lets me down, now and then,

usually when I'm tired. It all goes back to an accident I had when I was a child, or so my father told me.'

'You can't remember what that accident was?'

'No.'

'Nothing about it at all?'

'No.'

By now we had reached the gateway of Dune House and we stopped again. 'Bethany...'

'Yes?'

'The other day, when you fell, you said you'd already met that young policeman. I wondered...?'

'Why I was known to the law?' I laughed up at him but his expression remained serious.

That day, when he was walking me home, I had decided not to tell him about the 'hit-and-run' episode, it was too complicated. And, to be honest, if it really had been one of the young tearaways from the caravan park that was responsible, then it would only give Duncan further ammunition for his arguments against Paul's planned development.

And I didn't want to talk about it now. There was so much that I really couldn't explain and it might take too long and there were things I wanted to do.

So I said, 'Don't worry, Duncan, I haven't done anything criminal.'

He looked far from satisfied and I wondered why my knowing a policeman could be important to him but, at that moment, the bus pulled up just by the entrance gates and Mrs Doran got out.

Duncan shrugged. 'Well, I'd best be off. Goodbye.'

As I watched him walk away, Betty Doran joined me. 'So you've met the mad Scotsman, then?'

'You're the second person I've heard call him that. Why do you say he's mad?'

'Well, it's not right, I know, but the man's a mite strange ... all he thinks about is his work – and he's never made friends here as far as I can tell. He just stays along there in his cottage all the time.'

'That doesn't make him mad. Just dedicated. And he's perfectly friendly when you talk to him.'

'Just wait until you do something that annoys him.'

'What do you mean?'

'He's had more than one set-to with some of the young lads staying in the caravan park.'

'Perhaps there was good reason.'

'Yes, that's likely, but he goes way over the top.'

By now Duncan's vigorous stride had taken him a long way back towards his cottage but, even from this distance, there was no denying that his was a powerful figure. I realized that it was not hard to imagine him 'going over the top' with those he considered to be in the wrong.

Betty was smiling at me. 'So you've been up and out with the lark, have you? That's a pity because I thought I would come early and bring you your breakfast in bed – spoil you a bit.'

'As a matter of fact, I haven't had any breakfast yet. But why would you want to spoil me, Betty?'

'Oh, I don't know, habit, I suppose. I used to like to spoil your grandmother.'

'So I won't take it personally, then?'

She raised her eyebrows and looked at me askance and then she laughed. 'Come on, let's get inside. Orange juice and muesli, or bacon and egg?'

I had the orange juice – we both did, because I insisted that she join me – but we followed that with bacon, egg, fried bread and some mushrooms that Betty had brought with her.

When we had finished eating, we sat for a while with our cups of tea. My restless night was catching up with me and I was reluctant to move from the warm kitchen, even though I had planned to do much that day.

While I was sitting there, half-awake and trying to organize my time by making lists in my head, Betty struck.

'Those young policemen who came the other day...'

If I had been listening properly to the way she began, I would have realized that she was not about to question me – in fact, she was about to tell me something.

But I mistook her intention entirely and blurted out, 'Oh, Rob and Mac! Look, I'm sorry I didn't tell you straight away but I was still anxious about whether I should have bothered them at all...'

I saw her puzzled expression and something made me reach for her hands across the table and give them a squeeze. 'I should have told you, Betty, but you see someone else had already tried to persuade me that I was imagining things.'

'What ... who are you talking about?'

'Paul, Paul Mitchell... Look I'll start at the beginning...'

I told her everything that had happened on my first morning walk along the cliff road and into the dunes and afterwards. Not only because it was easier, but also because, in a way, it helped me. You see, I was still trying to sort everything in my mind.

Can you imagine working with a database in your computer and you have a huge mass of information in there, but you're not really sure what it all represents or what you should be looking for?

Well, I felt like that, and I didn't even have a wild card to start a search with. But I felt that I knew more than I thought I did, and it was just because I hadn't organized the information properly that I still had no clear pattern.

At that stage, the only thing I could do was to go over and over some of the things that had happened to me.

But I only told Betty about the things that had actually happened – I didn't say anything about the people and incidents that I was beginning to remember from years ago. They could mean nothing to her as she hadn't lived in Seatoncliffe then.

I didn't tell her that when I was balanced precariously on the cliff top with my ankle hurting and the crashing of the waves on the spiked rocks below filling me with terror, that I'd had the strangest feeling that I had lived through a similar situation when I was a child.

And another thing I didn't tell her was that I believed that whoever had knocked me down had done it deliberately. I hadn't even told my friend

PC McKenzie that.

When I had finished, it was a while before Betty spoke. She looked very thoughtful, and then she said, 'And so the police said it might be some young tearaway from the caravan park who didn't stop to see the harm he'd done?'

'Not in so many words. They said that that was a possibility.'

'And what do you think?'

'I suppose that that's a possibility.'

She didn't say any more. She just got up from the table and made another pot of tea and we drank it in what I suppose you would call companionable silence. Although both of us were fairly subdued.

Eventually, I changed the subject altogether. 'By the way, where's the door to the cellar?'

'Outside, next to the back door to the utility room. Why?'

'I just wanted to look around – and in the garage, too.'

'Well, I suppose that's natural. Although you won't find much. Your grandma had a big clear out when I first came to work for her. Anything that she didn't want to keep went to charity shops and jumble sales.

'I suppose she'd decided it was time to get rid of all the stuff that would never be used again. A lot of old people do that, you know, if there's nobody to treasure it.'

Betty had gone into the pantry to fetch the keys while she had been talking and I took them and hurried from the room. I was near to tears.

No matter what Frances Templeton's quarrel

had been with my father, for the first time I felt that she was my flesh and blood, my mother's mother, and she had loved me. Loved me enough to leave me her home even although she had not seen me since I was a small child.

We had both lost out. Whatever had happened here had robbed her of a family and me of her company. I knew there was no way back. No one can ever go back in time to right wrongs. But at least I could stay and try to lay the ghosts.

Betty was right. There wasn't much of interest in the cellar. The door gave onto stone steps leading down into a series of empty rooms, with no connecting doors, each one lit by a single light bulb that had come on when I touched the switch on the wall just inside the door.

It was obvious that stones from the religious buildings had been used in the foundations of Dune House. The founding Templeton father, like so many Victorians, had plundered the past to build his future and he was obviously not worried about the unquiet spirits he may have disturbed.

But most of the walls were brick and the rooms were clean and dry. The only beings I disturbed as I made my way through each connecting chamber were spiders who scuttled away into cobwebby corners.

There were a few old tea-chests here and there, all empty, but, in one room, there was a collection of broken furniture. There was one table leaning drunkenly on uneven legs, but it was mostly chairs and none of them was too badly damaged.

Perhaps my grandmother had not felt it right to

pass on something that needed mending and had intended to have them fixed before giving them away. I decided that I would ask Betty if this was the case and, if so, see to it.

I did not think I could have been down here before. No memories came to haunt me as I walked from room to room – until I reached the old wine cellar...

*Hold the torch steady, Bethany, let's see if we can find any wine bottles.*

Sarah and I were alone in the cellar. My grandmother had taken my mother to the ante-natal clinic at the hospital, my father had gone out somewhere and aunt Deirdre was as elusive as ever. Sarah had bullied me into exploring the cellar and I was most reluctant.

'There isn't any wine here, Sarah. It's years since they cleared it out.'

'I know that, but they might have overlooked something! And we might find other things.'

'What other things?'

'Oh, I don't know, old books, old papers, anything...'

Of course nothing had been overlooked, but Sarah still wouldn't leave the cellar.

'Gyp says there used to be a secret passage from the island to the Priory. He says some people think that now it comes right up into this cellar. Let's look for the entrance!'

She made me stay with her, tapping on likely looking stones to see if the wall was hollow and trying to turn and twist any protuberance that looked as if it might be the handle of a secret door.

190

After what seemed like hours, we still hadn't found anything remotely resembling a secret door or panel and, eventually, I rebelled. I headed for the stairs, going back through each room full of trunks, tin boxes and old chests.

Sarah called after me, crossly, but I hurried on. Through a room full of old sports equipment, skating boots hanging from hooks by their laces, quaintly shaped wooden-framed tennis racquets with broken strings, a couple of sets of golf clubs, a table-tennis table folded and stacked against the wall.

In the next room I brushed past a table and knocked a pile of sheet music to the floor. Some of the covers had drawings of glamorous couples twirling gracefully in each other's arms. There was an old gramophone and a stack of records. On the floor, nearby, a pair of silver dancing shoes...

All those years later, I stopped and closed my eyes but I could still see the sequined bows sparkling on the toes of the shoes.

I climbed back up the stairs and, when I put out the light, I tried to consign the memory of the way the cellar used to be to darkness.

It was too painful. If there was any more lost family history lurking in the garage then it would have to wait to be discovered on another day.

'Miss Lyall, Bethany, I'd like a word with you.'

Mrs Doran met me at the kitchen door. Her face was white.

'What is it?'

'Your hairdryer – when I went up to clean your room, I found your hairdryer on the landing at the top of the stairs...'

'So?'

'Well, it's dangerous, lying there like that with the cord tangled across the landing. You could easily trip and fall-'

'Yes, I know, and I'll make sure I put it out of the way. Betty, I meant to tell you, there's a bulb out up there.'

'I've already discovered that for myself, and I'll see to it. But don't avoid the issue.'

'Issue?'

'I'd rather you didn't leave your hairdryer there at all. Don't look at me like that – I'm only telling you for your own good.'

'All right, if it upsets you so much.'

And she was upset. In fact she was trembling.

'Betty, what's the matter? It's not just my carelessness, is it?'

Suddenly, she gave a great sigh. 'I was the one who found her, you know...'

'Found who?' But, of course, I knew the answer. Something came back to me, something Imran Hussain had said ... something about *the way she died...*

Betty's voice was low, tense, 'When I came in to work that day, I found your grandmother lying at the bottom of the stairs.

'The doctor said she'd probably tripped and fallen the night before. But God alone knows how long she took to die...'

# CHAPTER 12

'So that's what I was going to tell you before. It was the same two policemen who were the first to arrive the day I found your grandmother.'

Betty got up and wandered through into the hall. I followed her.

'There, she was lying there' – she pointed to where the reflections from the stained-glass window lay like pools of blood on the Turkey carpet – 'her poor neck twisted sideways and her arms and legs at angles like a broken doll.'

The description was all too vivid – it was as if I'd been kicked in the gut. I felt myself gasping for breath.

Betty turned to look at me, her eyes wide and her expression solemn. She continued, 'She must have fallen from the half-landing to the bottom, but that was steep enough, they told me afterwards.'

She began to climb the stairs like an old woman, clinging on to the mahogany handrail, and I followed her. It seemed natural when we turned and sat down on the top step of the first flight.

She stared down into the hall for a long time as if she could still see the body of my grandmother lying there.

Then she told me about calling the police and everything that had happened after that.

'It was like something on television – "scene of

crime" people swarming all over the house ...
more policemen, a doctor, a photographer–'

'Crime?'

'Well, they had to come. They had to treat it as
what they called a suspicious death, but I could
tell they were pretty soon satisfied that it had
been a straightforward accident.'

'Why?'

'Because your grandma's injuries were consist-
ent with the way she had fallen down the stairs,
that's what I heard them saying. There were no
other kinds of marks or bruises. And no reason to
think that anyone else would have been in the
house with her...'

'So, what do you think happened, Betty.'

'I think she fell down the stairs. I'd told her
time and time again about those stupid slippers,
high-heeled mules with nothing solid to balance
on and bits of feathery stuff trailing all over and
waiting to trip her up–'

'But why was she coming downstairs in the
middle of the night?'

'God alone knows. There had to be a post-
mortem, then an inquest, although they allowed
the funeral to go ahead.

'I'm not sure what the final outcome was, the
actual words they used, but you can trust Mr
Simpson, he would make sure everything was
legal.'

'Why hasn't Mr Simpson told me any of this?'

'I don't think he wanted to, until he knew
whether you're going to stay here or not. He said,
if you decide to give the house up and go back to
London, there would be no point in burdening

you with knowledge of the way your grandmother died.

'Unless you wanted to know, of course. He wouldn't have kept it from you, if you had asked.'

I hadn't asked. That day when I had sat in Mr Simpson's office, beginning to savour the fact that I was an heiress, he had given me the opportunity when he asked if there was anything I wanted him to tell me.

I hadn't even shown enough interest in my own grandmother to enquire about the way she had died. I felt ashamed.

'Mr Simpson said he'd show you all the papers in due course,' Betty Doran continued, 'death certificate and everything ... when the time was right. And that's the trouble...'

'What do you mean?'

'I wasn't supposed to say anything, I was supposed to leave it to him, but when you told me about your accident on the cliff road ... and then when I found the hair-dryer and it brought it all back to me... I just thought—'

'What? What did you think?' Suddenly, I felt very frightened.

Betty tuned her head and looked up the next flight of stairs to the first-floor landing.

'I thought, wouldn't it be terrible if you had an accident, too? I just had to tell you ... tell you to be careful.'

And perhaps she hadn't thought it out any further than that. That her employer, of whom she had been fond, had died as the result of an accident. And now, her employer's grand-daughter, of whom she was growing fond, was proving to be accident prone.

What if I had told her about my falling down in the dunes and nearly burying myself under tons of sand? Might she have said more?

But I didn't, and if there was something else worrying Betty, she didn't tell me. Not that day.

While we were sitting there, the phone rang and, God forgive me, even after what I had just learned, my spirits soared. Greg, I thought, please let it be Greg. It was.

'Did you read my translations? And my programme notes?'

'Yes.'

I was standing in the hall – the nearest telephone was on a table there. Betty had got up more slowly and I was conscious of her moving along the top landing to resume her cleaning duties.

'Well? What do you think?' He sounded amused, but eager just the same.

'About the poems or the programme?'

'Both, I suppose.'

'Well, the poems are ... interesting. I can honestly say I've never read anything like them before ... and I have to admit there were some things I didn't understand...'

'What were they? Tell me and I'll try to explain.'

'I couldn't possibly! Not over the phone!'

'Then, I'll come along and you can tell me in person. I could demonstrate–'

'That would be even worse!'

'Would it?'

'Greg...?'

'Yes, Bethany?'

'Are you flirting with me?'

What had given me the confidence to say that? Even before the words were out of my mouth I wished them back. When he didn't answer straight away, I felt mortified ... crushed.

I waited for the put-down, gentle or otherwise, but then he said, 'Yes, I think I am.'

I found it hard to concentrate after that. Greg told me that he really was interested in my views on the way he wanted to develop the script but that would have to wait, as he was going away for a few days.

He wanted to view some archive film of a programme about monasteries, made in the nineteen fifties, that he thought was by the archaeologist and television personality, Sir Mortimer Wheeler – but his friends at the BBC would put him on the right track.

'So is that a date, then?'

'I'm sorry...'

'Concentrate, Bethany. I said I'd call you as soon as I get back and we'll have dinner somewhere.'

'But not at your hotel?'

'Well, no...'

'Never mind, anywhere ... I'd like that.'

'Well, goodbye, then...'

'Goodbye, Greg.'

And I'm sure that he was as reluctant as I was to put the phone down.

'Betty, I can't make any decisions about all this, I don't have the right until ... until I've told Mr Simpson that I'm definitely going to stay here.'

'But you probably will be staying, won't you?'

I didn't answer her. We were standing in my grandmother's bedroom. She had opened the doors of a large built-in wardrobe, which took all of one wall and was filled with expensive-looking clothes.

This was a task that I had been dreading, sorting through my grandmother's clothes. I knew I would probably have to face it, eventually.

'There's all this, too, some of it's pure silk.' Betty had pulled open some of the drawers of a large chest. I stared, helplessly, at the neatly folded night-dresses and underwear.

'Mr Simpson took your grandma's jewellery, of course, but he trusted me to take care of all her clothes – until it's decided what's to be done with them.'

'What do people usually do?' I asked her.

'What did you do with your father's clothes?'

It still hurt. 'There wasn't ... he didn't have much... A friend came and took anything that was good enough, to add to a consignment her friends at work were collecting for refugees.'

'There now, I'm sure your dad would have been pleased about that.'

'Yes, that's what Josie said. She packed them up for me and – and she got rid of the stuff that wasn't worth keeping.'

Josie hadn't told me what she'd done with the couple of full plastic bin-liners that she had taken away from the flat I had shared with my father and I had never asked her. It wasn't long after that that she persuaded me to move in with her.

'Poor lass, now you've got to do it all over again. Well, I've had one or two friends who've lost their parents or their husbands and they gave whatever they or the family didn't want to the Salvation Army or one of the charity shops such as Oxfam or Save the Children,' Betty said.

She paused and frowned, doubtfully. 'Mind you, your grandma had some good stuff...'

'Well, when – I mean – if I get round to doing something, you must tell me if there's anything you want for yourself.'

I hoped she wouldn't be offended. It seemed so cold-blooded, so mercenary and yet so pitiful, standing here discussing the disposal of an old lady's clothes.

But Betty was more practical and experienced than I was, and she didn't seem to think we were doing anything improper. 'There's nothing there that would fit me.' She smiled faintly. 'Your grandma kept her film-star figure right to the end. But, actually, there is something...'

'What? Anything!'

'She had some pretty scarves, silk scarves, Hermès, I think she said they were...'

'Well, if it's up to me, you must choose what you want, and if there's anything else, like a handbag or gloves...'

Betty seemed to have taken it for granted that I was going to stay, even if I wasn't prepared to confirm it. 'Thanks, I will,' she said, 'and you might like to keep something like that for yourself.'

'Oh, no, I don't think I should.'

'Why not? I've guessed that you've begun to feel a bit guilty, but there's no need. Your grandma wouldn't have left you this house if she thought you were to blame for anything that happened years ago. After all, you were only a child.'

*She's just a child, David! She is not to blame. It's YOU, you that I shall never forgive!*

I leaned forward and grasped the edge of the chest to steady myself at the sound of my grandmother's voice. It was so strong, so clear that I wondered why Betty couldn't hear it, too, why she didn't say something.

I felt that, if I turned round, my grandmother would be standing there, eyes blazing in a face ravaged with grief as she faced my father.

And my father would be carrying me in his arms...

I was cold and very wet, I had lost a shoe and my ankle was hurting...

But, almost immediately, the image in my mind's eye began to waver and dissolve. When I turned to face the room, only Betty Doran was there.

'Are you all right?' she asked.

'Yes. Just tired probably, I didn't sleep well last night.'

'You know what? I've just had a brainwave.'

'What's that?'

'You should ask your grandma's friend, Mrs Bradfield, to help you with this job when you – I should say, if you get round to it.'

'Really?'

'Yes, they used to go shopping together, they had the same taste. She would know what to do.'

'Right.' Gratefully, I began to push the drawers closed.

I moved over to the wardrobe. 'I've been mean-

200

ing to go and see Mrs Bradfield, anyway. As a matter of fact I'd intended seeing her today, so–'

'Wait a moment.' Betty hurried over and stopped me from closing the wardrobe door. 'There's something that you can do, now, whether you're going to stay here or not.'

'What's that?'

She stood on tiptoe and reached up to take hold of a large cardboard box that was on a shelf at the top. 'Give me a hand down with this. This is the real reason I brought you up here.'

'What's in it?'

'Mementoes ... souvenirs, I suppose you would call them. Your grandma wanted to chuck them out years ago, but I wouldn't let her.'

'Why?'

'Because I hoped some day that there would be someone interested enough to see them.'

Someone had been here before me. As I sifted through the contents of the box, I had the same strange feeling that I'd had when I'd been sorting out my father's things.

Assorted papers with a rusty mark showing where a paper clip had been moved, recently. A certain disorder in an otherwise orderly collection.

My father had known that he was dying and he'd had sufficient time to put his papers in order, leave things organized for me and, perhaps, destroy things that he didn't want me to know about.

My grandmother could have had no foreknowledge of her death but, perhaps, like many old people, she had wanted to leave things tidy for those who would inherit the leftover bits and pieces, the remnants of her long life.

Once Betty had persuaded her to keep them, had she cherished a hope that the granddaughter she had lost would come back and want to see them?

Betty had suggested that the large formal table in the dining-room was the ideal place; she brought me a mug of tea, being careful to put it on a coaster, and left me to get on with it.

I looked down at some of the things spread out in front of me. They were a record of the life my grandmother had had before she'd been married and for a while afterwards. She had been an actress, at first on the stage and then in films.

There were theatre programmes, scrapbooks containing cuttings from newspapers, old and yellowing. And photographs.

She was so beautiful, so stylish. Some of the glossy black-and-white photographs looked as if they were stills from the films she'd been in. They showed her in various poses with other actors and actresses who seemed half-familiar.

Then a newspaper photograph caught my eye. It was of a bride and a very handsome groom, an army officer. My grandparents. My eyes misted over when I tried to read the report underneath.

I realized then that I could never give any of this up and, whether or not I stayed here, this box full of family history had to be mine to keep. My father may have robbed me of any knowledge of his and my mother's story but, at least, I could have this.

And yet, as I delved deeper into the box, bringing out more papers and photographs and trying to arrange them in some kind of order, I did find something of my mother's.

At first I thought all the letters, tied in neat bundles with bits of ribbon, were my grandmother's. The postmarks and the stamps made me think they were from my grandfather when he was serving abroad.

I couldn't bring myself to read them then, my discovery of them was too recent, it would seem like prying. But I knew that I would one day. So, I laid them out chronologically according to the date mark on the top envelope. One bundle was different from the rest.

I picked it up again. There were only three letters, the envelopes were slightly larger and the writing on them was not the same as on the others. The postmark showed they had been sent from London and they were addressed to Mrs Helen Lyall, my mother.

I looked at the postmark more closely. The date-stamps revealed that they had been sent to her in the summer of the year she died.

# CHAPTER 13

With the door of the summer-house open and sunlight streaming across the floor into the dusty corners, there was nowhere for ghosts to hide.

Even so, I pulled the old armchair away from the wall and into an open space. I dumped the rugs and most of the cushions on the floor and made myself comfortable. I wanted to be alone and uninterrupted when I read the letters that had been sent to my mother.

Just after I had found them, Betty had come into the dining-room to say that lunch was ready, so I stuffed them into the pocket of my jeans and followed her into the kitchen where we shared a meal of baked potatoes, cottage cheese and salad.

If I was subdued, she probably thought that I was overwhelmed by the things I had found in my grandmother's box and she wasn't at all put out when I said that I would take my coffee and sit in the garden.

I sipped my drink slowly, making myself finish it before taking out the letters. I had sensed that what I was about to read was important and I wanted to delay the discovery of things I might not like. I almost wished I hadn't eaten anything, because my insides were churning and I felt slightly sick with apprehension.

But, eventually, I placed my empty mug on the floor, took the envelopes out of my pocket and

204

laid them on my knee.

The date stamps were still legible so it had been easy to start with the first of the three letters that had been sent to my mother in the months leading up to her death.

The name, address and telephone number were on one of those little sticky labels stuck on the first page of each of the letters. Fourteen years ago, Mrs Jane Frears had lived in Ealing, in a house not too far away from one of the houses my father and I had once lived in.

I wondered, fleetingly, if I had ever walked by her in the street without knowing that she had known my parents. I wondered if she still lived there.

But then I began to read.

*Dear Helen,*
*You must be wrong! After your phone call, I thought and thought about what you had said and, really, it just doesn't make sense.*

*David has always adored you – and haven't you taken advantage of that fact! I can't believe that he would ever do anything to jeopardize your marriage at such a time.*

*Yes, I know, only too well, that it's when their wives are having a difficult pregnancy that some men do find comfort elsewhere (to put it delicately), and I'm sorry that my own situation is the worst of examples.*

*But, Helen, supposing David did feel tempted – and I really can't believe that he would – he wouldn't, absolutely wouldn't, ever be attracted to HER!*

*I think that he's probably a little depressed at the moment and needs to spend some time alone, away from you and your mother for a few hours, now and then.*

*After all, giving up his job was a major decision and, no matter how civilized he is, I don't really think he's the sort of man who enjoys being supported by his wife's family, even if he is a budding genius!*

*He needs you to have faith in him and his ability to make a name for himself as an artist. He doesn't want you complaining and trying to tie him to your side all the time when he should be working. For once in your life you must try to understand someone else's feelings.*

*If you've got this far without tearing my letter to shreds, please forgive me if I've been harsh, but I had to tell you what I thought. No one else will speak to you like this, not even your mother who, otherwise, is very sensible.*

*Now you can see why I had to write all this in a letter instead of telling you what I thought on the phone. Knowing you, you'd have slammed the receiver down before I'd said half of what I wanted to say.*

*I hope this isn't the end of our friendship because it means a lot to me. Life was never dull when you were around and you were the only one not to put all the blame on me for what happened in my own life.*

*Please use your intelligence and that forceful personality you have in a positive way. Don't destroy your life just when you have the baby to look forward to and everything seems to be so promising.*

*Write or phone. I want to hear from you, I really do, even if you're going to yell at me!*

*Love,*

*Jane*

I folded the letter and put it back in its envelope. Outside, I could hear the wind worrying at the overgrown branches of the shrubs. The gulls were calling shrilly, almost as if they were angry with the wind, and I tried to blot out their screeching as tried to make sense of what I had just read. It wasn't too difficult.

I felt as though I had been thrown headlong into the middle of my mother's tempestuous life. I read it many times after that first time and, even if I read it now, it never fails to move me.

But, even after that first reading, when I was reeling with all the implications of Jane Frears's intelligent advice, I had enough self-regard to be piqued that I wasn't even mentioned. Not once.

My mother's friend had begged her to think of my father, his work and the baby that she was expecting and was suggesting that she should be grateful. But what about me? Was nobody grateful that I was around?

I had never questioned my father's love for me and, with the confidence of childhood, I had assumed that my mother, of whom I had no memory until recently, would have loved me to. Now I was not so sure.

It was obvious what it was that my mother suspected and it fitted in so well with the incidents I had started to remember since returning to Dune House.

I couldn't wait to see how she had reacted to the letter and I took the next one out of its envelope.

*Dear Helen,*

*When you phoned me the other day I was so relieved. Many a time in these last three weeks I've been on the point of phoning you, but I was worried in case you would refuse to speak to me – ever again!*

*You were talking so quickly that, perhaps, I missed something, but I'm sorry that I didn't take you seriously enough, when you told me what you were thinking about doing.*

*Since we talked, I've given it a lot of thought as I promised you I would, and I still think that it's just not right.*

*To hire a private detective seems so, well, sordid. Would you be able to live with yourself, afterwards, if you paid someone to follow the man you're supposed to love and then found out that he was quite innocent after all?*

*That secret would be there between you for the rest of your lives together and I think that, basically, you're much too truthful to be able to live with that.*

*The thought of what you had done would niggle away at you, destroying your peace of mind until one day you would tell him. And I don't think David would ever forgive you. You really would be in danger of losing everything, just as you imagine you are in danger now.*

*For I still think that there must be a totally straightforward explanation for David's behaviour and I still think it might be something to do with the way you are behaving at the moment.*

*I know, I know! You feel nauseous and headachey and your poor fingers are so swollen that you've even had to take your wedding ring off. All you want is sympathy from the man you love, but the way you are trying to get it is driving him away and making you feel even worse. It's a vicious circle, isn't it?*

*But, please, please, please don't do anything that you'll regret for the rest of your life.*

*I've put this all down on paper because I want you to read it over and over as many times as it takes to convince you. And you must phone me any time you like, night or day. Most of the time I'm at home.*

*You know what my situation is – stuck here with two children whom I love but didn't really want. Now's the time for you to say, 'I told you so!'*

*I'll always be here for you.*
*Love,*
*Jane*

My mother was the recipient of these letters and yet it was her personality, even more than the writer's, that came across – jumped right off the page, as they say.

She was having a bad pregnancy and she was reacting badly. I guessed that, even without those circumstances, she must have been a tricky person to deal with. Her friend, Jane Frears, obviously cared for her enough to tell her some home truths but she knew she was risking her friendship by doing so.

Had my mother been difficult?

In spite of the changing weather outside, the summer-house had retained some warmth and motes of dust danced in the sun's rays. They were paler now. I closed my eyes, for a moment, and tried to remember, but nothing would come back to me.

Surely, if she had been harsh or peremptory in

her treatment of me, it would have left some mark? But, no, whatever the memories were, buried in my unconscious mind about my relationship with my mother, I did not think they were bad ones.

But were they good? Jane Frears obviously thought she was fun to be with, but was that vivacity reserved for her grown-up friends or had mother and daughter ever had fun together? I concentrated, but I could summon up no echoes of remembered laughter.

Once more, of course, there had been no mention of me in the letter. I began to wonder if I had even existed. Whether all those people were real and still perhaps living in some parallel universe, and I was a ghost, an intruder, an alien being who had no right to be tapping in to their lives.

I read the final letter.

*Helen,*

*For God's sake, what are you thinking of? You mustn't go wandering through the ruins and along the cliff road in your condition! Think of your baby, think of how you'd break your mother's heart if anything happened to you!*

*I'm so very sorry that I didn't believe you, that I didn't take your worries seriously. And yet, you're not a hundred percent sure of the truth of what you saw from the tower window, are you?*

*A man that looked like David – and yes, you ought to be able to recognize your own husband, even at that distance, but you've told me, yourself, that your vision gets misty sometimes because of your condition – and a dark-haired woman. You think you saw them embrace.*

210

*No, I'm not trying to talk you out of it. You believe that you saw that and, as I'm your friend, I want to support you.*

*As for the children, creeping about the house and garden, I'm sure they're just playing some game. David would never set your own daughter to spy on you and report back to him so that he could safely go to meet his lady love.*

*And I still find it very hard to believe that he is having an affair.*

*Do you want me to come and stay for a while? Roger will just have to cope at this end. He owes me that, at least.*

*Please don't try playing detective anymore and please rest and get your blood pressure down. For my sake if for no one else's.*

*Love as ever,*

*Jane*

I don't think I have ever felt such anguish. For with that one and only mention of me, in the last of the letters, no matter how oblique the reference was, I suddenly remembered how much I had loved my mother.

Until that last summer she had been bright, animated, vital and loving. She had not been uncritical and she had sometimes been demanding, but she was totally honest and forgiving, especially if she loved you.

And she had loved me. Child as I was, I had known that her increasingly irritable behaviour that summer was because of her pregnancy. My grandmother had assured me that, once the baby was born, everything would be all right.

211

And everything might have been, if only uncle Raymond had not been sent to prison and Deirdre and Sarah made homeless as a consequence.

My father had been withdrawing himself from the family scene even before they arrived. Gran had explained to me that he was working hard and that that was good and that she and I would spend more time together. And we had, at first.

But as my mother's pregnancy advanced, she demanded more and more of her mother's time and attention and it was left to Deirdre to look after me as well as her own daughter.

My poor mother. Had she really thought that Sarah and I had been spying on her...

*Look, Bethany, there's your mother.*

Sarah stopped and grabbed my arm. We were on the cliff road, heading towards the track that led to the caravan park, when we saw my mother hurrying along, ahead of us.

I was just about to start running after her but Sarah pulled me back. 'What are you doing?' she hissed. 'We're not supposed to be out of the house, remember?'

It was true. Aunt Deirdre had told us to play indoors as she was going upstairs to rest and then she had vanished. We knew that she had probably gone out and that she would not reappear for hours. My father had also gone missing and my grandmother had gone to visit her friend, Mrs Bradfield, so Sarah had dragged me out to go to try and find Gyp.

'But there's something the matter,' I said. 'Look at the way she's walking. Let go of me. I want to go to her.'

'Wait! It's just because she's expecting a baby. Pregnant women always walk like that.'

Sarah sounded so knowledgeable – after all, she was four years my senior – that I almost believed her. But then my mother stumbled, drunkenly, as if she couldn't see properly where she was going and I tore my arm from Sarah's grip and began racing towards her.

'Bethany! Stop!'

Sarah ran after me. She caught hold of the back of my cardigan and pulled so fiercely that the seams dug into my shoulders and into my armpits. I cried out in pain and my mother turned and saw us.

I saw her frown and blink. Her face was blotchy and the flesh around her eyes looked puffed and swollen.

'What are you doing here?' She was angry. 'You're always sneaking about the house and spying on me!'

She took a couple of faltering steps towards us but I saw that she kept turning to look back over her shoulder and down to the beach, below.

'No! No, I'm not!' I was so hurt by the injustice of it that I yelled right back at her. This made her even more angry.

'Oh, yes, you are. I saw the two of you listening outside my door the other day – and I'm sure it's not been the first time.'

Sarah was behind me and suddenly my mother focused her attention on her. 'Is it your mother that's put you up to this?'

I could swear that Sarah was genuinely surprised by the question. 'Put me up to what?'

'Spying on me ... following me around. Do you report back to her?'

'That's silly,' Sarah said.

'Don't speak to me like that! And another thing, it's no use sneaking around the house looking for Great-Grandfather's other will. It exists only in your mother's imagination.'

By now I was crying because Sarah was looking at my mother with something I recognized as contempt, even at that age.

'Don't look at my mother like that! She's ill, can't you see!'

What happened next? I heard my mother give a gasp of pain and I swung round to see her clutching her stomach. But she was looking at the beach again. I followed her gaze.

What was she looking at? Some children were running up and down the shore, dodging the waves; we could hear their excited cries. A dog, who seemed to be with nobody in particular, was racing up and down with them, barking excitedly.

But she was looking beyond them. Far to the north, past the causeway that led to the island, a man and a woman were strolling by the shoreline. They were coming towards us but were too far away for anyone to recognize.

Then my mother gasped again and I forgot about the people on the beach. Momentarily, as my eyes swung upwards, I noticed someone else on the cliff road. He was looking down at the couple on the beach. It was a boy, older than us and tall and slim with dark hair.

Was it Gyp? Suddenly it didn't matter, I forgot

all about him, and about everything else, as my mother clutched her stomach with both hands and retched violently. A moment later she sank to her knees, leaned forward, and vomited into the grass at the side of the road.

I was terrified and I must have cried out for my mother looked up at my face. Then, in spite of her distress, she became herself again. There were tears streaming down her cheeks, but she wiped them with the back of her hands and smiled weakly.

'It's all right,' she said. 'Don't be frightened, sweetheart. Here, give me your hand.' She reached out and her grip was strong, reassuring, but she looked dreadful.

'But ... what is it? What's the matter?'

'A pain ... but don't worry. It's not the baby coming, not yet. It's just something to do with the way I am. I must get home and lie down.'

She tried to get up, but she began to shake a little. 'Look, Bethany, you stay here and keep me company, and Sarah, you must go home and phone Mrs Bradfield. Her number's in the book in the drawer of the hall table. My mother is there. Tell her what has happened and she will come straight home.'

The effort of saying all that had almost been too much and, as Sarah set off, without a word, my mother pulled me down to sit on the grassy verge beside her. I leaned against her, drawing comfort from her softness, and we held hands as we waited.

That was the last time I was physically close to my mother and, as I sat alone in the summer-house, clutching the letters that had made me remember that day, I found that I was crying, great racking sobs, all over again.

I began to sense the sorrow that was to come and I was heartbroken. But I was also grateful, truly grateful, that I had been allowed to remember that my mother had loved me.

We didn't have to wait too long. My father found us before my grandmother had even arrived home. Where had he come from? He loomed over us, suddenly, looking shocked to the core.

'Helen, what are you doing here? What has happened?'

'Walking, David. Beth and I were walking. Take me home.'

At the time I never questioned her lie...

Why had my grandmother kept those three letters? There was the odd chance that she didn't know that she had them, that they had simply lain, unnoticed, amongst her papers all those years, since she had had the dismal task of sorting out my mother's belongings.

But I didn't think so. Had she kept them to fuel her hatred of my father? Had she wanted me to find them one day so that I should know what kind of a man he was?

But I still couldn't believe that my father was guilty of anything other than not dancing attendance on my mother as much as she would have liked. Surely my mother, feeling sick and miserable, must have imagined that he was being unfaithful.

I had remembered overhearing my grandmother telling her to be careful, not to nag, that she risked losing her husband if she did not change her ways.

Had my grandmother believed that it was simply a case of artistic temperament or did she suspect him too?

All the years my father had brought me up alone, he had never, as far as I knew, so much as looked at another woman. I had never questioned this. I should have done. But, when you are a child, and even when you are fully grown, you never think of your parents as sexual beings.

So, it was only after reading those letters, that I began to consider my father as a man, rather than, simply, a parent.

He had been tall, fair, loose-limbed and handsome. I could see that, now. He must have been only in his mid-thirties when his wife had died. Why had he not married again? Devotion to my mother's memory? Too heartbroken to care? Guilt?

If that was so, no wonder he had fled to London...

I pushed the chair back into the corner and replaced the cushions and the rugs. As I did so, something fell onto the floor. I bent down to pick it up. An earring.

In the doorway I examined it more closely. It was pretty but inexpensive, an amber bead enclosed in a geometric pattern of silver wire. But whose was it and how long had it been here?

Suddenly I remembered Sarah's words,

*We've made our own den in the summer-house... Gyp's going to bring food and something to drink...*

217

Was this still Sarah's den? I remembered the wine bottle which had been here just the other day – and then had vanished. I remembered the unusual musky smell; it still lingered. Was it Sarah's perfume? I couldn't be sure.

But why would she come here now? Was she still meeting Gyp and, if so, who exactly was he? Or was she still playing her secret games, this time watching the house and watching me? I could only guess at her reasons.

Betty met me when I was halfway back across the lawn. She had her coat on and she was ready to go home. 'I thought you'd fallen asleep in there. There's someone to see you, a gentleman.'

'Who?'

'No, not him.' She smiled. Was I so easy to read? 'It's Mr Mitchell, Paul Mitchell from Prior's Park.'

'Have you made your mind up yet, Bethany?'

'About what?'

Paul was standing by the drapes of the French windows. He had probably watched Betty and me walk back across the garden.

'About whether you're going to stay here, or not?'

He was trying to keep his voice light, trying to give the impression that he was merely being polite, but he was having some difficulty keeping his smile in place. Something was making him jittery.

'How did you know that there was a choice?'

'Well, I thought that your grandmother...' His words died away as my eyes widened. 'Ah.' He

218

laughed in a self-mocking way.

He walked away from the window and sank into an armchair. I went to sit opposite him. 'So you do know the terms of the will?'

'Sure.'

'Sarah told you, of course?'

'Why "of course"? Anybody can apply to find out the terms of a will.'

I had no idea whether this was true or not. I could check with Mr Simpson but, actually, it didn't matter. Paul knew that I had a choice and it was important to him.

'Paul, is the delay costing you money?'

'What do you mean?'

'The delay to your plans of expansion. Do you really need a decision from me so quickly?'

'No, Bethany, it's not that. We–ell, yes, of course, I've already spent a lot of money on the plans and I would like to be able to open up the cabin area for the next season, but it's you I was thinking about.'

'Me? What on earth do you mean?'

'Well, do you think it would be wise to come back here after all these years? I mean, you and your father made a new life for yourselves in London–'

'My father's dead.'

'I know, but you must have friends there – and a career. If you decided that you would rather not come back to Seatoncliffe, I'm sure that Sarah would be generous, that she wouldn't let you go completely empty-handed...'

He saw the way I was looking at him at him and, to give him credit, he held my gaze this time.

But there was a pallor under his tan and his brow was beaded with perspiration. I could smell his aftershave and there was a sour undertone to the expensive tang. Was it the result of drinking too much the night before or was it generated by anxiety?

'Is that her idea or yours?'

'Sarah's.'

But the long pause before he had answered me, convinced me that I had guessed right.

'I don't think so, Paul, and I don't know what makes you think you would ever be able to convince Sarah and her mother that they should part with anything that belonged to them. And furthermore I don't know why you should.'

I hurried on before he could frame an answer. 'Why are you so concerned about my well-being? Or is it just a way to speed up the development of your own plans?'

'No ... well, it's true that Sarah has promised... I mean, would probably agree to them if–'

I was angry. I sprang out of my chair and glared down at him. 'I think you'd better go now!'

He stood up and faced me. 'Bethany, I've always liked you–'

'Paul, please!'

'No, listen to me. I know you can't remember anything about it, but you were a sweet kid and I felt really sorry for you when–'

'I don't want to hear this.'

'Yeah, sure, I'm sorry...' He shrugged and then he turned to go.

I followed him out into the hall. I hadn't stopped him just because I was angry with him. I was frightened that, if he said too much about the past, he would read in my eyes that I had started to remember. I was more convinced than ever that I should keep that knowledge to myself.

Just before we reached the front door, he touched my shoulder. His hand was trembling, slightly, and, when I looked at him, his smile was wavery again.

'I hope I haven't blotted my copybook,' he said.

'You hope in vain.'

'Are we still friends?'

'Were we ever?'

I opened the door and he was halfway out when, abruptly, he turned and looked at me. 'You know, Bethany, when you're angry like this, you look just like Sarah.'

# CHAPTER 14

I met Imran Hussain when I was halfway into town. I had reached the junction of the cliff road and the main road into Seatoncliffe when his taxi pulled up beside me.

'Do you want a lift, Miss Lyall?

'No, thanks, I'm enjoying the walk.'

He looked at me askance, perhaps because I was not suitably dressed for walking. After Paul had gone, I had made a couple of phone calls and then decided I had better smarten myself up. I was wearing a beige wrap-around skirt with an olive green blouse. My hair was pulled back through a matching scrunchy and I was wearing Cuban-heeled beige court shoes which matched my shoulder bag.

I'd even clipped on my pearl stud earrings. Usually, I didn't wear earrings because, in spite of Josie's regular nagging, I was too cowardly to have my ears pierced and the clip-on kind began to hurt after an hour or two.

Imran leaned towards the open window and smiled up at me. 'I am not asking for a fare, you know. I am doing it out of courtesy.'

He made me feel that I would be very churlish to refuse. So I accepted, graciously, and got into the front passenger seat. I don't know if that was what he intended, but he didn't object.

'As a matter of fact, I have just taken your

cousin, Miss Templeton, back to Prior's Park, that is why I am coming this way.'

'Oh.'

I couldn't think of anything more to say and after a while, he continued, 'She is a very good customer.'

'Yes?' That was a little better, for the question in my voice at least invited further conversation.

'Oh, yes. Ever since she came back from Spain. At first when she was living with your grandmother, and then when she moved to the caravan.'

I remained silent but turned and smiled at him, encouragingly.

'Your cousin does not have a car, maybe she does not drive, but her friend, Mr Mitchell cannot always be chauffeuring her about.'

'No, I suppose not.'

'Her mother, too.'

'I beg your pardon?'

At last Imran had got a response from me that wasn't noncommittal and I think he was actually pleased to see how startled I was.

'She must be your aunt, I suppose, Mrs Templeton? She has taken an apartment overlooking the bay and I take her to the hospital to visit her husband. But, of course, you know this?'

'No. I didn't know, actually. We're not ... we're not a very close family.' That was the best I could manage but I saw that it had confirmed Imran's suspicions.

I had realized, very quickly, that his kind gesture had been motivated by curiosity about me and I didn't really mind. There was no harm in it and, in fact, he had done me a service.

Nobody else had informed me that aunt Deirdre was in England, although I suppose that if I'd had the sense to ask Mr Simpson more questions, he would have told me anything I wanted to know.

So, she had married again. I shouldn't have been surprised. I remembered her as a good-looking woman. She was somewhat deficient in charm, but that could have been explained by her circumstances at the time and, anyway, some men are more concerned with looks than personality.

*But surely not my father!*

I suppressed the thought immediately. I didn't want to worry about that now. I had decided to try to find out more about that summer from other sources and I wanted to face each problem in turn. I had to have some kind of order or my mind might go into overdrive!

Anyway, I had just learned that some poor chump had taken on 'dreary Deirdre' and, as yet, I had no idea whether this would have any bearing at all on my own situation.

'Are you liking it here in Seatoncliffe, Miss Lyall?'

'Yes, I am.'

My answer surprised me. I had only been here for four days and so much had happened. My journeys into that other country, the past, had not been happy. Even the present seemed to be fraught with some undefined danger, yet when Paul had suggested that I would be happier in London, I had known, immediately, that he was wrong.

I must have inherited a backbone from someone

– probably my mother – and I had no intention of being driven away from my home.

Then, of course, there was Greg. If I returned to London, now, I might never see him again. He was only interested in me because of the Priory and the television programme, wasn't he? In spite of his flirting, I didn't think that he would bother to continue our relationship, if you could call it that, if I went away now.

But I'm sure that that wasn't what swayed me. I was not so head-over-heels in love with him that I would have remained somewhere where I was unhappy just because I wanted to see him again. Or that's what I told myself.

'My wife, likes it here, very much, although, of course it is so different from Lahore.'

'Mmm?' I'd missed something but Imran hadn't noticed my discourtesy.

'My wife, Tahira. I brought her back here after the wedding. She had never been to England before.'

'Was your marriage arranged for you?' I couldn't help sounding surprised. Apart from his lilting way of delivering the English language, he seemed so westernized.

'Of course, and we are very happy.' He frowned and I thought I had offended him.

'Oh, I'm sure you are. I wasn't suggesting that–'

He glanced at my worried face and grinned. 'No, no, I have not taken offence. I was only thinking that, sometimes, it is difficult to convince some young fools that their families know best.'

Intuitively, I knew that he was thinking of only one young fool – his brother, Ahmed.

It had been a strange conversation. Imran had offered me a lift so that he could satisfy his curiosity about me and my family. No doubt we compared most unfavourably with his own close-knit background. I'm sure he had never intended to reveal anything about himself other than the fact that his wife was happy here so he was probably relieved that we had reached the promenade.

'Where is it that you would like to go, Miss Lyall?'

I glanced out and saw the illuminated sign of the taxi office. 'Just here will do.'

'Are you going to our shop? You should have just phoned my brother with your grocery list. One of us would have delivered it.'

'No, I'm going along there, to The Gondola. To see a friend,' I added mischievously, knowing that, no matter how curious he might be, he would be far too polite to ask me outright who I was meeting.

He tried, though. 'A friend? That is nice.'

'Yes, well, thank you very much for the lift. Goodbye.'

As I ran along the promenade to The Gondola, I knew that he was watching me and I glanced back. Imran waved as if he had been waiting on purpose just to do this, then he backed his car around the corner and into the parking space in the lane behind the shops.

'Hi! I'm just about to go off duty. You've just caught me.'

I loved the way that Mandy assumed that my only reason for calling in at The Gondola would

226

be to see her. She was right, of course.

'Have you time to have a coffee with me before you go? There are a couple of things I want to ask you.'

'Yeah, just wait until I take my pinny off. Go and sit down, over there, by the window. I won't be long.'

There weren't many customers; those there were seemed to be timing their comings and goings with the arrival and departures of the buses at the seafront terminus. I couldn't spot anyone who looked like a holiday-maker and I remembered Liz Davison's words about the summer season coming to an end soon.

Idly, I gazed out of the window and along the promenade. It was hard to believe that it was only four days since the last time I had sat here watching Greg walk away. I hadn't even known his name...

Soon, Mandy, dressed to go home, appeared with two coffees and a selection of sandwiches wrapped in cling film. 'Dig in to this lot. Save you making a meal when you get home.'

'Thanks, but–'

'It's all right. I didn't pay for them. Mrs Alvini's treat.' As she said that, Mandy gestured towards the dark-haired, middle-aged woman behind the counter. The woman smiled and nodded.

'Thank you, that's very kind,' I called and Mrs Alvini shrugged and gestured with her hands as though to signify that it was nothing.

'She insisted I bring you a cappuccino, too. She said you always liked it.'

'What?'

'She said that when you were a child and used to come here with your father you always asked for "frothy coffee"! Bethany, that's rude!'

'Rude ... what's rude? What are you talking about?'

'First of all, saying "what" instead of "I beg your pardon", and now, sitting there with your mouth open like a landed trout.'

'I ... I'm sorry...'

So I'd been right that first day when Greg brought me in here out of the rain. I had been here before.

'No, *I'm* sorry for being flippant,' Mandy said. 'There's something the matter, isn't there?' She got up and came round to sit on the bench seat next to me.

'No, there's nothing the matter,' I said. 'I was just remembering happier days ... at least they were happy until...'

I stared down at the shreds of chocolate floating amongst the bubbles in my cup. And, then, I must have smiled.

'That's better,' Mandy said. 'Mrs Alvini put extra chocolate on the top for you. She said the old lady always told her to, when you were a little girl.'

'The old lady was Mrs Bertorelli.'

'That's right. Frank Alvini was her nephew, he and his wife used to work for her and they took over when she died. That was long before I worked here, of course.'

'And they changed the name.'

'Did they?'

'Yes, they must have done. The café was called

"Bertorelli's" when my father used to bring me here. As a matter of fact he used to bring Sarah, too.'

'Yeah, Mrs Alvini said so.'

There was the same lack of enthusiasm in her voice as there had been on the day Mandy and I had met in the churchyard.

'Mandy...?'

'Yes?'

'What do you think of Sarah?'

'She's your cousin.'

'I know. But, you're my friend ... aren't you?'

Mandy moved back to the other side of the table and made a show of stirring sugar in her coffee, then she looked up at me and grinned. 'I've got nothing personal against her. Why should I have? It's part of a waitress's job description, being treated like a lower form of life.'

'But?' I was suddenly reminded of my friend, PC McKenzie, and the gentle way he had of questioning me.

'Well, I shouldn't really repeat gossip–'

'But you're going to anyway.'

She laughed outright. 'You know, I really like you, Bethany. I hope you'll be staying here.'

Fleetingly, I wondered if Mandy had applied to see my grandmother's will, too, but I dismissed the thought and decided I was in danger of becoming paranoid. Her remark was undoubtedly innocent.

'You were saying...' I prompted her.

'Well, it's Paul, Paul Mitchell. People here like him and it's not just because he provides employment and brings trade to the town.

'He's a good bloke – and it's a shame to see him going the way his dad went. And that was all because of a woman, too, as far as I've heard.'

'The same way as his father. What do you mean?'

'Drink. He's drinking too much.'

'And people think that's Sarah's fault?'

'Well, he always liked a drink, but it's only since her ladyship came back from Spain that he seems to have forgotten when to stop.

'You know she orders him about and he dances attendance on her almost as if ... as if she had some kind of hold on him.'

'What could that be?'

'Well, Liz Davison, she works at Prior's Park–'

'Yes, I've met her.'

'Well, Liz sometimes comes in here when she's waiting for the bus to town and she reckons it's because Paul's madly in love with Sarah – obsessed, more like.'

'And does she think Sarah's in love with him?'

'Liz doesn't know. But I hope Sarah's in love with somebody.'

'Why?'

'Because she's pregnant.'

'How could you possibly know that?'

'Liz told me – and to save you asking, no, Liz doesn't know for certain. But she sees Sarah every day and, apart from the fact that she's definitely heard her being sick in the shower block a couple of mornings, she reckons that she has that look.'

'Oh, come on, Mandy. "That look"?'

'I know. But Liz should be able to recognize it, if anyone can. She's the oldest of seven and her mother's expecting again – that's why she likes her job so much, she can stay away from home for months on end.'

'I don't think it's the only reason that she likes her job.'

Mandy looked at me and grinned. 'So you've noticed, too? Yeah, she's crazy about Paul, that's why she's been watching events so closely. She thinks that once Sarah has told him, they'll get married and her own hopes will be dashed forever!'

'So, she doesn't think Paul knows?'

'She's sure of it. He wouldn't be able to hide his emotions the way Sarah can.'

I was quiet for a long time and Mandy began to unwrap a couple of the sandwiches. She put them on plates and pushed one in front of me.

'Here, the cheese savoury's the best of this lot and, by the way–' she leaned across the table and lowered her voice '–there's no need to be overwhelmed by Ma Alvini's generosity, she didn't think she was going to shift this lot today, and she'd only have chucked them out at closing time.'

I nibbled at the sandwich experimentally and found it was quite good. I began to eat more enthusiastically; soon, I reached for another one.

'There's one cheese savoury left, or do you want to risk the chicken tikka in a bun?' Mandy said.

'What do you mean, "risk"? Is it awful?'

'No, but there's only one and it's my favourite!'

We giggled like schoolgirls and Mandy went to the counter for a knife and cut the bun in two and gave me half. After she had finished eating, she gave me a keen look and then breathed an exaggerated sigh of relief. 'Phew!'

231

'What is it?' I asked.

'For a moment, back then, I thought that you'd gone right off me.'

'Why should I?'

'Well, I like a good gossip, like most women do, but I'm not proud of it!'

'Mandy, I asked you about Sarah. You wouldn't have told me all that otherwise, would you?'

'Probably not.'

'So, let's forget about it, okay?'

'Okay. So what's the other thing you wanted to ask me about?'

'Oh, that. You've already answered it. I just wanted to know who had owned this café when I was a child.'

That wasn't the exact truth, but it was as near as possible without going into the whole business of my memory's missing years.

Mandy took our dishes back into the kitchen and then we left The Gondola and walked up through the town together. Mandy didn't have far to go and she said it wouldn't take me much longer to find my destination.

My grandmother's address book had still been in the drawer of the hall table. There were a sad number of neat crossings out followed by the one word, *deceased*, but this name and phone number were still there. I'd decided that it was only fair to warn her.

Mrs Bradfield's house was in the better part of town, so Mandy informed me. The easiest way, since I was walking, would be to go up Station Road and over the footbridge across the railway track.

'Yes, that's right, Elm Grove is at the other side of the tracks from where the O'Connors live!' Mandy laughed in that familiar, self-mocking way. We had stopped on the corner of her street. 'I'll be seeing you again soon, then?' she said.

'Yes, very soon.'

'You know, I'm not working on Sunday and I've always wanted to have a look inside Dune House.'

'That won't be possible.'

'Oh, I see.'

'Don't jump to conclusions like that and don't go all huffy on me, Mandy O'Connor. It's only because I won't be here. I've decided to go London tomorrow, to see my flatmate, Josie, and to sort various things out, get some more clothes, that kind of thing. I'll probably stay a night or two but I'll come and see you when I get back.'

'Okay. See you.'

As Mandy hurried along the street to her home I turned and made my way to the house of the woman who had been my grandmother's oldest friend.

From Mandy's reaction, I had been expecting something grander than the between-the-wars semi-detached houses of Elm Grove. But the tree-lined streets did look respectable and mildly prosperous.

The light was beginning to fade, but there were still a few older, confident-looking children, in fashionable casual clothes, playing on expensive bicycles and roller blades.

The gardens were well kept and tidy, although mostly given over to unimaginative and unexceptional bedding plants. I smiled at my own presumption.

Where had I suddenly got this superior attitude about gardening from? I wondered. Bethany Lyall, the girl who couldn't even keep a house plant alive. Obviously, I had been carried away by the discovery that my father had planned the garden at Dune House. I remembered that I would have to do something about that.

Most of the houses had bay windows and some of them had extensions built over single garages. Many had another car, or even two, parked in the driveway.

Mrs Bradfield's house didn't have a garage at all. In the space where it might have been, there was a tall fence and a wooden gate that obviously led to the back garden. All the houses must have been like that, originally, I thought.

The door opened almost as soon as I had pressed the bell. 'Come in, darling!'

Mrs Bradfield's voice was even more distinctive in person than it had been on the phone. It sounded as though she had ruined it with cigarettes at a very early age and had been soothing it with gin ever since.

She was tall, poised and elegant. Her silver-blonde hair was gently permed into soft pink-tinged feathers upswept from an elfin face. I guessed that she must have been around the same age as my grandmother, that is, in her seventies, and yet she didn't look a day over fifty.

She was dressed in a figure-hugging black dress made of something soft and silky; her one concession to her age was a pair of fairly low-heeled black court shoes.

'My goodness, the family likeness is unmistakable!' She stepped back and gestured gracefully towards a door at the front of the house. If that's the room where she was sitting, I thought, she'd probably watched me coming up the street.

The colour scheme of the soft furnishings and curtains was pale pink and apple-green. The carpet was a deep-piled luxury of creamy white. On small brass-rimmed glass tables, here and there, there were expensive ornaments and knick-knacks.

But the room was dominated by the portrait above the mantelpiece. It was unmistakably Mrs Bradfield, but when she was very much younger. She stood on some windblown cliff top, dressed in what looked like flowing chiffon, looking beautiful and romantic in the moonlight.

I walked over to have a closer look. The cut of her shoulder-length hair and the style of the evening dress placed the scene in the nineteen forties. It looked like a moment from a film. It was.

Mrs Bradfield came to stand beside me and she looked up at her former self, wistfully. *'I'll Wait For Dawn.* That was the last time your grandmother and I appeared in a film together. I was the star. My film name was Laura Lenore – perhaps you remember?'

She looked at me hopefully, then shook her head gently. 'No, of course not, far too young. But, anyway, even though she was playing second lead, your grandmother got the man – both of them, to be exact.'

Before I could ask her to explain, she had hurried on. 'The portrait was a gift from the director. Some time later, after I'd given up on Arthur, I married him. But you don't want to hear all this.'

'Oh, please tell me about it, tell me what you meant when you said that my grandmother got both of the men... You see, I've only just found out that she used to be an actress...'

'Ah, yes, Frances *was* an actress. I was what people were pleased to call a film star. But you must sit down, my dear. Over there, on the sofa, then I can sit beside you. Would you like sherry or something less ladylike?'

I convinced her that I really only wanted coffee. I intended to try and finish my design plan for Josie's friends' house, that night. I was going to London the next day and I wouldn't have been able to face her, otherwise.

It was easy to get Mrs Bradfield talking again. She told me that my grandmother, Frances Browne, as she had been then, had come up the traditional way through drama school, provincial rep and the West End stage before being offered film parts.

'I could only dance a bit, sing a bit and say my words prettily, but I loved the cinema and was determined to break in, somehow,' Mrs Bradfield said. 'Luckily, the camera loved me.'

'So, tell me about that last film, you did together, *I'll Wait For Dawn*.'

'It was a war-time escapade, brave British pilots, the women they left behind and heroic French Resistance fighters. I was the heroine who waved my pilot-fiancé goodbye and waited, steadfastly, after he was shot down in France, spurning all other offers, only to find that he'd fallen in love with the French girl who'd saved him.'

'Played by my grandmother.'

'Of course. With her dark good looks and sensitive face she was perfect for the part.'

'So in the film, you, nobly, gave up the guy–'

'And in real life your grandmother walked off with the hero, too, and married him.'

'I don't understand. She didn't marry an actor before she married my grandfather, did she?'

'No, the hero I meant was your grandfather. He was a serving army officer in an intelligence unit and he'd been drafted in to advise the film company about the Resistance part of the script. Couldn't have them giving any secrets away, unintentionally.'

'I see.' I sat back amongst the soft cushions and tried to put all this new information into some kind of order in my mind. It had happened so long ago but Mrs Bradfield made it sound like yesterday. She had done herself an injustice. She wasn't such a bad actress, after all.

'Here, drink this. I think you need something stronger than that coffee. She had poured me a large glass of brandy and, when I started to protest, she raised her hand and said, 'Do as you're told, child.'

I took the glass of brandy.

'Of course, I forgave Frances for stealing Arthur Templeton from under my very nose and we became the best of friends. When my George died so tragically young, it seemed the most natural

237

thing to come and live here, in Seatoncliffe, to be near to her.'

She paused for a moment and, when she spoke again, she sounded less animated. 'But you didn't come here to talk just about your grandmother, did you?'

'No.'

'I can't tell you, you know.' Her husky voice was suddenly muted, her expressive face grave.

'I beg your pardon?'

'I know you've forgotten what happened the day your mother died—'

*Not just that day, I'd forgotten all of my first seven years!*

'But Frances always believed that sooner or later you would remember. She made your father promise that he would tell her if you did. They wrote to each other now and then...'

I remembered going through my father's papers after he had died. I remembered feeling certain that he had been there before me, that he had already thrown so much away...

'She hoped that, when it happened, when you remembered,' Laura Bradfield continued, 'you might come back here, and that you and she could face it together.'

'But why? What is it that I have to face?'

'She didn't want you to feel guilty ... to punish yourself...'

*She's just a child. David! She is not to blame. It's you, you that I shall never forgive!*

My grandmother's voice, clearer now, tugging at my memory...

And then my father's voice, even louder, more

forceful, insisting that I obey him.

*It's all right, sweetheart, it wasn't your fault ... just try to forget ... forget ... forget...*

And I had. Whatever had happened that day was still hidden so deep that I seemed to be trapped in a time between the past and a future. I knew that I would always be a prisoner there until I could find the key that would release me.

I turned to look at Mrs Bradfield. She was watching me almost as if she was afraid.

'Mrs Bradfield, why can't you tell me?'

'Because I don't know, I really don't. The rest of us could only guess. After that dreadful day your grandmother refused to talk about it, even to me.

'The only person who knew for sure what had happened was your father.'

# CHAPTER 15

Laura Bradfield and I talked for a little while longer after that; what she told me was disturbing. Apparently, when my father knew that he didn't have long to live, he had written to my grandmother.

A short but intense correspondence had developed between them. Goodness knows the lengths he must have gone to conceal it from me. When no more letters came, she knew that he must have died. It was then that she decided to write to me and ask me to come home.

'But she didn't ... she didn't write to me,' I said.

'No, my dear, she died before she could put her plan into action.'

It was dark by the time I left, so Mrs Bradfield insisted on calling a taxi to take me home. As I was leaving, I remembered something else that I had wanted to ask her.

'The grave,' I said, 'my grandmother's grave, is it you who...?'

'Yes, of course. You don't think Sarah or Deirdre would bother to look after it, do you?'

'No ... and thank you.'

'You don't have to thank me, darling. I do it for myself.'

'But my mother...?' I couldn't bring myself to formulate the words. Fortunately, she knew exactly what I meant.

'A memorial plaque, inside the church. I think that's usual when there is no – when people are lost at sea.'

Suddenly she flung her arms round me and enfolded me in a soft, fragrant embrace. 'Bethany, darling, don't look so bleak, you know you can come and see me whenever you want to, don't you?'

All I could do was nod.

'Good girl.' She walked out to the taxi with me and leaned forward to close the door. 'Call me as soon as you get back from London.'

'I will. Goodbye.'

It was one of Hussain's Cabs but the driver, thankfully, wasn't as talkative as his boss. We sped through the town in blessed silence and along the road that curved around the bay. The shops had closed and it was a little too early for the wine bars and clubs to be busy.

Strings of coloured bulbs were strung between the lamp posts. The air had chilled and faint, misty clouds had formed around the lights giving the promenade an eerie look, like the deserted set of a Spielberg movie.

Once we reached the cliff road, the film turned into a horror flick. The only light came from the moon, and that was intermittent, as clouds scudded across the sky, blown by the rising wind. The silhouette of Dune House loomed up against the skyline like the Bates's house in *Psycho*.

Next time I planned to come home after dark, I told myself, I would leave some lights on – as many as possible!

I wouldn't have asked him to, but I was foolishly grateful when the driver got out of the car and saw me right to the front door.

'Thank you, but you needn't have bothered,' I murmured.

'Boss said I had to take care of you. Would have come himself when Mrs Bradfield called, but he was just going off duty. Dinner ready. Doesn't like to keep his wife waiting.'

When I'd paid him, I asked him to book me a cab for the next morning. I'd decided to take a taxi all the way to the Central Station in Newcastle. Hang the expense. I could afford it.

I finished the work on the designs for the house in Putney that Friday night. I even managed to do some rough – very rough – sketches of Dune House for Josie, as I had promised. But I didn't bother to write any accompanying descriptions. After all, I would be seeing her the next day.

I spread my work out on the kitchen table and attacked it with the help of instant coffee, some home-baked chocolate cake that Betty had left for me and sheer will power. There wasn't much left to do. It was a matter of tidying up the presentation.

But, before it was too late, I took a break and went into the hall to phone Josie. It was only fair to let her know I was coming. She might even tidy up the flat!

I dialled the number and waited ages, listening to the ringing tone. Eventually, I decided that she must be out, or working a night shift. I put the receiver down slowly. I was disappointed. I had needed to hear the sound of her voice. Before I was halfway back to the kitchen, however, the phone rang.

I turned, smiling, imagining that, in the last few minutes, Josie had arrived home from work, heard the phone ringing from outside, dropped her hold-all on the front doorstep, struggled to find her key in her mess of a handbag and opened the door.

Then she had dashed inside, negotiating the usual clutter in the narrow hall, only to have the phone stop ringing just as she was about to answer it. She would have guessed that it was me.

I could see her now, standing over the tiny telephone table, hot and flustered and probably shrugging her coat off as she waited for me to answer.

'Hi!' I called almost as soon as I had snatched up the receiver. 'Where the hell have you been?'

The pause was just long enough for me to realize that I'd made a mistake. With awful certainty, I knew whose voice I would hear.

'I thought I told you, I'm in London.'

Greg!

'Oh – I thought it was someone else... I'm sorry!'

Have you ever stood at the other end of a telephone line cringing with embarrassment, wishing that you could curl up and die?

His laid-back tone did nothing to help. 'I see.'

Don't do this, Greg. Don't go all distant on me, I wanted to scream, but I didn't, of course. Instead I mumbled, 'I thought it was Josie – the girl I share a flat with in London ... that's why, I mean...'

'Do you want me to hang up?'

'Why? Why should I want that?'

'Well, if you're expecting a call...'

'No, I'm not–'

'But I thought you said–'

*Aaagh!* It was getting worse by the second. 'No, I mean, I'm not expecting... I was just hoping that it would be her.'

'Umm.'

At that moment I could have hit him. He sounded so off-hand that I wondered why he had bothered to phone at all. Suddenly, my backbone stiffened. It had been growing stronger ever since I had arrived here.

'Well, anyway' – I hoped my voice sounded as cool and detached as his – 'why are you calling so late?'

'Is it late? Sorry, I get carried away when I'm working.'

'Working? Where are you?'

'Oh, staying with a friend.'

Silly of me to have asked. It was a foregone conclusion that he wouldn't give a straight answer.

'But I borrowed some tapes from the sound archives,' he continued, 'some old radio documentary programmes. I've been playing them and I found something that might interest you.'

'About the Priory?'

'Yes, well, about legendary love stories, actually. Doomed lovers. You know, Lancelot and Guinevere, Abelard and Héloïse, Edric and Alveva...'

'Edric and Alveva, are they...?'

'Yes, the young monk at Seaton who wrote poetry and the girl who inspired him.'

'She was a nun.'

'She hadn't chosen the religious life for herself. Her father gave her no option.'

'Poor girl, what happened?'

'There's too much to tell you now. I'll show you my notes when I come back. But, basically, they began to meet on the island where Edric was building a hermit's cell. She was supposed to be out gathering sea coal. When they were discovered and faced being parted, they chose to die there.'

'How?'

'Edric got Alveva to tie him to a rock and then she bound herself to him and they waited together for the tide to turn.'

'Greg, that's awful. And the coffins? The stone coffins in the ruined church?'

'Well, I'll be working them into the programme but I won't actually claim that they were the coffins of Ethic and Alveva.'

'Why?'

'For a start, as suicides they wouldn't be entitled to be laid to rest in consecrated ground. People like to think the coffins are those of the lovers, but I think that's just become part of the legend.

'But, even so, I'll get some moody shots of them in the moonlight, work out some atmospheric lighting. No harm in a bit of dramatic licence as long as I– Bethany? Are you still there?'

'Sorry. I was just thinking about them ... the way they died...'

'Powerful stuff, isn't it?'

'Yes.' So powerful that I was almost numbed by it. I had to force myself to speak at all. 'But was that the only reason that you phoned?'

'Just keeping in touch. I want to get copies of this tape and also some archive film about monasteries, so I'm not quite sure when I'll be back, when I'll see you again.'

'I see... Oh, but Greg, I'm coming up to London in the morning.'

'Are you?'

'Yes, just to sort some things out, I–'

'Oh, well, I'll see you when we're both back in Seatoncliffe. Okay?'

'Right. Bye.'

He'd rung off. Damn the man! What was the matter with him? He phones me late at night to tell me a story about doomed lovers and then he goes all stand-offish when I tell him that I'm coming up to London!

I remembered our last telephone conversation when he'd just about admitted that he'd been flirting with me and yet, now, he didn't even want to meet me when we would both be in London.

I went back to my work and tried to concentrate, but I couldn't stop brooding about it. I tried to make excuses for him. He was one of those men who are single-minded when they are working... His schedule is too tight to allow for anything but work...

But then I remembered how he'd taken me in his arms in this very kitchen. I was sure that he had been as shaken by the feelings that the kiss had aroused as I had been.

Did he regret that now? When I had answered the phone the way I did, did he believe that I really did think it was him and not Josie, and that

I sounded proprietary? Had that scared him off? Was he now trying to back-pedal like mad?

I soon realized that all this conjecture was getting me nowhere and I forced myself to finish my work.

It wasn't until after twelve o'clock that I packed everything away and made a cup of hot chocolate to take up to bed with me. I set the alarm on my travel clock for seven a.m.

But, of course, I couldn't sleep. When I had returned here to Seatoncliffe, four days ago – well, five now as it was after midnight – my mind had been like a blank computer disk as far as the first seven years of my life were concerned.

Then the memories had started returning and I still didn't know what exactly would trigger them. Sometimes it happened after somebody had given me a certain piece of information, sometimes there was no immediately obvious reason.

But the people, the places, the events, were still sorting themselves in my memory bank and I knew they wouldn't make sense until one more vital piece of information was added.

I had to remember what had happened on the day my mother died. The trouble was that that was what had caused my memory to crash in the first place. I knew that now. And I was beginning to suspect why.

I seemed to pass straight from a waking state to one of dreaming. One moment I was worrying about the fact I couldn't sleep and the next I was standing on the rocks at the edge of a deep pool.

All around was darkness, a chilling blackness

247

confining me so that there was no way back and no way forward, unless I stepped into the pool. I looked down into the water.

It was dark at first, but then the surface began to change, to lighten, and the effect seeped downwards until I could see a long way down.

Something took shape in the depths and began to rise towards me, turning and writhing up through the grey-green water. I tried to turn and run but I couldn't.

As the shape drew nearer it took on a recognizable form and, just as it reached out its arms to drag me in, the water rose, too, in a monstrous wave that engulfed me, swept me up and took me on, out of the blackness and into the open sea.

Now, instead of darkness, there were wide, grey skies above an endless ocean, but I only glimpsed them for a moment before I began to sink down through the water.

The last thing I heard was the never-ending screaming of the gulls...

Josie hadn't been on night shift when I'd phoned the night before, she'd been to Alison's leaving party. She told me that later, but, when I arrived, just after lunch, she was still sleeping.

I'd been away for less than a week, but already the flat seemed strange to me. But not the clutter – it would have been even stranger if the place had been tidy.

Quietly, without disturbing Josie, I set to and cleaned up. I cleared the table, washed the dishes and tidied the jumble of papers and magazines into one neat pile at the end of the coffee table.

About half a dozen video tapes were scattered all over the floor in front of the television, so I put them back in their boxes and stacked them on the bottom shelf of the small bookcase.

I even dusted and polished a little, but I didn't get the vacuum cleaner out, I didn't want to waken the poor girl too abruptly.

When I'd done what I could, I went into my own room to sort out a few more clothes to take back to Seatoncliffe. While I was in there, I heard Josie's voice.

'I must be dreaming!'

I hurried through. She was standing in her pyjamas, staring round at the tidy room. The expression on her face was half amazed, half scared.

Then she saw me and shrieked, 'Bethany!'

She was pleased to see me and I realized how much I was going to miss her. But we would keep in touch, I knew that. Like my mother and Jane Frears had kept in touch and, like them, we would always be there for each other.

Josie had a quick shower and got dressed, while I made tea and toast and we sat at the table together. 'You're going to stay there, aren't you?'

'Yes, I think so.'

Josie sipped her tea and nodded. 'You'd be mad not to. Now, tell me, tell me all about it.'

I told her all the usual things, the things she wanted to know about the place and about the house. She already knew about Greg, but I told her about Mrs Doran, Mandy, the Hussain family and even about Duncan and how impressive he was.

But it was when we got to the other people, the

249

people I ought to have known, that I realized I was going to have to tell her the truth about my amnesia.

When I did, she stared at me, solemnly. 'Why did you never tell me that you couldn't remember your childhood in Seatoncliffe?'

'Well, the subject never arose ... there was never any need to tell you, was there? And, to tell the truth, it didn't bother me very much.

'I suppose I'd blanked everything out so successfully that I never even realized that there was a problem most of the time. Do you understand?'

'Yes, I do. It's a survival technique.'

'That figures.'

Josie got up and filled the kettle to make another pot of tea. 'Look, Bethany, I think you'd better start at the beginning, I mean from the day you arrived in Seatoncliffe.'

It didn't take long. Josie is a good listener and she didn't keep interrupting. Soon I'd told her not only about Paul and my family, but also some of the things that had happened to me.

I had to tell her about the flashes of memory and how some of the events of the past had started to 'play back' almost as if I was re-living them. But I didn't tell her everything that I'd remembered. Or what I was beginning to believe.

Before I'd started, I'd thought that telling Josie would continue the process of sorting it all out, and it did. I'd also hoped that it would help me to feel easier in my mind.

But one look at Josie's expression, and I knew that I was right to feel apprehensive.

'For God's sake, Bethany, why didn't you

phone and tell me to come straight up there!'

'There was no need.'

'No need? You get knocked down and nearly killed—'

'It could have been an accident—'

'Someone is watching you from the summer-house and probably wandering about your house at will—'

'I don't know that for sure.'

'It's your cousin, of course. It's Sarah. She and her mother get everything if you back out or if something happens to you, don't they?'

'Yes. And I think that you're right about the summer-house and even getting into the house. But I think she has some crazy idea that there's another will somewhere, a will that would be in their favour.'

'But if there isn't another will, she would have to kill you.'

'Why kill me? Perhaps she's just trying to frighten me away.'

'Listen, Bethany. You've just told me that your grandmother was thinking of writing and asking you to go home—'

'Yes, that's right.'

'Don't you think it strange that she fell down stairs and died before she could?'

'It was an accident.'

'Oh, yeah? I know the poor old lady was wearing ridiculous slippers, but why was she going downstairs in the middle of the night in the first place?'

'Of course I've wondered about that—'

'And so you should! You said, yourself, that you

think Sarah has a key. There are all kinds of ways she could have lured your grandmother onto the stairs and then given her a gentle shove.'

'But how could she be sure she'd die?'

'It would have been a miracle if she hadn't. An old lady taking a fall like that and lying there all night? It happens.'

'But the police investigated it all, thoroughly. Mrs Bradfield told me that they questioned Sarah, along with anyone else who might have an interest. She obviously had an alibi for that night.'

'Paul?'

'Maybe. Why?'

'Because from what you've told me, he would do anything for her. And what about your own so-called accident?'

'I've thought about that. Sarah hasn't got a car–'

'She could have borrowed one.'

'I don't even know if she can drive.'

'Paul does.'

We sat and stared at each other. I couldn't argue with Josie because, of course, I had already thought of that possibility myself. If Sarah really was wicked enough to have killed my grandmother and now had turned her attention on me, she would need an accomplice. And maybe not just to give her an alibi.

I didn't want to believe that the accomplice was Paul. I thought that he really meant it when he'd said he liked me. Furthermore, if he was Gyp, and, by now, I was almost certain that he was, then, I had liked him.

But the boy, Gyp had been devoted to my cousin Sarah – just as Paul was now.

'Listen, Bethany, I think I ought to get some leave and come back with you.'

'What, and miss Tom and Alison's wedding?'

'I don't mind about that.'

'But I thought you were going to be a bridesmaid?'

'I'll tell her, she'll understand.'

'No, you won't, because she wouldn't and you would lose a friend.'

'Why wouldn't she understand? It all seems perfectly clear–'

'No, it doesn't. Alison would think your friend Bethany was being hysterical. I still have a nagging suspicion that that's what the police thought when I reported being knocked down.'

'But I can't let you go back there alone–'

'I won't be alone. I'll have people I can turn to for help, I promise you.'

'Who?'

'There's Mrs Bradfield and Betty Doran and Mandy O'Connor...'

Josie suddenly grinned. 'And Hunky Dunc the gamekeeper!'

'Duncan is not a gamekeeper, Josie, he doesn't breed birds and animals for rich oafs to take pot shots at. His job is to protect the local flora and fauna and their natural habitat.'

'Well, from the sound of him, Flora and Fauna are very lucky girls!'

I groaned in mock despair and began to clear our few dishes from the table.

'Let me do that,' Josie said. 'Do you know, we've sat here so long that I'm beginning to get hungry again.'

'Josie, why don't we get a couple of pizzas and a bottle of wine? My treat – I'll even get some chocolate fudge cake!'

'Oh, I'm sorry, Bethany. I should have told you... I'm going out...' Her face had fallen.

'Who with?'

'Matthew. You don't know him. I met him at Alison's party last night. He's an electronics engineer – Tom's cousin, actually. Look, I'll call him and tell him I can't make it.'

'What's he like?'

'Quite ordinary, actually. Only a little taller than I am, nondescript brown hair, neat and slim and not a bit hunky like the men in your life.'

'But?'

'I don't know how to explain this...'

'You don't have to. I get the message.'

'How?'

'The look in your eyes, the sound of your voice. And, of course, you're going to go out with him tonight. I wouldn't want to be the one to stand in the way of "tro-oo lurve".'

'Pack it in, Bethany.' But she was laughing and obviously relieved that I wasn't going to take her up on her offer.

As she got ready for her date – and this took most of the rest of the afternoon – we kept up the usual flow of backchat. But, all the while, I think both of us were aware that we might never spend time together like this again.

While she finished off her make-up, I flopped down in front of the television and, picking up the remote control, I began to flick through the channels.

'I don't suppose you know what's on tonight, do you?' I called out to Josie.

'Not a clue. But that reminds me! I've got something for you to watch. It was at home, my mother had it. You've never seen it.'

Josie knelt down in front of the television set and began to pull out all the videos that I had tidied away before. Finally, she held one of them up in triumph. 'Here it is!'

'What is it?'

'Just wait and see.' She slotted the tape into the video recorder and was just about to press the play button when she sat back on her heels and grinned.

'No, I'll leave you to watch it without me to distract you. There are times when a woman ought to be alone.'

'Josie, stop being so irritating. Tell me what it is.'

She totally ignored me and began to rummage through the pile of newspapers and magazines on the coffee table. Most of them ended up on the floor, exactly where they'd been before I'd tidied them up.

She found the one she wanted. It was an old, very much out-of-date television magazine. 'Here you are.'

'Thank you very much. Now explain.'

'The programme notes and some other interesting details are in the magazine. The film on the video tape was made by the one person you've been so careful not to talk about, so far. The one and only Greg Randall.'

# CHAPTER 16

'The pilgrims who followed this route in the middle ages, travelled in groups in case they were attacked by brigands...'

Greg was standing on a mountain road in a sun-blasted landscape, talking straight to camera. The floppy brim of his khaki sun hat had been tilted back at a ridiculously rakish angle, but, I suppose, that would be to make sure that his face wouldn't be in shadow while he was being filmed.

He was dressed in shorts and a loose T-shirt; a long-sleeved shirt was tied around his waist and he wore professional-looking walking boots. You could see the straps of his rucksack coming down over his shoulders. A pair of sunglasses hung on a cord round his neck.

I had started playing the video the moment Josie left. It was one of Greg's television documentaries. He had walked the ancient pilgrim route, the *Camino de Santiago*, through northern Spain, telling the history of it as he went.

Suddenly, he broke from his usual, slightly professorial, style and grinned. 'But, even though I hope I won't be meeting any bandits, I won't pretend that I'm travelling completely alone. I have my crew with me. One cameraman and one sound man.'

At a nod from Greg, the camera panned round to show a startled sound engineer and his recording equipment, and a dusty-looking back-up truck loaded with gear.

When the camera swung back to Greg he was laughing. 'You'll have to imagine what the cameraman looks like – he's shy – but I want you to know that I am really *walking* every step of the way.

'Those two jokers just follow on behind or sometimes go on ahead to book us places in the next hostel. I can't even persuade them to carry my rucksack when the going gets rough!'

An hour later, I felt that I had been every step of the way with him, along winding mountain roads, stopping at villages with ancient churches, going through towns and exploring their mysterious old quarters. Greg had the ability to make you believe you were there.

His communication skills were outstanding – except when he was on the telephone to me!

I pressed the stop button on the remote and went to put the kettle on to make some coffee. Josie had said that I could eat anything that I could find that was remotely appetizing. I settled for cheese and crackers, the last piece of a fruit-cake, probably made by Josie's mother, and a forlorn apple with a wrinkled skin.

I took my tray over to the settee. Then I remembered the television magazine that Josie had given me.

There was a two-page spread with photographs and more details about some of the places he had visited. The article told me that he had spent months living in Spain while he did the research and during the making of the programme.

Also that he had made many friends when he

was there, including some interesting expats – that is, English people who had decided, for one reason or another, to live out their days in Spain.

There was a panel on the second page enclosing a small article about the man himself. His education, erratic in the early years, his brilliant performance at university, winning all the prizes, then his burgeoning television career. But it was the photograph that caught my eye.

Greg and an older woman were in a garden. The likeness was striking. She was tall, slim, dark-haired and still beautiful. The caption underneath read 'Greg and his mother, former pop singer Pippa Randall'.

There followed a couple of paragraphs about Pippa, who now liked to be called by her given name, Phillipa, and how her brief chart success had been followed by years of touring round the northern club scene.

Apparently she had eventually found fulfilment in the Lake District where she ran a craft centre and art gallery. There was no mention of Greg's father.

I was too unsettled to watch any more television, read or do anything much after that. It was strange being back here, in this crowded cosy haven which had once provided a refuge for me. I don't know why, but I no longer felt truly at home.

But neither was Dune House my home, not yet. My grandmother's will had committed me to limbo, that place that is neither heaven nor hell, and where I must stay until I had redeemed myself by remembering and becoming responsible for my own actions.

The only consolation was music, but I was too unsettled even to make a choice, so I slotted in the first five CDs I came across and set the player to 'continuous'.

I lay and soaked in the bath while the flat reverberated to the sound of Enya, Vivaldi's 'Four Seasons', Simon and Garfunkel, Harry Connick Jnr and Mozart's 'Requiem Mass'.

After that, I went to bed.

Something had woken me up. I sat up and pushed the bedclothes aside. It was very dark, but, even so, I knew that I was not in London, I was in my bedroom in Dune House. The sound echoed eerily up from downstairs. I had to go and investigate.

I was puzzled because I didn't remember coming back here and, as I went out onto the landing, some deep inner consciousness told me that this was a dream.

The sense of relief did not last long because, to my horror, I could not force myself to wake up. I was going to have to act out whatever was required of me. The sound, which I now identified as moaning, was becoming more persistent.

The landing was dark and I felt on the wall for the light switch but I couldn't find it. My hand swept back and forth and up and down, then I tried feeling the wall at the other side of the doorway but the switch simply wasn't there.

Panic squeezed my heart and I could hear my own breathing. The moaning grew louder and I began to edge my way forwards, towards the top of the stairs. The darkness ahead of me seemed to be pulsing with a dull red glow.

I felt the landing give way to the first stair and I halted. Just as I began to go down, my ankles became entangled in some sort of cord and, when I tried to free myself, the cord wrapped itself tightly around my legs and jerked, sharply.

I lurched sideways to grab the handrail, but it was too late. I began to fall, spinning down into the darkness. I opened my mouth to scream but no sound came out.

Eventually, I came to rest on the hall-landing. The cord was still twisted round my legs and I had landed at such an angle that my head was hanging over the first step of the next flight.

All the while, the moaning had continued below me. I stared down into the hall. The red light now streamed down from somewhere high above me, like a stage spotlight, and formed a crimson pool around a body lying at the foot of the stairs.

It was my grandmother. She looked up and stretched her arms up towards me. I stretched my own arms down towards her but I could not reach her. And I could not move.

The next morning, Sunday, Josie was sleepy but happy and we didn't bother to get dressed for breakfast. We discussed what we were going to do about the flat.

I said that I would continue to pay my share of the rent for a while longer, until everything was sorted out, but that she could start thinking about finding someone else to share with, if she wished.

'Don't worry about that,' she said. 'I don't think that will be a problem – finding someone.'

She blushed, faintly.

'I see.'

'Don't look so worried. This is serious – for both of us.'

'But you've only just met him.'

'I know, but sometimes you just know, don't you?'

'Yes.'

I couldn't argue with that. I got up and walked round to where she was sitting and hugged her. 'I hope you know what you're doing, love.'

She pulled away from me and looked up into my face. 'I do, but what about you? I would say that Greg Randall is an altogether more risky proposition than my Matthew.'

What could I say? She was right. And, besides, from the way my usually sensible friend was acting, Matthew had obviously already made his intentions clear. Whereas I didn't have a clue where I stood with Greg.

I only wished that Josie hadn't been able to read me so well. But at least I could assure her that I would still return to Dune House and my inheritance even if I found out that I was never going to see him again. And that was true.

'Let's get out of here.' She got up suddenly. 'Look out there, it's a fabulous day!' She gestured towards the tiny window. Sunlight streamed in across the sink and bench top.

Josie dumped our breakfast dishes in the washing-up bowl and squirted washing-up liquid on them at the same time as turning on the hot water. 'Let's get ready and go and find a pub with a garden and have something to eat. My treat.'

It was my turn to disappoint her. 'I'm sorry, Josie, but I'm going out for lunch. In fact, it's time I got ready.'

'But who...? Not Greg? You did say that he was in London, but–'

'No, not Greg. I'm going to see a lady called Jane Frears. She was a friend of my mother's. I found some letters when I was sorting through my grandmother's papers.'

When we had talked the day before, I hadn't told Josie about the letters because they seemed so personal. Nor had I told her anything about my poor mother's fears during the last summer of her life and what they might have led to.

I had simply said that I now believed that my mother had been drowned as the result of some sort of accident. An accident which I had probably witnessed and reacted to very badly. Hence my loss of memory.

Josie was frowning. 'But those letters were written a long time ago...'

'I know. I realized that there was the chance that Mrs Frears may have moved. But when I found my grandmother's address book, it was the same address as on the letters. Gran hadn't changed it or crossed it out. I had to phone Directory Enquiries because the code had changed but, otherwise, her number was the same. I phoned and she was there.'

'But that's marvellous, isn't it, finding a friend of your mother's? She must have been thrilled when you got in touch!'

Not exactly thrilled, I could have said. When I had told Jane Frears who I was, I could hear how

262

shocked she was. And something else... Apprehensive?

But, after those first few moments, she had seemed genuinely pleased to hear from me and she agreed to see me. I could tell Josie that much, truthfully.

Jane Frears was probably about the same age as my mother would have been, I guessed, so that made her almost fifty. She was small and plump and, although she was still quite pretty, she had a faded air about her.

Her full, flower-patterned skirt was clean but it looked as if it had been washed in the wrong programme and the colours had run. Her blouse and cardigan were different shades of pink.

Suddenly, I felt out of place dressed in the unbleached, fitted linen suit and off-white leather court shoes that I had worn for my 'Duchess days' at Patrick Collings. I had teamed it with a maroon silk blouse and had taken my hair back into a soft bun at the nape of my neck. I was wearing the pearl clips again.

I had made a special effort before I went to meet my mother's old friend. I felt, somehow, that I mustn't let her down – my mother, I mean. I wanted my mother to be proud of me. Crazy, I know.

Mrs Frears had not been able to disguise her shock when she first saw me. She opened the door as soon as I had rung the bell, then she had gripped it with both hands for support. She stared for a moment, with her mouth open, then one small plump hand let go of the front door and clutched at the collar of her blouse.

Her first words were, 'I'm sorry, but you look so like Helen, you know. Your mother didn't have your height, but she was so beautiful, just as you are. But, please, come in.'

Her welcoming smile was subdued and she looked a little weary and careworn. I wondered if that was the result of bringing up the children that she had admitted to loving but not really wanting.

I could neither hear nor see any sign of these children as I followed her through the long, rather gloomy, passage into a little sitting-room at the back of the house. Of course they would be grown up now, and had probably fled the nest.

There was no sign of a husband, either, but then, having read Jane Fear's letters, I thought I knew why.

The sitting-room was sunny but it was faded, too. The loose covers on the chairs and sofa had bleached after years of exposure to tired city sunshine. There was a general air of neglect about the place, as there was in the tiny, overgrown garden that I glimpsed through the window.

Mrs Frears indicated that I should sit in one of the armchairs beside the fireplace. An old, three-bar electric fire stood in front of an empty hearth. It looked as if it might smell of burning dust if it was switched on.

There was a hostess trolley nearby, with plates of sandwiches and cakes. She gestured towards it, nervously. 'I thought this kind of thing would be more appropriate. We'll have so much to talk about – sandwiches are better than something more formal, don't you think?'

'Yes, it's very kind of you, Mrs Frears.'

'Jane, please.'

For a while she busied herself with pouring coffee from a thermos jug and making sure that my plate was filled. But, soon, haltingly, we began to talk.

'I'm sorry about your grandmother.'

'I ... I didn't really know her.'

'Of course, but, still, it's family, isn't it? There must be regrets...?'

'Yes.'

Very much so, I could have said. Regrets for all the wasted years. Wasted because something happened, something so terrible that my father had felt compelled to take me away from my home and endeavour to make me forget all about it.

'So, Frances still had my address in her book, then?'

'Yes ... but–'

'I'm so sorry that I didn't keep in touch with her. I haven't really got an excuse. Life, I suppose...'

'Had you and my mother been friends for long?'

'Since we were at school. We went to secretarial college in Newcastle together and got our first jobs in London, for the same advertising agency. It changed both our lives.'

'How?'

'Well, your mother met your father – he used to do some freelance art-work for them – and I met Roger, one of the partners.

'Your mother and father fell in love, got married and she soon talked him into returning to Seatoncliffe, even before you were born.'

'Did he want to go?'

'I'm not sure. But he would have gone any-where that she went. That much I do know.'

'What about his work?'

'He managed to keep some of his clients and he found some new ones, but your mother was con-vinced that he had great potential and that he was wasting his talent. She wanted him to become a "proper" artist, as she called it.'

'How did he feel about it?'

'Oh, he agreed with her. But he had a family to support and he knew what his priorities should be.'

'But she did persuade him to give up his other work, eventually?'

'Your grandmother was devoted to your mother and she had been lonely while she had been working in London. She was quite happy to sup-port you all, if it meant keeping you there.

'David gave in to your mother, as he usually did... But I think that was the start of all their problems...'

'Yes, I know.'

'You know? But how could you? You were too young to remember. In fact, after your mother died, your grandmother wrote to me and told me that you didn't remember anything very much at all.'

I took the three letters out of my bag and handed them over to her. 'I found these.'

I sat and watched her read the letters that she had sent to my mother fourteen years before. As I did so, I remembered the energetic, vigorous tone of them and wondered how on earth they could have been written by the same lustreless little woman who sat opposite me now.

When she had put the last one back in the envelope, she put all three together and held them with both hands in front of her body. She was gripping them so tightly that, for a moment, I thought she was going to tear them up.

'Don't!' I called and reached out for them. Very reluctantly, she put them into my hand.

'Bethany, have you ... have you remembered anything about that time?'

'Yes, a little, but it would help if you could explain one or two things.'

'I'll try, but I don't know where to start. I think you'd better just ask me anything you want to know.'

'Well my mother obviously wasn't well. I've remembered that – I mean, I seem to remember that she had high blood pressure...'

'That's right, she had toxaemia. It made her irritable, nauseous sometimes; she had head-aches, her poor legs and ankles swelled–'

'And her fingers.'

'Oh, yes, how did you know? In fact, she had to take her wedding ring and her engagement ring off. I don't think she ever wore them again. I don't know what happened to them...'

'Was her condition serious?'

'It could have been. Without proper treatment and care, toxaemia can be very serious. And, in fact, she made it so much worse for herself by not doing as she was told.'

'Resting, for example?'

'At one stage her doctor threatened to take her

into hospital, but she promised that she would rest at home.' Mrs Frears paused and shook her head, despondently.

'But she couldn't rest because she got the idea into her head that my father was having an affair?' I prompted.

'I just couldn't believe it. Not David – not your father – it was such a love match! I told her so in my letters, as you know, but she started wandering about, trying to find him whenever he wasn't dancing attendance in the house.'

'Dancing attendance?'

Mrs Frears flushed. 'Bethany, I loved your mother dearly, but she could be very – demanding. Until that summer your father had been a saint! I just thought that he wanted to escape for a while – have a breather, so to speak.'

'But you came to think that my mother's suspicions might be true?'

She paused for a long time, looking at me, assessing me, and then she said, 'I'm sorry, Bethany, but yes, I did – and so did your grandmother.'

'Why? Because my mother saw him with – with someone? You said, yourself, that her vision was impaired at times–'

'It wasn't so bad that she couldn't make out the figure of her own husband...'

'With a woman, I know, in the ruins of the Priory.'

'They were embracing, or so she thought.'

'She could have been mistaken, couldn't she?'

'But, Bethany, you saw them too.'

## CHAPTER 17

The sky had clouded over and everything looked dull and cheerless. Melancholy seeped into the room from the dated and discoloured wallpaper. I felt, not exactly weary, but lethargic, gripped suddenly, by a deadly inertia that made movement and even thought impossible.

Jane Frears's words had shocked me, and I half expected them to trigger one of my distant memories. But no voices came, no visual playback mechanism kicked into action. So, I just sat there and tried to understand the significance of what I'd heard.

She was looking at me, anxiously. 'Don't you think you should leave the past alone, Bethany?' she asked. 'There must have been a very good reason for you to have forgotten everything.'

'I'm sure there was, but I was a child then, I was seven years old. I was allowed to grow up with the first seven years of my life missing – the good memories as well as the bad.

'I'm not the same person I would have been if it hadn't happened, and I want those years back. I want my mother back. Don't you see?'

'Of course, dear.' She sighed. 'I can't deny you that, even if it means telling you some things that I know are going to hurt you.'

'So what happened the day I was supposed to have seen my father and ... and... Were they in the ruins of the Priory, as my mother told you?'

'Oh, no, you didn't see them, that day. It was a few days later. I'm not sure where it was. Your mother phoned and told me. It was the last time I spoke to her...'

'What did she say?'

'It's funny, she was quite calm, more like her old self, in fact. She just said that I would have to believe her now.'

'Why?'

'She told me that you had been out playing while she was resting and your cousin had come back without you. Sarah wouldn't say where you might be, but she looked as if she had been running and she looked sly, furtive, as if she knew something that she shouldn't. Those were your mother's words.

Without warning, I heard him. *Bethany, wait for me, I must talk to you!* My father's voice, at last.

And then mine. *No, no, go away, I don't want to listen!*

I looked at her, but, of course, Jane Frears hadn't heard the voices. She carried on as if there had been no interruption. 'Anyway, Sarah had come in through the French windows so Helen went to look for you in the garden. She heard you crying in the summer-house.'

'Before your mother got to the door she heard your father talking to you, he was trying to comfort you, to calm you down...'

I remembered his words and the way he was nearly crying himself. *Don't cry, Bethany, please don't cry.*

'But I saw you. I saw you kissing her. And Sarah

270

saw you too. Sarah says it's because you don't love us anymore!'

'No, no, she's wrong. I do love you, Bethany and I love your mother...'

'Then why were you doing that?'

'I don't know how to explain...'

'You're not supposed to do things like that.'

'I know, I know...'

'You can't love my mother, not if you kiss someone else. That's what Sarah says. She says you're going to leave us-'

'Forget what Sarah says. I am not going to leave you!'

'Then, why ... why ... why ... why...?'

My throat constricted as I remembered my childish sobbing.

But it was only voices, this time. There were no pictures, perhaps they would have been too painful. But with the voices had come the warm, resinous smell of the walls of the summer-house and the faintest drift of the perfume of roses and lavender from my father's garden.

The sounds and the scents faded...

I stared at Jane Frears. My flashes of memory were so real to me, that I still hadn't come to terms with the fact that nobody else could see or hear what I could.

She was not even aware that anything out of the ordinary had happened.

'What did my mother do?' I asked her. 'Did she...?'

'When she'd heard enough, she just turned around and went back into the house. She knew that you were safe with your father and she didn't want to have a scene in front of you ... to make you feel that anything was your fault. She told me that she felt ashamed.'

'Ashamed? Why?'

'Well, until then, she had even thought that your father might have involved you somehow. Set you on to spy on her, to report back to–'

I already knew that, but I was hurt that my mother had mentioned it to someone else. 'She told you that?'

'Bethany, she was ill, she wasn't always rational. You mustn't blame her!'

'I don't.'

'Well, now she knew she was wrong and she wanted to keep you out of it as much as possible.'

'Did she tell my grandmother what she'd overheard?'

'I don't know, but I don't think that she did, otherwise Frances would never have left her alone, not even for a moment.'

I thought I knew my mother well enough by now, to guess that she had not told my grandmother. She would have known that Gran would probably have packed her straight off to the maternity hospital and dealt with my father herself.

'So, one day when my grandmother was out she went looking for him again?'

'Of course.'

'And did she find him? Find my father with ... with whoever he was meeting?'

'I don't know. Nobody knows, except your father, perhaps, and maybe you.'

'Why? What happened?'

'One afternoon, she left the house. That's all

anybody knows for sure. When your grandmother returned from her friend Mrs Bradfield's
house there was nobody there. Nobody at all.

'I'm still not sure of the exact order of events
that day. I don't think anybody is, but the next
thing your grandmother knew was that your
father returned to the house carrying you in his
arms.

'Bethany, it must have been dreadful! You were
wet as if you had been in the water. He said that
your mother had fallen in the sea... There was no
trace of her...'

'But they must have searched?'

'Of course. The rescue services were called. The
search was continued as long as there was a
reasonable chance of finding her alive – and even
after that. But her body was never found.'

'How do you know all this? Did you go to
Seatoncliffe as you offered in your letter?'

'No, I phoned that very evening to see how she
was. Your grandmother was just about out of her
mind with worry, still hoping that the coastguard
would find her.'

'Did she say anything about my father? About
me?'

'Not at the time. She knew how much I loved
your mother and she wrote to me afterwards, a
long letter ... setting it out pretty much as I've
told you.'

'Did she say what had happened? How my
mother had fallen in the sea?'

'No. I don't think she knew for sure, she just
said that there had been a ghastly accident and
that no one was to blame.'

I frowned. Why had my grandmother told Jane Frears that no one was to blame? That wasn't the way that I had remembered it, was it? But there was something else I had to know.

'Did she say ... did she ever confirm that it was my aunt Deirdre that my father was ... was meeting?'

'No, I think we just had to assume that your mother had been right. After all, the ghastly woman was obviously up to something that summer, always sneaking off and leaving you and Sarah to run wild!'

'And when my mother heard me and my father in the summer-house, did I not mention Deirdre's name?'

'Do you know, your mother never told me, she was just so determined to let me know that she'd been right.'

'But what do you think?'

'I still find it hard to believe that your father would be remotely attracted to Deirdre. I'd only met her once or twice when I was a girl, before your mother and I went to London, but that was enough.'

'But who else could it have been?'

'That's the problem, Bethany, dear. Your mother saw him with a slim, dark-haired woman. I just don't see how it could have been anybody else.'

September in London is warmer than September on the Northumbrian coast. I had noticed the difference as soon as I had stepped off the train at King's Cross the day before, but the sky had clouded over and Jane Frear's small sitting-

274

room was becoming chilly.

She must have noticed me shivering slightly, and she insisted on making a fresh jug of coffee. She didn't attempt to switch on the electric fire and I saw that it wasn't even plugged in. The old-fashioned, cloth-covered cable was frayed. I wondered whether Mrs Frears had anyone to see to such things.

'Here, take this. Do you want anything more to eat?'

'No, thank you, the coffee's fine.'

She settled in her chair again. 'Has any of this helped you? You know, I'm still not sure if it's wise to drag things up from the past, like this. I mean, does any of it matter all these years later? Your mother, your father, your grandmother ... they're all gone.'

'But I'm still here and surely it's natural for me to want to know my part in it all.'

I didn't want to tell her any more than that and she seemed to accept that my motive was a natural, if somewhat morbid, curiosity about my parents and what had happened to destroy their lives.

There was no point in reminding her that Sarah and Deirdre were also still here and that I believed it was all far from over. Jane Frears was kind and telling her all that would only worry her. I had sensed that she had enough worries of her own.

She was holding her coffee cup in both hands, as if she was warming them, and staring wistfully at nothing in particular.

'I never went back to Seatoncliffe, you know. I

wanted so much to go to your mother's memorial service but I couldn't leave the children. Roger just wouldn't help out.'

'I'm sorry, it must have been difficult for you, bringing them up on your own.'

'On my own? What do you mean?'

'Well, I'm sorry, but there was something in one of your letters, saying how some men... I mean, you said that your own situation was the worst of examples... I thought your husband, Roger, must have behaved in the same way as my father.'

Jane Frears laughed bitterly. 'No, my dear, it was the other way round. I also wrote that your mother was the only friend I had who hadn't put all the blame on me, didn't I?'

'Yes, but...'

'Roger was a married man, you see, and I was the bit on the side. When his wife, Justine, found out, she went back to her family in France to have the baby and she stayed there. The two boys had already started school and were left with Roger. They went to their mother in the holidays.'

'But ... but he married you?'

'Of course. He needed a nanny and a house-keeper – I was cheaper. The divorce cost him his lovely house – he had to sell it – and it meant that we could never have children of our own. School fees for his children, you know, all three of them. He just couldn't afford another family.'

She saw my dismayed expression and she made the effort to smile. 'But I was happy. At the time I thought that I had everything I wanted. I loved him and I even came to love his wretched children. Roger and I saw them through school and

276

university and then he died.'

'I'm sorry.'

'I never see the boys now. They spend all their spare time with their French family, their mother and their sister. It's natural, I suppose.

'But don't look so sorry for me. Your mother wouldn't have done. She'd probably have pointed out that I got just what I'd asked for.'

She saw my shocked expression and smiled. 'But she would have said it completely without malice.'

As soon as I opened the front door of the flat, I was met with delicious cooking smells. There were candles, fresh flowers and wineglasses on the table. It was laid for two.

In contrast to the dining-area, which looked like a photograph in *House Beautiful,* the cooking-area – it wasn't big enough to be called the kitchen-area – was total chaos.

The sink was overflowing with assorted vegetable peelings. Various cooking implements were strewn across the bench. On the cooker top, every pan we owned was in use, with lids clattering, and Josie was red-faced and triumphant amongst the steam.

'Hi, it's about time you turned up!'

'What are you cooking?'

'Roast chicken, can't you smell it? With stuffing and roast potatoes, that's all in the oven. And here–' she waved in the direction of the pans '–we have a selection of fresh vegetables. Which, translated, means anything interesting they had left down at the corner shop!'

'Do you want me to finish things off while you get ready? Then I'll make myself scarce, if you like.'

'What are you talking about?'

'Well, if Matthew's coming over...'

'Matthew isn't coming over. This is for us.'

'But why?'

'Because I don't know how long it will be before we're together again like this, if ever–'

'Josie, we will be–'

'I hope so. But, just in case, this is a celebration – of our friendship, if you like. Now everything's just about ready. I'll dish it up if you open the wine.'

'OK. Where is it?'

'In the fridge, along with a couple of individual chocolate mousses. The wine, by the way, is a lively little bottle of fizzy white with a screw cap, so you don't need that corkscrew.'

In fact, there were two lively little bottles of fizzy white wine in the fridge and it was remarkable how easy it proved for Josie and me to finish one and most of the other over our meal.

After we had scraped the last little bits of mousse from their moulded plastic cups, we piled all the dishes on the bench and took what remained of the second bottle of wine over to the living-area. In other words, the sagging sofa in front of the television set.

Josie topped up both our glasses and placed the bottle on the coffee table, very carefully. She turned to look at me, solemnly.

'Have you thought about self-hypnotism?' she asked.

I stared at her. Had I missed something? What had we been talking about as we cleared the table? No, there weren't any clues there. We had simply agreed that it would be better to leave the dishes until the sink came back into focus.

'I'm sorry, you've lost me,' I said at last.

This time she spoke slowly, articulating her words very clearly. 'Self – hypnotism. Have – you thought – about – it?'

'No, no, I haven't, actually.' I waited, hoping that she would explain herself.

'It might be worth giving it a try.'

'I'm sure you're right.' We both nodded, sagely. 'But, Josie, why should I?'

'Well, if you want to remember, try to get more of your memory back.'

'Oh, I see.'

'I mean, it must be annoying never knowing when it's going to happen. When you're going to re-live the next exciting episode. This way you might be more in control.'

'But how would I go about it?'

'You have to stand in front of a mirror and imagine there's a dot in the middle of your forehead. You stare at yourself– I think you focus on the dot – and imagine that you're going down a tunnel.'

After a while I asked, 'Is that it?'

'No, but that's all I can remember. I read an article in a magazine that a patient left in the ward. It's probably still there. I'll send it to you, if you like.'

'OK.'

I leant back against the cushions and closed my

eyes. It was easy enough to agree. I didn't have to try and hypnotize myself right that minute. I didn't tell Josie that I wasn't sure if I wanted to. In fact, much as I wanted to know the truth, I was beginning to dread what I would discover.

I couldn't forget that angry scene when my father had carried me into the house.

My grandmother and he had faced each other and I had never heard such anger, such despair...

...*she is not to blame. It's you I shall never forgive!* And then my father saying to me, ...*it wasn't your fault just try to forget ... forget ... forget...*

Surely that could only mean one thing? For some time now I had suspected that I had been in some way responsible for my mother's death.

# CHAPTER 18

So, exactly one week later, I left King's Cross again but, this time, Josie hadn't been able to come and see me off. And, instead of a warm, sunny day, it was raining.

As the train headed north, the weather worsened. The rain was sheeting across the windows, making it hard to see what kind of terrain we were travelling through.

The lights were on inside the train and this made the outside world look even darker. In our hermetically sealed world of warmth and comfort, my fellow passengers and I, plucked from our everyday lives, could have been travelling anywhere; through any country, on any continent and in any time zone.

It was easy to imagined that, instead of simply returning to Seatoncliffe, I was also time-travelling back to my home as it used to be before the events of that fateful summer.

I soon abandoned this fantasy – it was too uncomfortable – and tried, instead, to recall some of the wonderful train movies I had seen. Especially the marvellous old black and whites that Josie and I watched on television at hours when sensible people are sleeping.

A speeding train provides a dramatic background for a film-maker and scores of sequences from suspense thrillers, comedies, Westerns, and seriously romantic movies, crowded into my mind.

What if this train was really the Shanghai Express, travelling through revolution-torn China, and was suddenly boarded by bandits? Would I be able to sacrifice myself to save my lover as nobly and as glamorously as Marlene Dietrich had?

Or if I was Margaret Lockwood, so British and beautiful and plucky, would I ever be able to convince Michael Redgrave that the old lady really had vanished?

Perhaps one of the little stations we hurtled through without stopping was the same dismal station where, against a background of swirling steam, Celia Johnson and Trevor Howard had said goodbye for ever in *Brief Encounter*...

After Doncaster, the rain eased off a little, but I still had that sense of being distanced from the real world.

I watched toy cars travelling along winding country roads, sending up huge sprays of water into the hedgerows. Toy farm animals stood patiently in drenched fields. Occasionally, we passed over rivers or canals where the water was the same steely-grey colour as the sky.

I had already bought myself a Danish pastry and a cup of coffee not long after the journey started but, when we reached Darlington, I went back along to the buffet car and bought a phone card. I used the pay-phone to call Hussain's Cabs and tell them approximately what time I would be arriving in Newcastle.

Imran was waiting in the station concourse. 'So

nice to see you. But, if you don't mind my saying, please be quick. The parking, here, is dreadful.'

The rain had stopped, now, but the road leading through the huge portico of the station was still shiny-wet. Imran was parked just outside. He eyed my two large suitcases speculatively as he stowed them in the boot of his cab and then he smiled. 'Come along, I will take you home.'

I didn't get such a warm reception from Betty.

'Oh, so you're back,' was all she said when I walked into the kitchen.

'Well, didn't you expect me to be?'

'I didn't even know you were going away. I had to find out from the likes of Mandy O'Connor.'

'Mandy? How ... I mean, when did you see her?'

'Saturday morning. I was waiting in the café for the bus to town. She wanted a chat when she brought me my cup of tea, she wanted to tell me how nice she thinks you are.' Betty didn't actually add 'Huh!' but I could hear it disturbing the air between us, all the same.

'Anyway, your friend, Miss O'Connor, assumed I knew you'd gone away and I didn't let on otherwise. But I was vexed, I'll be honest with you.'

I was in the wrong and I knew it. 'I'm very sorry, Betty. I should have phoned you before I left for London. I ... I won't do anything like that again.'

My apology and my truly abject manner softened her a little. 'All right, then. Have you had any lunch?'

'Not really, just snacks on the train.'

This time she did say it. 'Huh! Go and take

your coat off and we'll share this hotpot. I was going to put it in the freezer if you hadn't turned up.'

After our meal, while we were drinking tea, I asked if there'd been any messages, hoping that Greg had been in touch. But he hadn't.

However, Mr Simpson's secretary had called only that morning. She had said to tell me that Mr Simpson was away from the office for the rest of the week, but if I wanted to make an appointment with him for as soon as possible after that, she would be pleased to help.

My grandmother's solicitor obviously thought that I should have come to some sort of decision about my future plans by now and, of course, I had. In fact I was sorry that I would have to wait a whole week to tell him that I had decided to stay.

She almost didn't tell me and when she did I could see the effort it took. 'Oh, and that Mandy O'Connor phoned this morning. She said she would really like to see you today, and she hoped you wouldn't mind coming along to The Gondola.'

I was surprised that Mandy wanted to see me so urgently, but I was also upset that Betty, whom I liked, obviously didn't care for Mandy, whom I also liked, at all. Betty was behaving almost like a mother who didn't like her teenage daughter's choice of friends.

I didn't mind that she wanted to adopt a motherly role – in fact, I was flattered – but I wasn't a teenager and I thought I had enough judgement to choose my own friends.

'Betty,' I began tentatively, 'Mandy's all right, you know. I don't know what it is you've got against her... I mean, I know she makes jokes now and then about her family, but the girl, herself...'

I stopped because I saw that I'd succeeded in making Betty more cross than ever.

'Good gracious, Bethany,' she said. 'I've got nothing against Mandy O'Connor, she can't help it if her mother's given up the fight and her father's a no-good layabout. The girl's far too good for her own family.

'I was just cross that she seemed to know in advance that you were on your way home and I thought if you could tell her why couldn't you tell me!'

'But I didn't tell her!'

'How did she know, then?'

'Are you sure she knew? I mean, what did she say?'

'Well, I can't remember her exact words but she definitely said something like "tell Bethany when she gets home..." "When" she gets home, not "if".'

Suddenly, I thought I'd solved the problem. 'Betty, do any of the drivers from Hussain's Cabs go to The Gondola?'

'Yes, they're in there all the time.'

'Well, that's probably how Mandy knew I was on the way home. I phoned from the train to book my cab, you see.'

Betty's smile had been worth waiting for. 'That would be it. That's a proper little gossip shop, that is.'

I had already come to that conclusion. Almost anything that went on in Seatoncliffe would be discussed at The Gondola, sooner or later. And probably sooner rather than later.

Ever since the first coffee house had opened in London in 1632, gossip had been on the menu at such places. The Gondola was continuing an honourable tradition.

'Sit over there with Ruth. I'm due for a break in a moment.'

The café was busy and Mandy looked strained. She was carrying a tray laden with coffees and snacks, but she nodded her head towards a table in a partly screened cubicle near the entrance to the kitchen. A card leaning against a sauce bottle said, 'Staff Only'.

'Go on, Mrs Alvini won't mind.' She hurried away with her order.

I had hesitated because the other young waitress was engrossed in a large serious-looking tome, probably a textbook. But when my shadow fell across the page, she looked up and smiled.

'Sit down, do. Don't mind me. I'll be off as soon as Mandy starts her break.'

While I waited, I watched the people at the other tables and I realized, that with the partial screening of the cubicle, it was almost as if I was invisible.

I tried to close my ears to the conversation coming from the table at the other side of the partition, especially when I realized that the couple sitting there were having a quarrel.

But, by the time the girl got up and stormed

out, I had heard enough to decide that I really didn't blame her. I imagined that if he didn't come up with a pretty good explanation for his behaviour soon, he would be lucky if he ever saw her again.

Ruth was looked up from her book and grinned at me. Obviously she'd heard them, too. 'All human life is here,' she said. 'I think that's a misquote but you know what I mean!'

'Are you a student?' I indicated her book.

'Evening classes. This book is for A-level Psychology, but working here in The Gondola is as good as studying a hundred case histories.'

She closed the book and put it in a large shoulder bag; by the time Mandy came to join me, she was ready to go.

Mandy put two cups on the table and slid into the seat that Ruth had vacated. 'Here's your cappuccino, it's on the house.' She still looked strained.

'Thanks. Been busy?'

'Yeah.' She sighed and leaned back for a moment with her eyes closed.

After a while I said, 'You wanted to see me?'

'Oh–' another sigh '–yes. Mrs Doran gave you my message then?'

'Of course, that's why I'm here. Mandy, is something the matter?'

She didn't answer straight away. She leaned both her elbows on the table and rested her chin on her clasped hands, then she stared at me as if she were assessing me. Her amazing bluey-green eyes were wide and so solemn that I wondered what on earth she was summoning up the courage to say.

She must be in some kind of trouble, I thought, serious trouble. I'd already decided that, if she asked me to help her, I would do anything I could. But when she spoke, at last, she threw me completely off balance.

'Have you seen Greg Randall lately?'

'What?'

'I've told you about saying "what".' She gave a half-smile, but immediately became more serious again. 'I didn't know who he was the first time you came in here with him, but this morning I realized why he looked familiar. And something Sarah said confirmed it.'

'Mandy, what ... where is this leading?'

'In a minute. But have you seen him lately?'

'But–'

'Humour me.'

'I haven't seen him since he went to London a few days ago. He said he'd be in touch when he got back.'

'He's back. He was in here, this morning.'

'Oh.' I wasn't sure how to react. Greg had left no message at Dune House, but there was still time and what on earth was Mandy's interest in all this?

'And is it serious between you two? I mean, are you a couple?'

Mandy's first question was tricky. Whatever Greg felt, I knew what my answer would have to be. But the second question was easy, so that's the one I answered.

'No. Last Monday was the first time we'd met. I knew you'd got the wrong idea that day but you were so kind to me when you thought we'd had a lover's quarrel, that I didn't like to disillusion you.'

'And you're not ... erm ... you're not lovers, then?'

'Well, hardly.'

'Oh, I don't know. If that was really the first day you'd met him and you could get that emotional over a little tiff, it's not hard to imagine what could happen if you made it up.'

'Mandy, first of all we didn't have a "tiff", you only thought that we did, and, secondly, I wasn't being emotional about Greg. And since then we certainly haven't become...' I broke off when I saw that she was smiling.

'Only joking,' she said. 'But if what you say is true I feel a lot better about it all.' Suddenly, she frowned. 'At least I think I do.'

I realized then that I still didn't know what had worried her so much. 'Mandy, what happened? Why did you want to see me?'

'Well, when I saw them together and heard what they were talking about, I was furious. I didn't know then that you two had only just met and I thought your cousin Sarah had been carrying on with your boyfriend behind your back–'

Something in my face, some muscle twitching in spite of my rigidly controlled expression, made her stop.

'Look, are you sure that he's not ... that you and he...?'

'Yes, I'm sure. He's only interested in making a television programme about Seaton Priory. That's on my land, you know.'

'We–ell, OK.'

She still seemed reluctant so I prompted, 'I take it Greg and Sarah met here this morning?'

'Yeah.'

'And they looked... I mean, they looked as if they were...'

'No, it's not the way they looked, it's what they said.' Mandy looked embarrassed. 'You might have noticed that, when you sit here, you can hear the conversation at the next table?'

'I have.'

'It's a nice cosy little table, tucked away in the corner there and just the place to sit if you want to be private ... except nobody seems to realize that what they say can be heard, quite clearly if you're sitting *here*. Ruth says it's psychological – the partition gives them a sense of false security.'

Mandy paused and took a drink of her coffee. Now that she didn't think she was breaking my heart, she had lost her sense of urgency.

'Well, what did you hear?' I prompted.

'I was already sitting here when they came in. Sarah first and Greg only a few minutes later, so it must have been arranged. I was surprised but I wasn't too worried at first because I thought that you might have introduced them?'

She looked at me questioningly. 'No, I didn't even know that they knew each other.'

Mandy was nodding. 'Yeah, well if what I suspect is true they must have known each other for some time.'

'What do you suspect?'

'Just listen and you'll probably work it out for yourself. Well, they waited until Ruth had served

290

them before they started talking. Greg had espresso and Sarah asked for weak, milky tea. I can guess why–'

'Mandy! You don't have to tell me all the details. Just tell me what it was that bothered you.'

'Sorry! Well, as soon as Ruth had gone, Sarah got straight to the point. "Have you told Bethany yet?" she asked him and he said, "No." Well, I pricked up my ears, of course.'

Mandy was leaning across the table towards me and, I don't know if she meant to, but she was giving a pretty good imitation of their voices. I realized that she had a talent for acting. If I hadn't been so wound up, I would have enjoyed her performance.

She continued, 'Then Sarah said, "Why haven't you told her?"'

Mandy paused for dramatic effect. She had no idea how painfully my heart was thumping against my ribs.

'And what ... and how did Greg reply to that?' I managed to ask.

'He didn't answer straight away so her ladyship said, "What are you frightened of?" He told her that he wasn't frightened of anything, he just thought it was better for you to remain in ignorance a little while longer. Then Sarah asked him if he was keeping quiet because of his precious television programme.

'He tried to interrupt at that point but she told him not to worry, it suited her, too, that you should remain in ignorance. Then ... let me see if I can remember her exact words ... yes, she said, "At the moment I have no intention of telling

Bethany, anything, but if she starts asking questions, I might have to."'

Mandy paused and looked at me for some kind of reaction. I tried my best to keep my tone conversational. 'Was that it? Did either of them say anything else?'

'Not much. I think Greg said something about warning him if she decided to tell you what had happened and she said she'd think about it.'

'Did he say how... I mean, did he say how she was to get in touch?'

'Oh, yes. She asked him something about that and he said he didn't plan to move from the Bay.'

'The Bay?'

'The Bay Hotel, one of the new ones, next to that posh apartment block. But, anyway, Sarah said something like it was funny him booking in there and it must have been fate. I didn't understand that bit at all. Do you think it was some reference to a lover's tryst or something...?'

'I have no idea.' Greg had been so careful not to tell me where he was staying. Was that because Sarah was visiting him there?

'Not long after that they left,' Mandy said. 'But not together.'

Suddenly she gave me such a strange glance. 'Do you know, I think I am bothered about all this, after all.'

'Why?'

'Because I don't like the way you're just staring into space. You're upset, aren't you?'

'No, really. I'm just trying to work out what it all means.'

'I don't think that's too hard, Bethany. You'll

probably say I've got a dirty mind, but I think it can only mean one thing.'

'What?'

'Come on, it's obvious. Greg must be the father of Sarah's baby.'

'That's ridiculous. You don't even know for sure that she's pregnant.'

'Well, what else could it be? This whatever-it-is that they don't want you to know about yet?'

'I don't know.'

Without warning I remembered the article I had read in Josie's television magazine and my mind and my emotions began to play a game of 'what ifs'.

Greg had been in Spain for months making that programme about the pilgrims. Sarah had lived in Spain with her mother. What if she was one of the 'interesting ex-pats' that he had made friends with. But in this case something more than friendship had developed.

What if Greg had followed Sarah when she came home to Seatoncliffe – or she had come home because she knew Greg was going to make a programme here? It didn't matter which way round.

What if Mandy was right and Sarah was expecting Greg's baby?

The game came to an end with that. My head was arguing that it was all too logical and my heart was protesting that I just couldn't have been so wrong about him. At that moment I felt that nobody could win this game except Sarah.

'Mandy, do you think I could have another cup of coffee?'

'Sure, another cappuccino?'

'No, just black coffee, black and strong.'

While she was away from the table I did my best to pull myself together. I didn't want Mandy to know how shaken I was by what she had told me about Greg.

I had lied to her at the start of the conversation and there was no way I could tell her now that I had imagined myself in love with him.

# CHAPTER 19

After leaving The Gondola, I went to St Paul's in Seatoncliffe to find my mother's memorial plaque. Before I left Dune House I had phoned Laura Bradfield, who told me that the church would be open later, for evensong. I planned to slip in and out quietly before the service began.

The first door, which opened outwards, gave on to a stone porch with notice-boards on the walls at each side. The inner door opened straight into the church. It was warmly lit and the air smelled of polished wood and flowers.

A thin little woman in a shapeless cardigan was slipping along the rows of pews putting out hymn and prayer books and another woman sat quietly near the back with her head bowed as if in prayer.

To my consternation, when I let go of the door, it swung smartly and noisily shut. Both women looked in my direction. The thin woman smiled at me vaguely and went on with her task. The other was Laura Bradfield. She got up and came towards me.

'There was no need for you to come,' I said. 'I didn't mean to bother you.'

'No bother at all, darling,' she said in her distinctive smoky tones. 'I might have come to evensong, anyway. Are you going to stay for the service?'

'Er ... no. I don't think so.'

My father and I had never been to church together; the last time I had been inside anything resembling one was at his funeral. At the time I had been happy to let Josie and the undertaker arrange almost everything.

I was too grief-stricken to wonder if my father had any kind of religious beliefs. I just went along with what was expected.

'Did ... did my mother go to church, do you know?'

'I think she did, now and then.'

'And my grandmother?'

Mrs Bradfield smiled as if sharing a joke. 'Your grandmother and I found ourselves going more regularly as we got older. But don't worry, Bethany. Both your mother and your grandmother would have wanted you to make your own mind up.

'Come, dear. The plaque's over here.'

It was very simple. Only the words, 'In Loving Memory of Helen Louise Templeton', followed by the dates of her short life. No mention of her grieving relatives or the fact that she had been drowned.

'Your grandmother wanted it to be as simple as possible, that was her way. But, also, I don't think she could bear to be reminded of ... of the way...'

'I know.'

Laura Bradfield clasped my hands. 'Are you here to stay, Bethany?'

'Yes, I think so. I mean, I'm sure of it.'

'Good. But...' Her expressive actress's face clouded.

'What is it?'

'Bethany, dear, I'll come outside with you for a moment. There's something I want to tell you and it may lead to me having the most unholy thoughts!'

Just as we got to the door it opened to reveal a few early worshippers gathering in the porch and a blast of cool air. The branches of the trees surrounding the churchyard were dipping and swaying in the rising wind.

'I won't keep you long,' Mrs Bradfield said, 'but how much do you remember about your aunt Deirdre?'

'N-not very much. Why?'

'Well, I think you ought to know that Deirdre has always had some crackpot idea that her father-in-law was the rightful heir to Dune House and not your grandfather. I don't understand all the family history but, in her eyes, the house should have gone to her dreadful husband Raymond and then, of course, to Sarah.'

I didn't tell Mrs Bradfield that I already knew most of this, that would have been too complicated. I just waited to hear what she would say next.

'Well, I don't know how to put this, but I don't trust either of them. This sounds fearfully melodramatic but, if you want me to move in with you, at least until Blair Simpson has it all tied up for you, then I will.'

'That's ... that's incredibly kind of you.' And courageous and probably foolhardy too, I thought.

I wondered, if it came to the crunch, if Laura Bradfield and I, together, would be any kind of match for aunt Deirdre, Sarah and – and whoever it was who was undoubtedly aiding and abetting my cousin in whatever nefarious scheme she might have.

Sadly, I didn't think so, but I promised her that I would keep in touch and that I would let her know if there was any way that she could help me.

I had wondered, for a moment, if she had been going to tell me something altogether different about aunt Deirdre. But I decided that if she did know anything about my father and Deirdre having an affair, she must have decided that it would serve no useful purpose to drag it up now.

I had no idea of the times of the little local bus, nor where it stopped, except at the seafront terminus, and if I was going to walk that far, I decided that I might as well walk all the way home.

The wind was cold and I was hurrying through the pedestrianized market square when I tripped over one of the decorative cobblestones and fell heavily into a shop doorway.

'Ouch!' The old familiar pain shot up my leg from my right ankle. In that moment of agony I could hear the sarcastic voice of Miss Gibson, the PE teacher at school: 'If only you walked properly, in the first place, Bethany, you wouldn't be always falling over and making a fool of yourself.' I wonder how many teachers are hated for the rest of eternity for making remarks like that.

'Are you all reet, pet?' A muscular youth in

faded jeans, a grey sweatshirt and with his baseball cap on backwards, hurried towards me. The soft, Northumbrian accent was at odds with his fierce appearance.

'Yes, I think so.'

'Here, give us a hand. I'll help you up.'

He did so and as I started to thank him I saw that he was grinning broadly. I looked down at my skirt. It wasn't ripped and seemed quite clean. 'What is it?' I asked him.

'Well, I shouldn't laugh, but you've chosen a canny place to fall doon. In fact, me Da stumbles in and out of here regularly.'

I looked round and found to my horror, that the doorway in question was that of an off-licence. My good Samaritan was laughing openly now. There was something about the laugh that made me take a better look at him. His amazing bluey-green eyes reminded me of the eyes that had been staring into mine just a short while ago.

'Your Da – father, wouldn't be Mr O'Connor by any chance?'

He stopped laughing immediately and looked defensive. 'Aye, it would. Do you know him?'

'No, but I know your sister, Mandy. She's a friend of mine.'

That brought the smile back. 'Is that a fact?' He looked me up and down. 'Well, tell her to bring you home any time she likes. You'll be very welcome.' His glance was teasingly suggestive, but not in the slightest way insulting.

I couldn't help laughing. 'Thank you, I'll be sure to tell her.'

'Well, if you're all reet, I'll be on me way.'

As I watched him walk off I sensed the door behind me opening. 'What was all that about? Was Joseph O'Connor pestering you?'

I turned round to find Paul Mitchell standing there. He was wearing a pale blue cashmere sweater over a white shirt and stone-coloured slacks. The colours of his shirt and sweater accentuated his attractive tan, but there was a puffy look about his eyes which were now a decidedly watery blue.

'No, he wasn't pestering me. I tripped and fell, he was helping me up.' Paul began to smile. 'And before you say anything, it could have been any doorway. I wasn't on my way in.'

Paul was carrying one of those heavy-duty brown paper bags and, as he adjusted it, I heard the clink of bottles. I couldn't help looking at it but I had no intention of saying anything.

Paul answered me anyway. 'Not the kind of thing we sell in The Viking Bar. Some half-bottles of wine for my father.'

'But I thought... I mean, I'd heard your father was in hospital...'

'You heard that? Where did you hear that, Bethany?'

'Oh, I don't know...' I had to think fast. I didn't want to get poor, loyal Liz Davison into trouble for gossiping. But the best I could come up with was, 'I can't really remember. I think it must have been when I was having coffee in The Gondola. You know what a gossip shop that is.'

Paul smiled, briefly. 'Yes, I do.' Then as quickly as it had come the smile vanished. 'I wonder what else you've heard since you came back to

Seatoncliffe, Bethany?'

Now he was staring at me completely un-smilingly. The market square was empty and through the glass door behind him I could see that the salesgirl had temporarily vanished into the stockroom. There was an unmistakable air of menace filling the enclosed space of the shop doorway.

'I'm not sure what you mean ...' I edged away, slightly.

He sighed. 'No, I suppose not.' He paused. Then, 'You've decided to stay here, have you?' His voice was subdued.

'Yes.'

'Ah, well.'

It was as if he had suddenly decided to accept the inevitable, whatever the consequences might be. The tension between us relaxed.

Suddenly he raised a hand and brushed my cheek gently with the back of his fingers. The gesture was intimate and yet in no way threatening. He was looking at me wistfully.

'Bethany...'

'What is it, Paul?'

'We go back a long way, don't we?'

'I suppose so, but – but I don't remember everything, I think you know that.'

'You were just a kid ... Sarah was...'

'Older.'

'Yeah,' he sighed. 'That's it. Sarah was older more my age. If only...'

'It's never any good playing the "if only" game, Paul.'

'I know, but a man can dream, can't he?' He

was smiling again, more like his old self, but I couldn't help feeling that there was much more behind his words than he had actually said.

'I'd offer to run you home,' he said, 'but I'm on my way to visit my father. Yes, he is in hospital, by the way' – he patted the brown paper bag – 'and there's plenty of room to hide these in his locker.'

Paul set off to walk towards the bollards which marked the end of the pedestrianized area. There were a few cars parked in the street beyond. It was some distance from where I was standing but one of them looked like a maroon Jaguar. That's the one he got into.

I was limping quite badly by the time I got to the cliff road and cursing the fact that, knowing how uncertain the weather had been recently, I hadn't had the sense to bring an umbrella. I wasn't sure whether it was actually raining or whether I was walking into a sea fret. But I was going to be wet by the time I got home.

It wasn't truly dark yet, but visibility was poor, so the car coming up behind me had its lights on. I hadn't heard it – again, the wind was too gusty – but, suddenly I saw my own shadow appear on the gritty surface of the road in front of me. Dancing droplets of water were reflected in a pale swathe of light.

I dodged to the side of the road away from the cliff's edge and found that there wasn't much room to manoeuvre. There was a narrow ditch and then the drystone wall that edged the land once owned by the Priory and now all part of the Templeton estate.

The ditch was quite deep and full of long, wet grasses that soaked my legs and the back of my skirt. My feet were still on the road because I didn't want to step down into the ditch so I was leaning back at an awkward angle. As I pressed back against the wall, I was conscious of the rough stones digging into the palms of my hands.

I was frightened – no, terrified. How could I not remember the other time a car had come up behind me on this road? I had to fight the urge to drop my head and keep my eyes tight closed until the car had gone past but, to my horror, I could hear that it was slowing down.

I forced myself to turn my head and look. I was acutely aware that whoever was driving it could see me clearly in the headlights, whereas I was momentarily blinded by them. Nevertheless, I stared as if hypnotized.

What ... who was I expecting to see? I hadn't even had time to allow the answer to take shape in my mind before a dark green off-roader pulled up beside me. The driver leant over the empty passenger seat and opened the door.

'Hello, Bethany. You look like a startled rabbit.'

'Duncan!'

The relief was so great that I really did feel weak – not just at the knees, but all over. I sagged back against the wall so suddenly that I was in danger of falling into the ditch.

Duncan got out and came hurrying round the back of his vehicle towards me. He leaned forward, put an arm round my waist and the next moment, I found myself swept up into his arms. I had no choice but to fling my arms around his neck and hang on as he swerved round and lifted me clear of the ditch. He didn't set me down until he had walked all the way round to the front of the car.

The diesel engine was still turning over but the rhythmic throbbing was nothing compared to the painful thumping of my heart against my ribs.

Duncan smiled down at me, his eyebrows raised. 'Whatever's the matter with you, lassie? You were dodging about back then as if you thought I was going to run you over.'

'Oh, Duncan, if only you knew!'

'What? What is it? Are you saying that you did think I was going to run you over?' His smile had gone. I remembered how quickly his moods could change.

'No ... no, not at all!'

'But–'

'Duncan, please forget it. I was just being dramatic.'

He gave me a long, fathoming look and then he shook his head as if I was a foolish female far beyond the range of knowledge or perception of a reasonable man.

'Well, we canna stand here. I'll take you to your home, now.'

'What are you being now, Duncan, masterful or charming?'

He looked astonished. 'Whatever are you talking about?'

'Well, I've noticed that you make good use of your Scottish accent only when you want to manipulate some poor female.'

He burst out laughing. 'Och, away wi' ye.'

He asked me to stand aside while he moved his car forward and further away from the ditch so that I could get in at the passenger side. It was only a few minutes before we were at Dune House and he seemed content to drive in silence.

Soon he turned into the drive and took me right up to the front door. 'There, now. Get yourself inside and get dried off.'

'Do you want to come in? I can offer you coffee … a meal, even.' I knew that Betty had been busy filling the freezer with home-cooked meals that I should only have to warm up.

I had half opened the door, then turned back, waiting for his answer. Strangely, he was hunched over the wheel, his large hands gripping it tightly. He turned his head, slowly. 'I'm very tempted, Bethany.'

The words hung in the air between us but then he leaned back, stretching his arms and dropping his head backwards as he sighed. 'But, no. No, thank you. I've got some work planned tonight. Some photography.'

'Photography? But it will soon be dark...'

'Infra-red. I'll be setting up a camera with an infra-red beam as a trigger.'

'Trigger?'

'When the creature I'm after breaks the beam, it'll take its own photograph. I'll have to check the settings every now and then.'

'Isn't that very haphazard? How can you be sure you'll get the picture you want?'

He was quite serious when he answered, 'I usually do.'

After he drove off I realized that he hadn't told

me what wee creature he was stalking so methodically. I decided I would ask him if I could see the photographs next time I met him.

There was a message on the kitchen table in Betty's neat handwriting. 'Greg Randall called just before I left. I told him that I wasn't sure what time you'd be home so he said he'd call again. See you on Wednesday. Love, Betty D.'

I crumpled the note up and aimed it at the waste bin in frustration. It hit the lid, which swung open, but then it bounced off and slid onto the floor. I let it lie.

Did Betty mean that Greg had phoned or that he had called here in person? I wished that he could have brought himself to be more definite about the time he'd be calling on me or phoning me again. Or left a number so that I could phone him.

But of course he'd been very careful not to let me know where he was staying; now I thought I knew why. The fact that all I had to do was to look up the number of the Bay Hotel in the telephone directory didn't help at all. It was knowledge that I wasn't supposed to have.

Betty had left a pan of home-made soup on the stove and I lit the gas and left it on low while I went upstairs to change out of my damp clothes. I pulled on a pair of jeans and an oversize shirt in a soft lemon colour. I knew it flattered me. I wanted to look casual but also attractive – just in case anyone called by.

After a lonely meal in the kitchen, I wandered from room to room for a while, completely unsettled; at one point I contemplated going out to the garage. It was the only place I hadn't explored yet and I still had this feeling that it was important that I should look there. But I didn't go for, if I had, I wouldn't have been able to hear the doorbell.

At first I had thought that there was no television set in the house, but Betty had shown me that what looked like an antique cabinet in the sitting-room was, in fact, completely bogus. The doors opened to reveal a large screen and there was a shelf below, for a video recorder.

On the bookshelf behind the cabinet, a couple of rows of video tapes in false bookbindings revealed that my grandmother and Josie would have got along just fine. There were wildlife documentaries, Hollywood musicals and BBC classic serials such as *Pride and Prejudice.*

The only criticism Josie would have made of the collection was that there were none of Greg Randall's programmes. I shoved the tapes back on the shelf moodily, angry with myself that I couldn't stop thinking about him.

I used the remote to flick from channel to channel and realized that it was either watch the ten o'clock news or go to bed. I went upstairs. I didn't think he would call now.

Something had drawn me to the stone coffins.

I had fully intended to go straight to bed but, when I had gone upstairs, the moonlight falling across the landing had compelled me to go along to the window.

The window was at the back of the house and, beyond the garden wall, the arched outlines of the ruined Priory were alternately silver and black as the clouds raced across the moon.

A tall shape detached itself from the mass for a moment and seemed to be heading towards the roofless chapel, but then I lost track of it. Perhaps I had imagined it.

Then the idea came into my head that it might be Greg, going to the chapel to work out his ghostly lighting effects. He had said that he would probably shoot those bits in moonlight, hadn't he? Perhaps that's why he had tried to contact me earlier.

I should have stayed away, but I couldn't. I only paused to grab a cardigan from my room and then I raced down to let myself out the French windows. I hurried across the garden where the overgrown rose vines were tossing fiercely in the wind.

The old gate that gave onto the former Priory lands was slightly open. It was too heavy to actually swing in the wind but it was creaking on its hinges. I couldn't remember whether I had left it open the last time I had come home that way, but I didn't stop to worry about it.

God knows why I had convinced myself that the shadow I had seen going towards the chapel was Greg, but I was sure of it and I wanted to see him.

Was I going to confront him with my knowledge? Hardly. I sensed that he would only despise me for listening to gossip, but I thought that if I could just see him, just be with him, I would *know*. Somehow I would know, without asking, whether he was in love with Sarah.

The wind was even stronger and great luminous clouds sailed across the sky. Their shadows
raced across the rough grassland ahead of me as
if they were drawing me on.

The changing patterns of light and shade were
confusing. For a while I thought I saw a large,
moon-bleached hound bounding along ahead of
me. Benjy? Or a trick of the light? Whatever it
was, it had vanished by the time I reached the
chapel.

I saw that the door had been pulled open. I
paused for a moment to catch my breath, then I
went inside. 'Hello?' I called, but nobody answered.

I moved forward across the flagstones until I
was in the centre of the roofless building and
waited until my eyes had adjusted to the semi-
darkness, then I looked all around. The chapel
was empty.

But there was such an air of sadness. It seemed
to be emanating from the coffins and I walked
over to look at them. The moonlight only half
filled them and I looked down at the cold, grey
stone.

Greg had told me that the coffins could not
have been those of Edric and Alveva but, if the
lovers and the coffins had become bound
together in legend, and if people had believed in
the legend for centuries, was it too fanciful to
imagine that the old chapel could have become a
focus for their grief?

While I was standing there it began to rain. I
saw the first irregular spattering of raindrops fall
into the coffins and stain the old stone in larger

and larger patterns.

The wind, which had been growing stronger and stronger, seemed suddenly to blow up to gale force and I could hear it howling across the open land and around the corners of the ruins.

And then there was another sound. The door behind me slammed shut. The rain was getting heavier by the second so I turned and ran to open it. I grasped the old metal ring, turned it and pushed. Nothing happened.

I thought the force of the wind must have jammed the door and I pushed harder, even turning round and butting it with my shoulders until they were tender and aching. It was no use – the door wouldn't budge.

# CHAPTER 20

The top of the door gave a little each time I pushed, but the bottom remained firm as if wedged or blocked by something heavy on the other side. Eventually, I gave up trying to open it.

By now a full-scale end-of-summer storm was raging and I ran around the ruined chapel trying to find shelter from the driving wind and rain. But there was none to be found.

I ran to examine each window. They were open to the elements but they were either too narrow for me to squeeze through or, in the case of the larger ones, the lower sill was just too high for me to reach. I looked at the ancient stonework hoping to find a foothold somewhere so that I could climb up, but there was nothing.

I wondered if I could drag part of the broken coffin lid over to a wall beneath a window and prop it up and use it as a sort of ladder. But even the smaller portion of the lid was much too heavy for me to budge from its place at the side of the coffin.

I stood and looked down at the coffins in despair. Perhaps some crazy idea of getting into the larger of the two crossed my mind, but they were rapidly filling up with rainwater.

I found myself wondering if anybody would come and bale them out ... and bale me out while they were about it ... if I lasted that long...

I was deathly cold and shivering violently. I could hear my teeth chattering and I was sure that I was coming out in goose pimples all over. My clothes were soaked through and my jeans felt as though they were twice their normal weight, or more.

I began to walk round and round the chapel, keeping as close to the walls as possible to gain the little shelter they afforded. My sodden jeans chafed my legs and my right ankle protested at every step. Soon I lost all sense of time.

Had I been here for one hour, or two? Or more? Was it already morning and would it be getting light soon? How long could a storm last? Surely it must blow itself out, soon...

Keep moving, I thought. The storm must pass, eventually, and I must keep moving and not allow myself to huddle into a corner and curl up and give in to the more and more seductive desire for sleep.

And then, strangely, the sense of panic began to ebb away. I began to feel that everything would be all right if I could just lie down and go to sleep, conserve my energy.

Then, in the morning, I would wake up refreshed and strong again and shout my head off until somebody heard me and removed whatever obstruction the wind had blown against the door and let me out.

As I grew calmer, the wind seemed to die down, too, and the rain eased off to a fine drizzle. This convinced me that my attitude was right. I had stopped panicking and, as a result, my situation had become less dangerous. My own strength of purpose was controlling the weather!

Good, I thought, I can sleep now, I'll just go over and settle down beside the door so that I'm ready in the morning...

That decision probably saved my life. I was actually lying on the floor, as close to the door as I could get, when I heard a strange snuffling sound. It was coming from the other side of the door. I pushed myself up and listened.

I felt light-headed and began to laugh. It sounded so funny. Snuffle, snuffle, snuffle, at the bottom of the door. I stared at the gap between the door and the ground. Most of it was filled with some dark shape but at one end something was moving, quivering. A snout.

Obviously it's an animal, I thought and congratulated myself for being so clever. But what could it be? A rabbit? No, I doubted if a rabbit could snuffle that loud and, besides the nose wasn't furry and it was the wrong shape.

What then? What could be roaming the dunes at will? A fox? A dog? Benjy?

'Benjy! Benjy! Benjy!' I didn't realize that I was shouting his name out loud until I heard the echoes of my own voice reverberating around the chapel. And, at the same time, Benjy began to bark.

He was young and daft and he must have thought that this was a marvellous new game. The louder I shouted, the louder he barked. His scratching at the part of the door he could reach became more and more frantic and, eventually, he started howling like a wolf.

'Stop making that awful noise, Benjy!'

313

Did I say that? No, I didn't think I'd told him to stop. I leant forwards towards the door and listened. Voices ... two voices, but I couldn't hear what they were saying.

And then, 'Bethany? Are you in there?'

'Yes, yes, I'm here. I can't get out, something must have blown against the door.'

'Don't worry. We'll shift it. Get out of the way, you pest of a dog.'

No, he's a lovely dog, I thought. I'll have to put them right about that. Benjy's a lovely dog.

I heard scrapes and thumps accompanied by some grunts and groans and then, at last, the door was pulled open. Two people were standing there. One of them spoke.

'My God, Bethany, you look even worse than the first time I met you!' Mandy said.

Then the other person said, 'Oh, dear,' and Benjy came bursting into the chapel. He jumped up and began to lick my face enthusiastically. I staggered back and would have fallen if Mandy had not sprung forward to shoo off the dog and, simultaneously, put her arm around me.

'Ahmed, don't just stand there. Help me to get Bethany home.'

Mandy O'Connor and Ahmed Hussain. How strange that they should be out walking together, just when I needed them.

'Can you carry her?' Mandy asked him.

'Sorry, I don't think so. Miss Lyall is taller than I am.'

'Mmm, me too. We'll have to make a chair with our hands.'

'It's all right, I can walk,' I said and started

forward, but my ankle refused to support me and, once more, Mandy had to stop me from falling.

'Come here, Ahmed,' she said, 'grasp your own wrist, now grasp mine and I'll hold yours, that's it.'

They manoeuvred themselves behind me. 'Now collapse backwards, Bethany, that's my girl. Put your arms round our shoulders. Great. Now, hang on and let's get you home.'

We set off across the rain-drenched land, past all the ancient graves, with Benjy running circles round us and barking excitedly.

'Shut up, dog, do!' Mandy yelled. 'You're barking fit to wake the dead!' She giggled suddenly. 'And there's enough of them round here!'

By the time we reached the gate that opened into the garden of Dune House, I could hear Ahmed and Mandy breathing heavily. Then Mandy staggered slightly. 'The summer-house,' she gasped. 'We'll have to take her to the summer-house. Careful, up the steps, there – oh, no, stop him!'

Too late, Benjy had darted in ahead of us.

I watched as Ahmed shoved the door further open with his shoulder and my perceptions began to shift slightly. Things that had puzzled me suddenly fitted into new places. I waited until they had set me down and then I asked, 'Mandy, have you lost an earring?'

She gave me such a strange look and then she said, 'Shut up, Bethany. We've got to get you out of these wet clothes.'

'Don't be so bossy ... you're just like Josie.'

'Who's Josie, then?' But she didn't really expect an answer from me, or anything that made sense. She reached forward and stripped off my dripping cardigan and then began to undo the buttons of my shirt.

'No, stop–' Foolishly I tried to knock her hands away, but she took hold of my hands and held them firmly.

'There's no time for false modesty, pet, I've got to get you dry. And anyway, Ahmed's going now.'

'Am I? Won't you need help to get Miss Lyall to the house?'

'Yes, but not from you. If you're not home soon, your parents will go ballistic. You'd better go, but before you do, run into the house and phone my brother – it's all right, he'll be the one to answer the phone at this time of night and he knows all about us. Tell him to come here, pronto.'

'Shall I come back here?'

'Only if there's a problem. Otherwise go straight home or your dad might confiscate your car keys!'

Ahmed melted away obediently, but I saw the way they smiled at each other before the door closed after him.

Mandy soon had me stripped bare. She threw my sodden clothes into a corner and patted me dry very gently with something that looked like a tablecloth. Then she wrapped me up, or rather swaddled me like a baby, in two of the old rugs that had been dumped on the armchair.

'Shuffle back and sit down – careful, don't fall over!'

'Yes, Miss Gibson, I'll try not to make a fool of myself.' Mandy gave me a pitying look and I did as I was told.

She knelt down beside me. 'Get your feet off the floor and up onto this cushion.'

She tucked the bottom of the rug round my feet, then went over to the table. There was a candle stuck in wine bottle and it had burned right down. The flame had begun to flicker uncertainly. There were also a couple of smoking joss sticks in an empty jar. They filled the summer-house with a sweet, spicy aroma.

Wavering light makes everything you see waver, too. I was trying to make out Mandy's expression but the light didn't stay constant long enough. But, even so, I thought she looked troubled. Why? I was all right now, wasn't I? Or was it something else that was making her look so worried.

She poured some hot liquid from a Thermos flask into a cup. She turned round and saw me watching her. She thought my attention had been caught by the remains of the take-away meal on the table.

'I know,' she grinned. 'It's like kids playing house, isn't it? Here, drink this, it's only tea, hot and sweet the way Ahmed likes it, but anyway, you're not supposed to have alcohol if you've got hypothermia.'

'Is that what I've got?'

'I don't know, but I'm not taking any chances.'

I sipped the tea obediently and remembered those other children who had played house here in the summer-house ... Bethany ... Sarah ... and Gyp...

Mandy arranged some of the cushions on the

317

floor and sat down beside me. Benjy, who had been hiding under the table, crept out and flopped down next to her. 'Here, you great lump,' she said, 'mind where you put your muddy paws.' But she began to fondle his head.

'Have you been coming here long?' I asked her.

'Do you mind?'

'Not at all.'

'We've been coming here for a month or two – since Ahmed came home for the summer. Liz Davison told us about the place. She found it when this villain Benjy got into the garden one day. Your cousin Sarah doesn't always shut the gate properly.'

'Sarah?'

'She slips into the house now and then. I was going to tell you, but I guessed that you'd probably worked that out.'

'Yes ... yes, I did. But tell me ... you and Ahmed?'

'Ahmed's a good son and he respects his parents. He knows how upset they'll be when he tells them that we want to get married ... although I think his brother has guessed...

'Anyway, we don't want to flaunt it. It's not like being deceitful, it's more like being kind.'

'Kind?'

'Well, we're not going to change our minds, so we decided we'd wait until Ahmed has finished university before we cause his family any grief.'

'How long has he got to go?'

'Two more years. He's going back next month. When he's got his degree and found a respectable job, we just hope that they'll respect him and his choice. If not ... well...'

'But what about you, Mandy?'

'Oh, my mum and dad will be delighted. Ahmed's a good catch. I haven't told them because my mother would tell everybody!'

'I didn't mean that, I meant what about your education?'

'Yeah... Look, don't preach, Bethany. I'm working on that. Now, tell me, are you feeling any warmer?'

'Yes, a little. But, Mandy, how did you know I was in the chapel? I mean, you couldn't have heard Benjy from this far away, could you?'

'We saw you coming out of the house, earlier. We were in here when the light went on in that room at the back. Then you came haring across the garden like a demented ghost–'

'Ghost?'

'That shirt you were wearing. It stood out in the moonlight, I'm sure you could have been seen from miles away! You were so fast that we didn't have time to blow out our candle, but you didn't even notice, you went past like a flash and out into the Priory grounds...'

She paused as if she wanted me to explain myself, but when I didn't she carried on. 'We–ell, we thought maybe you were meeting someone. I mean, I know for a fact that there might have been something you wanted to say to the two-timing Mr Randall–'

'Mandy, I've already told you that you've got that wrong!'

'Yes, well, I've been thinking about that but, whatever the truth of it is, we weren't too concerned at first. After all, we had a lovely chicken biryani with lots of side dishes waiting! But all the time we were enjoying our meal, I suppose I was half listening for you to come back...'

'Nice of you to worry...' I yawned.

'Stay awake, Bethany. When the storm blew up I was really worried, but Ahmed thought you might have met Greg at the little car park and he might have taken you somewhere. That sounded reasonable, but I still couldn't stop myself worrying.'

'I didn't meet Greg, you know. I didn't meet anybody...'

Again she looked at me questioningly, but when I didn't say anything else she shrugged. 'Well, by that time the rain had just about stopped so I persuaded Ahmed that we should go out and have a look around. As soon as we left the garden we could hear Benjy howling.'

'Good old Benjy...'

The candle flared up and then sputtered out. Only the moonlight filtering through the dusty windows illuminated our refuge. I yawned again and my eyelids started to droop.

'Here, move over a bit.'

I looked up. I hadn't noticed Mandy getting to her feet but now she was standing over me. 'Why?' I asked.

'I'm going to sit in the chair.'

'Oh, yes, sorry, rude of me not to offer, it's your turn...' I began to struggle to my feet.

'Stop that, silly, the rugs are coming loose.'

'But...'

'I'm going to sit beside you ... cuddle you until Joe gets here... I'm not sure if you're warm enough yet so we'll try a bit of body heat.'

'Mandy ... I didn't know you cared...'

'Pack it in, Bethany. Here, put your head on my shoulder.'

Suddenly we started giggling helplessly as Benjy, thinking it was all a game, tried to get on the chair too. At first Mandy tried to push him off but then, when she realized he had dried off since coming into the summer-house, she let him stay, sprawled across our knees. There's nothing like a healthy young dog for added body heat.

Clouds must have covered the moon, for the inside of the summer-house suddenly became quite dark. It's funny how the dark makes you talk in whispers, but we did.

Mandy asked me about my work as a designer and said that she had got the job in The Gondola because it was the only one going when she left school, but recently she'd been thinking about getting back into education, starting with a Foundation Course at the Newcastle College.

'And then?' I asked.

'And then we'll see,' she said.

Benjy had gone to sleep and had been joining in our conversation now and then with gentle snoring. Suddenly he raised his head and swivelled it round to face the door. He gave a low growl.

The door was opening. A beam of torch-light pierced the gloom. 'Mandy? Are you there? What's going on?'

Benjy slid off our knees, still growling. Mandy stood up and grabbed his collar. 'Good dog, no need to make a fuss, it's a friend. Joe, what kept you?'

Mandy's brother didn't argue when she told him that she would explain later. He picked me up easily and carried me across the garden and into the house. He didn't stop until we had gone upstairs, with me issuing directions, and put me down on my bed. For such a tough-looking guy he was surprisingly gentle.

Mandy sent him downstairs again to make sure all the doors were locked and the windows secure. While he was away she got me into my pyjamas and made me get into bed.

Then she said, 'I'm going down to have a word with Joe, won't be long. Looks like Benjy will be keeping you company.'

He was draped across the bottom of my bed. There were muddy paw marks all over the pink candlewick bedspread. Well, I never liked it but just wait until Betty sees that, I thought.

Mandy came back with a mug of tea for each of us. 'What was all that about?'

'All what?'

'Checking the doors and the windows?'

'Just want to make sure we're safe for the night.'

'We?'

'I'm staying. Joe will settle it with my mam.'

'You don't have to. I'm all right now ... I think...'

Mandy smiled. 'Well, I want to make sure of that. But there's something else worrying me.'

'What?'

Her smile vanished and that anxious look that I had noticed in the summer-house came back.

'Bethany, I don't know why you went to the chapel in such a hurry?' She paused and there was a question in her voice. Then she sighed. 'All right. Perhaps you'll tell me when you feel like it. But I do know that it's no accident that you got shut in there. There was a whopping big stone pushed up against the door.'

'It must have been the wind–'

'I could be wrong, but I don't think the wind could have moved that stone. It took the two of us to roll it back.'

'What are you suggesting?'

'Someone put it there. Someone who didn't want you to come out alive.'

# CHAPTER 21

The sky was blue and cloudless and the air was filled with the fragrant scents of rain-washed grasses and wild flowers.

Benjy was following more earthy and interesting scents, probably those of rabbits, mice or voles. Nose to the ground, he tracked through the long grasses, swerving round the old graves with an air of utmost urgency. And he showed no interest whatsoever in heading for home – his home at the caravan park, that is.

Mandy had stayed all night with me. She was convinced that someone was out to get me and she thought that person was Sarah. Her motive: wanting Dune House, of course.

I didn't tell Mandy about the other incidents because I suspected that, if I did, she would have her brother, Joe, posted as a permanent bodyguard. I knew instinctively that that would only draw things out all the longer. I don't know why, but I sensed matters were coming to a climax.

But I had promised her that I would be on my guard at all times and quite soon after that we went to sleep. She'd borrowed a jogging suit – she wanted to be ready for any emergency! – and insisted on sleeping next to me to make sure my temperature, having got back to normal, stayed that way.

We had risen early, in spite of our late night,

and we two and the dog had breakfasted together – luckily Benjy liked cornflakes, or anything that was tossed his way, actually. Then Mandy went to work in The Gondola. She had made me promise to either phone her or call there later.

That morning I felt fine, but my legs were still chafed from rubbing against my wet jeans and my shoulders bruised from my attempts to force the chapel door. So, after my shower, I put on a light-weight gathered skirt and a comfortably loose navy cotton-knit top with long sleeves. I pulled on my training shoes and Benjy and I went out.

The storm had passed, the air was warmer than it had been for days and it was difficult to believe that I might have died the night before.

Mandy was sure that the combination of wind and rain had been enough to bring on hypo-thermia and that, if she and Ahmed hadn't found me when they did, I might have gone to sleep and never woken up again.

She had said that the stone blocking the door was too big for the wind to have blown it there. I wasn't sure about that. It had seemed to me that the wind had reached gale force and could easily have dislodged some bit of crumbling masonry.

So I'd decided to come and have a look for myself. I left Benjy happily hunting, I didn't think he would actually catch any small creature with even half its wits about it, he was making too much noise. I walked over to the door of the chapel to have a look at the stone.

There was nothing there at all – no small boulder, as Mandy had described it, no piece of broken headstone, nothing.

There was a small muddy area where the grass had worn thin just in front of the doorway and this was churned up. The grass at each side was flattened and, if I looked hard, I could imagine that a stone of some size could have been rolled away, round the corner of the chapel and in the direction of the more substantial ruins.

At least, that's the way it seemed to me but I wondered if I saw the tracks because I thought they ought to be there. I wondered if my friends PCs McKenzie and Robson would agree with me.

But I was still hoping against hope that Mandy was wrong. I looked up, half-expecting to find there was a gap in the pediment. But, of course, there wasn't even a pediment. The chapel was much too old to have any kind of fancy stone-work and there was no sign of recent damage. The stone face of the building above the arched doorway was as wind-blasted and smooth as it had been for centuries.

Nothing had fallen from above and, as I looked around, I realized that it would probably take a hurricane to hurl any pieces of broken stonework from the nearest headstones. And then, there would surely be a trail of damage in evidence, not just one stone. In any case, my hypothetical stone was missing.

So it looked as if someone had placed it there deliberately and then rolled it away again early this morning.

And somebody had come by quite cold-bloodedly this morning to remove the evidence. My death would be accidental... I had been caught in the storm and foolishly tried to take shelter in the ruins rather than run for home...

I walked into the chapel. The sun was streaming through the empty windows and last night's rain had dried into a few isolated puddles where the stone flags dipped and curved. The water that had gathered in the coffins was steaming gently and would probably evaporate in time.

There was such an air of peace in there, that I couldn't even summon up a shiver when I remembered how frightened I had been with the storm raging the night before.

But what a shock it must have been for someone to find the door wide open this morning and his victim fled. *His* victim. Sarah couldn't have manhandled the stone herself, not according to Mandy, so she had either had help or her accomplice had carried out the task himself.

My 'accidental death' couldn't have been planned. It had to be opportunistic, just as the 'hit-and-run' had been. Some one had seen me and taken advantage of the circumstances.

The first incident had happened in broad daylight, the second was at night, but Mandy had told me that the lemon-coloured shirt I was wearing had been just about luminous in the moonlight.

I could easily have been spotted by somebody out walking ... someone who went out regularly ... with a dog...

On cue, Benjy started barking and I heard a man's voice saying, 'Hi, there, dog.' The barking got nearer and I realized that man and dog were heading towards the church.

*Then* I was frightened. I glanced swiftly around

the chapel – stupid of me, I already knew there was no other way out – and then I backed slowly until I came up against the wall. I turned my face towards the doorway. Benjy raced in joyously, followed by Greg.

I eased forward slightly and my smile was one of pure relief but he took it for a welcome and hurried towards me. 'Hi, I've just been to call on you – I'm glad you're here.'

'Are you?'

'Of course. We said we'd get in touch as soon as we got back from London, didn't we?'

'You did.'

'What is it, Bethany? Why so frosty suddenly? When I came in just now I could have sworn you were pleased to see me.'

'*You* said that we'd meet up when we were both back in Seatoncliffe, not me.'

'I don't get it... Oh, yes I do. You told me you were coming up to London, didn't you? You expected me to say I'd meet you there ... that's it, isn't it?'

I couldn't deny it and I stood there trying not to look like a petulant child.

'Oh, Bethany, my love...' He closed the short distance between us and took me in his arms. 'I'm sorry. I've always been so much a loner – I'm not good at being accountable – as my mother will tell you...' He kissed me lightly as if tasting my lips. 'I was working ... I get carried away, but, I should have realized...'

And then he kissed me in earnest. I felt the cool stone of the wall behind me as he leaned in to me. I moved forward, aligning myself to him until our bodies seemed to be touching at every point.

One of his hands moved up and down my back, pressing me closer, and the other supported my head, not letting me turn my face away from his, even if I had wanted to.

I felt myself begin to tremble and it was nothing to do with the wild surge of longing that was racing through me. There were other emotions, fighting to surface. Eventually, the conflict became too strong and I tore my mouth away from his.

'Greg, no...'

'What is it? You're crying.' He kissed my wet cheeks, lightly. 'Have I hurt you?'

'No ... no ... but there's something we've got to talk about...'

He moved back and looked at me for a moment – there was no mistaking his look of alarmed unease.

'What's that, Bethany?'

'What is it that Sarah doesn't want you to tell me?'

'How ... how do you...?'

He looked so astonished that I couldn't help smiling, even although I was dreading what his answer might be. 'I have a friend who overheard your conversation in The Gondola yesterday.'

'I see.' He looked bleak.

'Greg?'

'Not here. Let's go somewhere where we can sit down. My car's over in the car park–'

'No, too public. We'll go home.'

Greg nodded and we left the chapel and walked towards Dune House – which had become 'home' to me and which I had no intention of relinquishing, whatever happened between the two of us.

Suddenly, he put his arm around me and we walked together as if it was the most natural thing in the world. I was surprised but I didn't have the strength of purpose to pull away. It seemed so natural to be close to him, even though there was so much between us that was unresolved.

Benjy, completely unasked, romped along ahead of us, stopping now and then waiting until we caught up.

Greg laughed. 'I seem to have acquired a dog.'

'It's Benjy. Don't allow yourself to be flattered, he's a fickle hound.'

'You know him?'

'He belongs to – to the caravan park. I might have to take him back later.'

I wondered why Liz Davison had not already been out looking for him. As far as she knew, he had been roaming loose for hours by now. It must have been about midnight when he turned up at the chapel, and it might have been him that I had seen earlier in the moonlight. But there were other things to worry about right now.

We went into the kitchen. I made a pot of coffee and Greg rummaged about in the pantry until he found a cake tin with some of Betty's raisin buns. And then we faced each other across the table.

'I realized almost from the start that you don't remember much, if anything, about...' he hesitated and his expression became guarded '...about that summer.'

This wasn't what I had thought he had been going to say. But perhaps it was a way of getting round to it. 'You mean the summer that my mother died?'

'Yes.'

'You were here, weren't you, you and your mother, staying in the caravan park?'

'Yes, we travelled around a lot in those days. My mother was a singer and she was engaged for the season at the Pavilion Theatre. It's closed now...'

I don't know what made me ask him, but I said, 'And your father?'

'We didn't need him, apparently.' He gave a wry grin. 'My mother didn't want to tie herself down to marriage – she didn't even tell him she was pregnant.'

'I'm sorry.'

'No, you don't have to be. It was an interesting life. And I met my father, eventually. We get on quite well. He used to play keyboards but now he's a music teacher ... married with children.

'But, Bethany ... that summer–'

'Did I know you?' I interrupted. 'Were we friends?'

'Hardly.' There was a hard edge to his voice when he said that and his lips twisted slightly. 'I hung about by myself most of the time. There were other kids at the caravan park but they were much younger, apart from Paul Mitchell, the owner's son. He was more my age but he was too taken up with ... with his other friends to bother about me.'

'With Sarah. We saw him when we were playing on the beach one day and he was dark and tanned and handsome ... Sarah was fascinated...'

Greg was looking at me, suddenly attentive.

331

'You remember that?'
'I just have.'

*You live in a caravan? Then you must be a gypsy!*
'No! I'm not!'
'Yes, you are. I shall call you Gyp!'
He'd hated it, but instead of having nothing more to do with us, Paul had become Sarah's devoted slave...

'Bethany! Come back!'
'What?'
Greg was half smiling, half worried. 'You seemed so far away, just then.'
'It's just that, ever since I came back here, I've been remembering things ... just snatches ... I think it's being here that started it ... it might not have happened if I'd stayed in London.'
'Did your father never tell you anything? Anything at all?'
'No.'
'That's what Sarah thought. She said that when she met you again it was obvious that your memory was a blank about what had happened–'
'More than that,' I interrupted. 'I'd managed to blank out the first seven years of my life!'
Greg shot me a look of concern but when it was obvious that my outburst was over, he continued, 'Sarah thought your father must have wanted to protect you and when she realized that you and I had met up, she told me that, in her opinion, it was better to leave things be.'
'But why? Why on earth should my cousin Sarah want to make it easier for me?' I must have

sounded bitter and Greg looked puzzled – I could have sworn the look he gave me was genuine.

'Out of kindness?' he suggested.

'Never.'

'Then I really don't know.'

'But you still haven't explained how you and Sarah came to be talking in the café yesterday.'

'Oh, she recognized me almost the moment I arrived in Seatoncliffe. She saw me going into my hotel – her mother has an apartment in the next building. She sought me out when she realized that you and I had met up.'

'How did she recognize you?'

'Apparently, apart from growing taller and, I hope, filling out a little, I haven't changed much in fourteen years.'

'But you said you didn't know us then.'

'I said I didn't know *you*. I'd bumped into Sarah now and then – she used to hang around the caravan park with Paul – and she knew ... she knew...'

'Knew what?'

Suddenly he reached across the table and took both my hands. 'She knew I was involved in what happened the day your mother was drowned.'

And, of course, this is where our conversation had been heading all along. Greg knew something – the same something that Sarah and perhaps everybody else knew – that would hurt me.

'I think you'd better tell me. It's better than guessing.'

'Yes.' He gripped my hands more tightly. 'I can only tell you what I saw. You and your mother were on the island...' He paused. He was looking into my eyes as if he was watching for some response, some sign that I had started remembering.

Then he went on. 'I was on the beach and I saw. I saw just the two of you on a rocky outcrop at the far side ... you looked as if you were ... talking...'

He waited again for some response but nothing that he was saying meant anything to me. He had seen a woman and a child talking on the island, he said they were my mother and myself. I was willing to believe him, but it was as if he was telling a story about two other people.

'Then, suddenly, you ... your mother fell and slipped into the sea ...'

'*Bethany!*'

I pulled my hands back quickly and rose from my chair.

'What is it? Greg asked. He was on his feet. 'Do you remember something? Do you remember seeing her fall?'

'No ... no...' I shook my head. 'Nothing...'

But for the briefest of moments I had known that something he said had not been right.

Time had started running backwards again. I could hear the gulls, smell the salt tang in the air, see – see-

But the impetus slowed and then stopped, stood still, then started forwards again until I was back in the present. The truth that I had just been about to grasp was lost and I looked at him helplessly.

Greg came round the table and took hold of my

shoulders. 'I saw you turn to run and I lost sight of you. But there was no time to lose. Your mother was in the sea, you were somewhere on the island and I knew it was time for the tide to turn. I had to get help. I ran to get your father.'

'My father? But how? I mean, did you go to Dune House?'

'No. I suppose you have to know. Your father was in our caravan.'

'Your...?'

'With my mother.'

'Your mother.'

All those memories of that summer that had never seemed quite right were explained by this one simple fact. My father had been having an affair with Greg's mother.

'I think I'd better sit down again,' I said.

Greg made me some fresh coffee and Benjy came and put his head on my lap. He looked up at me soulfully and I found myself bending down to whisper to him, 'Well, at least I'm glad it wasn't aunt Deirdre.'

'I beg your pardon?' Greg was standing over me with the coffee.

'Oh, nothing,' I sighed. 'But what ... I mean, please tell me what happened then.'

'My mother ran and phoned the police and your father went straight to the island ... I watched from the shore ... the tide was already threatening the causeway...'

Greg sat on the edge of the table just beside me, but I deliberately kept my head down over my coffee.

'There was no sign of your mother by then, but

the coastguard and air–sea rescue had been called and your father had to find you. You were in the cave at the far side of the island. You'd fallen and trapped your foot in some rocks.'

'My right foot...'

*Bethany! Where are you?*
'Here, daddy, here!'
I couldn't move, couldn't run away and the gulls were screaming their laughter at me as the waves crashed nearer...

'The tide was coming in rapidly and your father got to you only just in time. He had to race back across the causeway...'

'He told me  was safe now, that I should forget...'

'That's right. And from what you've told me, it seems that he devoted the rest of his life to making sure that you did forget.'

'And ... and your mother?'

'She knew it was over that day. Your mother's death would always have been between them. The guilt would have been too much for both of them.'

'Guilt?'

'He was with her when he should have been looking after Helen.'

'Yes, I can see that. So taking me away and protecting me from the knowledge of the things that happened that day was an act of reparation.'

'You could look at it that way.'

I stared down at the table for a while and fondled Benjy's silky ears absent-mindedly. Why did I have the feeling that there was more that Greg could have told me? There had been so many hesitations when he had been telling me what had happened. Was he just unsure how to go about telling me that I had been with my mother when the tragedy occurred or was there something else ... something he couldn't bring himself to tell me at all?

Suddenly he reached down and took hold of both of my hands. 'Bethany–'

I looked up at him. 'Yes.'

'If you ever do remember fully what happened that day, I want you to believe that you've – that we've all changed since then, that we're not the same people.'

'What a strange thing to say. What are you suggesting?'

'Only that you might blame yourself, I suppose.'

'But why?'

Greg looked as if he was searching for the right way to answer me and then he said, 'For being on the island in the first place, for surviving when your mother didn't ... people do that, you know.'

'I see.' But I didn't, not entirely.

'Do ... do you want to ask me anything?' he said.

'Yes, yes I do. When you decided to come here to make your programme, did you know Sarah was in Seatoncliffe?'

That was far from what he had been expecting and he looked astonished, or was it shocked? 'No, how could I? That all happened so long ago.'

'So what made you come here?'

'You know the answer to that. I've told you how I found the old manuscript in the cathedral library and it led me to Seaton Priory – that was pure chance.'

'Did you expect to find any of us here?'

'I've told you, I knew that you and your father had gone away. As a child I had only a very vague idea of the family set-up here. For all I knew your grandmother could have moved away, too.'

'But, of course she had died.'

'I only discovered that after I arrived.'

'And, almost immediately, you met up with me and Sarah and Paul again...'

'I haven't actually met Paul yet, but I might have to, soon.'

'Why?'

'When we start filming, we might rent some of his caravans for the crew. Smart hotels are out for that bunch of reprobates – when they came to me I told them that I couldn't compete with BBC-type expense accounts!'

He was deliberately trying to lighten the atmosphere and I was grateful for it.

'Talking of reprobates,' I said, 'I think it's time that I took this four-legged one back to his rightful home. Benjy belongs to Paul Mitchell, you know. Do you want to come with me?'

'I'd like to, but I've arranged to go into Newcastle to find a studio and arrange an editing suite – and also to see if anyone at the university has done any recent research that I don't know about.'

He looked at his watch. 'I've cut it fine, I'm afraid, I'll have to dash.'

'Oh.'

I suppose I looked disappointed because he suddenly grinned and said, 'Look, why don't you come with me? Spend the day with me. I'd like to show you all the things I have to do before the cameras even start rolling. At some stage we might even have time to find somewhere nice for a bite to eat, down by the quayside perhaps?'

'I'd like to Greg, but I really must take Benjy back. I'm a little worried about him and I can't just leave him here.'

'OK. But as soon as I get back, I'll phone you, no matter how late.'

Benjy and I were seeing him to the door when he suddenly stopped and, resting on the hall table, scribbled something on a piece of paper.

'Look, here's my number, I'm at the Bay Hotel – what – umph – what did I do to deserve that?' I had just kissed him.

'One day I might tell you.'

The sun was high and the sky blue and cloudless. I'd decided to cut across the open land beyond the Priory and meet up with the track that led to Prior's Park about halfway, rather than take the cliff road.

I'd improvised a lead for Benjy by looping one of my belts through his collar and he hated it. I was determined the young rascal wouldn't run away, but he couldn't understand – he took it as an affront to his dignity. He either pulled until I felt that the belt would snap or my arm come out of its socket, or he would stop suddenly, almost tripping me up and gaze up at me with a wounded expression.

'You need obedience training, my lad,' I told him on one such occasion and I tried to look very stern. But I spoilt the effect, immediately, by laughing when I saw how he cocked his head on one side as if he was trying his best to understand me.

I would have liked Greg to come with me but, at the same time, I felt that I had to face Paul alone. He must already be worried and wondering how I had got out of the chapel, I thought, and I wanted to judge his reaction when he saw me in perfect health.

I had no idea what exactly I was going to say, other than hinting somehow that I was 'on to him'. It sounded like something from a bad movie script, but I also planned to tell him that I had reported the hit-and-run incident to the police and that, as PC McKenzie had told me, it was logged in the computer. I would hint that my friends Mac and Rob would probably be keeping an eye on me.

What else could I do? I didn't think I had the nerve to come right out and say, 'Are you and Sarah trying to kill me?'

It all seemed so unreal in broad daylight. Instead of feeling worried and frightened as I should have done after recent events, I was enjoying the sunshine and my spirits were soaring. I felt that Greg and I had reached some sort of understanding. All because of a hastily scribbled number on a piece of paper.

There was no warning. No urgent music as in the best movies. No screaming of sirens – that must have happened long before I got there.

As I walked the last few yards along the track that led into Prior's Park at the seaward end, I slowed down. I could see men moving around the swimming pool, men in uniforms. The pool itself was taped off with blue and white striped tape, the kind you see on television news bulletins at a major accident, a terrorist incident or at the scene of a crime.

Within the taped area a man – he looked like a doctor – was kneeling by a stretcher. I couldn't see who was lying on it because of the other men grouped round him I hoped one of the children I had seen the other day hadn't had a serious accident but things didn't look good.

At the far end of the pool and beyond the tape, a curious crowd of holiday-makers had gathered. Two men, a policeman and a Prior's Park employee in the distinctive red sweatshirt, seemed to be answering their questions and trying to persuade them to stand back a little.

One large woman with hennaed hair and a lot of jewellery seemed to be arguing with the policeman. I could hear her strident tones even although I couldn't make out her words and I saw her gold bracelets move up and down her arms as she gesticulated forcefully.

One of the uniformed policemen at the near end of the pool turned round and saw me coming. He started walking towards me as if he was going to stop me, but was overtaken by Liz Davison.

'No,' she called. 'She's a friend of his – look, she's bringing Benjy back!'

The policeman hesitated and Liz reached me. Her face had been ravaged by recent weeping.

'Liz, what on earth's the matter?'

'It's Paul,' she sobbed. 'He's dead. They found his body in the swimming pool.'

# CHAPTER 22

'Liz, do you know how it happened?'

We were drinking mugs of sweet tea in the dining area of Liz Davison's caravan. Benjy had settled himself under the table and had gone to sleep, thank goodness. The sun was streaming through the wide, curved windows, completely at odds with our dark mood. But it warmed us and, as we sat and talked quietly, Liz calmed down a little.

She told me how she had been woken up very early that morning by Steven, the youth whose job it was to clean the pool. He had been almost incoherent when he banged on her door, but had apparently had enough sense to call the police before coming to get her. By the time Liz got there, my old friends Mac and Rob had arrived and were radioing for back-up.

Not very much later Prior's Park had been swarming with policemen, both in and out of uniform, as well as a pathologist and an ambulance crew.

'They've got to decide whether it was an accident or not,' Liz told me. 'They say that, so far, it looks as if it was, but there'll still have to be a post-mortem.

'Oh, Bethany, if only I'd waited and gone to him – he might not have done it!'

'Liz, I'm sorry, but I haven't the faintest idea

343

what you're talking about.'

She started crying again and it was a while before she was calm enough to speak.

'Paul might not have done what?' I prompted.

'Drunk too much. It's obvious that that stuck-up cow upset him so much that he just sat all alone in the bar for hours and got pissed out of his skull.'

'Are you saying that he fell into the pool and drowned because he was drunk?'

'It must have been like that. On the way back to his caravan – do you know that he didn't even lock the bar up after himself? It's a miracle that nothing's missing – he tripped over that damn pole and fell into the pool.'

'Pole?'

'You know, the one with the net on the end – the one that Steven scoops the litter out of the pool with. I'm always telling him not to leave it lying around.'

'But, Liz, you haven't told me yet. Who was it who upset Paul last night?'

'Sarah.'

I'd known she was going to say that – who else could it have been? But in view of what had happened to me the night before I had to know more. I poured Liz another mug of tea.

'What did she say to him?'

'Well, I arrived in the middle of it ... I was just going to say goodnight to Paul and ask him how his father was–' She broke off and frowned.

'What is it?'

'Nothing, really ... it's just that usually he would come and tell me as soon as he got back

344

from the hospital, but last night he didn't...'

'Does that mean you don't know when exactly he got back to Prior's Park?'

'Well, yes, I'd been on late shift and I was just about to lock up my office when I saw his car come back, but he didn't come to see me...'

'So he could have gone out again – say, walking with Benjy?'

'I suppose so. I came back here but I couldn't settle – it just wasn't like him not to say good-night. So, eventually I went...' she hesitated and looked embarrassed '...I went to Paul's caravan.

'He wasn't there. But then, on the way back I noticed that the door to the bar was ajar...'

'So you went in, but stopped when you heard Paul and Sarah having an argument. Liz, was this before or after it started raining?'

'It was after the worst of the storm was over, so it must have been after midnight. But does all this matter?'

'No, not really, I-I'm just trying to set the scene ... guess why he hadn't gone to bed ... work out what kind of mood he was in, you know...'

Poor Liz believed my lie. 'Oh, I see, you think he might have been depressed ... worried about his father?'

'Perhaps.'

'No, it wasn't that. It was something to do with Sarah. As I said, I went to say goodnight, but I stopped at the inner door when I heard him shouting. I should have turned round and gone away but I'd never heard him raise his voice to her before so I ... I...'

'You stayed to listen. Don't worry, Liz. It's a

345

natural instinct.' I nearly added, especially when you were in love with him, but I stopped myself in time. It would only have started her crying again. 'So what were they arguing about?'

'It didn't make much sense, most of it, that is. But one thing's for sure – the baby she's expecting isn't Paul's. Oh, I'm sorry, you probably didn't know that Sarah was pregnant!'

Liz had mistaken the cause of my shocked expression and I didn't feel like telling her that Mandy had already let the cat out of the bag. So I said, 'Er ... you're sure of that, are you? That Sarah's pregnant?'

'Yes, and Paul had only just found out. His father had told him at the hospital earlier.'

'But how on earth did Paul's father know?'

Even as I asked I knew the answer. I had had all the information I needed for days but I just hadn't put it all together.

When I had seen her arguing with the policeman earlier I hadn't recognized her because the years had been so unkind to her. The slim, elegant woman was now overweight and overdressed. Only her voice was the same. If I concentrated, I could hear her shrill complaining echoing down through the years.

'His wife, Mrs Mitchell, had told him. After all, she's Sarah's mother, isn't she? She must have guessed even before I did.'

Aunt Deirdre was married to Paul's father. That tied in with all the little bits of information I already had, like Deirdre was over here from Spain because her husband was in hospital...

But it also explained something else... Something was swirling around in my head ... something connected with the past but I just couldn't quite bring it to the forefront of my mind...

'So that's why Paul was angry, because of what his father had told him, can't you see?' Liz put her hands on the small table and leaned towards me.

'Yes, I can. Paul loved Sarah. He always has, ever since we were children.'

'Well, I don't know about that, but he suddenly shouted, "What a fool I've been. It's him ... you met him in Spain, didn't you?" I think those were his words.'

'Spain?'

'Yes. Sarah didn't say anything and Paul said that now he realized why she'd been so keen to come back to England, even though her mother had needed her to help with his father. Apparently Sarah had just been so damned awkward that her mother had chucked her out.'

Liz was frowning. 'After that, nothing made much sense to me. Oh, yes, you were mentioned...'

'Me?'

'Yes. Paul told her that even though he'd protected her in the past, now that Bethany was here, he was going to make sure that they didn't get away with it. I hadn't a clue what he was talking about, but I wondered if it was something to do with you two being cousins?'

I didn't have to try to explain because Liz stopped and her eyes widened. She was staring over my shoulder and out of the window behind me. I saw her flinch and grip the edge of the table and I turned to see the ambulance leaving the caravan park, followed by a police car. We sat in silence for a while and then she sighed and leaned back.

After a moment I said, 'Liz, I'm sorry to push you, but was that all? Can you remember anything else about last night?'

'There was something. Paul told her she had been wasting her time ... something like it was no good coming to him and asking him to say that she'd been with him that night. And, then, whatever she had planned she'd better forget about it. He wasn't shouting – he sounded very drunk by then. I didn't stay to hear any more.'

Poor Paul. I had been completely wrong in suspecting him of aiding and abetting Sarah in her attempts to harm me. The truth was that his refusal to have anything to do with her plans had almost certainly led to his death – murder.

Sarah had obviously gone to him to ask him to provide an alibi just in case my death, which she was anticipating, was treated as suspicious. Paul had refused, not knowing that I was already trapped in the ruined chapel.

What had Sarah done then? Paul had already started drinking heavily. Had she hung around, waiting for him to set off for his caravan and somehow tripped hint or pushed him into the pool?

She had contrived it to look like an accidental death, just like my grandmother's. My grandmother had been a frail old lady – easy enough to push her down the stairs once she had been lured out of bed in the middle of the night. I had no idea how, but I was sure Sarah had imagination enough to contrive such a plan.

But Paul was younger and stronger. Even if he was very drunk she would probably have needed help. Who from? I dreaded the answer. It could only have been the man who had been her accomplice all along. The man she met in Spain. Greg Randall.

'Bethany? Are you all right?' Liz was staring at me. Her face was blotched with recent crying and her friendly blue eyes were wide with alarm. 'You've gone very pale.'

Suddenly she drew her breath in and raised one hand to her face. 'Oh, Bethany, I'm sorry! You've known Paul for years, haven't you? Since you were children. I should have realized how much of a shock it would be for you!'

Luckily I didn't have to explain the full nature of my shock. Liz just assumed that I was upset because I had been fond of Paul. I realized then that I had been. When we were children, I had warmed to him and, even though I was so young, I had felt indignant on his behalf over the way Sarah had treated him.

But since I had returned to Seatoncliffe, my rediscovered feelings had been poisoned by my suspicions that he was Sarah's accomplice. My cousin had a lot to answer for.

Liz sounded anguished. 'Bethany, I'm so sorry. I've only been thinking about my own feelings...'

'It's all right, Liz. You have every right to grieve for him.' I should have added that perhaps I hadn't, but I would never have been able to explain. 'But, listen, there is one more question?'

'Anything. Just ask.'

'Well, what about Benjy? When you went to Paul's caravan last night, was Benjy there?'

'No. He would have barked when I knocked on the door. I assumed he was in the bar with Paul. He would often take him there after hours. This morning when ... when Paul was found in the pool, I forgot all about the poor beast until I saw you arriving with him.'

'He must have run off some time during the night, then.'

'I suppose so. Oh, Bethany, if only Benjy could talk. We might find out what really happened last night.'

At that moment Benjy woke up growling. At first I thought that it was because he had heard his name mentioned, but then there was a sharp rap on the door. Before Liz could respond, it opened and my aunt Deirdre heaved herself into the caravan.

She saw the two of us sitting there, but she spoke only to Liz. 'So, here you are. Get over to Reception, will you, there's a queue of people there who want all kinds of questions answered. I can't be expected to deal with everything.'

Liz leapt to her feet. 'Sorry, Mrs Mitchell. Of course, I'll go straightaway, but...'

'But what?'

'Does ... has anybody told Paul's father?'

'Not that it's any business of yours, but I'm going to the hospital as soon as the police are finished here. Time enough to tell him then.'

'Oh ... well ... please would you say how sorry I am.'

Aunt Deirdre didn't respond. She stood back

from the doorway. 'Off you go.'

Before she went, Liz leaned towards me and murmured, 'You don't have to leave straightaway. Rest here until you feel a bit better. Make yourself some more tea, if you like.' She smiled kindly.

'Thanks, Liz. I will.'

After she had gone, aunt Deirdre lingered. She looked at me quite impassively and I had almost come to the conclusion that she hadn't recognized me, after all, when she said, 'Well, Bethany. So you've come back to claim the Templeton inheritance.'

It didn't sound like a question and so I didn't make any attempt to answer her. An expression of extreme annoyance crossed her face.

'Well, if you decide to stay, no doubt we shall see you from time to time. It doesn't look as though we shall be able to go back to Spain for a while. Even when Mitch gets out of hospital, we'll be stuck here until we find someone to manage this place.'

I think that was the most she had ever said to me in our entire acquaintance. She certainly hadn't bothered to talk to me when I was a child.

And, even now, it wasn't so much an attempt at conversation as thinking out loud. She was entirely preoccupied with her own concerns, as she had always been. She had made no attempt to welcome me and, even more shocking, she expressed no grief for Paul who was, after all, her stepson.

Poor Paul. It was only later that I learned how much he had deserved better from her.

I didn't speak at all. What could I say? I had

never liked her as a child; I think at that moment I finally acknowledged how much I loathed her. That, at least, gave me a feeling of relief.

After she had gone I didn't make myself more tea, but I was grateful that Liz had said I could sit there for a while.

Was Greg duplicitous? Loving Sarah, had he wooed me, making me fall in love with him while all the time he was leading me into danger?

I only had his word for it that he'd arrived in Seatoncliffe just a couple of days before I had. He could have been in touch with Sarah ever since he left Spain. The fact that he wanted to make a television programme here could have been much more than a happy coincidence.

Well, I suppose I could believe that anyone could imagine themselves in love with Sarah. She was beautiful and she had always had a certain sexual allure, even as an adolescent. Paul had been her slave since the day we had met as children on the beach.

But supposing that Greg had fallen under her spell...? Was he also the kind of man who could be manipulated into helping her commit murder?

I groaned when I remembered how close I had been to him. Surely I would have known.

Benjy growled again, but this time he got up and ambled over to the door. He stopped growling and began to wag his tail even before he got there. There was a hesitant knock and the door swung open to reveal a tall, gangling teenager. I recognized the youth who had been cleaning the pool the first day I had come here.

'Miss Lyall?'

'You must be Steven. Are you looking for Liz?'

'No. She sent me over with a message. It's about Benjy. She was wondering if you'd take him until she can sort something out. She says Mrs Mitchell might just get rid of him – you know what I mean...?'

'I'm afraid I do. Don't worry, I'll take Benjy home with me. Oh, and Steven, tell Liz she can call at Dune House any time she likes.'

'OK.' Steven was halfway down the steps outside the caravan when he turned round and leaned in through the doorway. 'Miss Lyall?'

'Yes.'

'I didn't leave the net lying at the side of the pool, you know. I put it in the shed like I was supposed to. I wish Liz would believe me.'

'I believe you, Steven, and if it's any help I'll try to convince Liz, OK?'

'Thanks. Oh, and she said just to pull the door shut firmly when you go. She's got her keys.'

I still didn't have a proper lead for Benjy, so we had to walk home using my belt looped through his collar again. We cut across the Priory land and this time he was no bother at all. Perhaps he had sensed my mood and was trying to help.

I went in through the garden gate because I had remembered that I'd left my wet clothes in the summer-house the night before.

This time there was no warning at all. I heard the voices as I mounted the steps. Sarah's voice and my own. I pushed open the door and stepped straight into the past...

*Well, are you coming or not, Bethany? Gyp's waiting at the causeway.*

'But we're not supposed to go to the island. It's dangerous. What would we do if the tide turned?'

'I've already told you, Gyp's got the times of the tide from the newspaper. We've got ages yet!'

I wanted to go but, for as long as I could remember, the island had been forbidden to me unless I went with one of my parents. And this summer neither of than had had any time for me.

Sarah must have read my mind for she suddenly stopped bullying and became persuasive, seductive almost. 'It's a shame, isn't it, the way no one will take us anywhere? Your mother's always resting and your father and my mother are always out somewhere.

'Well, Gyp's almost grown-up and we'd be quite safe with him. He says he'll show us the cave ... you know, he thinks it could have been a smuggler's cave...'

I capitulated. 'All right!'

Suddenly we were racing out of the summer-house, across the garden and out of the gate. All the way along the cliff road and through the dunes and down the steep path onto the beach we expected to be hailed and called back.

We were excited, laughing, co-conspirators and almost friends. It wasn't until we arrived, breathless, at the causeway that we realized that Paul was nowhere in sight.

But Sarah wasn't fazed. 'Gyp will be waiting on the island. He said he might go on ahead if we were late. He wants to have plenty of time to explore the cave.'

Sarah wasn't as brave as she pretended to be; she looked as worried as I felt when we set off across the narrow causeway that joined the island to the mainland. The sea was calm, but the waves were lapping the rocks some distance away at each side. Each of us could not help looking now and then to see if they had come any nearer.

We were relieved when Paul appeared on the rocky outcrop at the southern end of the island. He was running towards us. When he realized that we had seen him, he stopped running and began to approach more casually.

When he spoke, he was strangely subdued. 'There's not much to see after all,' he said. 'We might as well go back.'

Sarah was astounded. 'Go back? Why?'

'Well, it's just a cave.'

'But I've never seen a cave on an island. I'm not going back. Come on, Bethany!'

She suddenly dodged round him and headed across the rocks. Paul turned to watch her and then looked back at me, helplessly. He shrugged and said, 'Wait here.' Then he darted after her.

How different my life might have been if I had waited.

I stood for a while, watching a large seabird hovering on outstretched wings before it swooped down into the sea to catch its prey. Then I began to walk across the rocks that circled the island.

I thought that I might meet Paul and Sarah coming back, but I had got all the way around to the seaward side. They looked as if they were crouched down behind a large rock not far away from the entrance to the cave.

At least that's what I thought at first but, as I got nearer, I saw that Paul must have grabbed Sarah and pulled her down because she was struggling to be free.

My instinct was to help her – God knows why. I ran forward shouting, 'Let her go!'

That was enough to make him lose his concentration for a moment and Sarah yanked herself out of his grip and ran towards the cave. Paul ran after her and I followed.

As I plunged from the bright sunlight into the dim interior of the cave I heard Sarah screaming, 'No! No! No!' And then she was silent.

Paul was sobbing, 'I told you not to come!'

When my eyes adjusted, I saw what they could see. Sarah's mother and Paul's father were lying naked on a rug on the rocky floor. They were in the act of springing apart and their faces portrayed total shock.

Aunt Deirdre pulled the rug up and frantically tried to cover herself. Mr Mitchell grabbed at his discarded clothes. He was tanned and muscular, a handsome man, but his face was contorted with fury as he shouted at Paul.

'Don't just stand there blubbering – get the kids out of here!'

And then, something even worse happened. We all turned to look at the entrance of the cave as another voice rang out. 'David, are you in there? You and Deirdre? Have I caught you at last?'

The rest of us were shocked into silence and immobility, but suddenly Sarah turned and shot out of the cave like a fury.

'Go away!' she screamed.

356

My mother backed away in fright. Her hands clutched at her stomach and I heard her gasp. Sarah took no notice of her distress and pushed her.

'Stop that!' I cried and darted forward, but my foot slipped down between two rocks at the entrance of the cave and I fell heavily. I was winded and tears were streaming down my face, but I twisted up until I could see what was happening.

Sarah had pursued my mother until they were standing at the very edge of the outcrop of rock. Even from here I could see that my mother's face was flushed and her jaws clenched in a strange grin. Her arms and legs began to jerk like a puppet with broken strings.

'Don't do that!' Sarah screamed but my mother took no notice. 'Stop it! You're frightening me!'

My mother ignored Sarah and called out, 'Deirdre ... Deirdre ...

Was she calling for help? Sarah didn't think so. 'You're not going to tell,' she screamed. 'Nobody must know!'

She pushed my mother into the sea.

Then there was only the dreadful sound of my mother screaming...

# CHAPTER 23

I sat hunched on the floor in the corner of the summer-house, whimpering with pain and fright. I had made myself come back to the present when I could bear no more. Benjy had come to sit next to me and he gazed up into my face as if he was trying to understand the strange sounds I was making.

What had my mother seen as she peered into the cave? Her friend Jane Frears had told me that her condition made her vision hazy sometimes. She must have seen Deirdre, because one of her last acts was to call to her for help.

But had she also seen that it was Mitch that Deirdre was with and not my father? I hoped so – oh, how I hoped so. For then at least she might have had the momentary relief of believing that my father was not betraying her after all.

If she had lived, she might have found out the truth eventually. But, in the event, perhaps it was better for her to believe a lie.

But the past was not finished with me yet. I knew that I would have to go back and act out that fateful last scene.

'Don't leave me, Benjy,' I whispered into the dog's soft ears, and I put both my arms around his neck as if I was making sure of a stake in the present. There would be some living creature, here and now, who would care what happened to me.

The sounds came first... The screaming of gulls and angry voices...

*Christ, what has she done!*

That was Paul's father who would have looked comical pulling on his trousers as he tried to run forwards, if it had not been so tragic.

Sarah ran back and stopped him in the entrance of the cave. 'Leave her,' she said. 'It's her own fault.'

'There's no need to worry about Helen,' Deirdre said. 'She's a strong swimmer.'

I twisted my head round and saw that she was smoothing her tights up her legs as coolly as if nothing untoward had happened. 'It's us you have to worry about, when she gets back and tells everyone what she's seen.'

'She's not going to get back, you stupid woman,' her lover shouted. 'She's heavily pregnant and the tide's on the turn – that's when it's at its most dangerous.'

Paul's father was sweating profusely. He wiped his face with the bottom of his shirt before he tucked it into his trousers without buttoning it. 'Deirdre, I can't swim, can you?'

'No.'

'Then we have to get help.'

'Have we? Are you sure?'

'What are you saying?'

They stared at each other.

Everybody was ignoring me completely. I was lying at their feet in agony as I tried to pull my right foot out of the cleft in the rocks. I couldn't see my mother at all and I could only hope that she had, indeed, struck out for the shore.

I turned round to see what Paul was doing. He was crouched against the wall of the cave with his head in his hands. I think he was crying.

'Paul!' I yelled. 'Come and help me.'

He raised his head and stared at me but he didn't move.

'Please – my foot's stuck – I want to go and get my mother!'

That caught their attention. Aunt Deirdre, Mr Mitchell and Sarah looked down at me as if they had only just remembered me. They watched in silence as Paul came across the floor of the cave towards me on his hands and knees.

It seemed to take ages before he reached out and put his hands around my ankle. He probed down with his fingers into the cleft of rock. 'I don't know how you've done this, Beth,' he murmured. 'Your foot's quite stuck. Here, try moving it this way.'

I screamed in agony.

'Leave it, Paul,' Aunt Deirdre ordered.

'But–'

'You'll break her ankle if you try and do anything. We'll have to go for help.'

'Right. You go, I'll stay with Bethany.'

'Don't be stupid, Paul,' Sarah said. 'The tide has turned. If you stay here you'll drown!'

'Be quiet, you stupid little bitch!' Mr Mitchell hissed at her, but it was too late. Paul was growing hysterical.

The others were edging further towards the entrance and he stood up and screamed, 'Don't leave her!'

'Shut up! We have no choice.'

That was Deirdre. She and Mitch drew together. She whispered something and he nodded. Suddenly he turned and hit Paul on the jaw with his bunched fist. Paul slumped and his father caught him and slung him over his shoulder.

I heard them talking quietly as they left the cave together. They must already have been making plans, getting their story straight. I was seven years old and they were walking away from me ... leaving me to die...

Already in the background I could hear the sound of the sea. Great masses of cold, grey water, rolling, shifting, getting nearer...

And, as the gulls screeched, I began to scream

I think I must have been out of my mind by the time my father came and found me. The water was already lapping around me and he knelt down and talked to me gently as he pushed his hand down into the cleft and eased my shoe off.

That enabled me to turn my foot and he helped me to pull free but the pain brought me to the point of fainting. He lifted me up into his arms and I just caught sight of his hands and fingers, grazed and bleeding, before I closed my eyes.

As he hurried across the rocks and around the island to the causeway, I suddenly jerked my eyes open and screamed for my mother.

'Hush, Bethany,' he said. 'It's all right now, you must try to forget...'

'But it's your fault ... she was looking for you, not me...'

But he couldn't answer me. We were both crying...

And with those tears my childhood was restored to me. I had remembered the worst of it; suddenly, everything – all the missing pieces of my life – was in place and I was a whole person again.

I wrapped my arms around my knees, sitting in the corner of the summer-house, and let the tears flow. Benjy whimpered and then sat up on his haunches and leaned forward to lick my face.

That made me laugh and that's how Mandy found me – crouched in the corner, both laughing and crying and trying to fend off a concerned and affectionate dog.

'Well,' she said. 'I suppose it's better to have a good cry, although I didn't realize you were that fond of him.'

'What are you talking about?' I got to my feet and tried to wipe my eyes with the back of my hands.

'Paul Mitchell. The whole town's talking about it. Dreadful, isn't it? Do you think it was suicide?'

I knew what I thought but, at this stage, it would be no use saying anything. 'I think we'll have to wait to see what the police decide about that.'

'You're right. But when you didn't come along to The Gondola or phone like you promised, I thought you might be a bit upset so I came here straight from work. Just as well I did, by the looks of you.'

Mandy gathered up the wet clothes that I had come here for and we went over to the house. I was happy to let her take charge. She dumped the clothes in the laundry room and set about making us a snack.

'I'm great at scrambled eggs on toast. Will that do?'

'Wonderful, as long as you make enough for Benjy, too.' I realized that I would have to buy some dog food and dishes and all the other paraphernalia if, as I was beginning to suspect, he was going to take up permanent residence here.

Luckily, Mandy didn't expect me to keep a conversation going as I sat lazily and waited for her to cook our meal.

My mind went back to the moment fourteen years ago when the others had walked out of the cave and left me to my fate. For all these years they had always kept up the pretence that they were never even there.

The day it happened they must have been terrified when they realized that my father had turned up in time to rescue me.

But then how lucky for them that the shock had made me blank it all out. How different all our subsequent lives would have been if I had been able to tell everyone what had really happened.

I wondered what they had planned to tell Paul if I had died. As it was, he would have been happy to cover up Sarah's part in the tragedy because, even then, he was besotted by her. He would have convinced himself that it was an accident and that Sarah must not be punished for causing her aunt Helen's death.

What if I had been drowned as well as my mother? Deirdre and Sarah would probably have inherited Dune House eventually, unless Paul said anything.

Now I like to believe that if I had died, Paul would not have kept quiet for all those years.

Poor Paul. My coming back to Seatoncliffe had forced him to acknowledge what he had always known. That Sarah was capable of murder. I had seen it in his eyes that very first day when he had rescued me on the cliff road. That flash of fear in his eyes was not because he thought I suspected him of trying to kill me. It was because he suspected Sarah.

After our meal, Mandy and I carried our coffee through into the sitting-room and Mandy insisted on staying quite late to keep me company. In fact, I was grateful. For when the phone rang, as I knew it would, I asked her to answer it.

'If it's Greg Randall, I don't want to talk to him,' I told her.

'What excuse shall I give?'

'I don't care. But make sure he doesn't phone again.'

That was a rotten thing to ask her to do, but she didn't complain. When she came back into the room I looked at her, questioningly, but she just shrugged and said. 'Don't ask. I don't like telling lies.'

I was glad that she was sensitive enough to gauge my mood. I couldn't have borne it if she'd asked me about him. I was not ready to tell anyone that I thought the man I had fallen in love with had tried to kill me.

I dreamed of Edric and Alveva. She had bound him to the rock and he was begging her to go, to

364

leave him to his fate. He was the one who should be punished for breaking his vows, he said, she had never wanted to take those vows in the first place.

She wouldn't leave him. As she bound the two of them together with a length of hempen rope, she reminded him that neither of them had wanted to live if they could not be together.

As the tide came in and filled the cave that had been their trysting place, their tears mingled with the salt water and Alveva's long hair floated out behind her in the waves.

But, as I watched, the outline of her face wavered and faded and then re-formed briefly into my own young face and then, finally, became my mother's, before it was submerged forever beneath the sea.

The next morning I found my father's paintings. I woke very early, so early that Benjy, who had slept across my feet at the bottom of the bed, merely raised his head and watched me, sleepily, as I pulled on a pair of jeans and a pale pink sweater.

I added 'dog basket' to my mental list of things to buy and slipped downstairs without him and out to the garage.

The building had once been a stable and there was still an upper storey where the groom and stable-boy had slept. Now it was simply a storage area full of old tools and garden implements. And my father's paintings.

They were loosely wrapped in either brown paper or sacking and it was obvious that no great care had been taken about the manner of their storage. I wondered who had put them here. My father? Grief-stricken and not caring any more? Or my grandmother, not wanting them in the house but not being able to bring herself to destroy them outright?

I wasn't ready to look at them. I was still very uncertain how I felt about my father. I had loved him all my life, both before and after that day fourteen years ago, and that hadn't changed.

He had been unfaithful to my mother and I would never know why – but he had certainly paid a high price for it.

I could only guess why he had turned his back on his career. I thought it might be because my mother had been his first inspiration and the person who encouraged him most. Perhaps he thought he didn't deserve to succeed alter she had died, especially as he thought himself responsible for her death.

So I decided to leave the paintings and sketches where they were for the moment. When the time came that I felt myself ready to deal with them, I would ask my former boss Patrick Collings for his advice. He would have the kind of friends who would know what to do with them.

It was still too early for Betty Doran to have arrived, so I decided to wait and have breakfast with her and, meanwhile, take Benjy for a walk.

Was he looking for his master? The dog ran backwards and forwards along the cliff road finding familiar scents and following them until, eventually, he reached the top of the stairs cut into the cliff that Paul had pointed out to me and plunged down towards the beach.

I followed at a more leisurely pace. It was a fine, sunny morning and the sea was calm but the air was damp. Long, transparent coils of vapour wreathed up from the water and snaked across the wave-ribbed sand towards me. Small waves broke gently on the shingle with a hollow slapping sound.

I tried my best to enjoy the simple physical experience of walking on an empty beach in the morning. I knew that I would have to acknowledge my turbulent feelings about Greg eventually, and that this was a delaying tactic. But – so what? I thought I owed it to myself to enjoy this moment of peace.

Benjy had brought us to the beginning of the causeway. He stopped and looked up at me as if asking permission and then, without waiting for my answer, he started bounding across.

'Benjy! Come back!' I called in exasperation. He ignored me.

I looked at the beach and the waves and tried to judge the state of the tide. I realized that I hadn't the faintest idea whether it was going out or coming in. But I couldn't risk that stupid dog being stranded on the island and perhaps trying to swim back and being drowned. I had to go for him.

I did try shouting a few more times – my angry commands could have woken the dead – but it had not the slightest effect on Benjy. I set off resignedly across the causeway.

By the time I reached the island, he was nowhere to be seen. I thought I had glimpsed him running up the grassy slope towards the highest point and I scrambled up. No sign of him. But there were plenty of rabbit droppings to show why he might have come this way.

If he had, then he had gone all the way down again, for when I reached the top of the hill I looked down and saw him bounding across the rocks on the seaward side.

'Benjy! Bad dog!'

That caught his attention. I don't think anyone had been quite so angry with him before and he actually stood and waited while I slipped and slithered down to join him.

When I got to the bottom, I found I was only a few yards away from the entrance to the cave.

# CHAPTER 24

The morning sun reflecting from the rock pools threw glimmering shadows onto the rocky walls of the cave and, as I stepped inside, I saw that it was much smaller than I remembered.

In my nightmares it had been cold and dark, but now it was sun-warmed and welcoming, the perfect trysting place. I wondered how many pairs of lovers had met there over the centuries, then the thought of Deirdre and Mitch's adulterous couplings soured my speculations.

So that had been the old scandal that Paul had hinted at. Deirdre must have run off with Mitch and then her husband Raymond had committed suicide. I wondered if the events of that day fourteen years ago had acted as a catalyst.

I looked down, trying to see the place where my foot had slipped between the rocks so disastrously when I was a child, but recent tides had covered most of the floor of the cave with crumbly sand.

At the back there had been a fall of rock at some time in the distant past. A huge pile of tumbled stones gave tantalizing glimpses of what might have been a dark passageway behind them. This was obviously what had given rise to the stories of another cave and a secret passage to the mainland.

It was no wonder that imaginative children had

always come exploring here. Benjy did not want to explore the cave at all. He was lying at the entrance, uncharacteristically quiet and docile.

Perhaps dogs can sense sadness or evil more easily than we can, and traces of the past still lingered. Whatever the reason, he would not come inside with me even when I called him.

But then he surprised me with a low growl. A shadow fell across the entrance and, the next moment, a tall, broad-shouldered figure appeared and stood there. He had his back to the light; at first, all I could make out was that he was wearing jeans and a creamy sweater.

I gasped involuntarily and felt my heart began to pound before he ducked his head and entered the cave. Now the sun fell across his strong-boned face and his spun-gold hair.

'Hello, Duncan,' I breathed.

'Now that's a bonny welcoming smile,' he said and I thought, again, what an attractive man he was.

'You've come to rescue me, I suppose?'

'Rescue you?'

'Remember you told me it was part of your job, rescuing damsels in distress?'

'So I did. And if you look out there–' he stepped back so that I could see beyond him '–you'll see that the tide has already turned. It won't be long before this cave is flooded.'

'I'll have to take your word for that. I'm no expert.'

His smile had gone and I felt as though I was being admonished. 'But, anyway,' I asked him, 'how did you know I was here?'

'Are you joking! We – I was out in the dunes when I heard you calling the dog. I walked to the cliff top to see who was making all the racket and I saw you crossing the causeway.'

'You were out early.'

'I usually am. Late and early. It's my job.'

Suddenly I remembered that when Duncan had given me a lift home he had told me that he was going to set up a camera to take night shots.

'By the way, did you get any good pictures the other night?'

'I haven't processed the film yet, but I'm not very hopeful. The weather was atrocious.'

I was relieved to see that he was smiling again and it seemed natural that he should take a step towards me. But the dog suddenly raised his head and growled. I laughed. 'It's all right, Benjy, Duncan's a friend.'

Then into my mind flashed an image of a large pale hound racing across the wind-tossed grass in the moonlight.

'When you do process that film, you might find you have some good shots of Benjy here.'

'Why do you say that?'

'Well, he was out in the storm that night…' I faltered when I saw the way Duncan was looking at me. 'What is it?'

'And you, Bethany? Were you out in the storm?'

And that's the moment that I knew.

I looked up into his attractive face. The face of a saint or the face of a sinner? His cottage had been like a hermit's cell, but all the time I was there I had not been able to deny that Duncan exuded a contradictory but powerful sensuality.

I flushed when I recalled that I had even imagined what it would be like to have him take me in his arms.

I had sensed almost as soon as I met him that Duncan would be obsessive. Until now I had imagined that his ruling passion was just for his work ... the conservation of wild life.

But now I knew that he had another passion ... a passion for my cousin Sarah.

I remembered his marvellous photographs whose colour and light could only mean they had not been taken anywhere near the British Isles...

And then the carafes... Duncan liked wine, I knew that, but these were the pale gold kind with long drinking spouts ... the kind people bring home from holidays on the Costa Brava.

But Duncan had not been on holiday, he had brought them back with him when he returned from whatever field trip he had been on when he took the photographs.

Duncan was the man that Sarah had met in Spain.

He knew I had worked it out. He leaned back so that his shoulders rested against the curved wall of the cave, but he looked at me warily. I knew then that it was Duncan who was responsible for the 'hit-and-run' and also for trapping me in the chapel on the night of the storm.

And then I remembered something else – the day he had walked home with me from his cottage and I had nearly been buried alive under the collapsing dune. Did I slip or was I pushed? And what would have happened if my friend PC McKenzie hadn't come along?

I looked up at him sadly. How could a man with such a face be evil? He was smiling, the same engaging smile as ever, but when I saw the look in his eyes it chilled me. I had never in my life been so frightened, for that look told me that the man was not entirely sane.

'The tide here runs south for so many hours, you know.' He began talking as if he was giving a lecture to some students on a study trip. 'Then it starts running north at about two knots...'

'Duncan, why are you telling me this?'

'Anyone who drowned off this island would probably turn up somewhere, eventually. Of course, some bodies are never found...'

'Stop it! Please stop!'

'There are underground caves near here. If a body was snagged in one of them, it could take twenty-four hours to come to the surface...'

'Stop! Stop! Stop!' I put my hands over my ears but I could still hear his voice.

'Or it might never surface at all.' He stopped and I lowered my hands and looked at him. He was shaking his head as if I was a foolish child.

'You shouldn't go scrambling about the island when you don't know the times of the tide, Bethany.' He bent down to pick up a large piece of rock. I backed away, but he moved round so that his powerful frame was blocking the entrance.

'It was silly of you to climb the hill like that. The grass must have been wet and slippery and you fell all the way down to the rocks and hit your head. You lay there unconscious while the tide came in...'

'Stop it! You're crazy! None of this has happened!'

Suddenly, there was a noise behind him and he turned his head. 'Oh, no,' he said. 'I told you to go back to the cottage and wait for me.'

He moved his body round slightly and I saw my cousin. I wondered how long she had been there. I had the feeling she had been listening for some while because she was looking at him impatiently.

Sarah was wearing jeans, just like my own, and a figure-hugging white top. The only signs of her pregnancy were her full breasts and a slight puffiness around her eyes.

'You shouldn't have come over here, the tide's on its way in,' Duncan said. 'I don't want you having to run.'

'Well, hurry up, then.'

If Duncan was mad, there was no excuse for Sarah. She was totally evil.

'What's the matter, Sarah?' I called to her. 'Don't you trust him? Did he make a mess of it the other times?'

I had made a grave mistake. Instead of causing dissension between them, Duncan turned his attention back to me. I saw him raise his arm, his fingers spread around the rock, gripping it tightly. Then, just as he began to bring it down towards my head, a sleek yellow shape sprang up from the ground.

I'd forgotten all about Benjy. He leapt high and sank his teeth into Duncan's arm. Duncan cursed, dropped the rock and tried to shake him off. But Benjy hung on, growling deep in his throat.

Then Duncan swung his arm back forcefully, smashing the poor beast against the wall of the cave. Benjy fell to the floor with a sickening thud.

'Oh, no!' I sank to my knees and cradled him in my arms. His eyes were closed but, thank God, his heart was still beating strongly.

I heard Sarah scream out, 'For God's sake, Duncan, the tide's coming in fast.'

Then I became aware that Duncan had stooped down behind me to pick up the rock. I half turned to see him swinging his arm back again and at the same time I heard Sarah give an indignant cry. I just had time to wonder why, before I realized that Duncan was bringing the rock down towards my head.

I tried to duck sideways but at the same time I didn't want to expose, Benjy, so I put both my arms across the back of my head and neck and waited for the blow.

But before it landed, I heard someone cry, 'Stop that!'

I turned to see Duncan being wrestled away and the rock falling from his hand. He struggled and the two men fell backwards out of the cave. I crawled out to see them picking themselves up.

'You OK, Bethany?' one of them asked. It was Greg. He was watching Duncan warily but the other man had eyes only for Sarah.

'You fool! You fool!' she screamed. 'Now what will happen?'

'Sarah, don't ... don't get excited like that ... you'll hurt the baby...'

Sarah gave a sob of rage and turned and ran. Duncan took off after her.

We watched them go and then turned to look at each other. I know I was smiling foolishly, but so was he.

'I'd like to linger,' he said, 'but Sarah was right about the tide. Unless you want to be stuck here for four hours alone with me, I think we'd better get a move on.'

'Let's go then,' I said and he looked hurt.

I walked up to him and kissed him, only breaking away when I realized that it would soon be impossible to do so.

'It's not that I don't want to be marooned with you,' I said. 'But I think we'd better get my other hero to a vet.'

Greg went into the cave and gently scooped Benjy up. He carried him carefully. By the time we got round to the landward side of the island, the waves were already lapping over the causeway.

'What do you think?' Greg asked.

I stroked Benjy's silky head. 'I think we've got to.'

'Well, for God's sake hang on to me.'

I did. The waves were washing over the causeway from each side and we trod carefully. I marvelled that my ankle had not given me even one bothersome twinge of pain.

Sarah and Duncan were already nearly halfway across. He had hold of her arm, but she was struggling to break away. Eventually, she did.

'Of course, you realize you'll have to explain all that drama to me,' Greg said.

The explanations had to wait for, at that moment, a wave much bigger than the preceding ones took Sarah unawares and knocked her off her feet. She was carried into the sea. Duncan gave a great cry and dived in after her.

We watched helplessly as their two heads bobbed about in the waves. They didn't seem to be making progress in any direction. For the first time that day I noticed the crying of the sea birds.

We looked towards the shore, scanned the cliff road. There was no one in sight. No one else had seen what had happened.

Greg sighed. 'We'll have to call for help.'

The search went on for the rest of that day and well into the night, resuming the next morning. The air-sea rescue Sea King helicopter came down from RAF Boulmer and the lifeboat from Blyth. But the bodies of Sarah and Duncan were never found.

Greg had phoned the coastguard from Dune House and he stayed with me until it was all over. He offered to go and tell my aunt Deirdre, but I said the police could do that.

I had called the Animal Hospital for Benjy, saying it was an emergency, and was chagrined to have him run to meet the vet when she arrived. She didn't mind at all and, after examining the rogue, she assured me that nothing much was wrong, but I could bring him along to the surgery any time, night or day, if I was worried.

'And that'll cost you a pretty penny,' Betty Doran muttered after she had shown her out. 'Do you realize how expensive this is going to be?' By 'this' she meant being a dog owner, but I could see that she didn't really mind.

We told Betty only that there had been an accident on the way back from a trip to the island. I didn't feel that I could tell her the full story then, or ever. But Greg had to know.

While the search continued, we waited in the sitting-room at the back of the house and, when the day cooled, we lit the fire. We tossed some cushions on the floor and sat at each side of the hearth, our backs propped up against the armchairs.

Betty brought us food on a tray and, from somewhere, she produced a bottle of wine. I remembered my fantasy the first night I had sat here and I could hardly believe that it might be about to come true.

But there was so much that we still had to tell each other. As the clattering of the helicopter came and went throughout the long hours, I told Greg everything except the one thing that I was ashamed of.

When I had finished my story and I looked into his eyes I saw that they were glittering suspiciously.

'Oh, Bethany,' he groaned. 'Can you ever forgive me?'

'Why? What is it that I have to forgive you for? You saved my life today!'

'It's that other day I'm talking about ... the day your mother died. I saw ... I thought I saw...'

Suddenly it hit me. I remembered what he had told me just the day before. 'You thought you saw me push my mother into the sea.'

'Yes. Now I know it was Sarah, but all these

years I've believed... When I met you again, you can imagine my feelings. I remembered that day, vividly. I'd seen an angry child deliberately push her mother into the sea. And yet ... and yet I found myself falling in love with you. I convinced myself you'd changed ... and all the time I was doing you a great injustice.'

No wonder he'd been so hard to fathom at first. I thought Greg had been blowing hot and cold out of sheer cussedness, but all the time he'd been wrestling with his own feelings.

And then something more appalling occurred to me. 'Greg, what did you tell my father?'

He knew straight away what I meant. 'I lied. I told him that it had been an accident. I couldn't have been so cruel as to tell him what I thought was the truth.'

Then at least my father hadn't thought for the rest of his life that I had murdered my mother.

'I made the same mistake again today, you know.' Greg was smiling wryly. 'I was on the cliff road and I saw Sarah hurrying across the causeway. I thought it was you, so I followed. Thank God I did.'

'But I don't understand. Why were you out so early?'

'Looking for you. I called at the house and Mrs Doran told me that you must be out walking.'

Suddenly I blushed. I remembered what I had asked Mandy to do the night before.

'It's just as well I took your friend's advice,' Greg said and that surprised me.

'What exactly was that?' I asked him.

'Oh, she told me who she was and that you

wouldn't come to the phone because you were in a right mood with yourself, but in her opinion I should leave things be and come straight along the next morning. So I did.'

'I don't know what to say.'

'Then don't say anything. But if you ever need advice I would go to Mandy O'Connor. She seems like a very sensible girl.'

'She is.'

Greg suddenly heaved himself up and came and sat beside me. He put his arms around me and tried to draw me close but I held myself away.

'Greg, there's something you have to forgive me for.'

'What's that?'

And then I told him why I felt so ashamed. I told him that, for a while, I had thought that he might have been Sarah's lover and that he had been her accomplice in her attempts to kill me. I couldn't look at him when I had finished and, as the silence lengthened I began to despair.

I had ruined everything. My lack of faith had spoiled things before they had properly begun. But then he put his arms around me and drew me close.

'Were you hurt when you realized that I believed you'd killed your mother?' he asked.

'No, it was a natural mistake ... the circumstances...'

'Exactly. Circumstances ... other people's actions ... do you realize how much better it might have been if your father had encouraged you to remember what had happened?'

'I'm sure he thought he was protecting me.'

'Everybody was affected by what happened that summer, Bethany. Your grandmother, your parents, my mother ... do you know, I think she had been hoping that she and your father were going to make a life together.'

'At my mother's expense!'

'We won't quarrel about that, Bethany. Now or ever. But we'll do much better for our children.'

'What did you say?'

'You heard me.'

And then I did go into his arms. I stayed there, only coming up for breath when Betty tip-toed in to remove the tray.

'I'm going home,' she said. 'I'll come back in the morning, but it looks as though you don't need me to take care of you, right now.'

Greg smiled up at her. 'That's right, we'll take care of each other.'

Later that night we took Benjy out into the garden. The air was cool but sweet and we stood for a while just looking at the stars.

'After I've finished work on my television pro-gramme,' Greg said, 'I'll help you get this garden into shape, if you want me to.'

'Yes, I'd like that,' I said. And we followed our dog back into the house.

The publishers hope that this book has given you enjoyable reading. Large Print Books are especially designed to be as easy to see and hold as possible. If you wish a complete list of our books please ask at your local library or write directly to:

**Magna Large Print Books**
Magna House, Long Preston,
Skipton, North Yorkshire.
BD23 4ND

This Large Print Book for the partially sighted, who cannot read normal print, is published under the auspices of

## THE ULVERSCROFT FOUNDATION